ALSO BY T. R. PEARSON

A Short History of a Small Place
Off for the Sweet Hereafter
The Last of How It Was
Call and Response
Gospel Hour

CRY

ME

A

RIVER

T. R. PEARSON

Henry Holt and Company
New York

Henry Holt and Company, Inc.
Publishers since 1866
115 West 18th Street
New York, New York 10011

Henry Holt® is a registered trademark
of Henry Holt and Company, Inc.

Published in Canada by Fitzhenry & Whiteside Ltd.,
195 Allstate Parkway, Markham, Ontario L3R 4T8.

Library of Congress Cataloging-in-Publication Data
Pearson, T. R.
Cry me a river : a novel / T. R. Pearson.—1st ed.
p.   cm.
I. Title.
PS3566.E235C78   1993   92-13860
813'.54—dc20   CIP

ISBN 0-8050-2200-7
ISBN 8-8050-3187-1 (An Owl Book: pbk.)

Henry Holt books are available for special promotions
and premiums. For details contact: Director, Special Markets.

First published in hardcover in 1993
by Henry Holt and Company, Inc.

First Owl Book Edition—1994

Designed by Paula R. Szafranski

Printed in the United States of America
All first editions are printed on acid-free paper.∞

3   5   7   9   10   8   6   4
1   3   5   7   9   10   8   6   4   2
(pbk.)

For
Stone,
Max,
Grace,
and D

CRY

ME

A

RIVER

1.

She wasn't even much of a beauty, wasn't possessed herself of the manner of features and accoutrements and contours that a fellow might conjure up and savor. She wasn't tall and leggy, wasn't terribly shapely at all, had a nose that was flat and a little canted off to one side and small deepset eyes the color of silt. Her lips were thin and altogether unvoluptuous, and her jowls were a little drawn and hollow though not gaunt after the fashion that's taken widely to be alluring. She usually left her hair to hang loose and fall upon her shoulders, black hair that was not terribly thick or appreciably lustrous and didn't reach far down her back, but she had a way of moving her head to pitch it about, a way of sweeping it off of her face with her fingers that was, I suppose, affecting.

She could do that, could accomplish with some trifle, some gesture, some movement of her hand or inclination of her head an insinuation of comeliness and grace that would pass like a scent on the air and be gone before a fellow could even begin to know what it was that had drawn him up and stopped him short and made him to look upon her with longing. But she wasn't much of a regular beauty and hadn't been born into loveliness though plainly she'd compensated, could manufacture well enough what she needed of seduction, fabricate what she required of charm. She didn't have much call to be beautiful too. That would have drained the sport from it.

I never knew anyone to tire of hearing the thing. There was evermore somebody clamoring about with a cousin come for a visit or a buddy passing through town who'd seen already the furniture mill and had eaten at the fish house and tolerated the panoramas up along the ridge, had become in fact fairly saturated with the local enticement but for our tale of woe that I would get invited, that I would get enlisted usually to narrate entirely or confirm at least the particulars of since I was the one who knew best of it, had endured the whole business to unravel before me. So they'd come to wonder of me might I speak of it please, might I share with their relations and with their buddies news of our own tragic episode which had gotten to be an object of civic pride suggesting like it did that we were after all, under the surface of things, a community of passionate people who sometimes slaughtered each other for love.

I'd found in a sticker bush, snagged on a thorn, a chunk of Wendle's head, a hank of hair attached still to a little pulpy scrap of scalp. Ellis had seen it first, had taken it for some venomous manner of creature.

"Kill it!" he'd wailed. "Kill it!" he'd shrieked, and we'd dodged about there in the undergrowth trying to keep from getting bit and tainted. Ellis had fairly jigged on out of sight before I'd managed to play the light back into that bush, before I'd come to be sufficiently emboldened to approach again that thorny shrub and squat before it from where I could see well enough that we would not likely suffer a bite, would not probably swell up and die, and I do recall how Ellis—from back in the trees, from down by the creek, from off and away in the darkness—yelled out once more to me, "Kill it!"

Ellis wasn't on the force. Ellis was a lush, not a consummate and debilitated sort of a lush but a lush chiefly of fortune and circumstance. Ellis, you see, had a sister who hardly approved of anything at all like would include Ellis and the majority of Ellis's habits as well which she was in a position to curb and influence since Ellis her brother lived under her roof in a room upstairs over the den and ate at her table and plundered through her purse which provided her, she figured, entitlement enough to tell him what he might do and tell him how he might act and muster up correctives when she saw the need arise. Ellis worked at the bottling plant out past the speedway, caught a ride mornings down on the truck route, met there in front of the Magic Wand a boy who carried him to work and hauled him home as well, dropped him off anyhow where he'd fetched him from which presented Ellis nightly with a dilemma since the Magic Wand itself was passably convenient to the state store where they sold pint bottles of Old Overholt which Ellis was most especially fond of and did not some nights figure he could do without.

So he'd walk home on occasion to his sister's house directly and would walk home on occasion only presently instead once he'd elevated his mood with fortified drink. Of course Ellis's sister harbored an especially low opinion of inebriation as a pastime and a pursuit and had made herself acquainted with the altogether sorry histories of several prominent national inebriates, statesmen and entertainers and industrialists, which she'd call upon for purposes of illumination once Ellis had arrived home lubricated, wondered anyway what in the world might become in time of Ellis her brother if men of actual character and legitimate substance could manage themselves to fall thrall to liquor. How soon, she sought to know, and how completely might her own brother Ellis, blessed with no reserves much of integrity and merely scanty traces of resolve, come at last to be ruined and done in by the effects and consequences of his passion for distilled spirits?

This proved precisely the sort of query Ellis was prone to make reply to with one of his resonant, thunderous, extended belches for which he'd come to be legend about the stationhouse as he could produce, with just a regular esophagus, a modicum of muscular pressure, and a measure of gaseous air, the sort of noise a giant mutated cricket might make. His sister was not herself so terribly fond of it.

Apparently the burp was prelude usually and preamble to the corrective that followed. Ellis, that is, was allowed to retire to his bedroom upstairs, was permitted to cross to his closet and unfreight like usual his wooden hanger that swung free and beat against the far closet wall, was provided occasion even to light upon the cane seat of his ladderback chair before his sister in the den, who gauged through the ceiling his progress and his pursuits, took up at last the receiver and dialed down to the stationhouse where she would make at Janice straightoff or make straightoff at Angelene that noise she was partial to, would discharge through her nose they figured a sort of a wan and pitiful toot.

We saw to him by turns, me and Wendle did, as an evening with Ellis could be at times a manner of trial and so alternated between us the duty of riding him around. That was all his sister ever wanted, was looking just to have him taken from her. She'd maybe hoped there at the first that the spectacle of getting escorted out across the yard by an officer of the law and deposited in the backseat of a cruiser might shame Ellis into sobriety and wholesome living, but she'd pretty shortly given over notions of that as Ellis's shame was apparently less concentrated even than Ellis's integrity and Ellis's resolve thrown together in a heap.

He was most usually delighted to get out of the house, would hear me or would hear Wendle mounting the steps in the hallway and advancing to the landing and would, I suppose, stand to greet us since he was always evermore standing when I went in, poised there before his ladderback chair with his brown fedora already in his hand and wearing of course, as was his custom, his black clawhammer jacket with the satin lapels, his black clawhammer jacket that he did not ever seem to wear but drunk. It was too tight for him in the middle and too short for him in the sleeves, but every time he took a taste he hauled the thing out of the closet and put it on since maybe it reminded him of those days back when he'd had prospects, attended soirees, entertained ambitions.

Wendle didn't ever much care for him but then Wendle was a

blowhard and Ellis himself couldn't usually be persuaded to shut up which likely made for an uneasy union. I was sort of fond of him myself. He'd worked once on a scow in the Ohio River and could tell, after he'd straightened up a little, scandalous stories about the places they'd put in and the things they'd done there. He'd taken jobs at a copper mine in Tennessee and in the coal fields up past Grundy. He'd sold shoes previously for a fellow from Winona, Mississippi, and had shoveled in a stint asphalt for the South Carolina department of highways. He'd panned for rubies out around Cherokee though he hadn't come across any gems much, and he'd near about drowned once in the French Broad River but had found there at the last a piece of tree to cling to. He was full of extraordinary lies about women he'd had his way with and worked his wiles upon and claimed even to have engaged in an intimacy with a verifiable duchess in the lavatory of a passenger train up in the wilderness of British Alberta where he'd gone, he said, to harvest hemlocks for an outfit from Georgia. Even half-drunk he could explain convincingly and in some considerable detail where in a railway lavatory a man and duchess all tangled up together in an act of passion might fit.

He wasn't even entirely useless in a law enforcement capacity, was surely largely useless but had effected on one occasion pretty much by himself alone the apprehension of a perpetrator. It was back a couple of summers past when me and Ellis had just come out of the bank lot there across from the Episcopal church and I noticed this boy up the road leaving the Ben Franklin at a trot. He was one of those fellows in for the cabbage harvest up on the ridge, was from Mexico or down in Guatemala and was fairly puny like most of them are and had that crop of dull black hair and that big broad head like the bulk of them tend to, and here he was loping out of the Ben Franklin that me and Ellis together took some notice of. He dodged off the sidewalk and into the street and was partway across it when Mrs. Caudill, the clerk and night manager, exited the Ben Franklin herself in a state of open irritation and struck out in pursuit of that boy as she shared with him her low opinion of his particular sort.

I stopped the cruiser alongside the curb and ran across the street myself so as to head off that fellow who was running towards me on the sidewalk, but he veered back into the road and was fairly bolting down the southbound lane when Ellis, who saw that boy coming towards him and ascended it would seem into a state of supreme agitation, stepped out from the cruiser as that fellow endeavored to pass and threw up on him. It terminated the pursuit and accounted pretty exclusively for the apprehension of the perpetrator due to how he came to be paralyzed straightaway with disgust and collapsed to the pavement where he found likely occasion to contemplate the unforeseen vagaries of American law enforcement since he hailed after all from a primitive land where justice was surely not so swift and malodorous.

Ellis himself, who'd not ever previously felled a man with an upchuck, was a little overcome as well and just stood there gaping at that boy on the pavement who pleaded with Ellis in broken English to retain please his fluids. He offered up in his extended hand the merchandise he'd lifted from the Ben Franklin, a red plastic hairclip and a Fifth Avenue bar that Mrs. Caudill arrived presently to identify as the purloined items in fact, though she didn't any longer believe she was hoping to have them returned to her. So we just stood there the three of us enduring the baleful aroma as we watched that boy on the pavement wipe at himself and rake with his fingers regurgitated items from his dull black hair.

Ellis, for his part, confessed at length that he was not persuaded he could make a career of upchucking on criminals due largely to the perils of dehydration, though he expressed a ready willingness to persevere in his habits and absorb his share of distilled rye so that he might, on a day of extremity and in a time of need, be blessed with reserves enough to hose off for me a fellow or two.

So he wasn't I guess the worst sort to have along that night when it all started to come undone, that night we found Wendle. We were responding to a call. Mrs. Heflin had spied a prowler in her shrubbery and had phoned in to the stationhouse with news of it. Mrs. Heflin possessed a gift for spying prowlers and could concoct from a murky

shadow and a couple of leafy limbs a most devious manner of ne'er-
do-well afflicted evermore with a spectacular array of unsavory intentions, set plainly on raping and pillaging and maiming and killing and
raising just a general and extraordinary fuss. I guess she saw more
prowlers than starlings even and gray squirrels and had called this
night at the dusk of the day on account of a man out back of her baby's
breath lurking in with the autumn olive.

He appeared to her to have on a dark-colored jacket and a pair of
light cotton slacks and cordovan loafers, and she was all but certain
that he was armed with a sizable scimitar, claimed she could see the
dwindling sunlight glinting off the blade of it. Mrs. Heflin had been
reading lately in a book from the pharmacy a story about a woman
who'd been forcibly removed from her camel and violated by a swarthy
bescimitared ruffian of the Sahara, so she'd assured Janice she was
acquainted well enough with the passions and wiles of the sorts of
fellows who would tote in the first place scimitars about. Naturally
she was concerned for her own virtue, but she was also appreciably
troubled as to the prospects of her sundry appendages and fleshy
outcroppings since that ruffian of the Sahara, when he was not inclined
to lay his blade to the tender pale throat of a damsel, had demonstrated
an extraordinary talent for lopping appendages and pruning and dicing
outcroppings. He'd even on one occasion ascended into a dudgeon and
seen fit to fillet a manservant.

Mrs. Heflin, then, was girding for some carnage, had turned off,
she confessed, the lights and taken up, she told it, from the hamper
by her chair that piece of maul handle she kept about to club intruders
with. So Janice put out the call to Wendle but, once she couldn't raise
him, she put out the call to me instead and told who was lurking out
back of the baby's breath and what he was lurking there with.

I inquired of Ellis, "What was it that last time?" and Ellis, who
drew up to the seatback and struck a contemplative pose, could not in
the end decide if it had been the dapper European assassin with the
machine pistol or the strapping dusky buck with the blowpipe and the
darts he'd rubbed on the belly of an orange frog.

7

We climbed in the cruiser up out of the river bottom past the lumber yard and the furniture mill and off across the junction where the rail lines mix and mingle from back in those days when the trains had come through and gotten shifted and shunted about to the docks. I turned up between the motel lot and the machine shop and crossed through town to the truck route where I set out to the west on beyond the country club and the memorial gardens and turned presently back to the right on a gravel road that ran down along the branch and cut through to the blacktop just shy of the interstate where Mrs. Heflin and her nest of prowlers lived.

The twilight had come to be general already, though down on the branch the night itself had pretty much taken hold what with the laurels and the evergreens above the roadcut and the hardwoods along the creek conspiring together to shut out the sky. I was fairly creeping along, was reaching there, I do recall, to switch my lights full on when I detected in the canopy before us an odd manner of flicker, noticed against the leaves up past where the road bent a wavering sort of a glow and I asked of Ellis, as we closed upon it, what he figured it might be. Ellis, however, inspired by talk lately of scimitars, was making to assure me how he'd skewered in his day a damsel or two and so did not notice the light and did not take heed of my inquiry engaged like he was in conjuring the details of one truly extravagant and fanciful bit of bladework.

As we rounded the ledgy outcropping, we spied together Wendle's vehicle there on the side of the roadway with the driver's door flung open and jittery flashes from the solitary blue beacon pulsing against the roadcut and the laurel thicket to the one side and the hardwood canopy to the other. I just figured he'd pulled some hapless citizen with a brakelight burned out or an expired sticker or had, God help her, endured some woman to turn in front of him without the aid and benefit of her signal. So I was guessing still he was up there ahead of his cruiser as I eased in behind it, just assumed he was issuing probably a citation, volunteering instruction, ladling advice, speaking maybe with his customary and undue gravity of the codes and courtesies of the highway. I'd even climbed out of my vehicle and gained Wendle's fenderwell before I realized that I was in fact quite altogether alone. There wasn't a car up there, wasn't anything up there at all. Wendle's chime was chiming and his clipboard and his summons book and his flashlight and his sleeve of saltines were laying on the seat. His shotgun was still wedged butt foremost into the rig on the passenger floor, but Wendle himself wasn't anywhere about.

I called to him, yelled up into the thicket, down into the woods, and I allowed myself as a source of ease to figure that maybe Wendle was feeling prankish, had slipped off to piss in the bushes and was hiding probably back of a laurel so as to pop out shortly and give me a fright, but Wendle wasn't truly the prankish sort, not the manner of fellow to leap out from a thicket at length and shriek. Ellis couldn't imagine where he might have gone, came out from the backseat to join me up alongside Wendle's open door and invited me to tell to him please if wasn't this a peculiar bit of business which I allowed straightaway it seemed to me to be.

I fetched Wendle's flashlight off the seat and shone it down along the creek, up the slope above the roadcut, and then played presently the beam out before the cruiser where I could make out plainly a tirerut there off the roadway in the pea gravel.

"He had somebody," I told to Ellis and squatted before that rut, poked my fingers into it, examined the tread impressions, and endured presently assorted queries from Ellis who was wanting to find out just where that rut had come from and what that rut had been made by, was anxious to discover was it fresh and recent, warm maybe still which moved me to inform him, "I'm no damn Indian scout, Ellis. It's a tirerut. A tire made it."

Straightoff Ellis confessed to growing uneasy, admitted to advancing qualms about standing there in the dark on the roadway hard by Wendle's abandoned vehicle as Ellis didn't suppose either one of us could know what it was that might be lurking off in the woods or up in the thicket, and he suggested that perhaps there was this night a strapping swarthy fellow loose on the land with a scimitar. "Was heading up towards the autumn olive. Stopped to run that boy through."

"Oh Christ Ellis," I told to him, "get back in the car."

But Ellis declined to retire to the cruiser, had concluded that probably the woods this evening were wholly infected with marauders and did not suppose that a doorlock and a windowglass would secure for him his salvation. He simply figured he'd just as soon perish upright in the open air which he made a declaration about, gripped with either hand onto a satin lapel and announced to me his intentions to go presently nowhere and do presently nothing at all.

I called out again for Wendle, yelled up along the road and down towards the fork and off into the laurel thicket but raised by it only a solitary rabbit that lurched out of the ditch and across the roadway and down the embankment and produced in Ellis some considerable consternation and alarm since a rabbit can after all, with its claws and its anxiety, kick up about as much of a fuss as a bescimitared infidel might. I shone Wendle's light all about his vehicle and fashioned for a time that I could see where he'd walked to and where he'd stood, but the gravel didn't hold truly much of an impression and looked just stomped on and stepped all over. I couldn't quite decide what I should do or how I might ought to proceed and was standing there in the soft pea gravel alongside the tirerut just sweeping the creekbank with the lightbeam when I noticed down in the scrub there among the stalks and the creepers a species of gleam that struck me somehow as pertinent.

I brought Ellis in to consult and indicated the thing to him in among the leaves and shoots, but he just tried to make a scimitar of it and worked himself into such an agitated state that he grew briefly wild with apprehension once I'd revealed how I was meaning to make my way down the embankment and wade the creek so as to find out for certain what exactly we were looking upon.

"I'm not going down there," Ellis told to me. "No sir," and once I'd allowed how he could wait up on the shoulder if he pleased, Ellis was quick to inform me, "I'm not staying up here."

So I said to him, "Well," said to him, "Ellis, do whatever is left to you," and I set out myself down the embankment through the nettles and the tangled vines while Ellis from the shoulder apprised me of how the woods at night were full of rats and vipers which was not of course even to mention the local concentration of bescimitared infidels. He did not guess he would chase a glint himself down into such a clutch of vermin, was announcing even how he'd remain just precisely where he'd come to be while he prepared, I suppose, for a descent of his own since he'd hardly even left off talking before he departed from the shoulder and passed me down the slope, came like he'd been pitched off the roadcut and arrived ahead of me on the silty creekbank from where he shared with me the news that I had carried off the light.

Fearful of what he might stir up, Ellis wasn't looking to walk in front of me and, fearful of what I might stir up, he wasn't too anxious to walk behind me either and so satisfied himself with walking all over me instead, caught up in his fingers a clump of my shirt and had me to pretty much tow him across the creek to the far bank where he scaled as best he was able my trouser legs and clung to me and breathed on me and belched at me and wanted to know of every little crack and rattle, "What's that?"

I couldn't tell just where I was, couldn't begin to gauge if I'd arrived after all at the place I'd set out to go. So me and Ellis wandered a little there in the brush, walked through the weeds and the leafy stalks first the one way and then back the other while I looked for the sort of item that might have glinted at me and entertained from Ellis queries as to what just lately he'd stepped on and what just lately he'd heard and what maybe please those creatures were off in the hardwoods back in the dark. I wouldn't have probably even come across it but for the fact that Ellis managed somehow to leave off walking on my shoetops just long enough to stomp squarely upon the thing. Of course it struck him as sufficiently exotic and unforeseen to cause him to vault into the air and howl after an unearthly operatic fashion which served straightoff to capture my attention and, while Ellis endeavored to scamper up onto my cowlick, I parted the leaves and reached down among the stalks and the vines from where I fetched out Wendle's hat with the shiny black brim and the platinum shield and the studs about the band.

Aside from having gotten just lately crushed and dented, it didn't look to me to have a thing else wrong with it, wasn't much beat up otherwise, wasn't stained or dirty or ripped through. I looked to see might there be some other article about, some additional item of Wendle's that had come maybe to rest down among the shoots, and I was playing the beam around my feet when Ellis caught sight in the wash of it the sticker bush, spied there snagged on a thorn what looked to him a portion of viper, the toothy end I suspect, and he was leaving even already before he told to me, "Kill it!" was selecting anyhow a possible path of retreat, a streak of scrub he might take for viperless and slip off into like he slipped shortly off into one as he told to me, "Kill it!" again.

It wasn't yet even crusty altogether, hadn't dried and drawn up and hardened and become by it curious chiefly but was largely pulpy still, an allurement for the gnats and the mayflies, was slick and supple and gruesome and held for me a manner of fascination there at the first since I'd not, in calculating what possibly I'd step down into the woods and turn up, anticipated at all a moist and thickly pelted scrap of scalp dangling from a thorn and quivering every now and again on the evening air. I took it even straightaway for a piece of Wendle's head, knew the hair to be his and could smell the tonic he used to plaster and persuade it, and as I watched the bugs light upon the thing and stalk about I entertained from Ellis back in the dark, down by the creek, encouragement further to do please away with that item.

I guessed he was hard by, didn't reason or calculate exactly but just suffered to come upon me like a sickness the notion that Wendle was surely about, and I shone the light off into a stand of poplars and down along the creek from where Ellis in his brown hat and his black clawhammer jacket stood blinking at me by the water. He lifted his fingers meekly into the air and favored me with a proposal, suggested that perhaps we would be wise to withdraw and invoked with passion and fervor the name of the holy Savior.

"Sweet," he told to me, "Jesus," and then told it to me again as he undertook with a jerk of his head to reiterate his intentions and amplify his desires.

But I just left him once more to the darkness, played the light-beam on up the creek a bit and then back into the scrub and round-about through the vines and the leaves where I wouldn't probably have taken any notice much of Wendle but for the column of gnats he'd attracted. They rose in a peppery shaft from a tangle of berry bushes just before me and, as a body, they swirled and twitched and bent in the breeze and lit by portions and lifted by portions as well. It was only presently and only at last that I spied beyond that column and through that shaft those shoetops in with the reedy stalks, those shiny black leather uppers standing toes foremost among the berries and the prickly shoots like some preposterous overripe manner of fruit.

At length I could make out a portion of trouser and a bit of shirt and, from along about the breast pocket up, what I took to be a general luxuriance of stain and seepage, stain anyhow and seepage enough to prompt me to reach with my thumb and switch off for a moment the light. I was wanting I guess the night simply to close for a time about me, was seeking I figure occasion just to breathe again there in the darkness with nothing to see but the beacon in the treetops and nothing to hear but the creek and the jarflies and shortly Ellis as well, Ellis who wondered where maybe I'd gone, Ellis who wondered what I was about, Ellis who called, Ellis who cried out, Ellis who presently whimpered and whined.

🖋

I'd seen already a world of dead people, the bulk of them killed along the roadways and the interstate where civilians routinely got crushed and compacted or pitched about every now and again and torn altogether to pieces. I'd seen the sorts that yielded of a sudden to a complaint, seized up out at the buffet or along the walk in town, fell over sometimes dead at home and lay undiscovered until the mail accumulated and the papers piled up when the neighbors would grow at last sufficiently fretful to call in. I'd seen the burned ones, seared and scorched and suffocated, and seen of course the forlorn ones too, the hanged ones, the poisoned ones, the gassed ones, the ones afflicted with misery enough to make of their shotguns and make of their revolvers unerring authentic narcotics.

I'd not, however, had much call to see too many murdered ones since locally we weren't given ourselves to that variety of mayhem. As a population we were maybe a little larcenous and prone I suppose to that manner of peevishness that blossoms on occasion into a thrashing, but we didn't often set out to kill each other, didn't usually even in our idle infuriated moments much want truly to see each other dead.

It seems to me I was a good half year or more on the force before I came across that fellow who'd suffered his wife to slice him open with a boning knife, gut him fairly much like a trout. I didn't know him, hadn't ever even once laid my eyes on him alive, but Dewey said he'd met up with him a time or two, Dewey who hadn't taken him for a bad sort, Dewey who didn't figure he'd probably done much to get killed about. Dewey had been around himself, had worked a stretch up in Salem and down in Charlotte, let on to have seen all gauges of crime and every imaginable manner of bloodletting, acts of passion, exploits of extraordinary meanness and almost sublime indifference. He claimed to have found the remains of a man who'd been set fire to by his neighbor, discovered a woman who'd been hacked by her brother to pieces and pickled away in a joint compound bucket, which would be of course in addition to the more conventional sorts of victims, the stabbed ones and the shot ones and the ones who'd been reduced with a length of pipe or a hunk of wood to a nuggety manner of gruel.

Dewey was one to figure aloud that he'd seen likely sufficient carnage to last a whole platoon of fellows the rest of their days and color pretty severely their opinions, poison probably their views of this world, and he could propose it all with such a surfeit of heavy and significant exhalations that a person might be forgiven for concluding that Dewey hadn't yet hardened altogether to the things some people just up sometimes and do to each other. But the plain truth was that Dewey had likely started hardened. He could blow well enough a breath and make a fine show of cloaked and buried anguishment, but Dewey at heart was probably about as soft and supple as a boat anchor.

Dewey was by disposition a hoodlum dangler. He'd evolved over time a technique of eliciting information and promoting confessions, had theorized and concluded that not even probably scum were terribly much anxious to be dropped from a considerable height onto their topnotches. So he'd hauled countless perpetrators and known associates out to the trestle alongside the old ruined rolling mill where he'd suspended them in turn by their ankles over what most people wistfully called a branch. Essentially it's all bed and no water and has a ledgy enough look about it to impress usually even hoodlums, impressed almost always hoodlums in fact except for a lone instance of muleheadedness when a suspect in a larceny neglected to volunteer his confession until he'd been already dropped and let go that Dewey determined to treat as the merest manner of technicality and wouldn't allow himself to indulge in doubts and recriminations, guessed that boy should have spoken up sooner, been prompt for once and timely like all those hoodlums otherwise.

Unfortunately for Dewey, he got discovered in the midst of an inquisition by a woman from Fort Mill, South Carolina, a lady who'd exited by accident the interstate and had gotten by accident off of the road she'd gotten by accident onto, had just blundered partway across the county and ended up at the rolling mill where Dewey was making inquiries of a fellow who'd boosted a Vega, was meaning not just to hear from him confirmation of the crime itself, but was hoping, as a point of personal curiosity, to find out why it was a man might go to the trouble in the first place to steal a Vega at all.

Naturally the confession proper was dispatched with in a forthright and uncomplicated fashion, that thief anyhow wailed and screeched and admitted how he'd done surely whatever it was Dewey was wanting him to own up to, but he could not formulate upside down and suspended off a trestle a satisfying explanation as to how he'd determined, out of all the vehicles roundabout, the coupes and the trucks and the sedans, to make off with such a contraption as he'd seen fit to make off with. As an altogether confirmed student of the vagaries of human nature, Dewey was simply curious to learn the reasons and hear the causes of this particular theft and, since that fellow was wiry and light, Dewey enjoyed the strength and the leisure to wait him out, was allowing that man the occasion to consider what circumstances he felt obliged to consider and factor in what influences he guessed he ought to factor in when that lady from Fort Mill, South Carolina, passed under the trestle on the road along the branch which she'd hoped might take her back to the road she'd gotten by accident onto after she'd left inadvertently the interstate.

Apparently she figured straightoff that Dewey and his buddy were fishing, and the notion even persisted with her as she laid her head out the carwindow and made herself known to the pair of them up on the trestle. She noticed shortly, however, that they were not either one of them in possession of a pole and didn't have below them any water much to cast into, noticed in fact that the wiry one seemed to be dangling upside down out over the trestle rail which was not truly an awfully prudent fishing posture. She was even set to wonder aloud what maybe that man was dangling about when she paid some regard to Dewey's hat and paid some regard to Dewey's shirt and interpolated from them Dewey's civic calling as an officer of the peace.

Dewey straightaway seemed to her guilty at least of a pretty severe breach of hospitality since she knew for a fact that down where she came from in Fort Mill, South Carolina, the lawmen were not allowed to carry on so. Oh they pursued and arrested and interrogated and incarcerated people in a regular sort of way, but free-lance perpetrator dangling was hardly encouraged or even so much as tolerated. She was bound, she figured, and obligated to speak of Dewey's infraction to Dewey's superiors, and she inquired up towards the trestle

16

after the stationhouse which earned for her a detailed account of how she might arrive there, an intricate description of the route to take there from the Vega thief whose hands were free to point with and whose interests were plainly vested.

So Dewey tolerated a reprimand and yielded to the wishes of the chief who did not want his officers indulging in practices and cultivating habits that they could not freely export to even such a place as Fort Mill. The chief himself was an enthusiastic student of advanced nightstick technique, had attended a conference in Baltimore, taken part there in a seminar on the topic of inventive restraint where he'd mastered the reverse inseam lever that he shared with Dewey the nuances of so that Dewey might fend off his urge to dangle hoodlums by levitating them with his nightstick instead. The substitute seemed to take and Dewey, I guess, mined in time near as much delight from the inseam lever, which he performed evermore with flair and infectious ardor, as hoodlum dangling had ever brought to him.

Everybody who came onto the force worked shifts for a time with Dewey, not because Dewey looked out for them or Dewey instructed them or Dewey set with his habits and actions a sterling sort of example, but largely on account of how Dewey knew no fear, would just roar on into most any species of difficulty and smother it on his own, extract from the turmoil the agitators, lever them maybe a little if he saw the need for it or was feeling sprightly and of a mood to lever, and allow the attending officer the opportunity to consider the matter in relative peace and figure what maybe he'd have done if Dewey hadn't been around to do everything himself. Dewey was a manner of insulation and provided by turns the rest of us the occasion to weigh and the leisure to ruminate and the freedom to calculate and ponder. So I was naturally ever so pleased to be in the company of him the night that woman found cause to take up her boning knife and apply it to her husband since I guessed I could endure Dewey between that enterprise and myself.

She was a Cathcart and lived down on the colored end of the river out past the mill and beyond the lumber yard, lived in a little frame house with a dirt front lot and a buckled slab walk and the skeletal remains of a camellia bush up alongside the porch. She had a puny dog that came out to the ditch and yapped and shivered at us. It looked to have been sired by a wharf rat. I'd spent even then already a gracious plenty of my time down on the river out at the colored end in my first half year on the force. It seemed that those people were evermore slicing each other up with knives and razors, were purely prone to lay flesh open, not often mortally and not usually to the bone but gravely enough to bring some resolution to their difficulties and satisfy the passions of the principals who'd go off to have their wounds seen after, sewn closed or flushed with fuel oil, and weren't ordinarily around anymore by the time we answered the call.

Almost from the first I was persuaded I had white people pretty much figured out, could reason on most occasions why they'd done what they did like they did it, could see through their lies and comprehend their motives, but down on the river out past the lumber yard even once the blood had been let and the culprits and the victims had been sorted and separated, I couldn't often decipher much sense in the explanations, couldn't find the causes, discover the sparks that had set the whole business ablaze. I simply had no feel much for the local social order with its implicit obligations and unspoken restraints, its ties of kinship and matrimony which were largely so casual and oblique that the queen's own genealogist would have been put upon likely to ink up charts enough for a fiefdom just to help a fellow find his first cousin.

Dewey, who never troubled himself to think too deeply about anything much, left off with even his meager functions down along the river at the colored end where he'd wade on into the crowd—there was always a crowd, even lacking a scuffle and lacking a crime there was without fail a crowd nonetheless—and make himself known to the conferees, the most of whom had been already dangled or levered themselves or were on friendly terms with somebody who'd had the pleasure of getting suspended the one way or uplifted the other. So down at the river out past the lumber yard Dewey alone could step in among a regular throng of people and produce an altogether magical effect, render himself instantaneously solitary.

I was given back in those days to creeping, had favored at the movies and on the TV the sorts of lawmen who crept, the ones who crouched and squatted and eased along when the prospect of danger impressed itself upon them, and the colored end of the river seemed so thick to me with threat that I was hunkering there usually before I climbed out of the cruiser, was taut and contracted and generally hit the ground in a manner of squat with my hand laid upon the hilt of my revolver.

Dewey had tried at the outset to break me, had wondered at me the first time I'd hunkered, "What in God's name are you doing?"

I'd told to him, "You know." I'd told to him, "Creeping," and he'd seen fit to share with me how I looked to him a man so far gone with constipation that I was half prepared to shoot myself in the asshole for relief. But I'd not been persuaded to stand just baldly upright, not anyhow by the night we went to find that fellow laid open when I was still inclined to stoop and slip along.

Dewey, I believe, was half disposed to hammer the head of that short-haired dog and called to it sweetly as he strode up the walkway and gained the front porch, but the creature apparently had sniffed out Dewey's intent and lurked just clear of head-hammering range while it yapped and snarled and shivered and dodged about. I lingered for the moment alongside the cruiser between Dewey up on the front porch with that mongrel and the crowd of spectators across the street under the vapor light where they'd collected to see what we might be up to, had collected anyhow to watch us be up to it since they evermore appeared to know already more than we'd ever find out, were acquainted themselves early on with who'd done what to whom and were knowledgeable as to why precisely, familiar with the intricacies of the motive, the inducements of the perpetrator, the offenses of the victim, and just came I guess to see us try to decipher the thing on our own.

Dewey beat the screen door with his nightstick, never knocked anywhere with his knuckles when the toe of his shoe or the buttend of his flashlight or the barrel of his stick was available to him to knock with instead. He rapped on the rail and called into the house for somebody to come please and lift the doorhook which he made a show even of waiting for somebody in fact to do before he poked through the screenwire with his stickend and let himself into the front room which prompted me to crouch and prompted me to tauten afresh and creep with my palm to my pistol on up the walk and onto the porch proper where I was meaning to be handy were Dewey to get into a scrape. Dewey, however, was prone chiefly to inflict distress and create for people otherwise enormous difficulties which left me usually to languish wherever I'd come to be handy at. He sounded, however, this evening to me a trifle put upon, inquired anyhow with some noticeable exasperation, "Now who is it that went and did this?"

I determined to enter on into that house myself, stepped into the front room where I took, as was my custom, an accounting, stood with my back to the jamb and peered slowly about for some trace of danger hidden and concealed. There wasn't, however, much place for danger to be as the room was small and crowded already with a settee and a pair of upholstered chairs and a geegaw cupboard off against the wall with pictures on the top of it of little toothy black children, nieces, I guess, and nephews and grandbabies. The oil burner on the hearth was lit still or had been lit lately and the air was stifling and close and extravagantly overheated, had a smell to it of must and dander, seemed stale and vaguely sweet.

In the kitchen Dewey was striking up a genuine inquisition, was wondering pretty much how it was things had come to the pass they'd come to and was tiring, it seemed, of the answers he was earning in reply. Now Dewey had not been blessed by the angels with patience and with charm and didn't much care for the course these sorts of inquiries often took. The customary format usually called for the witnesses to and the perpetrators of some species of lawlessness to throw in together and ponder exclusively whatever officer presented himself in advance of lying to him instead, and I could make out plainly from the kitchen the sound of two voices raised together in utter fabrication.

I eased on over towards the doorway where the green wall-to-wall left off and the yellow linoleum set in, and I was meaning to straighten up and stride into the kitchen proper so as to make if I might a stalwart impression when I detected the first traces of carnage, a splash of blood on the baseboard and a piece of that gutted fellow sticking out from under the dinette. He was sporting a fairly extravagant incision that set in at his windpipe and left off at his belt buckle, a deep and thorough-going manner of wound which proved for me an object straightoff of fascination since I'd not had occasion to see too many people laid open in a surgical sort of way, had come across a few unfortunates separated from their parts and pieces in collisions but had never run up previously on such a gaudy wound inflicted with intent. I couldn't help but wonder what a man had to do to get sawed longways fairly much in half but I made out pretty directly who it was he had to do it to.

She was a plump little woman in a housedress who was disputing at the moment with Dewey the sundry details of the matter at hand which Dewey, as was his custom, had misrepresented and misstated. That was Dewey's nature and his technique together. He would latch onto a suspect if a suspect were handy and narrate for him a fairly fanciful version of events, tell how he figured things had happened and why he guessed they'd transpired at all, but he'd get it all backwards and have it pretty much by design all wrong in hopes of being corrected and straightened out by the actual perpetrator since Dewey had learned from the chief, in addition to the nuances of the reverse inseam lever, that your guilty parties could be on occasion as intrusive and relentless as grammarians.

Dewey, for his part, could fire pretty miraculously wide of the mark, be wronger sooner than anybody might expect and demonstrate from the outset a misapprehension of causes and results that was oftentimes extravagant enough to take the perpetrator unawares, the perpetrator who would vent a cry and render a correction and suppress himself only once he'd as much as confessed.

The plump little woman in the housedress, however, was no longer looking to conceal her guilt, had resisted at first but soon enough admitted that she'd butchered her husband like a pig. She could not seem, though, to assist Dewey in the digestion of the causes, Dewey who endeavored to repeat to her most everything she'd told to him but was failing to keep the inducements straight and demonstrated no grasp much of the escalation of animosities. There was a woman otherwise over at the counter alongside the little plump one, a woman in red elastic pants who had not cultivated the sort of posterior that was terribly much flattered by red elastic. She was resting on her broad behind against the counteredge and was serving apparently an unwelcome advisory role, would interrupt the plump little woman from time to time with an augmentation or a personal impression or a contradiction outright and would hear invariably, "Ain't so," back.

I didn't even see the boy at all until he turned a page which reduced me straightaway to my creeping posture, and I squatted and I hunkered and could make out then under the plastic flower centerpiece on the dinette a portion of him across the table, a little scrap of shirt and a bit of forearm. I don't know if we ever found out exactly who he was. I mean we learned his name and got some notion of how he'd come to be there, but it wasn't ever made entirely clear to me if maybe he was related to that plump little woman and her dead husband on the floor or if he'd arrived instead with the lady in the red elastic pants who was apparently a neighbor from out across the way with no tie by blood to that plump little woman or that plump little woman's late husband. But he'd come somehow to be in the kitchen and was acquainted I guess with somebody there, had cause to be sitting at the dinette though he did not appear too terribly much attached to the proceedings or noticeably distracted by the corpse.

He was in fact reading a magazine and reading it with some attention though he would look from time to time over towards the counteredge to measure, I suppose, the progress of the debate, the stage of the confession which was complicated and elaborate and could not be just blurted and done with. His sneaker toe wasn't half a foot from the dead man's upflung fingers, wasn't awful far removed from the seepage and the gore, but that boy didn't seem much troubled by his proximity to that gutted fellow, didn't truly exhibit any detectable trace of distress, and once I'd given over my crouch and had grown sufficiently untautened to stand again altogether upright, that boy did me the honor of raising up from his periodical so as to look full upon me, stare blankly for a time in my direction prior to taking up again with his reading.

I just guess I'd expected a little more high feeling and a little less irrelevance considering how a man had been laid open and done in, a man with maybe engagements to keep, duties to fulfill, prospects and responsibilities he'd been relieved of and separated from by a six-inch boning knife in the grip of a woman I suppose he'd loved, a woman anyhow he'd seen fit to marry. I'd simply been led and conditioned to expect of the scene before me something a trifle more dramatic and compelling than what I'd ended up with, had figured the place would probably be alive with subtle revealing details which a trained professional eye like my own might fix upon instinctively and thereby come better to understand the motives and envision the act, where he must have been and how she must have slipped up on him. But near about all my professional eye could see at the time was the blood.

The place was fairly awash in it, more blood than it seemed to me likely a man could hold, and it looked as if everybody had walked through it and tracked it to those parts of the floor it had yet to seep and run to. I hadn't much expected the stench either, not the musty semi-sweet household aroma but those rank, sour vapors from the corpse, vented I guess out of the cavity or up from a punctured organ. They were thick and troublesome, smelled of rot and disease, and I didn't know straightoff if I could tolerate them with grace, maintain a suitable grave expression, not seem appalled, not appear disgusted, not look somehow uninitiated in the face of such casual and disarming ease on the part in particular of that boy at the dinette who left off regularly with his magazine to glance over and see what I might be about.

I'd just expected it would all be different, more glamorous maybe or at least sharper than regular life, incomparable somehow and distinct. But it was just, I suppose, another fellow killed, even here where nobody got killed much, and he didn't strike me as victimized truly. I wasn't anyhow stirred with compassion at the sight of him but caught myself trying to calculate how maybe he'd brought it on, why likely he'd had it coming. I was curious about him in an anatomical sort of way, interested to see his breastbone and a portion of his intestine, but I can't say I cared much that he was laid open. Getting murdered just didn't seem to me a savory sort of an enterprise, not the manner of undertaking to inspire any measurable pity. I'd thought the sight of the corpse might leave me charged with indignation, moved to righteous anger, but I wasn't much stirred one way or another. It all simply looked to me terribly untidy and inconvenient, common and lowly, no suitable fate for respectable people. I found myself wondering if that linoleum would maybe ever come clean.

Apparently he'd been out whoring, was given to whoring as a hobby and a pursuit which that plump little woman ordinarily tolerated, allowed him the latitude to indulge his urges as long as he observed the unspoken stipulations and played by the implicit rules. He'd committed, however, a breach of etiquette, had transgressed beyond the scope of his rights and indulgences, had been inspired somehow to wear this night the shiny blue shirt his plump little wife had driven clean to Roanoke to buy for him as a gift on the occasion of their wedding anniversary. It seems she'd never instructed him not to whore in it but had simply assumed he'd have more sense than to wear that shirt out catting around, had figured even once he'd left the house in his gray poplin blazer and his blue shiny shirt and his yellow twill pants and his imitation lizard skin shoes with the gold chainlink adornments that he was not probably intending to scour the county dousing, as was his custom, with his agitated member like a man hunting a vein of water.

She was persuaded he knew better, convinced he'd not required instruction after all which, it would seem, she held to and believed in until he arrived home, until he found her out in the kitchen before the sink where she was piddling still with the supper dishes, scraping the crud from a pot, when she caught a whiff of him, detected a trace of his spicy cologne that had come to be diluted by and folded into a conglomeration of scents otherwise, beer and smoke and treacly sweet perfume along with trace enough of vague, dank, fungal aroma to cause that plump little woman to reach into the drainer for her boning knife. She said she was meaning just to cut him, intending to whip around and slice through his shirt, sour his evening but she got rendered by her mood a trifle more decisive than she'd set out to be. She wished we'd seen his face. She guessed he'd had all the women he was likely ever to get.

Dewey asked me to take her on out to the cruiser. "See if you can raise Angelene," he told to me. "Have her send Lonnie out here with the camera and tell her we need Gooch to bring his wagon."

I gave him a roger, was as prone at that time to rogering as I was to hunkering and creeping, and at Dewey's instruction I left the hands of that plump little woman free to dangle at her side as I led her by the elbow out of the kitchen and through the front room and onto the porch. They were all of them still out there, more of them probably anymore across the road under the vapor light from where they watched us step down off the decking and onto the slab walk that had heaved up and cracked from the cold and had to be negotiated with some attention and care. I squired that plump little woman to the street, steered and guided her out to the cruiser where we endured the scrutiny of the crowd across the way, not one of whom spoke to us and not one of whom spoke apparently to anybody otherwise either as the night was still and the night was quiet but for that runt of a dog that wriggled and danced at the feet of the murderess and delivered itself from time to time of little short-haired high-strung sorts of noises.

I opened the driver's door, turned on the radio, and drew out the handset. I rested one foot in the doorwell and laid against the roof after as casual a fashion as I could manage while that plump little woman stood alongside me and instructed her dog, told to it at intervals, "Go on," in a low and wholly uninflected voice which proved somehow regard enough to delight that creature which bucked and shivered and twirled and raised with its nails a regular clatter.

There didn't seem to be anything but static on the channel. I couldn't for the life of me raise Angelene or bring anybody else onto the air, and I was fixing to sit down in the vehicle and tamper with the dials when I saw before me on the roof of the car what the trouble was though I made out like I hadn't maybe noticed, pitched the handset onto the seat and advised that plump little woman how I was meaning straightaway to squire her back into the house.

I took her up again at the elbow and steered her around the fender and along the walk and across the porch and through the front room to the kitchen doorway where we came upon Dewey squatting over that fellow with the major incision and the soured evening, Dewey who presently looked up at me in an inquiring sort of way and prompted me thereby to tell to him, "Somebody's made off with the antenna."

Dewey smiled straightaway, stood up pretty shortly but firstoff just grinned at me prior to lifting himself from his squat and laying his hand to his ribbed stickhandle, curling with grace his fingers and hooking his thumb in the particular configuration of his inseam levering grip. He said at length just out and just into the air, "Well these goddam people," but said it truly with no ire much, and as he stepped out of the kitchen and slipped by me through the doorway, I could detect plain enough the fairly giddy cast of his features, and remarked upon his face the sporting look of an enthusiast.

🍃

Wendle was in a terrible state out in the vines, off in the scrub, was a woeful thing to look upon. He was dead, of course, had been shot twice square in the face and the slugs had passed clean through his head and burst out the back, punched open his skull and ripped wide his scalp leaving the awfullest raggedy mess imaginable. I tried to keep Ellis from looking upon him, but Ellis somehow got hard set to see him and waded the undergrowth, braved the rats and the vipers, and slipped presently up behind me from where he gazed even a little upon Wendle before he came to be sufficiently worked up and disgusted to mount a headlong retreat and retire clean to the roadway.

Janice rounded up the lot of them, got a hold of the chief at home and Dewey out at the golf range, rooted Gooch out from a viewing and relieved Lonnie of his duties and obligations in the lockup where she figured those two boys in for mischief could make do this night without the sight of him canted back against the wall with his mouth flopped open and his adenoids exposed. She hadn't troubled herself to hunt up Clifford, but the chief had called him on his own since Clifford after all was the chief's wife's sister's boy and any time he got slighted, any time he got passed over and ignored, Clifford's disappointment and Clifford's displeasure traveled like a virus from sister to sister and infected pretty directly the chief as well.

Dewey was the first to arrive, had his lights pulsing and his siren wailing and was advancing at his customary heedless velocity when he rounded the bend and came up on us which was more of a thrill truly than Ellis required, Ellis who scooted about in the road like a squirrel, attempted as best he was able to run pretty much everywhere all at once but ended up at last where he'd started out from and was spared by happenstance alone as Dewey this evening managed one of his elusive semi-controlled skids and brought his cruiser to a halt clean athwart the roadway just shy of Ellis who'd near about, there at the end, augered himself into the ground.

Dewey had been playing carpet golf with his woman friend and was wearing still his carpet golf outfit, his striped sports shirt and his pleated shorts and his blue socks and his casual soft-soled shoes though he'd managed already to put on his gunbelt, had fetched the thing out of his trunk I guess at the golf range and buckled it round which naturally rendered him a peculiar sight most especially next to Ellis in his clawhammer jacket, Ellis who was grateful not to have been lately crushed and maimed and reported as much to Dewey alongside him, Dewey who jerked his head after that burly fashion he favored though the effect of it was largely diluted and diminished by his law-of-the-links ensemble.

"It was like this then?" Dewey asked of me and pointed towards Wendle's vehicle with the door flung open and the beacon on.

"Yeah," I told to him, "just like that."

We left Ellis up on the road and I led Dewey down the embankment and across the creek and off along the trail I'd tramped through the stalks and vines that carried us to the sticker bush straightoff, and I shone my light on that snagged scrap of scalp that Dewey reached out with his finger and touched. I showed him from there the shoetops, played my beam on the black leather oxfords and along the length of Wendle up to where the seepage was plain in advance of stepping over to the corpse itself where me and where Dewey sat together on our heels and viewed the carnage, considered the wounds, inspected the vicinity and breathed at each other in a telling sort of a way, exchanged little significant noises.

We guessed we could figure well enough what had happened to Wendle, didn't truly feel the need to speak of it since it appeared clearly the manner of thing we dreaded for ourselves, endeavored to plan against, suffered in the black of night troubled dreams about. With me it's always a Ford, usually a Torino, a blue one or a gold one or a red one with primer on a fender and rust along the doorpanels. The tag is out of state, Georgia sometimes, South Carolina, New York. There's been a mild infraction, an improper turn, a failure to yield, an expired sticker, nothing too grave and troublesome, and I figure I'll just speak of it to the driver and let him go on. So I fall in behind that Torino and switch on the beacon. He sees me straightoff. They all see me, and the two of them in the backseat twist around to look out the window as the driver eases off the roadway and onto the shoulder.

I can make out four of them altogether and they're engaged plainly in a debate, are meeting at the front seatback in an animated conference which rises to a pitch but leaves off sharply once the driver has lifted his open hand and conveyed his instructions. They all of them slip a glance at me back in the cruiser where I'm taking up my hat and taking up my stick, marshalling my paraphernalia, and they've decided already I'm on the radio, I'm talking to the stationhouse, the state police, the federal bureau, Interpol. I know what they've done, am acquainted with what they're suspected of doing, have cultivated some notion of what likely they mean to be up to. I've got them as good as apprehended. I step out of the cruiser.

They all sit now facing forward. The driver watches me in the side mirror as I drop my stick into the hanger and settle my hat on my head. He says something to the rest of them low and sidelong and I lay by habit my palm upon the hilt of my pistol. The tires are bald and the tailpipe is wired to the bumper. The flap window is shattered and the antenna is a coathanger. The driver is black sometimes, white sometimes, caramel-colored every now and again like those boys up for the harvest, and he is extravagantly polite and pleasant, says to me, "Evening, officer," and shows me his teeth. He can't begin to imagine what he's done, lives, he lets on, to be lawful, and the rest of them all grin. They want themselves to be slick one day and nervy like him.

I ask for his license, for his registration, and he tells to me, "Yes sir," tells to me, "Surely," and lays his far hand upon an item, extracts from under his thigh, produces from off the seat cushion always a revolver that he trains straightaway upon me, points at the bridge of my nose. I see the rounds in the chambers, watch his knuckle whiten on the trigger. I'm going to duck. I'm going to draw. I'm going to plead and beg. The hammer falls to the pin. I'm going to die.

"Might have come down off the interstate," Dewey said to me and he gestured with his nose chiefly up across the roadcut and off through the woods in what he figured for the direction of the exit, at the head of the truck route, over by the pancake house and the motor hotel and the discount shoe outlet. We liked to believe our trouble was largely transient and imported, inflicted on a whim by some lowlife from the highway, some fellow from up north of here, down south of here who'd stopped for gas or stopped for hotcakes and had carried down the ramp his impulses and his inclinations.

"Wendle caught him in a violation," Dewey told me. "He was up to no good. Got jumpy. Popped him."

"Yeah," I allowed. "Maybe so."

"I'm persuaded of it," Dewey declared and stood full upright again.

Clifford had swung by the stationhouse partly to fetch away Lonnie but primarily to pick up the generator and the light standards that he'd requisitioned himself and insisted all along we needed though they'd been only so far employed in the chief's backyard at a lawn party. Here, however, with Wendle dead in the woods out of the reach of headlamps and considerably removed from all power sources, Clifford realized the triumph of his foresight and his preparation, and the thrill of being a man of vision, if even for one night alone out of all the nights otherwise when he was just Clifford the chief's wife's sister's boy, got away with him a little and introduced too awful much sprightliness into his mood to suit the circumstances. Clifford came, that is, fairly prancing down the embankment and through the brush and near about stepped flush upon Wendle at the belt buckle in his zest to speak to us of the halogen lamps that shortly would illuminate the darkness and bring probably evidence to light.

"Every bug in the county's going to be here," Dewey told to him in advance of directing Clifford to refrain please from stomping on the victim which brought at last to Clifford's attention Wendle laid out before him.

Clifford wasn't a regular officer and didn't drive a cruiser or wear often a uniform. He was our investigator and largely passed his days instructing people who'd been robbed in how best they might lock their doors and secure their windows. He wore usually a brown suit when he did not wear a blue suit instead, and he evermore smelled to have applied his after-shave with a bean sprayer. Clifford wore a shoulder holster he'd ordered from a catalog that had straps and stays and buckles all about it and held his pistol upside down in his armpit after a fashion that promoted, it would seem, some habitual chafing and appreciable discomfort which Clifford would never own up to but went around with his hand to his hip and his arm crooked and uplifted which the boys at the station found fetching and sweet.

Clifford was not by disposition of an investigative bent, was blessed in fact himself with all the native intuition of a hubcap, though he could make a fair show of deducing and pull the manner of face that might prompt a fellow to take him for calculating and incisive. He'd managed to solve a case or two; they'd come anyhow undone before him and he'd been in the end convenient to scoop up the culprits. Naturally Clifford never tired of making mention of his successes, found most days cause to refer to them as a means of illustrating how an officer might proceed were an officer hopeful of advancing in the department, an officer with no prospects of becoming somehow related to the chief by marriage.

Clifford guessed he was most especially accomplished in the finer points of vehicular pursuits and would without solicitation speak at length of his most memorable high-speed chase which had culminated in the apprehension of a species of auto thief and a woman who Clifford was likely as not to let on to be a moll but who was in fact the Presbyterian minister's daughter and sweetheart of the boy who'd not exactly stolen the vehicle in question but had only instead borrowed it from his grandmother who'd allowed how he could and then, due to an infirmity, had forgotten she'd allowed it.

She figured it had been pilfered in the night and provided Clifford with pertinent information on her green four-door Cavalier, even conjured up for him two of the letters and one of the numbers off the tag which proved sufficient to lead nearly straightaway to the identification of the vehicle itself as Clifford came across that green four-door Cavalier out on the bypass on his way back to the stationhouse. The grandchild and his Presbyterian moll were sitting in the middle lane waiting to turn left into the shopping plaza, were meaning to visit the Diamond Mine and look at engagement rings and wedding bands which served for them as a manner of hobby since they both entertained hopes and harbored intentions of cementing at length their association with binding nuptials.

Clifford recognized the vehicle once he'd come up alongside it, and he slammed on his brakes and backed up there in the roadway so as to identify himself to the perpetrators and suggest to them how they were surely cornered and caught. Naturally the grandchild and the Presbyterian moll did not directly take Clifford for an officer of the law given the suit and the plain tan Chevrolet and the flagrant disregard for the rules of the road and given as well that expression Clifford was prone to, that defender-of-justice and instrument-of-truth face he could pull when the sap was up and the juices were flowing, a cast of his features which was oftentimes zealous enough to look a little maniacal and appear to be the product of impure and unstable urges.

I guess he would have waved his badge if he'd not been sitting on it, if he'd not been persuaded that he was dealing after all with felons which inspired Clifford to show for identification his revolver instead which was itself a nickel-plated .357 with an oversized grip and an extended barrel, sufficient of a firearm to persuade that grandchild and convince his moll that they were enduring a legitimate menace. Understandably enough they got frantic, did not wish this day to perish out on the roadway before the shopping plaza. The grandchild anyhow hoped to save his girlfriend and preserve himself long enough at least to enjoy the rewards and partake of the favors that his delivered sweetheart might see fit to bestow in the passionate abandon of her gratitude. So he was persuaded by his reason and his hormones together to accelerate down the turning lane which straightaway compounded his infraction since the turning lane clearly was designated for turning only.

Clifford, of course, gave chase in his tan sedan, came up again abreast of that Cavalier and made once further a demonstration with his weapon and an exhibition with his animated features, instructed the perpetrator to brake his vehicle before Clifford saw fit to deal severely with him, told that is to the grandchild, "Stop that goddam car," and conveyed with his revolver, that he flourished and pointed, sufficient of a threat to render the grandchild unruly, the grandchild who accelerated further still and excited thereby the genuine ire of Clifford in his Chevrolet, Clifford who in the excitement of the moment managed, it seemed, to squeeze off a round, discharged his weapon into the roadway and bounced a slug off the pavement, sent somehow a ricochet up under the Cavalier and into the oil pan which drained straightoff through the puncture leaving that grandchild unlubricated.

That grandchild, however, was in no position much to heed his lights and gauges as he had his sweetheart to deliver and his hormones to quell, was fearful that him and fearful that her might come together to be exterminated and so disregarded the knock and the clatter and the bitter unwholesome aroma from up under the hood and kept the gas to that Cavalier until the motor grew so strained that it seized up on its own and caused the vehicle to lurch to a halt down between the Magic Wand and the Shell station with the big flag.

Since assassination seemed to them in the offing, that grandchild and his Presbyterian moll fell together into a desperate embrace and kissed and panted and issued by turns extravagant declarations of their affections, declarations in fact far more colorful and farfetched than their customary variety along with extended soulful kisses that were about equal parts respiration and saliva. That grandchild even touched without recrimination a portion of his sweetheart's brassiere, lavished tender palpations upon a little piece of hardware that attached a strap to a cup, and he was only persuaded to let at last loose of the thing by the nickel-plated six-shot revolver which Clifford stuck in through the window and laid barrel foremost against the neck of that grandchild who gave over in fact his brassiere buckle presently and in time.

I guess maybe a terrible clamor would have surely ensued had it not been Clifford who'd fired into the pavement and apprehended at gunpoint the grandchild and the minister's daughter once he'd effectively destroyed the green four-door Cavalier that had not in the first place been stolen. And it wasn't even that the chief, his momma's sister's husband, had to intervene for him. Clifford had no call for intervention due to how Clifford was one of those rare and wholly unaccountable sorts of fellows who was never somehow visited by consequences. He could manufacture all grades of mayhem and commit the most flagrant and grievous indiscretions without enduring the least little portion of them to come back sometime and bite him. He simply enjoyed blessings and dispensations, was party to a mystical grace. Of course Clifford guessed instead he was shrewd and guessed instead he was cunning, but if a man could be constricted and struck down with stupidity, stroke from wrongheadedness, Clifford would reside already in the memorial garden.

Clifford himself had never had much use for Wendle. We'd none of us in fact ever had much use for him, but Clifford alone lacked altogether the grace to pretend even to some distress and feign a little outrage. He was put off surely by the gore and the pulpy effluvia, but he plainly couldn't find less use in Wendle dead than he'd found in him alive. I guess me and Dewey and maybe even the chief too, once he'd come down across the creek and through the brush to view the carnage, couldn't help but believe straightoff it might just as well have been us shot through the face and dragged off the roadway, but Clifford, ignorant and charmed, didn't appear to be persuaded that he would ever get dead.

"I brought the lights, Chief," Clifford announced. "Brought the generator. Just figured all along we'd have some call for them," and Clifford turned his attention towards the roadway where Lonnie, surrounded by the light standards and holding the camera bag in his hands, was entertaining presently from Ellis news of the manner of vermin that were plainly about, rats and vipers and bescimitared infidels which was not even of course to mention the fellow with the gun who'd laid Wendle low.

"I wouldn't go down there," Ellis said. "I've been once already and I'm here to tell you if I was you I wouldn't leave the road."

"There's infidels down there?" Lonnie inquired.

"Yes sir."

"Where?"

"Back in the trees," Ellis told him and indicated a particularly impenetrable stand of yellow poplars where Lonnie was attempting to make out if he might an infidel or two when Clifford persuaded him to bring on the camera and haul down a standard or two as he came.

Clifford hadn't bothered to carry with him the generator manual since he was after all a guy and the generator was a mechanized contraption, and he just guessed guys like him could manipulate a contraption like that without a book to instruct and illuminate him. He'd made the thing work well enough at the chief's lawn party, but he could not in truth recall how in fact he'd managed to do it as there were valves to open and valves to shut and dials to set and switches to throw. He figured it would come to him shortly, was waiting there on the shoulder still for it to come when Ellis, who had appreciably more guy to him even half-drunk than Clifford ever would stone sober, manipulated the valves and set the dials and threw the switches and choked the carburetor and pulled the starter cord and brought thereby that contraption to life.

The lamps came on all at once and lit up, it seemed, the entire creek bottom which inspired a great wealth of creatures to decide of a sudden they'd prefer to be elsewhere and be there, if they might, pretty directly. Lonnie, setting his aperture alongside Wendle, attempted to hover and float in the air as the rabbits and the opossums and the rats I guess and the vipers went off to recover the night. Lonnie thought straightoff he saw an infidel over in a white oak up on a rise, but he turned a lamp on it and found it to be just an unaffiliated raccoon instead.

It was surely an odd and dreamy sort of a scene there before us, appeared too peculiar to be grave and in earnest. The woods about us were lit up clean to the treetops, saturated with white relentless light that was bright and crisp and stark and revealed to us more of the brush and more of the vines and more of the wounds and the seepage than we were among us anxious to see. Wendle had plainly been dragged from the road, drawn it appeared by his feet on down the incline and across the branch and up through the vines and the stalks that he'd bled on and bent back which we could tell clear enough now he had. His holster hood was snapped shut still over his pistol grip, his stick was in his hanger, his wallet was in his hip pocket. He'd been shot in the left cheek and shot in the roof of the left eye socket but had bled chiefly out the back of his head, down his neck, onto his shirt.

The chief, with his customary excess of feeling, apprised me and apprised Dewey and apprised Lonnie as well how we had before us a tragedy, and he spoke of the broad proportions of it, touched upon the aspects and the implications, bemoaned the troubles and ills of this world that would bring a decent and lawful man, an official of the community, an officer of the constabulary, to such an end as this. Then he apprised us of pretty much the same thing all over again but in an altered and abbreviated form which the chief found he preferred to the extended version and so repeated it and polished it and rendered it by means of a breathy moan ripe with empathy and ripe with grief and tinged I guess with appropriate indignation.

It seemed to strike him, as a sentiment, ever so successful, the sort of thing he might tell to the newspaper, speak of on the AM station, have maybe even occasion to share with the correspondent from Roanoke, the one with the square teeth and the blue eyes who came down usually with her cameraman in her Wagoneer whenever a local calamity beckoned. The chief had a way with anguishment, and he shaped his features and made himself elaborately forlorn there in the bottom off by the branch, rehearsed his grief, practiced his desolation.

Clifford wanted to lay out a grid, had read lately in a procedural guide a chapter on grids and had carried with him a ball of twine which he produced from his jacket pocket as he attempted to contaminate us with his ardor. He indicated where the corners of the thing might go and had calculated the number of stakes he'd require which Clifford was meaning for Lonnie to hunt up once he got done photographing. He was, in fact, in the midst of treating Lonnie to a manner of gridstake primer when Dewey stepped over to wonder of Clifford if he might briefly hold in his fingers that twine which Clifford was pleased to allow and gave over the thing to Dewey, left even off for the moment with stakes altogether and spoke instead of the tensile strength of nylon fibers, was just undertaking to concoct for Dewey a general history of twine when Dewey turned about and flung that ball of string as deep into the woods as he could fling it, pitched it on over a rise and back among the conifers which Clifford straightaway exclaimed about, whined that is to his uncle the chief who could not be sufficiently roused from his show of deep feeling and profound regret to tell to his wife's sister's child anything beyond the "Aw" he usually told to him.

Gooch arrived in his wagon up on the roadway, the white one with the gauzy curtains that he did not drive too awful much anymore due largely to a rattle in the motor which he'd not been able to cure, a persistent and irritating manner of rattle, an intrusive sort of clatter that we all heard as he came up. He exchanged a word or two with Ellis prior to stepping off the shoulder and picking his way down the embankment where he demonstrated what was very likely a newly heightened appreciation for the prospect of rats and vipers and the odd lingering infidel.

Gooch was an undertaker, was in fact a kind of conglomerate since he not only embalmed and becasketed the deceased and provided, if need be, a modest handsome chapel for the ceremony, but he owned outright the memorial garden on the truck route and shared with a cousin a significant interest in a vault company out towards Sparta. Gooch liked to think of himself as a general purpose liaison between his clients and the everlasting, was fond of proclaiming that he did for the dead everything they'd probably do for themselves if they weren't too dead already to do it. He had a manner about him that was calm and consoling and he could fashion at a moment's notice a species of deeply tortured expression that plainly beat the chief's all to pieces.

Gooch didn't have any neck much, appeared to be attached by the jowls to his collarbones, but he'd come lately into possession of a glorious crop of shiny black hair which could hardly get taken for native, failed under scrutiny to look even to be hair most especially when Gooch put on for reading or put on for closework his spectacles that caused invariably his sideburns to pooch out. But then Gooch was so exceedingly fond of his new forehead, which did not extend anymore clean back to his cowlick, that detached perpendicular sideburns did not strike him as too high a price to pay. Coming towards us across

the creek and up through the brush and the scrub in his customary
gray suit and his green and blue striped tie and with his stiff, deliberate carriage and his newly abbreviated forehead, Gooch looked like
a preacher or a two-term governor, had a veritable cloud of sincerity
about him and upon his arrival he greeted us each softly by name and
extended to us his fingers to take up and shake.

I don't suppose Gooch had previously found occasion to get
illuminated by halogen light and so had no way of anticipating the
effect of it upon his coif, the resulting iridescence most especially up
along Gooch's hairpart where the display was truly prismatic and gay.
Clifford, of course, became straightaway enchanted and studied that
vivid hairpart fairly gracelessly for a time in advance of mustering the
wherewithal to speak.

"Gooch," he said, "your hair's all shimmery," and Gooch engaged straightaway in a bit of gazing of his own and raised his hands
so as to lay them each with unguarded feeling upon Clifford's knobby
shoulders as preamble to telling presently to Clifford, "Thank you,"
but Clifford allowed how it was nothing, insisted it was hardly in fact
anything at all.

Gooch served as county examiner by pure default. We couldn't
seem to keep an actual doctor in the post, had lost a while back the
intern we'd baited and lured and had made do for a time with a
dermatologist instead, but he'd not had much stomach for the calling,
could abide a pustule well enough but possessed no tolerance truly for
drainage of the manner and magnitude beyond your regular inflam-
matory sort. It was Wendle himself who broke that dermatologist in
the end, called him out one night there below the gap where a truck
had wrecked. A boy hauling beer had determined to sneak his rig
down the blacktop instead of easing off the ridge on the interstate
where his general tonnage called for him to be. He'd figured, I guess,
on saving maybe a quarter hour and so had decided to brave the pitch,
but his truck had gotten away from him partway down and his brakes
had fairly incinerated which left him to endeavor to preserve his hide
in a turnout, run off the road and onto a sizable ramp of sand along the

shoulder where that rig in fact came straightaway to a halt, mired up clean to the axles and lurched dead still though the beer demonstrated an irresistible inclination to travel further itself, punched most of it through the front wall of the trailer and into the cab herding naturally that boy before it, ramming him on through the windshield and over the hood and burying him at last deep in the sandheap.

We couldn't even find him at first what with the busted cartons and the broken bottles, the punctured cans, but we rooted him out at length and laid him bare. He didn't appear to be whole any longer and was greasy and gritty, looked like something you'd come across in a catbox. Wendle, I recall, was fascinated with the sight of him and showed him off to Harnett from the state patrol, Harnett who was himself ripe with grisly tales of mayhem and vehicular malfeasance and seemed to find with Wendle a certain allurement in the grotesque, would swap readily yarns of dismemberment and conjure up with animation bloody collisions he'd worked, pileups he'd heard tell of.

They could hardly between them get enough of that boy bathed like he was in beer and dusted over with sand and come plainly to pieces before them. They hadn't even this night dared hope for such a sight and were reminded by him of assorted travelers they'd seen disassembled previously which I left them alone to tell each other about and went off to look to the remaining contents of the trailer since I do recall a crowd had collected. Every fool with a police scanner had brought his neighbors and his relations down ostensibly to see the wreckage, had heard those magic words "beer truck" over the airways and had come to make off with whatever of the load hadn't been already crushed and busted.

They were a thirsty bunch with convictions about their endowed rights as they pertained most particularly to beer in the back of a wrecked vehicle, were persuaded the progenitors of the commonwealth had seen fit surely in their wisdom to allow by law and decree for unlimited pillage along the roadways, had identified as community property any disabled conveyance parked or upended off a thoroughfare. So when I moved to stop the plunder, arrived at the back of the trailer where the doors had been pried open and what of the load remained was being spirited away, when I charged that crowd of folks to cease straightoff and desist, they none of them showed any shame much in their thievery but pretty directly pelted me with their scholarship instead, informed me as a group what part of the law possession seemed to them to be.

The examiner of the moment arrived just after the rescue squad. He drove a German sedan which he did not like to park near a crowd or a gathering or an accumulation of even so much as two people together due largely to the doctor's fear of blue jean rivets and pocket buttons and his knowledge of the sorry way most people have of pitching themselves against a fender panel to lounge and lay. Consequently, he was generally a bit of a laggard when it came to his duties as examiner since he couldn't even bring himself to park his sedan convenient to the scene of the crime or the mishap on account of how crimes and on account of how mishaps proved invariably a magnet for rivets and buttons and backsides. So he'd drive generally past the scene, find himself an unpopulated place off and away to park, and walk back to us.

Wendle didn't have much patience with him and he'd managed to pollute that trooper Harnett, had persuaded him to disapprove of the dermatologist as well, the dermatologist who had money, lived in a big brick house up on the ridge, kept a boat down at Lake Norman, drove an expensive imported car, had married a handsome brunette with delicate features and a flat stomach, and smoked an elaborate hooked pipe plainly more for the look of the brier than the effects of the tobacco. Wendle just wanted to be too much like him to do anything but resent him outright, so once he'd learned that the doctor was squeamish, Wendle rarely missed an opportunity to bring him unprepared and wholly unforewarned into the presence of an oozing wound or a grisly laceration or, as was the case with the beer truck driver, hard up on a fellow who'd been disjointed like a fryer.

It seems to me they told him they were caught up in a puzzlement. Wendle that is and Harnett threw in together to appear perplexed and greeted the doctor at the rim of the sandheap with the news that the beer truck driver looked to the pair of them deceased though they could not between them tell for certain if he was after all dead and done in as they did not either one of them possess so much as a scrap of dermatological training. They wondered consequently if might the doctor step over and hold a mirror to that boy's lips or a finger to a vein and judge thereby the liveliness of him which that dermatologist allowed he'd be pleased to oblige them in.

He felt plainly a little proud to be privy himself to the mysteries of the medical brotherhood, got a trifle haughty there by the sandheap and made a regular demonstration of drawing upon his brier, discharged into the air a cloud of sweet fruity smoke and then advanced at length with his veinfeeling finger extended, allowed himself to be ushered by Wendle up among the cartons and the cases, the bottles and the cans, and into at last the presence of that boy who was not of course lingering much at all but had come instead to be pulverized and mangled, so thoroughly exterminated that there did not appear to be enough of him left to fill up a grocery sack. Wendle played his light upon him and made even to have spied out a vein for that doctor to press, if that doctor saw fit, his veinfeeling finger against, but before even Wendle could offer if he might his veinfeeling finger suggestion that dermatologist collapsed in a faint with such intemperate precipitation that he could not have fallen quicker and with more unmitigated success if Wendle had reached down his throat and snatched out his skeleton.

His brier landed atop him and spilt coals upon his shirtfront that began shortly to smoke and smolder and excited thereby the attention of those boys with the rescue squad who shifted their efforts from the pulverized driver, who they were persuaded they could not save, to the dermatologist instead who they guessed they could revive or at the very least extinguish. Wendle was the one that had them haul him to the truck, was the one that had them strap

41

him to the gurney and carry him clean back to the hospital for X-rays and observation as Wendle had seen him fall and Wendle had seen him hit and so had cause he guessed to be concerned for that dermatologist's brainpan which likely had been jarred and probably had been jostled though Wendle could not say for certain how much of either or how much of both a brainpan might endure since he allowed how he was not after all a dermatologist himself. Wendle was, however, persuasive enough to send those boys off with the examiner which provided him the opportunity to bring along at length that German sedan that Wendle parked in the hospital lot snug between a Pinto and some massive manner of dilapidated Dodge where there was not room enough truly for a German sedan to fit.

In the wake of that beer truck and the dismembered driver and the assorted indignities he'd endured there at the rim of the sandheap at the hands of an officer of the law, along with the ding in his doorpanel, our examiner saw clear to bring to a close his association with the county, and as we could not entice any manner of doctor otherwise to serve a term or two in his stead we recruited Gooch, our local mortician conglomerate, to take the post since Gooch possessed the disposition and the stomach for it and the wagon for it as well. He even had a nephew who'd attended previously medical school for the better part of an academic year, a nephew who was available usually for consultations and confabs whenever Gooch was feeling doubtful and inadequate.

Of course there was a genuine doctor or two about we could call on in a pinch, but Gooch most times was able enough to discover on his own the reasons that pertained to a happenstance, could tell the stabbed victims from the beat ones and the beat ones from the crushed ones and the crushed ones from the mangled ones well enough and was not prone to misplace the facts or cloak them over with fanciful theories but would come out square and plain and declare precisely what had been squashed or what had been punctured to let flow the blood and extinguish the spark.

Gooch had a way with corpses, had apparently surrendered to

time and exposure any native fascination with death and had come to the point where he could take hold of a clammy appendage or pluck up a piece of entrail with no more aversion than the rest of us might muster for yesterday's socks. Of course accustomed as he was to grieving, disconsolate relations, Gooch had developed a manner or bearing that was wholly unobtrusive, rendered him practically invisible in as much as a sizable sort of a fellow with synthetic hair can be made in any fashion to go largely unnoticed. Gooch could just slip and creep around with unusual grace and admirable posture since he was constrained anymore to keep his back straight so as not to dump off his coif.

Straightaway he squatted hard by Wendle's bloody carcass and extracted from his coatpocket a penlight he carried. He fetched out as well his eyeglasses and slipped them with care and exceeding deliberation onto his face so as not to disturb his sideburns beyond the lifting and the pooching that was plainly unavoidable.

Clifford was slightly offended that Gooch did not find with the halogen lamps illumination enough to suit him, and he would have likely issued a strident objection to the need for a penlight at all if the spectrum of Gooch's iridescence had not shifted so noticeably with the coming of the squat as to re-enchant Clifford altogether. The purples and the mauves and the teal greens had not previously been so lively and vibrant, and the onset of them in vivid streaks forestalled Clifford from issuing, as was his wont, instructions and declaiming, as was his custom, opinions but left him instead quite thoroughly engaged like a child given a bauble to wonder at and admire. Gooch, consequently, was free to perform uninterrupted his examination, and we watched him shine his light all about Wendle's person and poke on occasion with an ink pen at clotted bits of effluvia.

He studied the wounds with unflinching attention, probed them a little with a reedy piece of stalk so as to find how they ran and cleaned at length about them with spit and a noserag, cleared enough crust and stain to reveal the burns from the powder. He felt around for injuries otherwise in advance of rolling Wendle with Dewey's assistance over onto his stomach which made available to him the back of Wendle's head which gave even Gooch some pause, cracked as it was and splintered like a piece of crockery, a regular confusion of scalp and bone and gore and matted hair.

I showed Gooch the sticker bush hung with the piece of head and endured from him a rueful grin prior to flinging my arm to indicate the place I'd found the hat. Then I left Gooch to step alone down to the bank and the creek where he shone his feeble light up towards the roadway, off along a flattened track through the weeds where it seemed to him likely the corpse had been dragged.

"Hauled him by the feet looks to me," Gooch told to us, and he came back again into the light proper and stood hard by where Wendle lay. He lifted upright his thumb and extended his foremost finger, brought the very tip of it flush against his cheek. "Bang," he told us. "Bang."

They claimed they didn't know her, could not seem among them to recollect having properly made her acquaintance, didn't feel that is sufficiently friendly to ride to her house and tell her her husband was dead which called they guessed for a chum, called they supposed for a buddy, called they figured for me. I'd gone through school with her, had run with her brother for a time, endured still her daddy to come up on me every now and again and grab me at the back of the neck that way he always did, but I didn't truly know her anymore, hadn't ever in fact known her much at all. She was just Dale's little sister, the one we wouldn't carry anywhere or have hardly anything to do with. I'd see her every now and again at the drugstore and the market, come across her and Wendle out at the fish house or the triplex and pass maybe with them the time of day, but I wasn't myself much acquainted with her either.

They lived out north of town in a house they let from a Stuart who cultivated cabbages clean up to their wellhead. I didn't stop the first time by, hardly even slowed, but just looked up across the yard towards where the lights were burning in the front room. I attempted to fashion what I might say and how I might say it, auditioned assorted condolences and long grave expressions but hadn't truly landed on a suitable combination when I swung about and came back up the blacktop, turned into the drive. I don't guess she saw my lights, don't suppose she heard my tires on the gravel as she didn't get up and come to the door but stayed there on the settee before the television where I could spy through the window a little piece of her.

I figured if it was me I'd probably want to hear it flat out and straightaway, and I told to the mirror, "Wendle's been shot," told to the mirror, "Wendle's been killed," told to the mirror, "I'm sorry to say that Wendle's met with a misfortune," which I found that I favored in conjunction with a pained face and a deep and demonstrative exhalation that seemed together to establish a mood and promote an eventuality.

I was tinkering still with my tone, casting about for a direr inflection when Clifford came onto the radio in a state, Clifford who me and who Dewey and who Lonnie as well had contrived to send out to Mrs. Heflin's, had let on how maybe she'd seen a thing, had come across earlier in the evening a swarthy sort of a fellow which we insinuated was odd and proposed to be significant and had baited thereby Clifford to ride in his tan cruiser on down along the branch to Mrs. Heflin's house where he'd wheeled apparently into the drive and stepped boldly up onto the porch without troubling himself to flash his grill lights or sound his horn, without giving Mrs. Heflin proper cause to believe him an officer of the law.

In eyeing Clifford through the doorlight Mrs. Heflin, it would seem, failed to detect about him much trace of his official capacity but just saw instead another affiliate of the brotherhood of the gland armed with his wiles and his ways and cloaked plainly in deception, laying surely for her after the whim of his deceit. I guess he appeared to her purely alight with unreined desire and as she'd left off

surely figuring that the law would come to thwart him, she determined I suppose to go on ahead and thwart him herself. Clifford
anyhow had been persuaded to retire to his vehicle and, above his
frantic yodeling on the radio, I could make out the dull tattoo of the
maul handle upon the Chevrolet roof, the slap and thump of it on
the sheeting that provided for Clifford accompaniment as he wailed
into the handset and pleaded with Janice, pleaded with Lonnie,
pleaded with Dewey and me to say to him if we would something,
tell to him if we might anything at all.

Dale's sister was watching on the television the show about the
tycoons who were relations the clan of them by blood and relations as
well by marriage and who largely passed their time building empires
and chasing women of easy virtue in addition to scheming and plot-
ting and conniving to contaminate happiness and undo well-being
wherever they might come across them. As I arrived on the slab porch
before the aluminum storm door, the crusty old patriarch was comb-
ing his moustache with his fingertips and casting for the moment his
lot with his least girl's husband, hatching with him some manner of
deviousness against a fellow named Frederick who the pair of them
spoke ever so malignantly about.

I guess maybe I rattled or clanked, made with an implement some
detectable racket because she heard me there at the door, stiffened
abruptly and swung around on the settee in a fright. She caught sight
I suppose of my patches and caught sight I suppose of my badge and so
took me straightoff for him, yielded up directly an endearment and had
struck out even to loose the latch, had stood from the settee and circled
about the endtable when she saw I wasn't him after all, saw I was just
me instead with my face made long and grave and my hat before me
in my fingers which I guess she found to be articulate and found to
be revealing judging from how she stopped herself midway between
the sofa and the door and laid her open hand ever so lightly upon
her breastbone.

I don't think I'd even spoken yet, hadn't told her surely of
Wendle's misfortune when she saw fit to turn about and retreat to the

sofa, settle again upon it and just sit for a time leaving me atop the slab beyond the latched door where I held to my hat and maintained my expression and listened to the patriarch and listened to his girl's husband swear an oath together to fall upon that Frederick like the night.

2.

They gave it out as just a regular domestic, didn't let on it was anything otherwise, failed to allow it was anything else but just told me a neighbor had reported a spat and dispatched me to bring peace without even so much as suggesting that maybe it wasn't a husband and wasn't a wife. I was new still on the force back then and had made, I suppose, a poor impression. I was pretty fresh out of the army and guessed I'd seen everything, was persuaded I knew about all there was to know as I'd policed on a base in Kentucky and had come to be convinced that soldiers were fairly much like people and the army was fairly much like life. I'd picked up from Dewey a pointer or two on questioning suspects and compressing testicles but hadn't proved otherwise an eager student, just supposed I was likely acquainted already with most everything I needed to know. Consequently, as a prank, I guess, and a lesson, they gave me the number and they gave me the street, had Angelene to send me out there alone like it was just a straightforward and ordinary thing, some simple sort of matrimonial eruption.

Likely it had been once a fine house, had a handsome design to it, a deep wrap-around porch, fretwork in the gables, slate on the roof, but it had come at last to be done in with neglect and clutter. The front lawn was weedy and ragged and strewn about with odd bits of concrete block and trash and little pitiful piles of firewood with the plastic rain sheeting flung back. There was a lawnmower carcass in the shrubbery keeping company with a section of porchrail, and a dinette chair had been brought out onto the walk at the foot of the steps, a metal dinette chair with a speckled vinyl seat and a piece of board for a back. The porch proper was encumbered with sundry items, boxes and crates, old newspapers, a mismatched pair of side tables, and a rust-eaten washtub full of twigs and shavings. The doorscreen was punched out at the top and ripped through at the bottom and the panel door was standing open even though it was spring yet and the night had some bite to it still.

I couldn't hear anything straightoff, couldn't see anybody and knocked at first to no answer. I detected, however, what struck me as the sound of a woman in distress. She was drawing shallow breaths of air and whimpering after a fashion, venting occasional throaty cries that suggested to me mischief outright, so I hammered on that door with my stickend and heard from off deep in the house, "Back here."

It was all I could do to pass along the hallway towards what I took to be the source of those cries that had come just lately to be rhythmic and syncopated. There were cartons and sacks either side of the runner and a couple of straight chairs midway back that proved an appreciable constriction, but I marshalled my paraphernalia and slipped and sidled so far as the sitting room opposite the back stairs where that distressed woman was plainly hard by and, judging from the tenor of her discharges, increasingly put upon. I stepped into that sitting room proper and straightaway came upon both Talmage brothers together who told to me fairly harmoniously, "Hey."

Curtis, I was to discover, was the one over by the woodstove with the plate in his lap while Royce was the one in the La-Z-Boy before the television, the one most convenient to the door, the one I made initially inquiries of, asked him anyhow, "What's going on here?"

"Well," Royce told to me and indicated with his foremost finger the TV screen, "she's his wife's little sister and a buddy of his bet him he couldn't fuck her clean in half, but he was persuaded himself he might could, figured anyhow he'd make a go of it."

Of course I was perplexed straightoff and stepped around to where I could see on the screen a man and a woman engaged in an intimacy, a lively and vigorous sort of an endeavor which had been captured for posterity by an indisputably intrepid cameraman who'd recorded surely at peril the particulars of the act and was probably fortunate he hadn't been clapped snug between the thrusting pelvises and crushed like quarry stone.

"I don't believe I get that station," I told to Royce in the La-Z-Boy, Royce who held up the plastic moviebox and waved it at me.

He appeared set to contribute a piece of talk further but came to be distracted by an uncoupling of the participants who separated with an indelicate manner of noise and suffered their glands to be profiled individually and committed to film which prompted Royce to declare with feeling, "If I had me a bat like that I could lead the league."

I might have volunteered a manner of reply but for a curious contortion of the sister-in-law in conjunction with some deft and daring camera work that served together to render me a little addled and unlubricated and in no fit state to speak which, as a condition, was not in any way relieved once that brother-in-law saw fit to reapply himself with replenished zeal and extravagant leverage which me and Royce Talmage and the upended wife's sister all shrieked a little together about.

Naturally I felt a bit foolish having figured like I did that a woman was in some sort of legitimate distress only to discover, once I'd crept and hunkered and squatted, that she was just instead being fucked in half on a bet. Furthermore, I couldn't discover much in the way of a disturbance there in the sitting room down the hall where Royce Talmage was taking semi-decorous pleasure in his movie and his brother Curtis, over by the stove, was pondering quietly the plate on his lap, considering anyhow an item on the plate that was smoldering in fact and appeared clearly the source of a troublesome aroma, the source anyhow of that particularly foul, pungent, irritating stench which likely cloaked and concealed those sundry stenches otherwise that come usually with squalor and filth.

I informed the pair of them how we'd received lately word from a neighbor that there'd been a dispute which gave Royce occasion to scoff with exceeding animation, and he invited Curtis his brother to throw in and scoff if he might with him, but Curtis did not appear of a mood for it and contemplated exclusively the plate on his lap while Royce in his La-Z-Boy guessed which neighbor it was and spoke uncharitably of her. He characterized her in fact in the vilest sort of way and enlisted once more his brother Curtis to join him please in the undertaking, his brother Curtis who lifted at last his head and did in fact speak, informed the both of us, "All I said was it didn't seem to me John Gavin had ever been better."

Royce was in an instant afoot, sprang up out of his recliner with alarming vigor and, insensible of a sudden to the ecstatic discharges of the semi-vivisected sister-in-law, reminded Curtis his brother in the strongest language possible how he'd mentioned already previously that he did not this evening wish to hear again the word "John" and the word "Gavin" wedded together and uttered in a breath.

Curtis just gazed forlornly upon the smoldering heap on the plate in his lap in advance of informing his brother, "It isn't even *Back Street.*"

As an officer of the law and no kin of Royce Talmage's by blood or marriage, I just figured his admonition did not likely apply to me, or failed anyhow to guess I'd get berated for saying like I did, "John," and saying like I did, "Gavin?" which Royce launched straightaway into a genuine tirade about, wondered of me was I deaf, wondered of me was I simple, wanted to know if hadn't he just made plain how he did not hope this evening to hear that name again that I was compelled to confess to him he had which left Royce to wonder why I'd seen fit to drop my jaw and say it. He sputtered, he spat, he aired some savage and aimless profanity prior to becoming all at once quite thoroughly becalmed and returning directly to his recliner and the escapades of the merry in-laws who by this time were hanging the pair of them off the bedstead all stuck and bound up together like a couple of cockleburrs.

I took occasion to step over and visit with Curtis at the woodstove, Curtis who in his assorted enticements resembled Royce his brother, was unshaven and balding and appeared fairly near to term, but was as well a little tidier than Royce, not necessarily cleaner since, to judge from his shirtfront, it appeared that Curtis had taken maybe his supper by tossing it into the air and running under it with his mouth open, but at least his buttons were buttoned and his zipper was raised and his shirttail was tucked into his pants which lent to Curtis a meager air of dignity and refinement that distinguished him from Royce across the way, Royce who was presently acknowledging some unforeseen and wildly dexterous exploit on the TV with a yelp and a burp in combination.

I was hoping maybe to learn from Curtis the cause of Royce's poor opinion of Mr. John Gavin which was shrouded for me still in mystery most especially since Royce seemed ready enough to admire the likes of the brother-in-law who'd demonstrated surely a manner of unflagging enthusiasm but was plainly no showcase of admirable impulses. I was even set to utter at Curtis the dread name itself, had leaned in close to speak ever so discreetly that word "John" and that word "Gavin" but got directly forestalled from it as Curtis held up towards me his plate and wished I'd look at what it was his brother had gone and done to the Duke. The thing he had been pondering and studying, the item that had been letting off the reek turned out to be the remains of a videocassette, a charred and semi-melted videocassette that had lately begun to cool and stiffen, had managed to recoagulate into a mound and was smoldering still a little and seeping from its folds and creases a slick and oily manner of juice.

"*Fighting Seabees*," Curtis told to me, and I tried to make to look illuminated as Curtis spoke briefly of the chemistry of the leads that seemed to him, for chemistry, altogether unmatched.

I was inclined to make inquiries of Curtis when I came to be put off and forestalled by the in-laws on the TV whose efforts sounded to be yielding fruit at last. They were wailing anyhow and moaning and invoking from time to time the Lord Christ Himself as a means, I guess, of conveying their utterly miraculous sensations. They sounded to be colliding and clapping to with all the velocity of a reciprocating saw which carried them presently to a riotous culmination, the sort of simultaneous eruption that's captured routinely on grainy film but is, I believe, pretty rare and elusive among amateur fornicators in the undocumented privacy of their own bedrooms.

Curtis, once the uproar had ebbed, went on ahead and confided to me what the trouble was at heart, saw fit presently to share with me in a low, conspiratorial voice, "He's never much cared for her."

"Who?" I asked of him.

And Curtis leaned in close and told to me softly, "Miss Hayward."

"Miss Hayward?"

"Susan," he said and eyed Royce and eyed me and eyed Royce again.

Straightaway Royce in his La-Z-Boy wanted to hear from his brother who it was he'd said that Curtis appeared reluctant to reveal to him, and Royce grew directly so thoroughly livid and precipitously enraged that I could not see the harm in telling to him who it was we'd spoken just lately about and persuade him thereby that it had not after all been John Gavin. So I told to him, "Susan Hayward," myself and he confounded me altogether by leaping bolt upright and undertaking to pitch a truly spectacular manner of fit that far outstripped his previous exhibition replete like it was with arm flailing and hair pulling and rancorous scorching epithets.

Curtis appeared inclined to abide the abuse with a measure of grace and restraint, maintained his seat by the woodstove and held lightly still the plate atop his lap with the melted cassette upon it as he endured his brother's tirade. It seemed that Royce could not likely have thought more poorly of Ms. Susan Hayward than he did, found her deceitful and found her conniving, hardly approved of her wiles and ways and apprised me and Curtis of how she was not plainly so encumbered with charm or ripe with allure as the wife's little sister on the TV who knew, Royce informed us, how to treat a man right.

In an effort to persuade Royce to keep in the future his scandalous opinions to himself, Curtis took up from alongside the stove a length of what looked to be dogwood and flung it across the room at his brother who was adequately acquainted with Curtis's impulses to know to duck and dodge and allowed thereby that stick of wood to sail on past him and fetch up against the baseboard. Royce figured he could have been struck maybe senseless, supposed he could have been killed outright had he not been able to slip deftly aside, and the threat to his well-being impressed itself so upon him that he decided to deal his brother some sort of answering blow. He stepped consequently over to the cupboard alongside the television where he drew open a drawer and selected from it an item, a plastic moviebox from which he extracted straightaway the movie itself and charged with it towards the wood-stove but was intercepted by Curtis his brother who handed to me his plate.

They fell in together like wildcats and moiled and yowled and grunted and imprecated, and Curtis attempted to relieve Royce of what turned out to be *Beau Geste*, which Royce appeared ever so hard set to commit to the flames. They exchanged, of course, personal estimations of Ms. Susan Hayward. Royce anyhow would muster the breath to offer an opinion and Curtis would see fit straightaway to correct him about it which would prompt Royce to let on to be quite utterly unpersuaded and he would restate his view with advancing conviction and rejuvenated malevolence and endure his brother Curtis to counter with a contrary assessment. The general racket surged and swelled and became unendurably clamorous, but I couldn't figure how best to intercede, failed to make myself heard and wasn't able to introduce my person between the two of them, was contemplating in fact some freeform species of inseam lever when the brother-in-law and the little sister on the TV provided between them my salvation.

It seems the brother-in-law had come across a manner of strop, a foot and a half's worth of leather thong which he'd been by the little sister invited to apply to her bare backside. While he'd set out with reluctance and made at the first a couple of timid swipes, he'd warmed pretty directly to the enterprise and was providing anymore his wife's sister with just precisely the variety of flogging she seemed to favor. She greeted each blow with a little breathy cry of delight, and as her sister's husband gained a feeling for the chore before him, his stroke accelerated and he produced a pretty fabulous response.

In a show of gratitude the wife's sister reached out blind and backwards and wrapped her fingers around her in-law's upraised organ which was cause quite naturally for a display of thanksgiving on the part of the sister's husband who undertook several exclamations of his own which served, in conjunction with the quivering cries otherwise, to capture outright the attention of Mr. Royce Talmage who guessed he could tell well enough when a fellow was having his organ groped and he pined so to see for himself the sight of it that he gave over *Beau Geste* and retired to his La-Z-Boy allowing Curtis to return to his chair by the woodstove and gaze tenderly upon his videocassettes, his *Beau Geste* in his fingers and his *Fighting Seabees* on his plate, his *Fighting Seabees* that he held up presently before me and wished I could see for myself that look she gives to Michael O'Keefe, that way she tosses her head and smiles when he lays his cloak upon her shoulders.

"It's plain poetry," Curtis informed me, and I allowed how I did not doubt it was.

"Look at him," Curtis said, and we eyed together Royce his brother who was marveling just presently at a manner of contortion the wife's sister had found cause to execute, a maneuver somewhere between yoga and traction which had left her in an altogether novel position, sort of cranked around backwards and upended which presented to Royce vistas he'd not previously had the pleasure to see.

"I let him run that mess, don't tell him what trash it makes him out to be. I don't say the first word to him about it, and I don't want him turning around and speaking," he told me, "of her," and Curtis tapped firmly once with his fingerend upon his melted *Fighting Seabees*.

I just stood and looked at him, heard somewhat of the in-laws grunting and panting and laboring at their passion but paid chiefly mind to Curtis himself who seemed an unlikely sort of romantic what with his stubble and his belly and his dubious hygiene and ensconced like he was in unrelieved squalor. It just didn't appear that he would be prone to adore a woman so, especially a dead one he'd only seen in pictures, but there he was in his straight chair alongside the woodstove with his fingers upon his *Fighting Seabees* and a pleasant distracted look upon his face as if he could not maybe believe his fine fortune, had not in this lifetime hoped even to come across such a glorious creature as the one in the melted case before him.

I was struck, will admit outright that I had not expected to answer this call, step into this house, and find what I found which was only the battling Talmages somewhat but not essentially and at the core the battling Talmages much at all. You see I was back then a married man, had taken a bride in Kentucky, a woman I'd met on the base, a civilian typist with long shiny hair and green eyes. I'd wooed her, had not exactly selected her specifically to woo, as I'd been engaged at the time in a manner of saturation wooing, but she'd proven the one intoxicated by my charms, agreeable to my advances. Her name was Karen. She was fond of my cologne, confessed to an affection for the way my hair laid on my neck, laughed at the foolish things I'd tell her, thought I had a noble nose.

Karen was a sunny sort, liked to mine the good in people, advocated stoutly the benefit of the doubt. She copied into a bound notebook with pink scented pages inspirational phrases and touching lessons of the heart that she came across in magazines. She collected tiny glass geegaws, kept stuffed animals on her bed, believed everything she heard on the television and read books about women who overcame long odds and intolerably poor fortune to marry potentates and princes. She was quite altogether sincere and near about inexhaustibly spunky which maybe would have given me some qualms straightaway but for the effect the sight of her had upon me those nights when she'd step out of her dress and stand before me in her underclothes a little meek still and girlish and beautiful beyond belief.

She was a graceful thing with a long elegant neck and lovely slender fingers that she'd lay ever so lightly upon my chest once I'd flung my arms about her, and she demonstrated in bed sufficient passion and adequate longing and desire to make a fellow ignore the things she might say after, persuade a fellow to suspect that maybe she wasn't so terribly giddy down deep but was afflicted like him with urges that were dark and a trifle unholy. I just thought sometimes there in the halflight once we were spent, once we were laying silent together in a weary embrace, that perhaps we felt about this world the same way after all. I can't now even begin to say why maybe I thought it.

We married in the Baptist church she'd grown up in. The service was performed by the preacher who'd baptized her. He was elderly and frail and could hardly seem to remember what he was up to from one moment to the next, called me Darrell twice, thought she was her sister and cried when we exchanged vows, blubbered outright and then felt obliged to stand there upon the altar and reveal to us that he was mourning still for his wife who'd died, missed his girl who'd moved to St. Louis, was troubled as well by the effects of a recent surgical procedure, and he explained to the guests and explained to the wedding party, explained most particularly to me and to Karen how his condition had been remedied with a length of tubing that caused him still some discomfort.

I was persuaded I wanted just every little thing that Karen saw fit to want for me, embraced there at the first her expectations as I was simply too dazzled by her charms and her allurements to be in the least contrary. Of course I have like many men a sorry history of partial sensory failure in the presence of uncloaked agreeable women, which is to say the germ of my being gets so constricted and concentrated into the vicinity of my inseam that I go selectively deaf and passably blind and can readily cobble together a dose of utter and uncritical enchantment with little encouragement to speak of. Sometimes the condition wears off pretty quickly and, once the urge has been exorcised, the troublesome humors discharged, and the blood loosed to circulate afresh, I find myself of a mood to revise claims I've made and oaths I've sworn there when I was feverish and needy. But with Karen the enchantment seemed to settle and take, and she demonstrated a talent for keeping me fairly idiotic with desire.

I carried her away from Kentucky once my discharge came through, away from her friends and away from her people and down here where my mother was, here where I'd come from and guessed I could get on well enough. We let a house from Wade's brother, a manner of bungalow out off the pike, a handsome little item situated down in a crease of terrain with apple trees and spruces in the yard and a wet-weather spring off at the head of the lot where the ground stayed boggy and the grass stayed high. The place had come free once the previous tenant, a bachelor gentleman from up around Christiansburg, had managed somehow to get himself incinerated at the power plant. We found a pair of his shoes on the closet floor and a book of his on the hamper by the toilet, a well-fingered and semi-dilapidated instructional guide on the topic of fabulous wealth and how to accumulate it.

It's funny the things you think about sometimes. I mean there I stood listening to the brother-in-law grunting like a longshoreman as he thrusted and pounded away at his wife's sister and watching Curtis Talmage touch lightly with his fingerends his semi-melted cassette while he displayed upon his features the sort of expression I'd seen men display before, that little smile some fellows are prone to in the presence of the women they'd chosen, the women maybe they've forgotten they admire until some paltry and undramatic bit of business, a gesture, a turn of phrase, a singular inclination of the head, which by chance they witness and take notice of, reminds them of their affection and suggests to them their extraordinary luck. Curtis just appeared to feel blessed by his association with even a dead starlet, and there I had a live wife I'd begun to entertain doubts about. You see I'd never not believed that long slender legs and a flat stomach, handsome contours and fleshy lobes wouldn't always somehow be enough alone. It's funny the things that come to mind, the things you think about.

I got to be wistful for my old life and nostalgic for my former ways, set in to contemplating what possible appeal pure girlishness had ever held for me, dropped off in fact into a regular study that I managed only presently to be jarred out of by an exploit of the wife's sister who mounted a dressing table and set to performing upon herself, with the aid of a hairbrush handle, an intimate service, reamed assorted of her nether features with candid delight which proved quite naturally to agitate the unemployed brother-in-law who, being at loose ends, was free to engage in an extravagantly undelectable commentary.

So I came again shortly to myself and grew once more acquainted with my immediate purpose. Accordingly I wondered of Royce and inquired of Curtis if couldn't they both of them see clear, at least for the balance of the evening, to endure each other in relative peace if not harmony outright, mute perhaps their mutual abuse and forego any further temptations to grapple and wail which Royce and Curtis together allowed they would possibly entertain as a prospect, grunted anyhow their tepid assent without troubling themselves to interrupt their pursuits, without paying to me any mind much truly at all even as I took my leave of them, bid them a pleasant evening and retreated through the sitting room door and out into the back hall where I sidled and slipped along towards the parlor and let myself shortly out onto the porch.

For a time I just sat in the cruiser and listened to the chatter on the radio, Dewey talking to Angelene, Wendle talking to Dewey, and the pack of them waiting to hear from me. They were plainly all atingle with the prospect of my reduction, and I listened for a time to them trade their opinions and sundry remarks before I took up the handset and made myself known to them and so endured from Dewey and endured from Wendle and endured from Angelene as well encouragement to own up to my lapses and confess to my ignorance in some things still. They wanted to know if I'd taken in the squalor, if I'd witnessed the animosities, remarked Royce's taste in feature films and Curtis's inclination for his dead starlet, were anxious in short to

learn if I'd come across a piece of this life I'd not learned of in the
army, and straightaway I told to them, "Yes," allowed pretty shortly
how I had.

My neighbor upstairs is a homosexual who calls himself Desmond
though I know from his mother that his name instead is Bob. Desmond is not a bashful and retiring sort of a fellow and seems quite
proud of his orientation, incorporates the news of it into every introduction he makes for himself, announces his name and identifies
his alignment as stoutly and forthrightly as if he were maybe
just a Freemason or a practicing Republican. Desmond is not a dainty
manner of creature and I evermore hear him stalking about overhead,
pounding the nappy carpet with his ball-peen feet. He can never
seem to light and linger in one place or another but wanders and
circulates most of the evening hours until I guess he gives out and
collapses at last. Desmond owns a pair of tufted boudoir chairs, a
couple of clawfooted tables, an empire settee and a carved mahogany
bed along with a handsome armoire where he keeps his stereo and
his extensive collection of recordings, cast albums chiefly from
musical productions that sound through the ceiling to have been com-
posed by organ grinders.

Early on Desmond had me up for a drink, came down while I was
still unpacking and told to me his name and revealed to me his
tendency and fairly conscripted me to join him for a cocktail, as much
as drove me before him up the stairway and into his apartment where
I was encouraged to lounge upon Desmond's settee and sip Desmond's
gin and listen with Desmond to a touching duet sung by a woman and
sung by a man with identical brassy voices. Theirs apparently was a
forbidden love and they were pretty much tortured about it, or agitated anyhow and feverish and given in their extremity to the higher
registers. Desmond indicated to me the parts that were in his view
particularly lilting, and he swayed on occasion and dipped with the

rhythm and sang sometimes along with the woman and sang sometimes along with the man and then invited me to savor with him if I
might a manner of musical meditation embarked upon by the mother
of the boy. Desmond for my benefit turned up the volume excruciat-
ingly high and promoted thereby the sensation that we were not so
much in the room with that woman as lodged maybe in her esophagus
instead. I suspect he would have played me showtunes all the night,
got the feeling from the way he saw after my drink and the general
agitation he displayed on my behalf that Desmond didn't often meet
with the chance to entertain, that his introductory proclamation served
pretty regularly as a punctuational device.

My own apartment downstairs had been occupied by a foul strain
of Crowder and his common-law wife who'd squandered their rent
money on a cherry red Trans Am and had provided me thereby occasion to preside at their eviction. I'd been taken with the features of the
place, the gold speckled carpet, the glass shower door, the coppertone
appliances and the view out of the bedroom window of the dumpster,
or the view anyhow of the interceding stockade fence where assorted
dead bushes and brittle expired climbers served together as the residue
of a wholly thwarted experiment in decorative horticulture.

I didn't have much to move, left Karen with the curtains and the
fuzzy toilet seat cover and furniture but for my Naugahyde chair. I let
her have the throwrugs and the wedding pictures and the pots and the
pans and the dishes and the flatware and took for myself a laminated
endtable and the quilt my aunt had made for me. She peppered me
there at the end with emphatic declarations and saucy scraps of prose
she'd culled from a book about women who love the men that they do
and why in the first place they love them. I got the feeling she wished
I'd been lured from her, been driven by desire to take a mistress that
way princes and that way potentates will, got the feeling she'd rather
I'd strayed since, proving a man of urges and fiery passions, I could be
forgiven and I could be redeemed, but it wasn't truly that clear and
wasn't remotely that simple. I couldn't explain it to her, could barely
explain it to myself. So when she pressed and when she inquired I

shrugged and made grave faces and endeavored to let on that it wasn't anything she'd done, wasn't anything she'd failed to do, that it was me exclusively, was somehow me alone instead.

I bought a little TV at a tag sale and it had there at the outset a bright, crisp picture, but come one Saturday afternoon I wrenched off the antenna trying to bring in the bowling which I took as a sign and a visitation and concluded on my own that a fellow who'd watch people bowl on television probably doesn't deserve an antenna or have much claim to decent reception. It wasn't even like I could so much as hear the thing in the first place due to Desmond upstairs whose schedule seemed often enough to coincide with my own. Whenever I was disposed to lay about and watch some species of idiocy on my TV Desmond would invariably grow inspired to tour his premises at a trot, race sometimes between rooms or up and back along the hallway and raise on occasion his voice with the cast members who would sing alone or sing in pairs or join all up and sing as a chorus with near as much modulation and charm as a sack full of piepans dragged along the ground.

Desmond only ever lit and settled for a portion of the news hour which allowed me peace enough to take in the events of the day, those events anyhow that the news team in Bluefield saw fit to make mention of. I could see through the static the news desk and nearly make out on the back wall the Bluefield news team logo, and I could tell invariably which was the anchorwoman and which was the anchorman since, even through the snow and the interference, that newsman's extraordinary head of hair was apparent still to me. It was thick and shiny and as black as roof tar and looked to have been parted with a miter saw.

I took usually my supper in my Naugahyde chair and read for diversion those magazines that came still for the Crowders, *American Rifleman* and *Hot Rod* along with a couple of hefty beauty monthlies, the sort that advise women how to make their breasts perkier and their backsides flatter and their thighs altogether more sleek and comely and feature usually each month a frame-by-frame makeover of a regular housewife into a semi-domestic strumpet. I was provided as well the opportunity most evenings to exchange views with the Crowders' mongrel, a mongrel anyhow I took to be the Crowders' due to the way she came to me there at the first, showed up on the landing shortly after my move and bumped against the door until I stepped over and opened it. She didn't seem to care that I wasn't a Crowder myself, failed to sniff me at the outset or pay me any regard but simply stepped on into the apartment, crossed the front room, proceeded up the hallway, and stretched out on the bathroom floor back of the toilet and under the tank.

I didn't much want a dog, surely didn't want a shaggy black mongrel with a greasy snout and mats on her haunches and a notice-able stink about her, a manner of *eau de* compost that vanquished the scent even from my perfumed toilet paper which I had not suspected any stench could do. Fortunately it turned out that she didn't herself much want an owner, was not looking to get fed or adored or rubbed on her belly but required simply the door to be opened as she could not work the knob. I had that first night designs to put her out and attempted to lure her from the bathroom with a piece of chicken that proved to be inadequately decomposed to suit her and so did not figure as a temptation, though she did presently step out from under the tank and looked by turns at me and the toilet bowl until I grew sufficiently illuminated to lift the lid and raise the ring and make available to her her beverage.

Naturally we got a little friendly after a while though hardly that way most people and dogs get friendly. We weren't, that is, affec-tionate truly but grew to be passably congenial, and she got shortly to the point where she would linger in the front room and entertain from me a piece of talk, sit there on the carpet by the laminated table and tolerate my opinions and endure my views and favor me in time with that expression of hers that appeared to be thoughtful and contem-plative. I took it anyway there at the outset for an uncharacteristically pensive sort of a look for a dog but learned at length that it was simply a byproduct of her digestive process, was invariably the expression she

63

worked up and displayed whenever she'd mined the opportunity to notice herself break wind.

She was in fact an extravagantly vaporish creature, couldn't be persuaded to eat dry food from a bag or wet food from a can but dined daily instead at the dumpster, feasted off the overflow and the spillage and was partial to most any sort of savory that had rotted quite entirely beyond recognition. For a starter she was particularly fond of cantaloupe pulp and rind and favored for an entree most any species of fat and gristle she might come across along with a stray bean or two and a withered hunk of potato for balance. She took usually her salad in the European fashion once she'd sniffed out all the entree she could find and enjoyed often for dessert a brown scrap of apple along with a dram or two of iridescent cordial which she'd lap up from depressions in the asphalt.

Understandably the rubbish she saw fit to ingest did not simply leave off decaying and fermenting because it had come to be gobbled up and deposited in the stomach of a mongrel. The introduction in fact of sundry canine gastric juices seemed only to accelerate the rot, and that dog could transform the likes of a slick brown chunk of cabbage into a veritable fog of wholly corrosive vapors almost before the thing had passed entirely through her neck. She never sputtered or chugged or made with her duct any manner of detectable ruckus but simply grew grave of expression and became for a dog quite altogether still and what looked to be reflective as she furtively discharged her byproduct which served usually as comment upon and noxious reply to whatever sort of complaint I'd found cause to air or frustration I'd managed to speak of.

So it was in the end a variety of conversation that passed between us most evenings. She would bump the door and I would admit her and she would display the courtesy to linger at the laminated table and pay apparently some notice to my views and my opinions, endure from me news of the discouragements of my day prior to characterizing the lot of them with a dose of pungent wind and then wandering off at length to the bathroom where she quaffed customarily a bit of commode water prior to stretching out under the tank and back of the bowl.

When I called her anything I called her Monroe only because she'd carried home one evening in her mouth a dog collar with a little metal fireplug tag fixed to it, a little metal fireplug tag stamped with the words "Hello, my name is Monroe." The collar itself was a trifle gamy and ripe, and I couldn't help but figure she'd probably eaten the occupant, found him maybe done in in a ditch and feasted on him from the assend up until all that was left to her was the collar and the tag, and she carried them home that way people sometimes come away from the steak house with their plastic swords. So when circumstances dictated an introduction or a formal dressing down, I went ahead and called her Monroe and she made sometimes like she knew who I was speaking to, considered me anyhow with her customary gravity and attention while she blessed me by habit with answering blasts from her atomizer as a manner usually of comment and rejoinder.

It was almost like having a buddy, an intimate who was not maybe much on nuance and provided invariably the same advice but was willing anyhow to look attentive and appear concerned while I spelled out my troubles and identified my irritants and earned in the end unwavering comment and response from that scrawny black dog with the greasy snout that roomed with me and boarded at the dumpster and seemed to have mounted through constant gastric distress a claim to wisdom and a claim to repose quite uncommon among creatures that drink from a toilet. Of course I couldn't grow to love her aroma or adore her discharges and I truly didn't much care for that way she had of laying her nose against my naked thigh whenever I lit upon the ring to make my own business and read for distraction an article on chrome header maintenance or a discussion of powder loads or an apologia for lip gloss, but I never wished she hadn't come and bumped against the door, grew at length a little attached to her and found myself every now and again disposed to scratch her atop the head or stroke her back though she usually prevailed upon me to resist the temptation.

That night we found Wendle I was late getting in and she was waiting for me on the landing, was stretched out upon the slab with her head on the doorsill and that peevish expression on her face which often gave service as a rebuke. The cement made her stiff and achy and she managed a production of just rising to her feet and stretching herself, hobbled about a little for my benefit and watched me hunt for my doorkey with a look in her eyes of truly heightened anguishment. She got, however, a whiff of me soon enough, visited straightaway the toilet bowl for a bit of elixir but caught, I recall, the scent as soon as she'd come back down the hallway and arrived alongside the laminated table.

I guess she could smell him, could smell anyhow the death about me, and was driven by the aroma to demonstrate a manner of keen curiosity in most especially my left shirtsleeve which had become spotted and stained with Wendle's blood, not greatly spotted or extravagantly stained, hardly ruined outright, but just smeared and speckled a little here and there. She laid her nose flush upon it and grew shivery and animated, just altogether worked up like I'd never seen her get. It was all I could do to keep her off of me, persuade her she'd best sit over by the table and break like usual her wind, and though she did sit at last and did at last vent her gases, she looked upon me with what I could not help but take for emotion, appeared quite entirely transported by the sight of me, figured I guess she'd found at last a kindred spirit, a suck-egg creature like herself.

❧

Come morning we got a call at the station which no one was handy to see to but me as the chief and Dewey were out at the scene and Clifford was at the mortuary while Lonnie was down in the lockup sleeping against the wall. Angelene was working the switchboard and was looking grim and forlorn. She'd come through the chief to be acquainted with poignant displays of high feeling and had cultivated great personal skill as far as shows of anguishment went. She proved, however, fairly indiscriminate in the application of her tortured expressions, and her poor-dead-Wendle look didn't appear to me much different at all from the faces she pulled when the Redskins lost or we ran out of Creamora. She informed me she'd received a call from down at the *Ledger*, our local news daily, had heard from Mrs. Tyree that she had a little trouble, some manner of disputation on her hands. It had a thing to do with Wendle. Angelene couldn't say just what but proposed that the murder of an officer of the law was spawning already fear and promoting apparently distress among the population.

"People are edgy," Angelene told me. "People are worked up," and she favored me with a stirring measure of supplemental torment.

I walked down to the offices of the *Ledger*, couldn't suppose that even a wild disputation was anything worth hurrying myself about. I'd attended at disputations at the *Ledger* before, the sorts of affairs that were often set off by an unbecoming turn of phrase or a glaring indifference to fact or just a poorly lit unflattering photograph in the back pages of an issue that the subject would find he could not abide in silence and so would stop in to speak to Mr. Chapman or speak to his sister Mrs. Tyree who together through sheer tactlessness could make of a mild disappointment a disputation outright.

I'd relieved them last from the fairly virulent displeasure of Mrs. Millard Baumgardner who'd been featured on the social page, had been photographed by Mr. Chapman himself who demonstrated evermore an altogether uncanny knack for training his lens on the fleshy backsides and considerable flanks of the local matrons and mature women of standing who did not usually care to have their posteriors profiled so and published in such fine and revealing focus. Mrs. Baumgardner took particular offense as the affront to her was plainly of a compound variety; she'd been made to endure an unbecoming low-angle photo and a snide incriminating caption as well.

Mrs. Baumgardner had organized a barbecue for the volunteer fire squad that had done her the service of extinguishing her carshed once Mr. Baumgardner had inadvertently set it ablaze. She'd hoped to demonstrate her appreciation, raise a little money for the unit and provide her Millard the occasion to prove that he could in fact light the charcoal alone without touching off any adjacent structures. She'd designed and posted the announcements, sold the tickets, marinated the chicken herself and had made of the whole business a thorough-going success, had helped to generate for her local fire squad money enough for legitimate softball pants and handsome striped leggings which she guessed was the point and figured was the news and had assumed would be the gist of the notice in the *Ledger*.

They did in fact manage in print to make Mrs. Baumgardner seem to be at least a little noble and selfless, approved anyhow of her motives while taking clearly issue with her marinade which Mrs. Baumgardner likely would have tolerated and probably would have endured but for the accompanying photograph which appeared to Mrs. Baumgardner quite plainly intended to highlight her spread. And as if it wasn't offense enough for a woman of some girth and mature years to have her largess tainted with the publication and distribution of an unambiguous photograph of her least dainty feature, she was made to suffer an additional barb in the caption where her posterior was iden-tified as Mrs. Millard Baumgardner and the gentleman beyond her was given out to be the Reverend Mr. Doakes to whose name was attached the parenthetical observation, "partly obscured."

So while maybe she would have endured with grace the objection to her marinade and tolerated in silence the portrait of her posterior, Mrs. Baumgardner could not so much as begin to abide the crowning insinuation of the caption itself, the news that she had not just over-salted her chicken and overnourished her thighs but had managed as well to fairly eclipse a full-sized reverend and hide him with her backside from view. She guessed she could detect well enough the hand of Mrs. Tyree in the caption, Mrs. Tyree who was infamous roundabout for her parenthetical abuses, wielded often enough her qualifiers like a lance and worked to puncture and labored to deflate which Mrs. Baumgardner failed to find on this occasion near so amus-ing as previously she'd been inclined to find it.

She guessed she was humiliated, was certain she was incensed, and she marched directly downtown to the offices of the *Ledger* so as to have if she might a word with Mrs. Tyree and a word with Mr. Chapman, air her grievance against the parenthetical, her objection to the photograph. Of course Mrs. Baumgardner was likely a tad shriller than maybe she'd intended to be and advanced presently into mild hysteria once Mrs. Tyree and Mr. Chapman together attempted to persuade her of the healthful, aerobic properties marching downtown in a snit likely possessed.

I seem to recall that once Mrs. Baumgardner and Mr. Chapman and his sister Mrs. Tyree had swapped assorted uncharitable rejoinders and Mrs. Baumgardner had started to insist upon a printed retraction, a manner anyhow of clearly worded wholly unparenthetical technical explanation as to why it was she'd looked to be broad and rotund, the whole business veered of a sudden into the realm of the disputational as best anyway as Mrs. Tyree could tell, Mrs. Tyree who took usually upon herself the chore of separating the insignificant antagonisms from the disputations outright. So she threatened, as was her habit, to call the law and have an officer remove Mrs. Baumgardner from the premises which Mrs. Baumgardner endured the news of well enough until Mrs. Tyree saw fit, upon reflection, to propose it might take in fact a pair of officers together which served to draw from Mrs. Baumgardner a highly impassioned and wildly unflattering rebuke.

So Mrs. Tyree called Angelene and Angelene called me and I made my way downtown to the offices of the *Ledger* where, by the time I arrived, Mr. Chapman and Mrs. Tyree were badgering Mrs. Baumgardner with their rights and privileges under the constitution of these United States, were attempting to educate her as to why precisely they could be as low-angled and parenthetical as they pleased, and were making Mrs. Baumgardner out to be a seditious and treacherous scoundrel, Mrs. Baumgardner who was full well in the midst of a heated and fairly regrettable statement on the topic of the founding fathers when I managed to intercede.

I simply carried her home in the cruiser, made her out to be petite and apologized on behalf of Mr. Chapman and on behalf of Mrs.

Tyree who I let on to be kindly people at heart afflicted on occasion
with poor impulses and lapses in taste and surely girth enough apiece
to blot out the Pope himself which proved for Mrs. Baumgardner a
soothing line of talk.

Naturally on this occasion I feared some relation of Wendle's
might have stopped by all done up with grief, and I was relieved to
discover when I arrived at the office that it was only instead Mr.
Shumate the poet and sonneteer as distinct from Mr. Shumate his
brother the motorgrader driver and Mr. Shumate their father the
dairyman. Mr. Shumate the poet and sonneteer was himself in fact an
employee of the department of transportation like his brother the
motorgrader driver, had mowed shoulders and right-of-ways for a
number of years until, by some stroke of fortune and happy luck, he'd
enjoyed a promotion, had given over his orange tractor and his yellow
plastic hardhat for a half-ton pickup and the duties and obligations of
a department of transportation foreman and overseer which proved, as
far as duties and obligations go, appreciably shy of strenuous.

Mr. Shumate the poet and sonneteer was charged essentially with
watching other people do the sort of work he used to do himself which
did not require on the part of Mr. Shumate so terribly much concentration and effort. Straightoff he was led to suspect that perhaps he'd
not been after all intended for management on account of how Mr.
Shumate did not truly take to the tedium and savor the aimlessness of
overseeing that way the foremen otherwise appeared to, failed to discover much fulfillment to speak of in laying against his doorpanel and
drinking icewater from his Igloo while fellows mowed and graded and
paved and resented plainly being watched at it. Mr. Shumate simply
wanted something to do, some manner of undertaking that might
focus his faculties and occupy his mind, and it was by sheer happenstance alone that he discovered one morning his gift for versifying.

He'd been watching a boy scrape up some fill to pack around the
ends of a low-water bridge where the stream had surged and washed,
and Mr. Shumate had taken in his leisure notice of a gauzy veil of mist
that lay upon an eddy up the waterway, though he'd not figure it

70

straightoff for a gauzy veil in fact but had been charmed simply by the sight of it and, in casting about for some way to speak of that mist to the boy scraping fill, he'd concocted "gauzy veil," had concocted in fact "gauzy patch" there at the outset but had seen fit shortly to renovate his phrase once he'd landed in his musings upon "veil" instead. He featured it in a declaration, was obliged to intone it twice and even then only earned from that boy on the backhoe a pinched and sickly expression.

I don't suppose he'd ever had cause to suspect he was fecund in a poetical sort of way, guess Mr. Shumate was as surprised at his advancing passion for versifying as anybody might have been, and maybe he even figured it would wane, likely he even suspected it would play out, but he busied himself in the meanwhile constructing conceits and fabricating metaphors and rendering his syntax ever so gaudy and oblique. There at the first he contented himself with making the odd phrase, stringing together clumps of words that might at some juncture serve him well as radiant modifiers. Of course he worked all along on his declaiming, practiced his breathing and exercised his diaphragm so as to come to be able to produce the species of full, round tones that bombast most usually calls for, and he fired off every now and again some bit of business he'd worked up and gilded. In the midst of a conversation he would oftentimes see fit to air a loosely pertinent lyrical scrap of verse and thereby manage most usually to stultify his companions who were decent enough themselves not to lapse when they could help it into tortured metaphorical forms of expression and so expected the likes of Mr. Shumate to treat them in kind.

Mr. Shumate, however, in the tradition of poetical sorts the world over, was far too transported by the delicate beauty of his declamations to take much notice of their anaesthetic effects which allowed him in time to become, in the hoary tradition of poets, friendless and solitary but for the occasional company of versifiers otherwise of which there were assorted local specimens who were prone to exchange sumptuous poetical phrases like mortar rounds. Blessed consequently with the disposition and the occasion both to work largely undistracted by regular human commerce, Mr. Shumate began to enlarge the scope of his endeavors and progressed presently beyond mere lines and phrases, improved his leisure by cobbling together entire stanzas and full-scale poems outright.

He embarked upon his oeuvre with a manner of meditation that concerned itself partly with gauzy veils of mist and the like but took up in time the case of a groundhog who'd expired beneath the wheels of a Dodge there in the presence of Mr. Shumate himself who responded to the thump and the gore with a clutch of dainty rhetorical queries designed to probe in meter the oh so flimsy nature of life on this earth where one creature can thrive and prosper while another can spring from a ditch and dart directly under a radial tire. He couldn't exactly figure the causes, was able himself to make little sense of the vagaries of cruel fate which proved of course to be a boon and a blessing providing him like it did occasion to discover how poetry at its core is the art in fact of not making sense of anything much. Apparently it's largely the confusion that's poetic, which proved for Mr. Shumate an awfully happy circumstance since he was by disposition routinely perplexed and certain of almost nothing at all.

Pretty directly Mr. Shumate determined to eschew rhyme and declaimed as much to anybody who was convenient to hear it. He was hoping to go unfettered by the assorted constrictions of traditional poetical form and made his position plain to most especially the local versifiers otherwise who were partial themselves to doggerel outright and the strictest manner of meter and grew of a sudden uninclined to consort with a fellow who would openly promote free verse. Mr. Shumate, consequently, came to be even more friendless and solitary than he already was and fell back for a time upon Mrs. Shumate, assaulted her anyhow with meditations and pastoral reveries until she managed to refresh him as to the provisions of their legal union, the vows they'd taken, the promises they'd made which could not be construed to oblige her to suffer near constant declamations.

It came to be Mr. Shumate's custom to settle in the evenings at the table in the kitchen and compose his verse in pencil on yellow legal paper, verse about people he'd met, creatures he'd seen, sensations he'd imbibed, verse even about items he could spy from the table including an altogether stirring appreciation of the dish drainer and a cycle of sonnets inspired by the contents of the spice rack. He accumulated fairly directly poems enough to fill a tome, as best as Mr. Shumate could tell, and he paid a woman to type for him his oeuvre and hired Mr. Dunleavy to offset it and staple the collection together into handsome slender volumes that Mr. Shumate carried around himself and gave away. We had one down at the stationhouse for a while. It stayed usually on the table off alongside the drinkbox and several times over a soda and a sack of nuts I'd taken the thing up and dipped into it.

I'll confess to having been myself a little put off there at the first what with Mr. Shumate's native perplexity in conjunction with his resolution to eschew rhyme that together served to render his poems troublesome and odd, but in time I'd come to be acclimated and could tell well enough that there was considerable heart to the whole business, that Mr. Shumate was sharp and shrewd and couldn't begin to figure it was adequate occupation just to lean against a truck and watch the roads get improved. He was wanting I guess to discover some way to make the world add up and took consequently heed of what he saw and heed of what he heard and heed of what he found himself just idly thinking about. With obvious care he shaped and honed his impressions, set them down to keep as a means of persuasion, as a manner, I suppose, of testimony. I recall I was most especially fond of his poem about a bug on a stalk and found quite genuinely touching his sonnet on paprika.

Mrs. Tyree at the *Ledger*, as an adjunct to mangling dignity and mischaracterizing posteriors, in addition to her duties as keeper of the parenthetical and defender of constitutional freedoms, served on occasion as a cultural critic and reviewer. She wrote up the stage shows at the high school and gave out usually the plots of the movies at the triplex so as to preserve I guess the rest of us from having to sit in the theater and wonder what might happen next. She attended on occasion concerts up in Roanoke and proved evermore astounded at how people she'd heard on the radio were oftentimes in life far shorter than she'd figured they'd be. She visited restaurants and reported on the food she'd been served and the hygiene of the people who'd served it, and about once a month she took to task the steak house out at the interchange where they'd replaced their buttery captain's wafers with regular saltines; it seemed doubtful she'd ever recover altogether from her disappointment.

Every now and again Mrs. Tyree read a book and provided the population with her impressions. She valued most especially a good story and could come in fact to be pretty frankly transported by the manner of novel that allowed a man and allowed a woman to triumph together over their difficulties and over their misfortunes and flop at last naked onto an actual bed where the woman would respirate most tellingly and fairly wail her approval while her lover tinkered with her assorted parts and pieces and coaxed her at last into paroxysms of passion outright. They were tales essentially of ladies with pluck and men with tongues, and clearly they spoke to Mrs. Tyree, who gave them out to be grand and stirring.

Mrs. Tyree was not, however, overfond of poetry largely on account of its murkier qualities and fanciful turns of phrase. She could stomach well enough the verse of Mrs. McElroy from out at Ivanhoe, Mrs. McElroy who wrote poems chiefly about her savior and His wondrous love which were not in fact too terribly afflicted with murk even though Mrs. McElroy allowed herself the occasional excruciating construction and the odd convoluted interjection. Her redemption came largely in the fact that she rhymed like a regular lunatic and provided fairly faultless syncopation which seemed to find favor with Mrs. Tyree who would take oftentimes occasion to recommend to her readers the verse of Mrs. McElroy and print as an advertisement a sizable snatch of it, usually some bit of business about the unrivaled beauties of the world and the glorious predilections of the Maker.

Naturally, back when he was distributing his slender volumes,

Mr. Shumate stopped off at the *Ledger* and gave one most expressly to Mrs. Tyree, as he'd taken her apparently for an advocate of enlightenment and had empathized with her campaign to bring back the captain's wafers that he'd been himself more than a little fond of. Mrs. Tyree in fact read Mr. Shumate's slender volume and she wrote up in the *Ledger* her estimation of it which was ripe with vitriol. Plainly Mrs. Tyree had anticipated that Mr. Shumate's oeuvre would be pretty much like all the local oeuvres otherwise, that Mr. Shumate was himself the sort to observe the regular restraints, the manner of versifier who could speak of his Lord or the dawning of the day or the sheer and rapturous miracle of birth or even a gauzy veil of mist on a stream and remain as well mindful of the strictures of poetical construction and ever so closely attentive to his beat. She'd been, however, bitterly disappointed and found cause in the slender volume to lament with considerable bile and excessive feeling Mr. Shumate's wayward impulses. She took most particular issue with his sonnet on cumin; it had only nine lines to it and not even the first trace of punctuation.

Mr. Shumate had read about Wendle in the paper. Mr. Shumate had heard about Wendle on the radio and he'd grown as a consequence inspired and had undertaken in the early hours of the morning an ambitious and timely bit of verse which he'd foregone overseeing to carry to the offices of the *Ledger*. He'd hoped Mrs. Tyree, as recompense for her vicious notice, might consider his poem for publication, might find it to be a suitable expression of civic loss and personal grief together since Mr. Shumate had been himself acquainted with Wendle, had been caught by him anyway in an illegal turn and cited. Mrs. Tyree did Mr. Shumate the courtesy of scanning his poem and made in fact to weigh its qualities in advance of offering up an explication, as preamble to dismissing the item altogether and observing how Mr. Shumate was still plainly eschewing rhyme and neglecting punctuation, and she advised him to go on home if he might to his spice rack and leave the poetry to genuinely poetical people.

Understandably, Mr. Shumate begged to differ, sought to explain to Mrs. Tyree and explain to her brother Mr. Chapman that what he'd concocted was a manner of hybrid, something between an ode and a panegyric that was meant both to mourn the violent death of the officer and the advancing extinction of the world of gentlefolk. But Mrs. Tyree and Mr. Chapman just tossed their heads and laughed their little collegial laugh as a means of suggesting to Mr. Shumate what a trifling sort he seemed to them to be with just his unrhymed half-breed bit of verse to offer which was not plainly itself ode and not plainly itself panegyric and hardly as well any useful sort of union of the two.

As was their custom, then, they subjected Mr. Shumate to their own manner of ridicule, were snide and jolly together at his expense and expected him I guess to retire from the offices of the *Ledger* as was usually the habit with people whose views they'd mocked and whose intentions they'd derided. However, having long since eschewed rhyme and given over meter, Mr. Shumate had already become an object of fun for the local poets otherwise and their assorted patrons. Consequently he had hardened to abuse and answered it more often than not with a declamation, intervened on his own behalf with an unrhymed stanza or some wholly meterless snatch of verse that he was proud to have penned and pleased to intone.

So he did not retire, failed to slink in humiliation from the offices of the *Ledger* but set in instead upon a recitation of his hybrid item, established himself in a dramatic declamatory posture and got shortly underway with his panegyrical ode which Mr. Chapman and his sister Mrs. Tyree took between them for an altogether invidious brand of dissent and so trotted out from reflex their rights and privileges under the constitution of these United States and confronted Mr. Shumate with declamations of their own though they could not truly find a right or discover a privilege that protected them from exposure to free verse.

By the time I'd arrived, Mr. Shumate had run through his pane-gyrical ode twice and was attempting to illuminate most especially Mrs. Tyree as to the aptness of a phrase he'd concocted. Of course they wanted me to pitch him out the door, insisted they had on their hands a genuine disputation and a regular trespass and wanted me to take up that scoundrel Mr. Shumate and fling him down the steps and out into the road where he belonged. But Mr. Shumate, for his part, was more of a mind that they were engaging together in a dialectic and begged quite naturally to differ with Mrs. Tyree and Mr. Chapman, who threw in both to wonder of me if didn't I find free verse to smack of leftist tendencies.

Mr. Shumate wanted little more than to be if he might in his own defense permitted to declaim once further which seemed to me reasonable enough, and Mr. Chapman and Mrs. Tyree guessed together it might since I'd not yet had to endure a declamation and so couldn't likely anticipate the trials and the torments before me, the wretched conceits and lacerating convolutions that would bring me nothing truly but unhappiness and confusion. But I guessed I was sufficiently girded and resolved and sought the indulgence of Mrs. Tyree and her brother Mr. Chapman in advance of instructing Mr. Shumate to go on ahead and declaim away.

Straightoff I did glean sense from the thing. It was a little about Wendle but was mostly about the uniform and mostly about the badge and was concerned largely with the general deterioration of authority as suggested in the sundering of an officer of the peace from his vital vapors and fluids. Mrs. Tyree interrupted to identify the whole item as an anarchistic screed and accused Mr. Shumate of some noticeable fomentation which Mr. Shumate failed to dignify with a response but merely persevered with his declamation and arrived shortly at a piece of it he was most especially pleased with, a turn of phrase he lifted his finger to emphasize so that I in particular might take some notice of the sundry qualities of it which I endeavored with a look to insinuate I had.

He capped the thing off with a flourish, a passionate rendering of the final line with tremulous voice and upraised finger working in union together to produce a stirring effect, and directly beyond the culmination Mrs. Tyree and Mr. Chapman jointly concluded and harmoniously announced that they liked the thing less even on this occasion than they'd liked it previously and they'd not, they insisted, liked it previously at all. I, however, allowed straightoff that I'd been genuinely moved which Mrs. Tyree and Mr. Chapman appeared distressed at the news of and could not likely have thought at that moment more poorly of me if I'd made to them claim to be related by blood to Karl Marx himself.

Mrs. Tyree reminded me how none of the words rhymed and none of the lines measured out and she made plain that she'd be pleased if I might reconsider and climb on board with her and her brother who guessed they could well enough tell between them art when they heard it and tripe when they heard that instead. But I persevered in my approval of Mr. Shumate's panegyrical ode, and before Mrs. Tyree and Mr. Chapman could keep me from it I went ahead and proposed to Mr. Shumate that maybe he'd best declaim that poem of his one time further which they both of them straightoff attempted to prevent, but it would be surely just as easy to stop the wind from blowing as to choke off a poet who's been asked to recite.

Of course they weren't persuaded to publish Mr. Shumate's panegyrical ode, but I'd been pleased to have occasion to cause them to endure it further, and I suggested at length to Mr. Shumate that me and him both retire to the street which Mrs. Tyree and Mr. Chapman were pleased to construe as the triumph at last of their rights and privileges and so exulted together and gloated and barked by turns certain passages of the constitutional preamble that they found to have particular charms, while for my part I escorted Mr. Shumate out from the offices of the *Ledger* and down the steps to the sidewalk where I loitered with him a moment there by the paperbox.

Mr. Shumate guessed there wasn't any market much for panegyrical odes which I could hardly help but throw in with him about, and we made a point of longing together for days of yore back when people were prone as not to sit down of an evening and take up some verse. I informed Mr. Shumate that I'd read in fact his handsome volume myself and had been touched and affected by his poem about the bug on the stalk, his sonnet to paprika. Straightaway Mr. Shumate was buoyed by the news and offered to do me the honor of a joint declamation which I couldn't begin to bring myself to resist and refuse and so watched Mr. Shumate draw his breath and strike his pose and drop his chin to intone.

He was passionate and emphatic and, by the culmination of the sonnet, pretty wholly rejuvenated, felt I suppose like a man once more of letters, looked again spry and vigorous and not so terribly done up with rejection. He guessed at me he had phrases to manufacture and polish, lines to construct, stanzas to assemble and, up past Woodlawn towards the airstrip, the laying of a culvert to marshal and oversee. So I watched him buckle on his orange mesh vest and climb into his truck and, as is the way with licensed poets, pull out directly in front of a Buick whose driver braked and veered and shouted which Mr. Shumate, listening likely already to his muse, hardly appeared to notice.

I walked back up to the stationhouse to make out my report on the disputation and intended, in honor of Mr. Shumate, to bring a little rhetorical flair to the thing which caused me to pace and stalk about since I'm not customarily so blessed and agile as to be ever ready with flair but am put upon most usually to extract gaudy expressions like eyeteeth which sets me often upright and afoot and sends me touring about. Consequently, I found myself inclined to wander and arrived shortly back at the conference room in pursuit of a highly descriptive clause. Clifford, I figured, had collected a little evidence out at the branch—a bloody stick, a sausage tin, a spent blue twenty-gauge casing, a sack of rocks from the road, along with the desiccated scrap of scalp. He'd laid it all out on the tabletop, and I took up that casing and held it in my fingers as I debated with myself the aptness of an adjective. I was just beginning to spend some regard on that scrap of scalp as well when I noticed an envelope off beyond the sausage tin, a moderately freighted legal-sized one with the flap unclasped. I picked it up and peered inside and found it to hold Wendle's effects which I spilled out onto the table.

I examined Wendle's penknife. I examined Wendle's keys. I

shook his rubber change purse and plucked up his buckeye that I left for a moment to lay on my palm. Wendle's wallet was in a sorry state, was worn and misshapen and coming unstitched, and I was loath to take it up there straightaway since I feared that Angelene might happen onto me and misapprehend my motives, figure maybe I was just prying and nosing around and not in fact up to an investigation. So I stepped into the hallway to listen for and place her before I returned to the conference table and began to investigate.

I extracted Wendle's bank card, Wendle's credit card, Wendle's video club card and his driving license. He had a picture of his girl as a baby, his wife as little more than a child, a book of stamps that had come from the damp to be altogether stuck shut and a register receipt from the Western Auto for fourteen dollars and thirty-seven cents. He'd squirreled away odd scraps of paper, lists and notes and assorted chits and stubs, and had been carrying back with his folding money a coupon for barsoap. He didn't have but twelve dollars which I laid on the table and was feeling about to see if that wallet was genuinely empty when I came across some manner of thing off along the back, an item stuck under the sateen flap beyond where the bills go, the spot most fellows would keep a thing they ought not probably to have.

It was stiffer than a bill, had made an impression in the sateen and I couldn't truly much figure what sort of an item it might be as I worked my fingers beyond the flap and plucked out at length what proved a photograph, a portion anyhow of a Polaroid that had been shaped and trimmed and made to fit. It was her. Of course straightoff I couldn't say who it was exactly but I could see plain enough it was hardly Dale's sister, could see it anyhow presently and could see it anyhow in time once I'd recovered a little from the effects of the general vista, once I'd gotten pretty well over the fact that the woman in the picture I'd found in Wendle's wallet back of Wendle's sateen flap didn't happen to be wearing so much as the first scrap of clothing.

One of her knees was half-obscured by a fold of flatsheet, but her pertinent parts were altogether exposed and she was, I'll admit, a fairly arresting sight, not that she was a ravishing manner of creature, one of those women with miraculous contours and legs clean up to her eyesockets, but she was more than adequately handsome and shapely, and I examined her with the variety of care and attention I do not often by habit display. I was deliberate and I was thoroughgoing and I lingered, I'll confess, over most especially the delicate private features but managed in time to surrender the glands and relinquish the lobes and proceed after my own glacial fashion to that girl's pale shoulders and her long comely neck and her actual head as well which she held a little cocked and ever so coyly pitched and canted.

She didn't appear to care that she was naked, didn't look much bothered that she was altogether uncloaked, had been able somehow to muster for the lens a wholly unself-conscious expression, a trifle of a smile as if she'd just for the moment been diverted, as if she'd just for the moment been amused. I'll confess I was charmed and taken, allow I was more enchanted truly than I had any call to be since she was hardly herself a beauty outright. But I could surely feel the pull of her well enough, was sufficiently acquainted with the sensation to detect straightaway the ache, identify the longing, and I don't in truth believe I knew I'd make off with her until I had my own money out, my sateen flap unlifted.

3.

I used to be the golden boy, but that was early on, back before Dewey learned to lever and came to be transformed. The chief wanted me to be the one to do what he did and think like he thought. Maybe the way I'd hunkered at first had served to charm and deceive him. Of course he was partly to blame for my fall since he was the one who made us carry pistols off the clock, had us to go around armed in our leisure so that we might be ready to thwart whatever mischief we happened across. I packed a little Browning myself, a .25-caliber semi that I carried in my glovebox or my windbreaker pocket. It was a puny gun to start with, and I'd gone and lost the clip, so short of persuading a perpetrator to swallow that pistol and pass it, I didn't see that I could make a danger of that thing. So I didn't guess the chief should care I'd threatened to harm a boy with it, had pressed the bore to his forehead and proposed to open an airway.

It happened on a Friday night when Monroe, apparently, had found at the dumpster a discarded hunk of foodstuff that was some way or another too spoiled and caustic for even her to digest. By the time I let her inside and she took up her place near my chair, she was breaking already near ceaseless wind and belching and moaning as well, and I asked her in an idle way just what she'd dined upon. As a means of reply, she commenced directly to retch and heave and so disgorged onto the speckled carpet some manner of slimy item which I enjoyed in fact scant pleasure to gaze upon on account of how Monroe, after that endearing fashion of dogs the world round, set in straightaway to dining afresh, devoured that discharge with relish enough to cause me some agitation myself.

Dog wind, however, and dog throw-up would never be enough alone to send me to the triplex of a Friday evening, the night young couples traditionally see fit to take their urges on an airing. However, I was having at the time trouble as well with my television, had not on the news been able even to make out the anchorman's hair, and on the muck-raking semi-journalistic pseudo-magazine show that followed, while I'd heard well enough accounts from the Lutherans who'd engaged with their pastor in illicit, unnatural acts right there in the sanctuary just beyond the narthex, I'd been prevented by excessive snow and near ceaseless vertical roll from seeing for myself even the first frame of the lurid, salacious accompanying footage that I'd in the advertisements been well assured I'd see.

Understandably I was disappointed and more than a little worked up and was in no mood to endure through the ceiling the musical review about the petty despot which Desmond had been throughout the week displaying an undue fondness for, notwithstanding how the despot himself sang in a voice that had to it all the lilt and allure of an airhorn. He'd killed his enemies and tortured his detractors and ignored his children and abused his wife and, in a dream, they all rose up before him to haunt him in song until he awoke and repented and was joined by the happy peoples of his nation in a hymn of rejoicing. I was sick to death of the sound of him croaking his remorse like a freighter, and I discovered that Friday with the despot above me and the vertical roll before me and the rancid air all about me incentive enough to take up my jacket and fairly bolt from the premises.

I didn't still even then drive straight to the triplex, but just instead toured town for a time and fell in presently behind a LeSabre, a well-traveled, moderately delapidated sedan, a yellow two-door LeSabre that appeared to be molting, was shedding anyway its vinyl top in strips and ribbons that flapped and fluttered. Directly I noticed that vehicle was veering and dodging about, would drift towards the shoulder or the oncoming lane, venture into gradual peril and get jerked sharply back and even steered briefly with attention and some success before it began again to stray.

I assumed the driver was maybe about half-drunk as it was after all a Friday evening and I guessed he'd been paid and gotten lubricated which I figured I'd best at least speak to him about, and I blinked my lights at him and I blew my horn and endeavored out the window to indicate to him that he might best pull off the road. It is, however, a terrible chore to attempt behind the wheel of a Chevette to seem a figure of authority. That fellow in the LeSabre didn't in fact appear even to see me at all and just kept ranging about the roadway avoiding barely the ditch to the one side and the oncoming traffic to the other until he turned off at last past the Magic Wand and back into the triplex lot.

I followed him off the road, was meaning to render him privy to at least some nugget of my accumulated wisdom on the topic of highway safety and civic responsibility which I was working up already my face about as I rolled in alongside him and parked, my grim and vaguely pained expression that I was wont to show to violators so as to insinuate the effects upon me of their disregard and their infractions. So I was working to shape and coordinate my features as I stepped around the rearend of my Chevette and approached that LeSabre, was far too occupied, in fact, to pay much heed to the general festivities that were proceeding in that vehicle apace and, consequently, had arrived at the doorpanel and rested already my near arm upon that rotten vinyl roof before I peered into the vehicle proper and thereby discovered that the driver was not precisely intoxicated, was impaired surely and distracted, but presented to the trained eye evidence enough that he was hardly in any fashion drunk.

He was a strapping sort, a big, broad, barrel-chested manner of guy, and he was grunting and wheezing and breathing with palpable feeling due to how he had a Spivey in his lap, was savoring the ministrations of who I took there at the first to be Donna on account of how Donna was the blonde one who'd started blonde and Sherry Lee, her sister, was the blonde one who'd been born instead a brunette and was prone to neglect her roots. I was, however, mistaken, as Sherry Lee had lately undergone a tinting which she lifted her head and told me about once I'd called her by her sister's name, said to her anyhow, "Donna?" ever so meekly and largely from reflex alone as I don't in fact believe I'd been meaning to speak. It was just that I'd been expecting simple intoxification, had my face ready, my comments prepared, was fixing to shame and castigate that fellow when it became too awful plain to me that he'd not after all been driving drunk but had only been driving aroused instead which didn't make him safer or maybe even lawful but rendered him less congenial than probably he would have been.

So it was me and it was him and it was her, the three of us there together enduring as best we were able the complication of that boy's aggravated implement that Sherry Lee gripped and held to and did not appear at all inclined to let loose of but instead ran her thumb across the head of it as a means, I suppose, of keeping it aggravated. She wasn't a harlot exactly. Her and her sister neither one ever took money as best I could tell, but they were happy enough to be treated to movies and treated to meals and kept at the lounge at the motel fairly awash in wine cooler. They were merely the pair of them tramps but they honored routinely between them the obligations of the order and serviced as a custom those men who went to the expense to squire them about.

Of course they were possessed of standards and guided in their endeavors by an altogether mystical strain of scruples that they observed religiously and so kept themselves, as best they might, relatively pure and unsullied. It was, for instance, common knowledge that Donna Spivey did not ever take her shirt off entirely, would open it or lift it but would not get altogether shed of it and only allowed her panties to be removed completely from one leg alone. Sherry Lee was a little less exacting and would go sometimes naked altogether but was saddled on occasion with whimsy enough to cause her to retain her socks or insist on keeping her arms through her brassiere straps. Neither her nor Donna would ever commit the act itself within the confines of a motorized vehicle. Full and relatively uncloaked consummation most usually required a room at the rock lodge up on the parkway where the maids left at night chocolates on the pillows and folded handsomely the endsheet of the toilet roll.

It was little wonder, then, that the expense and trouble of outright intercourse drew the bulk of men up short as Donna and Sherry Lee, no matter their standards and regardless of their fanciful scruples, were widely considered to have consummated in fact a little too freely between them to be worth hauling clear to the rock lodge when a fellow could enjoy their ministrations easily enough in his own vehicle, could purchase after a fashion and savor what was regarded roundabout as their most enduring gift. You see they'd earned with their talents and their techniques considerable fame as a pair of women who each alone could likely suck a stump clean out of the ground.

Sherry Lee didn't appear much troubled by the fact that I'd arrived to witness the amours. Upon the sound of her sister's name, she merely reared up there straightoff and looked at me like maybe she'd lifted her nose out of a good book. She didn't even sit up altogether or wipe off her mouth before she began to speak to me of her own particular tint that had been applied lately clean to her scalp so as to render her a more natural seeming blonde. She even rustled for me her tresses and appeared set to speak further of hair matters when her date, with whom I was not personally acquainted, inserted himself into the confab by way of a request, saw anyhow fit to instruct Sherry Lee, "Shut up," prior to reaching out the LeSabre window and endeavoring to catch up a fistful of my windbreaker for purposes, I had to suppose, of drawing me into proximity for harm.

I considered with attention my circumstances, weighed my assorted options, and determined pretty directly to dodge and to flee as dodging and fleeing appeared to me the least complicated course of action. Naturally I was straightaway meaning to leave the scene in my Chevette, but since I'd only just lately shut it off, I knew it wouldn't fire up. So I retired instead towards the triplex where I introduced myself into a fairly appreciable knot of people collected before the ticket window and watched to see if that boy might be still inclined to get me or if perhaps Sherry Lee had charmed him again with her stroke. I went ahead and bought a ticket and moved into the lobby where I lingered by the plateglass until Sherry Lee and until her date climbed together out of the LeSabre and advanced towards the triplex themselves when I made my way to the middle theater and took a seat in front of a pimply, well-cologned boy and his girl with her hair piled up in a do.

I'd selected the high-concept comedy-drama about the Laplander and the New York detective and the New York detective's dog, Wayne. They'd already started the movie about the creature with the melted face and the spiny protrusions, the enthusiasm for camp axes and the appetite for lithesome young women, while the sequel to that film about those crochety old people who get blessed by an alien race with more vigor and strength than they'd ever imagined they'd have to be crochety with wasn't quite over from before. I was a little agitated and a trifle concerned, but once the movie started I'll confess I came to be pretty thoroughly caught up in it. Of course I knew from Mrs. Tyree how it would all play out and the dialogue was foolish and the subplots fairly lame, but the music was loud and rhythmic and the New York detective's dog, Wayne, turned out to be an appealing sort of a creature capable of the most extravagantly soulful gazes.

The Laplander naturally was unacquainted with the habits and customs of urban American life and so entered with the detective into a course of instruction which seemed to consist largely of lessons in how precisely to say "motherfucker" with bile and flair and venom enough to come off seeming a native. It struck the crowd there at the triplex as an awfully jolly gag, and the most of them dissolved into mirth once that fellow had tried out his lingo on the desk clerk at the Sheraton. Of course that Laplander and the detective got around at length to dealing with the swarthy villain of the piece, or had begun anyhow to pursue him with some vigor and attention when I found cause to commit my offense to judgment and thereby brought my viewing experience to an end.

The trouble was primarily that boy and girl back of me who discovered, once the lights lowered and the movie started, that they had in fact no end of things to chat about and enjoyed in common the thoroughgoing inability to hold in their minds from one minute to the next any single morsel of information. They could not seem to remember who anybody in the movie was except on occasion for the Laplander and except on occasion for the detective if they'd neither one of them changed clothes. They were less certain altogether of the swarthy villain whose appearance on the screen would prompt invariably commentary as the boy and the girl back of me would feel at the sight of him evermore compelled to ask of each other, "Who's that?"

They seemed as well constitutionally incapable of absorbing together any scrap of dialogue, though one of them would generally hear what was said well enough to mangle and corrupt it in the repetition. The demands upon the pair of them became in time more strenuous than they could bear up under and they lapsed together into abject confusion, became pretty simultaneously disoriented and didn't seem either one to know what was happening or who it was happening to or why on earth it was happening to them. They entered as a consequence into a manner of syllogism and fairly chanted harmoniously how it seemed to them that if the short one was the Laplander and the tall one was the detective and the mottled one was the soulful dog, Wayne, then the swarthy one was maybe the villain and the loud one was likely the lovable street urchin which left the prissy one for the desk clerk and a whole array of vulgar ones that they could not place and identify though God knows they attempted to.

So even though that comedy-drama was a trifling and idiotic business blessed with only brief vivid spells of bloodshed, it proved in fact to be hardly trifling and idiotic enough and cast that boy and his date into such a thoroughgoing quandary that they could not for a time bring themselves to shut up and so sparked and spurred me as I was after all primed to get touched off. I mean I'd endured already vile mongrel discharges back at home along with the vertical roll and the honking dictator, and then I'd come out in public and interrupted an intimate act between a woman with a rare and unusual gift for intimacy and an outsized sort of a patron. So I guess I was ripe to relinquish my grip, and I'm sorry to say I did in fact let go for a time once that boy back of me and his date began to confuse the Laplander with the vicious swarthy villain who didn't have truly the first Laplandish thing about him. Although I believe I was only intending to swing around in my seat and request if I might the indulgence of that couple back of me, ask of them if couldn't they, for the sake of everything sacred and fine, just please, please, shut up, I'd fetched out already my pistol by the time I'd turned about and made straightaway application of it to the forehead of that pimply boy who fell in fact quite silent.

I explained to him in as calm a tone as I could manage who precisely was the Laplander and who precisely was the villain which that boy let on to be grateful to hear, and he endeavored to ply me with a pleasant expression as he told to me softly, "Mister, now mister," and began to spill in fact from his seat, appeared on his way to dissolving and shifted and slid and descended while I shared with him a sampling of my own favorite movie house rules and courtesies. That boy was beginning even to look at least a little contrite when I pulled the trigger one time and caused him to faint dead away. He as much as poured onto the floor and his vacant seatbottom sprang up.

His girl apparently figured he was killed and murdered outright and appeared intensely fearful that she would get it next which she moved to forestall with an ungodly yelp, the species of discharge a man might raise from a hound with the appropriate torment. But nobody seemed there at the first to pay her much regard as her yelp just happened to coincide with a scene in the comedy-drama comprised almost entirely of lively profanation joined with extravagant bloodletting which struck I guess the audience as reason enough for a yelp. She saw fit, however, to add a dose of hysterical shrieking that did not seem much called for by the action on the screen where the New York detective was demonstrating his assorted sensitive qualities by indulging in a show of self-reproach over the scantily cloaked voluptuous body of the swarthy villain's concubine who the detective had happened to cut in half with wayward rifle fire.

So that girl yelped and shrieked and shrieked and yelped and persevered at it for longer even than the audience at the triplex could endure, and one acutely fastidious soul went off at last and fetched back the manager who, at the sight of the pimply boy piled up on the slab, instructed the projectionist to stop the movie and turn up the lights which served pretty directly to illuminate the whole sorry business at hand.

I fled out about like I'd fled in already which was not, I'll confess, a boon to me later when I was attempting to manufacture as best I might my case, but I had to figure Sherry Lee's fellow might be laying for me and I had to suppose that pimply boy would come shortly to his feeble senses and him and his date would set up together a fuss about how they'd been abused for exercising their God-given right to talk out loud at the movies and demonstrate, if they so desired, how they were between them as dumb as carps. So I charged up the aisle and into the lobby and out to my Chevette in the lot which had sat long enough to turn over directly and carried me past the Magic Wand and onto the truck route proper.

The chief never seemed to cool off entirely and I couldn't get him interested in my side of the thing. I attempted to persuade the chief to think of all the people I'd resisted the temptation to lay my muzzle to, explained how I'd failed so far to take aim at my neighbor who'd certainly abused me with his musical selections. I'd not plied yet with my pistol that girl out at the Hardees who crammed into my takeout sack whatever food proved handy regardless of what I'd ordered and paid to carry off. Beyond a couple of searing epithets, I'd spared that

90

boy who drove the truck that emptied out the dumpster even though he came at two in the morning and dropped the bin onto the lot so that we might all of us sit upright and savor the concussion. And I hadn't even been so much as short with that girl at the food store who could drag a package of chicken parts across her barcode scanner until the friction alone might fricassee them. I liked to think I was blessed with uncommon forbearance and campaigned to make the chief see what a patient sort I was.

Maybe he just got too awful much of that pimply boy and his people, heard more from that shrill, indignant girl than he truly cared to hear. Maybe it was just that Dewey started to come along with his nightstick and did not appear to long and pine for those afternoons at the trestle with an ankle in each hand. It could be the chief just took at last a proper measure of me, saw that he'd miscalculated, learned he'd had me wrong. All I know is I didn't find much favor after that. Me and Lonnie led by turns processions to the graveyard, marked tires with the chalk stick, and pulled the midnight shift.

🌾

Her bedsheets didn't match. The flat one had a yellow stripe. The fitted one was blue. The printed pillowcases were all blossoms and bamboo. I just figured it for her room, guessed her sort would not much care to sprawl so but at home. There was a tumbler on the nightstand, a brassiere on the bureau, a mirror hanging on the wall with photographs fixed to it—a white-haired man in a seersucker coat, a woman in a speckled blouse, a pair of young boys posed together, just teeth and cowlicks mostly. The topsheet was crumpled and flung back. That girl had a scar on her knee, a mole next to her navel, freckles on her breastbone, a chain around her neck with some bauble hanging from it. The flash had made her eyes go red and she was grinning slightly, had a look upon her lips of awfully mild amusement, with a trace to it of boredom, a suggestion of disdain.

I guessed that Wendle had trimmed it, had sheered away the top so that the thing might fit behind the money, back of the sateen flap. The border at the bottom had smudges all across it where I figured Wendle had held the thing about the way I did. I supposed he'd been the one to take it, had asked her would she smile. I just couldn't help but wonder where he'd found her in the first place, marveled that he'd had the means to charm and to beguile her. I hoped she'd been intoxicated or deranged beyond all reason. Compromised or even deeply beholden would suit me well enough. I just didn't want to think she'd been enchanted from her clothes, not by the likes of Wendle with his habits and his ways.

As I sat at home in my Naugahyde chair perusing her features and listening to the news, I was put in mind of a photograph my uncle used to have, the one Aunt Connie had married between the judge and the carpet king, the wiry one that golfed, not in a gainful sort of way but as a hobby and a calling which he saw fit to pursue with a pure and truly unspoiled strain of idiotic fervor. His name was Dean and I recall the first time that I met him he was down on Connie's living room floor reading the lay of the worsted pile. Dean was some stripe of policy man, traveled around in a Riviera suggesting coverage and collecting premiums and addressing rocks and bits of clod with his shoulders square and his knees bent slightly and his arms extended but relaxed. Though Connie was hardly the sporting sort, she'd sometimes of an evening put on her shorts and pour a rum and sit out by the wellhead to watch her Dean chip balls.

Unfortunately Dean possessed himself no talent much for golf, made lovely swings at rocks and clods, practice strokes out on the links of rare, surpassing grace, but over an actual ball in a round he grew somehow transformed. Dean suffered from impact anxiety. It undid his rhythm entirely. It compromised his form, induced him to stiffen and lunge and produced thereby too awful much variety in fact. He could hook and could slice and could skull and could sky and, if his nerves were with him, he could shank his drives and leave them almost back of where he started. Dean was just a regular golfing blunderbuss and his talent for the game proved largely editorial. Dean could distill from any round a couple of moments to savor, shots he'd struck nearly square, putts he'd almost made, and he'd narrate his adventures in true epic golfing fashion which seemed to keep and hold him until he paid his fee again and stepped up on the tee to lacerate his optimism.

Naturally Dean had cause to figure that life on this earth must truly be grand for those sorts who hit the ball first and always the ground later, those fellows on the tour who could draw and who could fade, could lag a putt, leave a trap, hit a fairway wood. Dean bought the brands of clothes they wore, used the balls they played, and he'd been once to Augusta with a buddy for the Masters. They'd followed slamming Sammy Snead all about the course on account of Dean's pure reverence for slamming Sammy's stroke. It was sweet and simple, long on fluid grace with no fuss at all about it as best as Dean could tell. Slamming Sammy just stepped up and purely spanked the ball.

Dean had had his buddy to take a photograph, a picture of Dean and Sam Snead outside the scoring tent. Sam had on his straw hat, a drinkcup in his hand. Dean had his arm about him as if maybe they were chums. Sam was peering at the camera with a wan and feeble grin while Dean was turned in profile gazing at Sam's head with a look upon his face of undiluted adoration. He'd had the thing enlarged and framed and Connie let him hang it in the den above the settee on the wall with her attachments. Dean and Sammy ended up between my cousin Grady and Connie's second husband's mother back before her stroke.

He always showed it to us, took me and took my brother in before the settee and pointed out the thing. "You know who that is?" he'd inquire.

We'd say it was Sam Snead.

"And who's that with him?" Dean would ask.

"That's you, Dean."

"Yeah. That's me."

We weren't of course but boys with no special claim between us to sensitivity and refinement, just your ordinary manner of dull and heedless creatures, and yet even we suspected our new Uncle was pathetic. We listened to him tell us about slamming Sammy's swing, slamming Sammy's native gift for perfect syncopation. We heard the yarns he spun about the laughs they'd shared together. We saw the look he lavished on the side of Sammy's head. And when the time came for it, that way it always came, we'd square our shoulders, flex our knees, and leave our arms to hang. We'd simply watch our Uncle Dean and stand the way he stood.

The Polaroid just seemed to me to have that flavor to it. That girl looked to be indulging in a favor for a fan, enduring inconvenience for the sake of an admirer, a boy behind the lens who she'd lately tolerated. I laid her on my chairarm, perused her planes and contours while my mongrel sat and watched me from beside the TV table and cast her customary pungent pall upon the evening, vaporized the repast she'd lately hunted up. I couldn't say what use I'd probably best make of that picture. I mean I figured I should give it over to the chief, but I feared he'd maybe be a little free and easy with it and the thing would circulate and the news would get around here now that only Wendle was the one to be past harm. I tried to weigh my options but had dog wind for distraction and the racket from the TV where the Roanoke public station was bleeding through to interrupt "P.M. Magazine." There'd be a scrap of talk about a waterslide in Tampa and a little piece of film of people sluicing down a flume, and then a fellow would break in speaking of the Berber nation. He had the manner of a waiter and eyebrows like marsh grass.

So I couldn't truly concentrate that way I'd hoped I might, though I made attempts to calculate the course that I should take clean past "P.M. Magazine" and partway through the show about the beautiful accountant who righted wrongs at night. She worked ledgers in the daylight but come the evening time she put on a body stocking and black boots up past her knees and went out to fight injustice and pummel lawless sorts. I couldn't help but watch her, peered through the bleed and static. She was one of those rare creatures with a body stocking body, more compelling on occasion than the girl atop her sheet. Her legs went on forever. Her hair maintained its wave. She could kung fu with her bootheels all the ne'er-do-wells about, almost make a fellow wish he was a thug in gotham. I settled in and watched her and didn't even care that she couldn't make it seem she'd held a pencil in her life.

❧

We wore our dress blue uniforms with the tailored jackets and, down along the pantlegs, the handsome sateen stripes. We wore our shirts with the epaulettes, our collar studs, our moleskin gloves as well as the sorts of peaked hats a singing petty despot might favor. We'd been charged to carry the coffin, me and the chief and Dewey and Clifford and Harnett as well who was done all up in state police gray with a Sam Browne belt and a campaign hat and a bright ceremonial revolver. We sat up front across the aisle from Dale's sister and her people along with Wendle's mother who they'd carried from the home. We sang, we prayed, we listened to the Reverend Tarpley soothe us, and then me and the chief and Clifford and Lonnie and Dewey and Harnett as well got directed to roll Wendle on his carriage so far as the doorsill where we became obliged at last to in fact take him up.

Wendle was purely a load which was largely, no doubt, on account of his coffinry, his sizable gaudy encasement that had been selected on his behalf by his wife and by her mother who'd settled together on an item of fairly arresting extravagance. It was thick enough from bottom to top to hold a couple of fellows and broader again by half than the bulk of corpses probably have call for a coffin to be. The thing struck me as unduly showy, busy most especially about the lid with brightwork and relief, nearly everything short of a brass knocker, and the rails along the sides were so girthsome themselves and so fulsomely decorated that they were next to impossible to grip and hold to with much success.

Except for Dewey, who possessed still the sculpted physique of a hoodlum dangler, we were not as an assemblage much accustomed to strenuous lifting, could climb well enough from our cars and raise ourselves with skill and success from our chairseats without much strain, but we hadn't the most of us made lately any appreciable use of our toting muscles, and I can only suppose that the pallbearers otherwise had simply like me assumed that surely even sleep everlasting had been renovated and transformed by some vagrant species of space-aged technology. I just guessed that there was likely a casket polymer about, some sort of extruded substance suitable for purposes of eternal repose, something lightweight and durable and maybe as tough as a milkjug. I wasn't, consequently, prepared at all for my share of the burden which proved more extensive truly and more profound than I'd anticipated, than any of us plainly had figured on and we groaned harmoniously together but for Clifford who was, there at the first, making merely himself a show of pall bearing, had caught the eye of a young thing in the back pew and was preening still and posing for her benefit as we hoisted Wendle off the cart.

We lurched and staggered out across the doorsill and fairly much careened down the steps and along the walk, as good as flung Wendle into the back of a wagon where he skidded across the fuzzy carpet and collided with the partition which served to give rise to an undiluted strain of chagrin on the part of Gooch at the wagon door, Gooch who could hardly condone with grace the flinging of the dear departed as even an abstract and a theoretical proposition on account of his personal feel for bearing and his definite ideas on decorum. When he was put upon to watch us toss an actual client into the back of the wagon, Gooch quite naturally found cause to quake and almost ejected his hair which was likely itself space-aged and probably extruded.

There's little I recall plain about Wendle's burial service when I think back now upon it. I don't have much clear idea of what the reverend told us, and I can't truly say whether or not we prayed or sang or endured scripture. I remember that Mr. Darnell from the VFW had a word or two to share with us at the graveside, read from a scrap of paper, but I don't have much idea anymore of what was on his mind, and while I have some recollection of a fuss there in the cemetery, seem to recall that some stripe of relation fell out in a faint, I can't for the life of me conjure who it was or say anymore why in the first place it came about—if it was from grief or from sun or maybe low blood sugar. I do remember hauling Wendle to the canopy, do even remember riding at the head of the procession interrupting traffic and insuring safety and venting regular invocations that Wendle had bought maybe one of those plots just along the roadway.

He turned out, however, to be insulated from the thoroughfare by a regular conglomeration of his mother's people who were laid out willy-nilly roundabout an elaborate pillar of granite. They made the pack of them for some treacherous footing, and I can cast back easily enough to the anguish and sundry hardships of the expedition we were obliged to undertake between Gooch's blue hearse and the open grave where we struggled ever so gamely under the ponderous weight of Wendle and his grand ducal casket, rested the thing even briefly on a ledge of the granite pillar so as to renew our grips and thereby inspired Gooch to a glorious show of abject consternation as he was hardly the sort of mortuarian to tolerate with grace from his pallbearers unanticipated, unadvertised, and wholly unscheduled stops. Ours was intended to be, quite plainly, an express excursion.

I'm mindful still of the veritable jubilation with which we greeted our arrival at the graveside, remember how Clifford fairly yipped once we'd settled at last Wendle upon the webbed slings. I don't, like I said, recall what went on during the graveside service. The reverend, I know, harangued for a time further and Mr. Darnell read from his scrap of paper and maybe we sang and likely we prayed and probably we endured scripture in advance of the salute the chief's wife had incited, had wondered anyhow of her husband the chief if wouldn't it be a fine thing to fire on Wendle's behalf a shot or two which the chief had slipped up and made mention of to his nephew Clifford who'd organized a squad. As we didn't have at the stationhouse much use for rifles, Clifford had determined we'd make do with our riot guns instead and the six of us, including Harnett, would fire each three rounds and then the chief and Clifford and Dewey would let off the fourth so as to make for a proper twenty-one-gun sendoff.

I had, I'll confess, my misgivings. I couldn't say, if it was me who'd come to be bereaved and forlorn, who'd suffered a loved one to be shot twice dead through the face, if I'd be much disposed for gunplay at the service, even honorable gunplay with pomp and ceremony. Moreover I couldn't truly imagine that the bulk of the assorted mourners were too terribly anxious to be this day favored with six simultaneous rounds three times over of twelve-gauge fire. As it turned out, however, my reservations were partly unwarranted and misplaced since we the six of us proved utterly incapable of shooting all our guns at once. We'd rehearsed in the lot out back of the stationhouse, had been drilled by the chief and Clifford together in gun-raising technique and had worked up in fact a stylish bit of business, a means of shifting and whipping about our gunstocks so as to raise our weapons and bring them to bear with some snap and some polish, but we'd not bothered to squeeze off any actual rounds, had assumed we were capable of serviceably harmonious triggerwork, were unaccountably contented that we would upon the signal fire all our guns at one time precisely, and there at the first we even almost did.

Lonnie lagged a little but the rest of us let loose fairly much all together and were instantaneously deafened by the concussion which impaired of course our ability to hear from the chief the signal and caused us with the second round to become after a fashion incohesive outright. The third round was less harmonious still and the fourth consisted of three shots fired consecutively which proved a suitable culmination to our ragged and sorry display, brought anyhow our part in it to a close although, across the way on the far side of the memorial garden where a fellow and his wife had come to pay respects to their dead relations, the shot began to rain down from the sky, began to fall about upon them upon the grass and upon the markers and upon the tops of their heads which induced some dodging and darting about on the part of that fellow and on the part of his wife who hunkered and crouched and endured the shotfall as best they could in advance of offering a scalding and unwholesome stripe of reply aired with vigor and volume both by that fellow across the way, a colorful bit of profanation that we most of us managed to regain our hearing in time to make out and savor.

I can't anymore conjure much else of the whole affair, recall that Gooch was fairly undone, that the casket was ever so heavy, that Wendle's mother didn't know exactly where she was, and that the gunfire stirred some local dogs that barked and yelped in wonderment, I suppose, that somebody'd found cause to shoot up the graveyard.

They most all of them wanted to learn our views and hear our suspicions. Once we'd arrived at Wendle's house off at the edge of the cabbage field so as to eat and to chat and to try if we might to put from our minds what we'd just been about, nobody wanted anything of us but to know what we figured and sample what we thought which provided most especially Clifford occasion to hold forth and speculate. Since I hadn't myself found out much or figured anything I was inclined to air, I didn't prove a draw for the mourners and was left free to wander about and stand apart and watch what people were up to and listen to what people were telling each other which was primarily some variant of the reverend's lament about how it seemed lately this world had gotten full anymore of trash, rife with meanness, lawless and cruel. The chief, of course, had a face and a patter for this particular sort of affair and passed about the room disarming the mourners with his wounded expression and his low dire strain of talk.

I fell in over by the table at the molded salad with a man who'd lost his Lawnboy and his buddy who'd had his tractor battery stolen twice. They were still the both of them keenly irritated most especially the one with the Lawnboy who, longer even than he could remember, had been in the habit of keeping his mowers off alongside his cellar steps under his upended wheelbarrow. He'd never known anybody to mess with one of them until just this past spring when he'd gone out one morning to cut the grass and discovered under the wheelbarrow not a thing in this world to cut it with. He wished he could find the fellow who'd made off with his mower, was anxious still with his bare hands to thrash and pulverize him. He was assured straightoff of the assistance of his buddy with the tractor who'd been rendered by larceny of a mood to whip some butt as well.

"Take the sons-of-bitches apart," the fellow with the tractor declared and earned for it a rousing salute from that man who'd lost his Lawnboy.

Soon enough I was ready to leave that place myself, was wanting to pay my regards to the widow and slip out the kitchen door to the yard, but Dale's sister didn't appear to be about. I looked for her in the front room, sought her around the dining table and had stepped a little ways down the hall before I decided it would be indelicate of me to proceed any further. I was turning back and meaning to retreat among the mourners when I took notice of the pictures on the wall, the portraits and the snapshots all matted and framed and hung plainly with care and art along the length of the hallway. There were pictures of Wendle and Dale's sister apart, pictures of Wendle and Dale's sister together, pictures of their girl as a naked baby, as an infant crawling across the rug, as a child upright in a lacy little jumper and shiny black shoes. There was a snapshot of Wendle standing in the yard in his hunting pants and his hunting jacket, a photo of his wife in her red prom gown with her hair down her back and her eyelids painted, a picture of their daughter flopped on her stomach in her plastic wading pool. And there in the midst of the whole assortment was a proper portrait of some size and effect, a fairly formal grouping of the three of them together.

They had back of them a skyblue screen and they'd been plainly posed and situated. Wendle anyhow and Dale's sister were sitting like people hardly ever sit, half turned about and shifted around with their heads lifted and cocked. They were holding the both of them to their child between them who'd plainly proved reluctant to get situated herself and had had to be persuaded not to squirm and jerk about, and they were all of them grinning, looked to be genuinely happy and pleased. This surely wasn't the Wendle I'd known, him of the vile opinions and the unsavory dispositions who'd not been often prone to such a sweet, kindly smile, wasn't remotely my Wendle who'd found,

I had to guess, a way to leave it in the cruiser or at the stationhouse.

I was put in mind of a call we'd taken the both of us together. He'd come down off the truck route and I'd come up from the river and we'd met shy of the hospital where a couple of boys on a tear had been busting open leafbags and knocking over mailboxes. And it wasn't even like we had to chase and catch them, wasn't even like we had to hunt them down since a few of the residents had banded together and apprehended the pair of them, had shut them up in a toolshed to keep until we came. So we just recorded a few statements, made a brief tour of the destruction and took officially charge of those boys who were only a couple of kids with more bald spunk than sense. They didn't want to look to be fretting, didn't want to seem the least cowed and contrite, and put on surely more bluster than was seemly as we ushered them to Wendle's cruiser and shut them up inside.

I followed Wendle down towards town and I don't believe we'd gone too awfully far when Wendle pulled his vehicle off the roadway at a stand of trees, eased onto the shoulder, and before I could even stop behind him he was out and upright and around to the back where he hauled one of those boys off the seat and into the weedy ditch and set straightaway to tossing him about, flung him down onto the ground and kicked him and stomped at him while he informed him whatever it was Wendle saw fit for that boy to know. It was a remarkable sight and I was a little too astounded to do much at the first but watch Wendle thrash and beat that boy though I did at last manage to speak, came out from my car and around to the ditch where all I could say was, "Wendle!" at first and then "Wendle!" again and only in time and only at length did he leave off with him and turn about so as to tell to me, "What?"

I'll never forget the tone of it, how even and steady it was, flat and altogether unruffled, baldly conversational like Wendle hadn't maybe been lately himself up to a thing to speak of. I'd thought he'd be gone with the juices, figured there'd be a trace at least of bile and ire about him, but he was utterly calm and placid and delivered one last blow before indulging me with the news of how this one had seemed unruly. I couldn't work up anything in the way of a reply and just stood there watching Wendle who passed behind his cruiser and favored me with that look of his, the one with the eyebrows elevated and the teeth exposed, the one meant to take me in and make me party to whatever it was he'd been about.

I hardly knew this Wendle all posed and situated with his head lifted and cocked, the one with the regular grin and the air of contentment, and I was studying him still when Dale's sister came up on me, stepped out of the back room and into the hall and joined me before that portrait, gripped me at the arm and held to me. She was puffy and congested and clutched in her free hand a little knot of Kleenex that she'd worried near to tatters. She tried to share some manner of thing Wendle had done for her once, an item she clearly cherished but was in no state to tell. So we just stood together there viewing Wendle on the wall, and I managed to speak admiringly of his jacket and his tie while Dale's sister raised her tissue and dabbed it at her nose.

4.

I guessed I could anticipate how it might play out. The chief would call in from Roanoke the correspondent with the square teeth and the blue eyes and the Wagoneer and she'd in fact drive down and speak to him once he'd shared with her the news of how he had anymore not just an officer shot through the face but evidence as well of lasciviousness outright which is just the sort of thing to dress up carnage, give it a little zip and heighten its attraction since that correspondent from Roanoke could go on the television and suggest how ours was maybe a case of lethal wanton desire. She could show to her viewers the streambed, what of the Polaroid decency might allow, favor them with a theory from the chief and maybe a quarter minute's worth of one of his stirring expressions that would make in the end for precisely the sort of package to beat plain carnage all to pieces. And it didn't even matter who that naked brunette might turn out to be since the news on television can render in an instant anything true, so it would evermore in people's minds be Wendle and be her, would ever after be them both together.

Naturally Mrs. Tyree and Mr. Chapman would run the thing in

the *Ledger.* They might crop it or blot out the offending portions and render it thereby presentable, but they'd surely run it above the fold and make undoubtedly the strain of stink they were the pair of them partial to since they had together no use for lust, no patience to speak of for hussies and harlots, and they took plainly as dim a view of lurid uncloaked poses as they usually were known to reserve for Godless communism. They'd been previously provided occasion to make their opinions plain. A girl from out towards Fries had appeared in *Playboy* magazine in pretty much the altogether. She'd been wearing a blouse but had neglected to button it and was holding her shirthem up around her navel which had served to confirm that she had in fact left her underclothes at home.

It wasn't any sizable picture but was part of a portfolio of coeds, a half-dozen pages of glands and organs and supple flesh along with assorted scraps of text and unparenthetical and wholly unironic italicized captions designed to convey the news that the delectable naked creature atop the fencerail with the fetching white sneaker and hair ribbon ensemble harbored an abiding enthusiasm for harmony among nations and skydiving while the young thing in the bathtub with her legs lifted and splayed was altogether keen herself on modern dance and steeplechasing. Mr. Chapman, who penned the article in the *Ledger,* suggested the strain this manner of undertaking put upon our national moral fiber and his sister Mrs. Tyree brought her considerable descriptive powers to bear upon that coed from Fries in particular (radiology and spongecake) who she let on should have remained cloaked for reasons beyond decency alone, insinuated that her blotted parts and her obscured pieces were hardly so firm and well-developed as to merit national exposure.

I suspected, then, I knew what they might have to say on the topic of Wendle's sort of woman with her red eyes and her languid posture and her uncoordinated bedlinens, the type who looked even to me like she could take up a bolt of moral fiber and gnash it to ribbons and shreds. I guessed it would be an ugly business, figured it would be an unsavory display most especially for the likes of Dale's sister who subscribed to the paper and watched the TV and lived among a population that was treated already to enough ugly business and favored with adequate unsavory displays to divert and occupy them. I just couldn't imagine they had much call for this bit of scandal as well if scandal even was what in fact it played out to be. So I determined to make inquiries on the sly, poke about discreetly and discover as best I might the identity of this creature in the Polaroid, this woman atop the flatsheet with the comely features and the thin, indulgent smile, but I was persuaded I'd need at least a little help and landed at length upon a fellow I guessed might suit, the only one about I supposed I could confide in and trust.

It would have been better there at the first if he hadn't yelped so, if he'd resisted somehow the temptation to whoop and wheeze which served straightoff to jar and unnerve me on account of how Ellis had sworn an oath he'd keep himself from shrieking. But plainly he'd passed so awful many evenings lately alone with his sister that he'd near about forgotten what women could look like. She reminded him a little of his duchess, the one he'd enjoyed in the locomotive lavatory, and he recounted for me how they'd come to be tangled and how they'd come to be situated and spoke of the blessed syncopation of the steel wheels on the seamed track that had concealed their impassioned cries and ecstatic discharges from the duke himself who was dozing hard by in the smoking car. This one didn't appear to him near so delicate as the duchess had been, but then Ellis guessed he had no call to acquaint me with how your basic aristocrat is as much as bred for dainty features, hails usually from a long line of high cheekbones and proper noses.

I harbored some regret at having lifted my sateen flap and produced the thing for Ellis to gaze upon, and Ellis seemed to sense my distress and plumb my disappointment and consequently whistled through his toothgaps with more seemly discretion than he'd shown just previously talent for. Even full well intoxicated, Ellis detected plain enough my mood and my misgivings and managed to mute his respiration and resist the temptation to ejaculate further while he attempted instead to focus his vision and pay for a time some unannotated regard to that girl with the lank hair and the red eyes and the exposed glands and organs. He couldn't be sure he knew her, couldn't be sure he didn't know her either, couldn't in truth see her well enough to decide, had remembered too awful well his rye and forgotten altogether his spectacles which served in combination to render him effectively blind which Ellis suspected we could remedy and Ellis proposed that we could cure if I'd just ride him around for a time with the windows down and stop off maybe at the mini-mart so as to buy him a cup of that rancid concoction they like to let on is coffee.

I'll confess I was doubtful myself that a breeze and some coffee might bring him around but then I'd managed to put from my mind the assorted properties of the mini-mart brew, the fact that it was boiled outright and proved evermore to be dependably caustic, could in an instant replace the heedless merriment of intoxication with such thoroughgoing and wholesale discomfort that a fellow was soon enough likely to forget that he'd ever even been drunk in the first place. It was the acids, I guess, that did the trick, the ones that assaulted the stomach lining and set about decomposing the intestinal tract. I was reminded shortly of them by the color Ellis took on in the midst of his first cup, by the involuntary gurgling of his insides which Ellis withstood and which Ellis endured ever so stoutly, proved bold and bluff in the face of the creeping corrosion, concealed completely from me his pangs and his anguishments which surely went a ways towards confirming the wisdom of seeking Ellis's help.

Naturally Ellis was put upon directly to retire for a time, helped himself to the key to the lavatory, the one with the tire gauge fob, and fairly trotted on out the door and around the corner, but he came back pretty shortly a new man, was purged and was improved and was altogether willing to own up to and proclaim it, appeared playful even now that the torment had passed, sufficiently fit and able to toy with the girl at the register who he undertook to impress and woo with a brawny fabrication, some tale about a boy he'd thrashed and a damsel he'd serviced and satisfied which Ellis let on to be in the way of a regular enterprise for him, fairly sprawled upon the countertop there alongside the jerky jar and assured that girl at the register how he was evermore thrashing one sort and servicing and satisfying the other, was blessed with a talent for each and both.

We made together a couple of circuits roundabout the far pump island, took in the heady petroleum fumes that appeared to finish for Ellis the job the coffee had started and soon enough he was near about coherent, was no longer anyhow less coherent than most people otherwise seem usually to be, and Ellis pulled up short alongside the high test and declared how he was set at last to be a help to me, guessed the unevacuated rye and figured the unevacuated coffee had blended by now and married into a tolerable sort of a stew. So we retired off alongside the cruiser and I produced again for Ellis the Polaroid which, lacking his spectacles, he still could not make out unaided and alone, though once I'd held the thing before him and backed with it partway across the lot he could see it, he guessed, clear enough since it wasn't so much that his eyes were bad but more that his arms were too awful short.

I didn't truly figure he'd know her, hoped maybe he might have seen her somewhere but didn't expect he'd be likely acquainted with her himself since Ellis was anymore pretty long in the tooth and hadn't, I suspected, thrashed lately in fact any boys or serviced and satisfied any damsels to speak of though plainly he was acquainted with that ilk out at the bottling plant who knew probably women themselves, were given maybe even to running on occasion with the manner of creatures that would sprawl and pose in the altogether which they might have shared with Ellis the news of so as to bait and provoke him, compensate Ellis for all that near ceaseless talk of the ecstasy he'd in his day inflicted.

So I held her up at around five paces for Ellis to see, hoped he'd maybe just know somebody who knew her, but Ellis of course couldn't straightoff allow he'd not had her himself, seemed to recall an evening of passion he'd passed not so very long back with a raven-haired temptress though the details anymore were murky and vague and kept him from saying for certain if this was perhaps his temptress in fact.

He confessed to me how sometimes when his humors were raging and his musky fluids were boiling and coursing about, when some damsel with her attractions and charms had produced an effect upon him, he paid usually ever so close regard to assorted of her particulars, attended to certain features and allurements each in their turn and so made himself acquainted with the parts and made himself familiar with the pieces but came often away with no solid and useful impression of the entire creature seeing as how his stripe of Lothario, out like he was to service and satisfy, had call to be strictly heedful of an ever so limited range of items. Ellis simply thought he recognized the slope of the neck, believed the lay of the torso familiar to him, was persuaded he'd been in intimate proximity to that birthmark on the left thigh which I found to be merely a fleck of grunge the Polaroid had picked up in my wallet and, in wiping the thing away, fairly undid for Ellis the notion that he'd seen this girl before since she looked to him, grungeless, like a different sort of a temptress altogether.

Ellis thought maybe that boy he rode with might be acquainted with her, the one that picked him up mornings and dropped him off nights out by the Magic Wand. He wasn't, Ellis informed me, afflicted with too awful much savoir-faire, had failed over time to come to be burdened with manners and beset by charms but had nonetheless a way with the women, held somehow a mysterious sway which Ellis admitted he could not truly begin to fathom and grasp.

"They surely mine something," Ellis told to me but he guessed he had no means of saying just precisely what they mined since he was hardly the sort himself to be tempted to passion and spurred to romance by thoroughgoing unrefinement. "That boy's as rough as a cob," Ellis said, "but there's girls about who plain can't seem to hope to live without him."

Naturally Ellis was curious to know what maybe she'd been about, laid up over the seatback once we'd gotten underway and shared with me the news that she appeared to him devious and shrewd, confessed how she'd seemed just naked there at the first, admitted he'd

chiefly felt straightoff the lure and the potent pull of her, but he
guessed anymore he could make out plain how awful conniving she
looked, was hoping I'd see fit to up and tell what she'd done, wanted
to know whose life she'd ruined, wanted to hear whose marriage she'd
spoiled, guessed he could tell by looking at her that she'd soured some
harmony somewhere. Of course I couldn't say for sure if she'd been
about anything at all and was hardly inclined to share with Ellis where
I'd come across her, so I made out to be fairly saddled with ignorance
as far as this naked creature was concerned and supposed, as long as we
were casting about, we might as well hunt up Ellis's buddy with the
coarse appeal and the mystical allure who Ellis figured we'd likely find
out at the lounge at the motor lodge where often enough he was
inclined to pass his leisure hours, exude his manner of charm off
beyond the bar at the ninja machine where he tended usually to
bivouac with his Budweiser and his quarters and his all too hardy
fervor for video kung fu.

But for that lounge and the gaming machines and the Friday and
Saturday night shrimp buffet, the whole motel complex would long
since have been boarded up and shut down as there never seemed to be
any actual lodgers to speak of, nobody around to let a room except for
those occasions when snowsqualls kicked up or car engines failed or
Donna Spivey or Sherry Lee had been somehow prevailed upon, plied
and persuaded with sufficient wine cooler to give over for an evening
their assorted proscriptions and retire upstairs to dally and cavort, pass
in the veritable altogether upon a proper and seemly bed an entire
night of relative abandon in the company of some fellow with a semi-
deathless ardor and nineteen dollars for the room.

Largely, however, the accommodations went pretty much unemployed, and even with the lounge and even with the buffet the place
was generally a picture of desolation. I couldn't myself ever step full
into the motor lodge lounge proper without enduring one degree or
another of creeping despair. The sight of the patrons, the smell of the
smoke and the stale beer, the flat, toneless clamor of the video games,
and the full-fledged assault of the general decor were usually enough

together to blacken my disposition, and I don't even claim to entertain much hope still for this world. I routinely wavered at the double lounge doors prior to stepping at length inside where I knew the stink and the clatter would greet me, the swiveling heads, the hard spiteful laughter, the purest distillation of decay.

For his part Ellis had proved truly eager to strike out for the lounge, had never previously performed there an investigation and staged an inquiry but had only ever, back in his beer-swilling days, mounted a bender or two and trolled in his regular fashion for agreeable damsels, the manner of wenches that could see clear enough when a fellow had wit and a fellow had style, rare creatures, Ellis informed me, plain scarce at the lounge at the motor lodge which tended to attract those girls who put so awful little stock in wit and style that Ellis's stripe of *bon vivant* could barely begin to hope at all to dazzle them with his social grace and melt them with his banter. Apparently Ellis had experienced as well some trouble with the prevailing house beverage, found at the lounge too awful much employment for his bladder and his tracts.

"Fairly beat a path to the toilet," Ellis told me and eyed me beyond it in such a way as to let on and reveal how that sort of steady traveling was often enough to undo whatever the wit and the style and the grace and the banter had accomplished. Ellis was simply persuaded that a man could either urinate or woo and could hardly afford to blend the callings and harmonize the avocations.

Consequently Ellis had given over his evenings at the motor lodge lounge, but saw fit to relive en route assorted of the highlights for me, was especially attached to his memories of the elegant piano player, the woman the owner had hired some years back in an effort to inject at least a little class and a trifle of polish into the local nightlife. The hope was to draw in sophisticates, supplant maybe the usual rabble at the bar with a seemlier set of people. They even set out free nuts and served a few wines that were near about dry. Of course didn't any of it take since those among us with the means and the inclination preferred to be sophisticated up in Roanoke or down in Mt. Airy and weren't much tempted to pass an evening sipping chablis and throwing back cashews out at the motor lodge lounge even given the incentive of an actual piano player, a slinky, winsome, horsefaced creature from up about Poplar Camp who accompanied the Methodists Wednesday nights and Sundays and played the upright at the motor lodge lounge two shows Friday and Saturday each.

I heard her a couple of times myself. She was largely a tinkler, adorned her melodies and filled in her pauses with regular cascades of fluttering trills. Her sense of rhythm had gotten, I guess, tainted at the sanctuary keyboard because most every selection she attempted ended up somehow in march time which could naturally render an evening at the lounge more stirring than likely people were hoping an evening at the lounge would be.

Ellis confessed it was the gown that got to him first. Ellis allowed how that night he met her he'd hardly anticipated he'd step in through the double doors and spy there at the upright off between the pay phone and the cigarette machine a woman in a green sequined floor-length dress with the back scooped out of it clean down to her kidneys and her flaxen hair coiled and piled upon her head. He admitted the sight had drawn him up short, declared he'd been arrested outright and had stood there pretty much still in the doorway admiring her tonality and perusing her lower back, savoring, he recollected, the haunting strains of "When Your Lover Has Gone" which proved a suitable vehicle for fluttering adornments and bouts of syncopation outright. Ellis was simply accustomed at the lounge to the ever so twangful music from the eight track back of the bar with the fiddles and the steel guitars and the plaintive, adenoidal vocals about loving hard women and drinking hard liquor and having your life turn out in the end more than a little flinty and tough. He just hadn't supposed he'd come at the lounge across a lady given to trills and wayward tinkles, partial to four/four time, a regular siren with her back laid bare, her dressend upon the floor.

They weren't doing this evening much business to speak of at the motor lodge lounge, didn't of course most evenings manage any grand sort of commerce, but there were only this night a couple of trucks in the lot along with a Buick sedan and Donna Spivey's red Toyota, Ellis, however, identified the half-ton beyond the lightpost as his buddy's vehicle and so guessed we'd find him after all camped out at the ninja machine. I had a manner of scheme in mind, was hopeful that I could depend upon Ellis to step by himself into the lounge and fetch out his buddy, share discreetly with him the news that I was wanting to see him out front which Ellis let on to find to be a splendid sort of a scheme, assured me he'd make a pure success of it and insisted we exchange smart salutes there in the lot alongside the cruiser which probably should have made plain to me that the mini-mart coffee and the cool night air had failed between them to undo the rye altogether. But I just guessed Ellis was wanting to feel properly deputized and so obliged him in a salute and then watched him fairly march off towards the double lounge doors with the tails of his clawhammer jacket twitching and flapping behind him.

I even waited expectantly for a time, figured for a considerable while that Ellis would just any moment step back through the double doors with that buddy of his in tow, though at length it dawned upon me that I'd dispatched Ellis not simply into the company of distilled and fortified enticements but into the immediate proximity of some fleshy ones as well in the person of Donna Spivey who, compared to that horsefaced piano player, would prove likely for Ellis a ravishing sight. So I guessed he might get put off from his duties, come in the lounge to be instead preoccupied with iniquity outright, but I didn't bother to conclude it straightoff and even for a while anticipated that Ellis would shortly show up and present to me his buddy until I caught at last a glimpse of him through one of the narrow lounge windows, spied Ellis flapping an arm in the air and cutting what appeared to be a caper.

I provided him occasion to recover if he might his sense of obligation, hoped anyhow he'd possibly recall what he was supposed to be about, but I kept seeing through the window parts and pieces of him in various states of regalement and was persuaded in time to give over hopes that Ellis would maybe find cause to act even a little deputized. I made, consequently, my own way across the lot and lingered by custom and disposition just shy of the double lounge doors prior to pushing through to the deep pile landing alongside the bar where I enjoyed the close study and perusal of the assembled patrons who lifted each of them their heads and swung about sufficiently to favor me with their undivided regard, including of course Ellis himself who did not appear to recall precisely what he was supposed to be about but recognized me nonetheless for a pal and a chum and summoned me on down along the bar, wondered if I might join please him and Earl and Donna who were sharing together what looked to be a bucket of sangria.

Earl appeared beside himself with stifled irritation. The strain of acting civil seemed just about more than he could hope to bear up under, and he shot regular, sidelong, lacerating glances in the direction of Ellis just down the bar, Ellis who'd apparently introduced himself into the midst of Earl's amours and had mucked up for the time being whatever designs and intentions Earl had been hoping to act upon with the acquiescence of Donna hard by him, Donna who'd abandoned her tumbler and was drinking, when she felt parched, her sangria straight out of the bucket with a cocktail straw.

Ellis had been put by the concoction in mind of a tigress he'd previously known, a woman who'd fallen prey to his charms, succumbed altogether to his potent appeal which Ellis managed to speak of at length in advance of proceeding to the purely exotic wiles and ways of that fiery damsel who Ellis had to figure had taught even him a thing about the passions of the blood. He provided as a courtesy an instance or two of lascivious educational information that Donna Spivey blew with her straw bubbles in the bucket about and let on to be too altogether taken with Ellis's sort of a tale to suit Earl beside her, Earl who tried to make out like he'd had once a tigress himself, but Earl could hardly hope to lie with the dash and prevaricate with the vigor that Ellis evermore managed to muster.

Donna was the sort to favor a fellow who had a little training

behind him, and she clearly demonstrated a growing fondness for Ellis
and his pedigree, sprayed playfully through her straw a dose of sangria
at him as a token of her affection and laid oh so coyly her fingerends
upon Ellis's satin lapel which I hated to punctuate and was loathe to
interrupt but felt nonetheless obliged to step down along the bar and
speak lowly in confidence to Ellis of what precisely he'd saluted in the
first place about.

Being himself of a gentlemanly persuasion, Ellis undertook directly proper introductions, presented Miss Donna Spivey who wiggled at me her fingers and Earl hard by her who was clearly inclined
to hope I'd come to make an arrest, seemed set to propose a candidate.

I wondered if Ellis might we the pair of us retire for a moment
and consult, let on that me and Ellis were due for a pressing exchange
and then laid my own fingers to a satin lapel and drew Ellis off towards
the window well where I was set to be stern with him, had begun even
to make a sharp inquiry pertaining to that buddy of his when Ellis
managed an interjection, informed me in a low, grave voice how just
presently his buddy was suffering from a complaint, had seen fit at the
buffet to provide his constitution with a helping of the breaded oysters
which had only lately commenced to exact from him their tribute.

"He's been on the crapper since I got here," Ellis informed me
and disclosed his annoyance at having not just to wait for his buddy to
finish his own evacuation but at being as well kept and prevented from
evacuating himself since he was, he reminded me, harboring a blend
of Old Overholt and mini-mart coffee which were proving to be uneasy
companions and prompted Ellis to disclose to me how he could do
directly with a sitdown as well.

We stepped together over to the video ninja machine so as to be
the both of us handy to welcome Ellis's buddy once his bowels had
seen fit to clench up, and he came to us soon enough, was detained
briefly at a booth by a couple of boys who wanted to hear from Ellis's
buddy if hadn't they tried to warn him off the breaded oysters, pre-
dicted precisely the cleansing effect a helping of oysters would have,
which Ellis's buddy made ever so ginger allowances about prior to

taking his leave and proceeding on a course towards the ninja machine where me and Ellis waited to greet him and did shortly greet him in fact though perhaps, on the part of Ellis, a little more robustly than that buddy with the bowels could gracefully endure.

Ellis's buddy appeared to believe that a round or two of video ninja warfare might settle and soothe him, and he produced from his coatpocket a fistful of quarters that he slapped down onto the laminated ledge alongside the lever which moved his own personal ninja warrior about. Me and Ellis even stood by and watched a dollar's worth of battle though I'll confess I never myself got much feel for the rules and the scoring. A little cartoon man in a robe and baggy pants went all about the screen with his right foot lifted and cocked, and Ellis's buddy steered him into thugs and clutches of terrorists and made him to kick and leap and incite, apparently, mayhem which in turn caused the clangers to clang and the beepers to beep and the score to swell extravagantly, but I could never figure exactly just how much mayhem was worth and got prevented from dwelling upon it by the twelve-bar ninja theme which that machine insisted on playing in the event of a kick or upon the occasion of a leap and as a ready companion to most any instance of wholesale carnage that Ellis's buddy, with his lever and his button, managed to effect. The entire business just seemed to me very nearly as consummate a waste of quarters as that full-color national news daily which I'd in the past been known to be tempted to buy from the box at the Kroger.

I can't say that boy looked to me too awfully much of a prize. Even once I'd attempted to compensate for the peculiar attractions women are prone to, tried, that is, to see in him what an actual girl might see, I could hardly mine in his aspect and discover in his general unrefinement the coarse appeal and mystical allure that Ellis had told me about. He was foul and dirty, had machine oil all over his shirt and what looked to me to be a self-inflicted haircut, and every time he moved and shifted about I got a pungent whiff of him, was made privy to a stink that was a blend of sweat and noxious breath together, not remotely the manner of musk that seemed to me likely to lure a mate or bring on even the rutting season. I didn't guess I'd want to be acquainted with the actual variety of female who could manage to discover Ellis's buddy's appeal, entered even into silent prayer that Wendle's naked brunette would turn out please to be a different sort of female herself, didn't figure I could likely stand there in the lounge and tolerate from Ellis's buddy a look of triumph and savory conquest as he held in his greasy fingers my piece of Polaroid.

Of course he just yelped and whooped and wheezed himself which I had to suppose was a considerable part of his charm for Ellis since plainly in the face of exposed glands and uncloaked fleshy lobes they shared the pair of them a tendency for hyperactive exclamation notwithstanding the oaths of restraint they might have just taken and sworn. But it was pretty clear as well that he didn't know her, was not anyhow intimately acquainted with the assembled allurements south of her gullet which bedeviled and enchanted him so there at the first that he could not manage to bring himself to digest her northerly features, failed to be persuaded to shift his gaze and render himself helpful until him and Ellis had exchanged their fill of lascivious remarks and managed each their complement of wry, articulate expressions when Ellis's buddy allowed himself to fall sufficiently unemployed to have to figure he could maybe now look at the head itself.

He guessed even straightoff he'd seen her around, insisted he'd previously come across her though he needed, he believed, incentive to conjure up just where, and he showed to me his yellow teeth and made with his thumb and forefinger the universal gesture for lubrication which I attempted at the first to overlook and ignore, mustered even a feeble and anaemic appeal to Ellis's buddy's sense of justice and civic obligation but gave it over directly once Ellis's buddy revealed to me how he was only harboring hopes of two dollars worth of quarters and maybe a fresh longneck from the cooler behind the bar. I made out to be torn and let on to be balky but went ahead and relented soon enough, fetched from the bar the change and the beer and purchased with them the news of how Ellis's buddy had seen Wendle's brunette in the company of a fellow he knew.

"This very one?" I asked of him, and Ellis's buddy felt obliged to expend upon her a confirming gaze in advance of telling to me, "Oh yeah. It was her all right."

He named the boy, just called him Crouse, told me he was a sorry prick, didn't let on to have for him any use to speak of and couldn't even begin to imagine what a woman with measurable sense and appeal might manage to see in him. "It was her," he told me. "It was him. It was the both of them together."

"You know where he lives?" I asked of Ellis's buddy who jerked his nose towards the far wall and told me that boy had a house out past the parkway towards the gap.

"But he isn't at home," he assured me.

"Well where is he?"

"He's here," Ellis's buddy said and plugged his mouth with his bottleneck permitting me and permitting Ellis to gaze about the lounge without the benefit of illumination and commentary, eye Earl at the bar and the boys in the booth and a doughy man off at a table by the window with what looked to be his doughy wife.

"Which one?" I managed at length to inquire of Ellis's buddy who made himself unstoppered just long enough to inform me, "Not here. Over there," and he jerked his nose again as if it were a legitimately edifying enterprise and then wrapped once more his lips around his bottlespout in advance of advising me how that Crouse worked some evenings at the motel office across the lot on the chance that somebody one night might just happen in and stay over.

Ellis fairly exulted, wanted by the time we'd reached the double doors to know if wasn't he proving already of incalculable and untold worth as an investigational asset which I was pleased to pause in the doorway and assure him, to the lush accompanying strains of the twelve-bar ninja theme, he most decidedly was. As we stepped out into the lot proper, Ellis felt called to enumerate for me those assorted personal qualities that he suspected accounted most directly for his extraordinary usefulness, and he commenced with his profound powers of deduction which he found he could not make just brief mention of but felt compelled to hold forth about and so held consequently forth about them as we crossed the lot towards the motel office which was a little block building off to itself halfway between the motel proper and the road.

The window blinds were open and on the neon "Office" sign above the door only the consonants were lit. I could see the top of that Crouse's head, spied the fingers he raised to scratch it with, could make out the gray wavering light from the television he was watching and hear the all too frequent bursts of sharp manufactured hilarity intended to distinguish the zany TV fun from standard droll and sensible proceedings.

I held the door for Ellis, ushered him in ahead of me, figured the sight of him in his old brown fedora and his formal black clawhammer jacket might serve to concentrate that Crouse's attention. He was sitting behind a low counter and was largely hidden from me there at the first by a freestanding cardboard placard designed to advertise the local attractions—the golf club, the fish house, the grist mill on the parkway—but Ellis saw him plain enough himself and told straightoff to that Crouse, "Christ buddy," told straightoff to that Crouse, "Well Jesus."

He was a mess. Once I'd slipped past the placard I could see on my own that he'd been pummeled and he'd been thrashed. He had a butterfly suture high on his cheek where his skin had been laid open against the bone, a Band-Aid across his nose and a couple of legitimate stitches in his bottom lip which was puffy still and outsized. His one eye had blood in it, the one he could open. The other was blueblack and swollen full shut. I could see that his right hand was a trifle discolored and his knuckles were scraped like maybe he'd even given a little back. He wasn't any puny sort of a fellow, was tall and stout and had some bulk to him, didn't look much of a candidate for a beating which was plainly what struck and stayed with Ellis who proved anxious to hear just what manner of creature had visited upon that Crouse abuse, that Crouse who endured Ellis's inquiries and tolerated Ellis's ejaculations but did not appear inclined at all to speak to Ellis back.

I asked him was he Crouse and he told me he guessed he was prior to shifting about to take in the antics of a gentleman on the TV who'd shut himself out of his house in just his undershorts and was making a manner of jumper from a black plastic leafbag, was proving in fact to be the object of such appreciable canned amusement that I was put upon to ask of that Crouse if couldn't he please see fit to reach over to the set and turn down the guffawing. He obliged me at his leisure, presently grew persuaded to switch the thing off entirely prior to asking of me and asking of Ellis what maybe it was we wanted.

Plainly Ellis himself was still primed to hear who'd thrashed and pummeled that Crouse, and I saw on my own clear to wonder of him what maybe he'd lately been about and who maybe he'd lately been about it with, but that Crouse at length just told us both, "I fell down."

"Well you got a little help, didn't you bud?" Ellis said to him.

And directly that Crouse informed Ellis back, "I tripped."

Ellis entered into an elaborate show of his outright skepticism, pulled for my benefit a face which he exhibited after such a fashion as to allow that Crouse a glimpse, that Crouse who volunteered how he'd been going along one second all upright and regular and had caught the next second on a treeroot and pitched hard over to the ground.

Ellis plainly didn't much care for the tone of the explanation and he turned about to advise me how the time seemed to him ripe for one of those nightstick applications that Dewey my colleague was known to favor. He guessed the one that crushed testicles to a pulpy liquid would suit and encouraged me to go ahead and make what preparations that sort of levering might require. I chose instead to produce from my pocket that piece of Polaroid which I handed across the counter to that Crouse as I wondered of him if he were perhaps acquainted with the lady in the picture.

He didn't yelp himself, failed to whoop and wheeze but provided for me revelation enough in just the way he looked upon her with that one bloody eye, or the way anyhow he left off shortly at it so as to study instead the blotter before him and pick with his fingers at a corner of the thing while he made to me his declaration, swore unbidden an oath that he'd never himself met up with such a creature before, and then he asked me, "Where'd you get this?"

"Don't know her?" I said to him, and he told to the blotter corner, "No."

"Never seen her?" I said to him, and he took occasion to look at her again, lingered even over her a time prior to shaking at length his head and offering back my Polaroid which was when I saw the ring.

"Maybe your wife's run up on her," I proposed and watched him pause to consider what precisely to tell me back, watched him weigh his sundry denials, his assorted prospective responses, and at length he saw fit by way of reply to tell to me, "Maybe so."

"But you don't know her," I said to that Crouse. "Never seen her before."

"No," he insisted. "Not me."

And I guessed I could decipher well enough what it is exactly that makes us men such loathsome creatures on occasion since here we are afflicted with a talent for following our upright organs pretty square into the thorniest sorts of complications and the blackest manner of deceit and we can't ever even seem to be much bothered to lie about it to good effect. Probably it's the juices and the hormones that benumb us since I've known any number of fellows who could evermore work up the energy to marshal and manage altogether baroque fabrications when it came to a larceny or a simple assault but who grew invariably and utterly transparent when there proved to be some woman in the mix, some creature they were stealing to woo or robbing to keep, nobody usually they wanted for good, just a girl they guessed they could stand to have now.

So that Crouse offered me his denial, shook with some vigor his head, regarded me with his bloody eye, and made a success of giving himself away. I took down his home address. I took down his telephone number. I suggested how I was meaning soon to stop in and see him and the wife together maybe once his swelling had subsided and his vision had cleared and he was fit truly to make out a buck naked woman which I insinuated maybe he might best mull and might best stew about while Ellis, for his part, advised that Crouse to stay clear for a while of the woods where those troublesome treeroots tended to thrive and made often of themselves a nuisance and a danger.

Ellis wondered had I heard him. Out in the lot with the cruiser before us and that Crouse behind us Ellis confessed to me how he'd always had a flair for barbed remarks and so hoped I'd been paying just lately heed to him as he spoke since he'd as much as speared that Crouse clean through which in truth I did not need to have heard the first time at all since Ellis favored me with a stirring encore that was only scantly overhauled and a little improved. He guessed we'd between us pumped that Crouse pretty good, had demonstrated to him what a proper inquisition was in fact all about, and Ellis persevered at soundly congratulating the both of us together until we'd settled into the cruiser when Ellis laid across the seatback and wondered what precisely we in fact knew now that earlier in the evening we'd maybe not known.

I made for Ellis a show of consulting my notepad, perused those pages where I'd seen fit to set down an item or two, and presently I rendered for Ellis my professional determination, informed him how it appeared to me we knew exactly dick.

Ellis of course considered such news a rebuff and a blow since he was of the opinion that dick was pretty much what we'd started out knowing, had figured we'd gotten by means of that Crouse well past dick altogether which I resisted straightoff the temptation to dispute but instead as a courtesy consulted my notebook once further and made only in time to be persuaded to my unwavering satisfaction that clearly dick itself was all we were acquainted with. Of course I attempted to point out to Ellis that there was among officers of the peace an ancient and vaunted tradition of knowing pretty much just dick alone, of blundering fairly blindly along with little more than dick to guide us until miraculous fortune or sheer happenstance served to reveal a motive or lead to a perpetrator, but Ellis couldn't appear to draw much solace from the institutionalized ties between the professional constabulary and, truth be told, dick and squat both together. He'd just guessed we'd gotten somehow this evening smart already and was distressed to hear my own estimation that we'd likely stay stupid for a while yet.

"Oh," Ellis told to me, and laid back towards the window well from where, once he'd adjusted his hat and tugged a little forlornly at his satin lapels, he informed me one time further, "Oh."

Not this past spring but one before it Desmond my neighbor upstairs threw a do, put on what he gave out to be an unmitigated bash, what he advertised on his invitations would prove doubtless the liveliest affair of the coming social season, and maybe even it did. I attend myself so awful few bashes as to be no fit judge of the liveliness of them but can only attest to my recollection that Desmond's do was a regular corker. He'd strung crepe and hung balloon bouquets, had made on his own assorted finger sandwiches and curried sausage balls, had melted the shredded cheddar cheese onto the whole-grain crackers and had personally concocted the sour cream dip which he presented on a platter with a handsome arrangement of carrot sticks and cauliflower florets and two-inch lengths of celery stalk he'd rinsed even most of the grit from. The punch was a brew of his own devising, a blend of Wink and ginger ale that, along with the aid of assorted fruit juices, cloaked the rum and concealed the Everclear and seemed fit to carry off the curry, tasted in fact so remarkably unalcoholic that a number of the guests got straightaway reduced, chased from the getgo so awful many sausage balls with so awful much punch that they came to be rendered effectively senseless while the evening was fresh yet and young.

Desmond's invitation had made altogether plain that the theme of his bash was "A Night in Rio" and he'd encouraged the bashees to go if they cared to latin, but Desmond was the only one to dress up proper, wore a painted moustache and a pleated shirt with puffy sleeves, a pair of clingy black trousers and stub-heeled boots, and he told to the guests as they stepped through the doorway, "Babaloo," or something like it which he routinely adorned and amplified with a manner of singular pirouette, lifted his arms and snapped his fingers and twirled himself round in advance of stomping with his boot heels upon the gold speckled rug and venting himself of a yip.

Naturally Desmond had selected suitable music for the occasion. It was all trumpets and syncopation along with a variety of intermittent vocalizing that sounded the work of a Mexican bowling team out on a spree. The singers hooted and howled and yodeled and let on to be having an awful swell time, let on of course to be having it at an altogether excruciating volume which at first prevented the guests from hearing anything much in the way of talk except on occasion for the proclamation of Desmond's orientation which Desmond was prone to announce to spouses and reveal to dates there in the doorway at the shank of his pirouette and the culmination of his yip when he was feeling still likely too worked up to lean in close and speak in semi-confidential tones.

I hadn't myself been meaning to attend, had hoped to draw a shift but couldn't bring Dewey to make way for me, Dewey who was at the time weathering woman-friend problems and was desperately wanting to work so as to keep from passing the evening in earnest, sincere dissection of his own personal rich pageant of accumulated insensitivities. I'd figured I might even take a little trip, venture up to the parkway and pass a night of luxury in the rock lodge, but I was having at the time trouble with my Chevette that was sputtering and missing and stalling at stops, and I didn't suspect I could likely afford the rock lodge and a tow both together. So instead I determined just to make to be away, bolt my door and draw shut my shades and read my latest beauty monthly.

But then early on Desmond came looking for me, was seeking some pre-bash assistance and knocked on my door and tapped on my front windowlight and inquired idly of Monroe, who was out herself dining about the dumpster, where possibly I could be. I guess he'd heard me come in, spied my Chevette in the lot, and calculated he'd maybe not manufactured enough of a ruckus and so set in afresh to pounding my door and rapping upon my windowlight which he left off at only long enough to step upstairs and call me on the phone. I just didn't see how I could hope to stave him off and opened at length the door to him, was meaning to tell him that I'd been napping and was feeling ever so poorly, was nursing I suspected an inflammation, but Desmond didn't allow me the occasion truly to speak as he was presently enduring a balloon bouquet crisis and required my assistance straightaway, fairly hauled me on up the stairs so that I might help him to figure how best with a clutch of balloons to insinuate Latin romance.

I confessed at length to Desmond that I was feeling in fact feverish, was nursing a galloping inflammation, was not persuaded that I could manage this night with balloon bouquets much insinuating to speak of. Desmond, however, appeared too frantic to desert and abandon and he pleaded and begged so pathetically that I stayed to help him with his balloons, inflated them and taped them and tied them and, once Desmond had hung them himself, made how I could see their charm and detect their insinuations. Desmond had me to help him move his dining table as well and rearrange his boudoir chairs and his settee, and he enlisted me there at the last to attach his pinata to the overhead light. It was a blue and orange donkey that Desmond had stuffed full of condoms, lubricated Sheiks.

Desmond dubbed me honorary co-host and sent me off to change into my Latin ensemble notwithstanding my protests and my strident objections along with mention once further of my advancing inflammation. Of course I owned no Latin ensemble to speak of, had come one Christmas into possession of a pair of red socks with palm trees on them but couldn't hope to put together a shirt and trousers that would do much insinuating themselves, and I'd hardly as well been looking to get dubbed since I did not wish to share even nominal duties with the sort of fellow who was likely to hover by the door greeting his guests and broadcasting his proclivity. Desmond, however, couldn't seem to bring himself to leave me be, was convinced he required my assistance and my support and came down to fetch me back once he'd figured I'd had time to dress and primp.

He had me to stir the punch and sample the sausage balls, set out the ashtrays and the mixed nuts and make with him soothing conversation in advance of the first guests who arrived precisely on the hour and got pretty ferociously babalooed by Desmond, who performed his pirouette, vented his yip, hugged his workmate and made directly known to her husband his persuasion, her husband who spied me off by the settee and favored me with a little grin.

I'd figured it would be an enduring torment, but it didn't turn out to be a torment exactly. I can't say I knew but two of the guests. One of them cashed my checks at the bank and the other I'd arrested drunk on the bypass. He was a little ill and vengeful there at first but came in time to be chummy enough once the punch had taken effect. The rest of them were pretty much strangers to me though I'd seen a few of them here and there and heard tell of a couple more, and they all seemed for the most part regular sorts, didn't appear any of them to be themselves of Desmond's gland and persuasion. They worked apparently with him out at the new industrial park or had arrived in the company of somebody who did, were employed the pack of them by an outfit that manufactured wallboard which was, there at the first, the topic of some appreciable discussion as all the industrial parkers felt straightoff obliged to talk some shop. Presently, though, they managed to weary of wallboard themselves and joined the rest of us in regular chat which proved for me a welcome diversion from my broken television and my flatulent mongrel.

I met a girl who'd dated once a boy I'd run in on an assault and a woman who lived alongside people who'd previously gotten beaten and robbed. I came across a fellow who'd been a few years back wrongfully incarcerated and fell in at last with a gaggle of folks who were debating when I happened upon them Sheetrock screws but proved shortly to share among them an interest in law enforcement and let on to be curious to know why it was a man like myself might have seen fit to swear the oath and join the force. I don't suppose they

125

were casting truly about for a probing reply, and I had me a shrug and a look of bemusement that I was accustomed to air in response, but the punch I guess had rendered me chatty and before I knew what I was about I was off on my tale of Wade, the one I usually kept close and rarely gave an airing.

You see Wade had been previously on his own an officer of the peace, not as a career and an occupation, but he'd managed to get once conscripted into a sort of a posse. When my mother came to know him he was employed at the hardware store and sold her a set of strap hinges for our crawlspace door, even threw in a hasp and a lock which my mother failed to take straightoff as a prelude to courtship. Of course she'd found by then reason enough to swear off men as a breed and a species since the one she'd married firstoff, the one that was father to me and my brother, had just up one day and left her, explained how he couldn't be bound up and saddled, claimed to be suffocating and just packed his clothes in a grip and lit out. He called a time or two sober from somewhere down off the ridge, showed up one Christmas, came by one Easter, called a time or two drunk, but presently he left off with us entirely. My mother took a job at the municipal hall and, since me and my brother weren't but puny tykes both, she left us days with a woman in Woodlawn who kept children in her front room on the floor.

So me and my brother didn't see ourselves so awfully much of our mother at the time, passed just our weekends with her and passed just our evenings and weren't I guess much looking to have the likes of Wade come wandering in and muck up our routine. Straightoff, then, we didn't take to him. He just showed up there one night along about suppertime, tapped meekly upon the doorrail and called out to make himself known to my mother who recollected in fact with prompting how Wade himself had been the one to sell her the strap hinges and make to her a gift of the hasp and the lock. Wade simply let on to be wanting as a custom to check in and learn had the hinges proved to suit, had the lock and the hasp turned out in the end to be of any use at all which induced my mother to confess how in truth she'd failed yet

126

to take them out of the bag which proved a considerable incitement for Wade, who assured my mother that he'd with pleasure see to her hinges and affix her hasp.

Naturally she protested, but Wade by then had set already to retiring from the porch, had commenced directly to make for his vehicle in the drive which was one of those vans with fender skirts and chrome all about it, and he fished out his toolbox and his light and encamped at the crawlspace door where our mother delivered her hardware.

Apparently our mother had never had occasion to stand hard by and observe the work of a man who knew what he was about. Her husband, our daddy, had not been himself a handy sort of a fellow, evermore clenched hinges and hasps with bent nails, never demonstrated any patience much for screws. So our mother, I suspect, was taken straightoff with the nature of Wade's endeavor, the care and the economy of it, the sure progression, the steady pace, the thoroughgoing absence of ire and agitation. She held his light for him, watched him level and mark his hinges and punch his pilot holes, draw tight his screws, regarded I imagine the care he took checking the swing of her crawlspace door and the consideration he demonstrated in placing the hasp so that a lady might squat just a little to reach it and not have to stoop and bend full over.

Doubtless she paid some heed to the way that Wade went about the entire business, and I figure it had an effect upon her. I'm aware, of course, that charm and dash and wit in a fellow are taken widely to be allurements but am persuaded myself to believe that sometimes competence alone can hold sway with a woman, most particularly the manner of creature with a history of hapless men.

Our mother asked him to supper and Wade made his noises like he might resist and decline, but our mother led him on into the house and apparently me and apparently my brother objected to him straightoff, were still at the age when we were disposed to screech and wail, did not yet even between us suspect that events sometimes might play out contrary to our wishes and to our desires which we framed and expressed by screeching and wailing or failing to screech and to wail. And though I don't actually remember what transpired that evening, I can imagine the assorted indignities me and my brother inflicted, so I guess it's a regular marvel that Wade could see fit to take up with our mother. But we failed in fact to put him off and our mother began to keep regular company together.

He'd sit with us nights before the television and drive us Sundays up to the lakeside where Wade taught me and my brother to fish, hooked anyhow fish for us and then handed to us the poles. He carried our mother every now and again to dinner, not at the steak house or the buffet but clean up to Wytheville to the continental restaurant in town while me and my brother were left in the charge of the Feenys' girl Margaret, who watched the TV and talked on the telephone and entertained on occasion guests in the bedroom once she'd bought off me and my brother with a sack of caramel squares.

Wade and our mother plain courted for a goodly while, decided to wed, and then courted a while longer so as to allow Mr. Lyles the lawyer from town to hunt down our father and serve papers on him. They were married at length at the municipal hall off in a little room set aside for civic ceremonies. It had blue draperies and folding chairs and a laminated table with a lectern upon it and looked for all the world like an algebra classroom, though it served to suit well enough for Wade and our mother whose vows were administered by the honorable Mr. Gilmer Royce Dow who extracted from Wade and our mother pledges and secured from them solemn vows.

Wade had been letting a room from a lady in town and had been sharing with two fellows otherwise a bath at the end of the hallway. None of the furnishings were his except for a straight chair he'd come across somewhere and had developed an abiding affection for due, Wade informed us, to the burl in the seat which Wade found to be as odd and comely a burl as he'd yet come across. He had a few pictures of his people, his mother and his father and his dead sister, Irene, along with an uncle or two which he kept in an envelope stuck in a book, and he'd accumulated over time several suits of clothes and pairs of two-toned shoes that our mother prevailed upon him to deliver to the bin in the shopping plaza lot.

Wade wasn't by nature the sort of man to indulge and dote on children, which isn't to say he didn't have it in him to be tender and kindly, but Wade was just a little too meek and self-conscious to engage a child in the variety of exchange that children for the most part seem to take to and demonstrate evermore a fondness for. He wasn't, that is, much interested in my brother's species of inquisition and didn't prove truly any count at explaining the mysteries and puzzlements of this life but was prone to defer to our mother who was able herself and sufficiently willing to field our inquiries and talk our talk. Wade was the one that drove us to the lakeside and carried us Saturdays to the show, brought home some nights ice cream from the dairy bar and encouraged us on occasion with a look and a nod to leave off resisting what of our mother's wishes we'd seen fit to throw in together and resist.

Wade owned a rifle he'd carried with him from his previous digs, an old Remington breechloader that had come to him upon the death of one of his father's brothers. It was an awfully handsome item. The flat of the stock had near itself as much burl to it as the seat of Wade's straight chair and the gunsteel had been burnished and greased and treated over time with exceptional care. Wade, however, didn't seem to be much attached to his uncle's breechloader, kept it in a gunsock in the closet at the first and appeared altogether contented to leave it there, didn't anyhow let on to feel inclined to put the thing on display and would probably have happily left it in the sock if our mother hadn't managed to prevail upon Wade to bring that rifle out and hang it over the mantelpiece. She believed that the general decor could stand a touch of manliness about it and figured maybe Wade had just been too polite to suggest as much himself which left her to perform the service of suggesting it for him.

I don't imagine, however, that the tenor of the decor was anything Wade troubled himself about, and I can't recall him demonstrating much affection for that weapon even once our mother had hung and situated it. I don't even believe he'd ever as much as fired the thing himself though his uncle had left him a carton half full of bright brass cartridges for it. Wade just didn't hunt and hadn't somehow cultivated much trace of that frothy hormonal involvement with guns that men are known for. He was happy simply to fish a little sometimes for sport, and I can't recall him paying much heed to that rifle at all except for every now and again when he'd stand on the hearth and trace with his fingerend the swirl of the grain.

Clearly Wade wasn't personally afflicted with any yen to speak of for police work, which is often itself frothy and hormonal at heart, and I don't recall that he was even prone to get much exercised when some rascal roundabout would find cause and occasion to indulge his wayward impulses, manufacture a measure of harm and havoc, a dose anyhow enough of each to come to be locally known and reviled by the citizens at large who were not themselves famous for their patience with rascals or celebrated for their graceful tolerance of wayward impulses. Wade just never appeared too awfully surprised at the things people would up sometimes and do to each other and was not himself the sort to make pronouncements about just where in a handcart this world of ours was going.

Consequently, Wade hardly seemed a likely candidate to throw in with a manhunt and probably would have refrained and resisted had he not been put upon to entertain from the sheriff his appeal there in the hardware store along with those fellows who most usually tended to linger and loiter back by the sheetstove between the housepaint and the fencewire. I just have to believe that Wade himself got pressured and swayed by the pack of them as Wade was not so stout a sort that he couldn't be moved and persuaded and caused at length to take up and do what everybody else was taking up and doing.

It seems the law was after an Akers who'd gone apparently off his keel and come to be a danger. The sheriff had complaints sworn out by that Akers's own uncle who'd been thrashed and by that Akers's own cousin who'd been violated. Naturally, they'd spoken together poorly of their relation and had given the sheriff to believe that that Akers

130

presented a considerable threat to regular unaffiliated people as well. They thought he had a pistol. They knew he had a knife. They guessed between them his sap was up and suspected he'd be scouring the county for women to have his way with and force his desires upon which the sheriff stood in the hardware store, back between the paint and the fencewire, and passed along to the fellows there who of course got whipped up straightaway and guessed they could stand to curb a fellow loose on the land with his sap and desires, guessed it I suppose with such high feeling that Wade himself got maybe a little stirred and agitated.

He threw in anyhow with them and they all went off and fetched their rifles and then met up north of town near the reservoir as the uncle and the cousin had indicated that the offending Akers had taken along about there to the hills, was figuring, they imagined, to hunker down until nightfall when he'd probably emerge with his sap and come forth with his desires so as to prey upon whatever women he happened across. The prospect of it proved altogether galvanizing and prevented the sheriff from having himself to concoct incentives otherwise since sheer gallantry served as motive enough for his corps of recruits who raised their hands by the roadside and swore an oath in advance of following the sheriff's men up around the water and into the woods where they fanned out across the hillside.

Wade's uncle's breechloader only held one bullet at a time and the rest of Wade's ammunition was rattling about in his trouser pocket which served to render Wade less surreptitious than probably he was hoping to be as him and his buddies from the hardware store moved pretty much like skirmishers through the trees, driving the rabbits and the quail and the odd deer and turkey before them. Once they gained the ridge they split in half and advanced in opposite directions for a time prior to sweeping down the far slope and moving through the creases and the gulleys and out into a stretch of pastureland where they broke off into pairs to investigate the hedgerows and the scrub along the creek. Wade ended up with a Skiles who let on to be anxious to loose a little blood to flow, and as they poked about in the bushes and the

vines and dodged around the clammy locusts that Skiles advertised his
disposition and made against that Akers assorted hard remarks which
he persevered at and improved upon while him and Wade passed together out of the pasture and down into a nectarine grove.

That Skiles was prattling still as they rounded a shed and came
there in the dooryard of it flush upon that Akers himself who was out
there messing with a hound that was chained to a stake, his own
hound, it turned out, his own shed, his own piece of land. He had on
the coat they'd said he'd be wearing. He had on the cap they'd told
them he favored. Wade could see the knife sticking out of his boot,
the pistol on his hip, and him and that Akers and the Skiles as well all
stood there for a palpable time and just gazed at each other without
moving to offer a challenge or a threat.

That Akers just didn't seem to much act hunted, didn't look to
Wade pursued which gave him, quite naturally, pause, and he was
meaning to make inquiries, to wonder of that fellow was he in fact the
Akers who'd beat his uncle and violated his uncle's child, find out was
he inclined to ride into town and face the charges, but before he could
bring himself to speak that Skiles alongside him raised his rifle and
vented simultaneously a remark which served together to provoke that
Akers who in a single motion drew and leveled his revolver as he laid
to the hammer his thumb. Wade himself fired from the hip and liked
as a consequence to get his arms wrenched loose at the shoulders on
account of the buck of that breechloader, and he was privy straightaway to the enthusiastic approval of the Skiles alongside him who sang
to Wade his praises and offered up his gratitude for having been
salvaged and saved even before that Akers had collapsed altogether
into a heap on the ground where his spotted hound sniffed his wound
and licked his fingers and shortly grew anxious and throaty.

Of course they all came running, the whole pack of them came
crashing and stampeding through the woods and across the orchard
and down around the shed to where Wade and the Skiles and that
hound together stood gaping at that Akers. The Skiles took directly
upon himself narrative duties and indicated how him and Wade had

come and where him and Wade had got to before they'd slipped up on that Akers himself who'd been lurking, the Skiles told it, laying pretty much for the pair of them as best as that Skiles could figure. He wondered could they all of them see the pistol there in the grass that that Akers had drawn. He invited them please to picture if they might the nimble reaction of Wade himself who'd levered up his Remington and cut loose before that Akers could manage to squeeze off a round.

It turned out, however, that the uncle and cousin had hardly wanted that Akers laid low. They'd only been peeved and irritated. They'd quarreled, it seems, with that Akers over money, that Akers who'd in fact violated his cousin who made of violation a going concern, offered up evermore her favors for profit and was not disposed to provide even kin with complimentary service. So it wasn't so much that that Akers had in fact engaged with his cousin in an unwholesome act but more that he'd neglected to take it for commerce and had withheld pay which him and his uncle had remonstrated together about with the uncle getting clearly the shortest possible end of the remonstration. So they'd gone the pair of them to the law and they'd filed a complaint against that Akers who they'd hoped to inconvenience and persuade, teach maybe the ins and teach the outs of fiduciary obligations.

They had not at all been looking to get him killed and so pitched together a holy fit when word came to them of the fate of that Akers who'd been both a cousin and a customer to the girl and a moderately loving nephew to the uncle who'd only gotten thrashed by him once or twice. They were together mightily upset and showed up soon enough in the hardware store to apprise Wade of their disposition, arrived there two days after the shooting, found Wade back with the auger bits and laid pretty much siege to him, had to be lifted and carried from the store and set out at the street by those fellows at the sheetstove who made themselves a point of bringing to Wade's attention what a noble strain of manly bastard they still found Wade to be.

I can't say I recall just exactly how Wade took it. I mean I don't remember firsthand much about the entire business at all except for the travels of Wade's breechloader which he could not bring himself to hang again over the mantelpiece and so retired it to the closet, stuck it in the gunsock and left it, we supposed, off behind the hanging clothes and back of the shoes where we'd all of us guessed it had stayed until later, considerably later, well after Wade was gone, when I was out in the carshed looking for a board and found the thing laid up across the rafters. I guess he hadn't been able even to bear it in the house. Our mother insisted he was changed and altered though she could not herself say exactly how, but then there's not much doubt that killing a man can have an effect on a fellow, most especially a fellow like Wade who'd just shown up like usual at work expecting maybe to tidy up the bolt boxes and mix a little paint and hardly intending to go off on a manhunt and fire a slug clean through an Akers.

So I figure by the time I was old enough to know him proper he was a different Wade already, not anymore the Wade at all we'd screeched at and tormented but a Wade instead who'd undergone a manner of transformation, who could not probably help in the end but get a little overhauled, not just because he'd reduced with his Rem-ington that Akers to a heap but largely instead on account of how he was known for nothing else, had pulled one time his trigger with purpose and with effect which proved in the end undertaking enough to distinguish him for good.

When me and my brother were bigger boys and were out in the company of Wade, men we'd come across roundabout could not often keep from wondering if we were together acquainted with what pre-viously our stepdaddy Wade had done which they'd set in straight-away to crowing about if Wade didn't stop and prevent them, Wade who they'd manage to let on to be one flinty, hard-boiled son-of-a-bitch that they guessed we should know and figured we should hear.

For his part I only once knew Wade to speak to what he'd done and I can't exactly say what had spurred and induced him. We hadn't been talking about anything much. I don't seem to recall that we'd been in fact speaking to each other at all. I was just sitting at the

dinette eating saltines and Wade was standing over the sink sucking
the pulp from a tomato and looking out the window into the yard. I
have to figure the elements maybe conspired to prompt and remind
him, that perhaps the light fell and the breeze moved and shifted the
branches and the birds chirped and called after such a fashion together
as to prove for Wade striking and reminiscent, Wade who left off
sucking his pulp and just stood for a time gazing through the windowlight.

He told me they'd come down through the orchard, him and the
Skiles, had crossed a rail fence and eased up to the shed beyond it
where they spied that Akers out in the dooryard messing with his dog.
The Skiles brought his bore to bear on him and directly plied that
Akers with a remark, that Akers who Wade didn't figure was the sort
to get with grace remarked at. He drew his pistol, Wade said. He
raised and trained it, settled his thumb to the hammer, appeared set
to do some harm, Wade said and then fell for a time silent, just stood
there at the sink peering through the windowlight into the yard.
Presently he told me it was funny, presently he told me it was strange,
but he couldn't recall even so much as hearing that rifle go off and
wasn't truly certain he'd shot it until him and that Akers together took
notice of the wound, the hole through the jacket and through the shirt
and clean through the breastbone as well which that Akers studied and
that Akers perused, lifted even his jacket flap for an unimpeded view
in advance of raising again his face and paying his last scrap of heed on
this earth to Wade alone.

"He looked right at me," Wade said. "I can see him," which he
declared in such a voice and after such a fashion that I was persuaded
for a moment to believe I might step to the window and see him
myself.

It had upon me an effect, made upon me an impression that's
lasted and that's endured. Out of the general fog of my boyhood
there's not terribly much I can conjure still plain except I suppose for
Homer our dog that died of distemper, our mother's green Ford with
the soft suspension, the striped cotton shirt with the stain on the

pocket that my brother favored and wore near to rags, and Wade standing at the sink holding his tomato. I guess even there at the dinette I was deciding already and calculating, determining how I'd be the one to make it all right and do it all proper which I didn't suppose that Wade would have occasion to make it and to do it himself. The whole business just managed to prove somehow seed enough to suit, persevered as cause and inducement and allowed me, when people grew from my badge and my stick and my gun inquiring, to tell to them how my daddy Wade had been once a lawman himself.

Of course that bunch at Desmond's was more than a little besotted themselves, had quaffed among them adequate punch to come to be sluggish and slow, weren't in short the ideal crowd to let on and imply at and were proving in fact pretty faulty and dull which I feared might lead to some inquiring further that I was girding myself about when a fellow off under the lightglobe manufactured a saving distraction, reached up unbidden and with his fingers ripped open Desmond's donkey which straightaway disgorged its Sheiks upon him, its Sheiks that he managed to mistake entirely for handy moistened towelettes and so opened one up to wipe if he might the sausage ball grease from his fingers which a lubricated Sheik is truly not so very well suited to do.

Naturally at last when I came across her I wasn't even looking to find her. I mean I was still in a general way hoping to run up on her, but I was hardly actively searching her out when she finally showed herself to me. Wendle had been dead a week and a half or closer maybe to two and we didn't officially have anything in the way of actual leads though the chief and Clifford and Dewey and Lonnie and Harnett from the state police as well had cultivated among them theories and suspicions that they were growing prone to snipe and inclined to battle about. Most any time a couple of them came across each other they'd fall directly to speculating, air varying opinions and competing suppositions and exchange with advancing enthusiasm wildly differing views.

We'd ventured truly the pack of us deep into the land of dick and squat. I had my Polaroid and had hardly yet finished with mining that pummeled Crouse, but they couldn't the rest of them find in truth much concrete to clutch at themselves which was causing legitimate trouble for the chief whose store of significant and telling expressions was dwindling and draining away. As a group, then, our prospects for the speedy capture of the bloodthirsty perpetrator were evermore slipping from view, and I was coming myself to be set to go and bring to that Crouse's happy home some grief and some trouble together when I just up and blundered across her out at the shopping plaza.

She was squatting in the Wal-Mart in the kitchenwares before the assorted utensils, was studying a long-handled slotted spoon, paying it truly her undivided regard and so did not straightoff take any heed much of me, not anyhow like I took truly heed myself of her though I can't say I saw in her straightaway that naked thing from the picture. I mean I found her just handsome and found her appealing and was prompted I suppose to draw up there at the mouth of the aisle and gawk and gaze on account of how she struck me as rare and comely, wasn't wearing one of those pastel sweatsuits the women roundabout seem to favor and appeared willing to let her hair hang and lay, hadn't troubled herself to tease and to wave it. She just didn't look to me much at all like the rest of them tend to look, and I'll confess I had no suspicions about her when I stopped to soak her in.

I'm a steady and reliable visitor to the Wal-Mart, am put upon to stop in about every third week on behalf of my Chevette which has proven an extravagantly seepy sort of vehicle. It tends to lose its fluids out along the roadways and drip and discharge off at the apartment and over at the stationhouse lots. The motor oil pretty much runs straight through it, loiters maybe long enough to lubricate a little, and at high revolutions the antifreeze is wont to shoot in a stream from the necks of the hoses. I can't say what becomes of the brake fluid which gets after its own fashion gone or figure how the grease in the crankcase manages to evacuate the basin, but I can evermore depend upon that car to get in short order dehydrated once I've taken the trouble to bring all the fluids up to their suitable levels. The idling engine has the look of a fireboat, throws off its liquids in a festive display, and though I've replaced any number of gaskets and clamps and refitted hoses untold, I've never been able to produce myself much effect upon that vehicle.

So I'd stopped off on my way from work to accumulate fluids, as was my custom, and I'd failed like usual to see much need for the use this evening of a buggy, had declined by habit to accept one from the lady in the smock at the door whose job is to make us at the Wal-Mart welcome and offer to us buggies as we come in. Consequently, I was obliged to pay some appreciable mind to my sundry containers to assure that they were balanced and suitably situated as I made my way from the automotive section on towards the registers at the front of the store, proceeded along the wall by the tropical fish and the fuzzy throw rugs prior to hanging at the bedsheets a hard right and crossing into kitchenwares proper where I found myself put upon to stop and adjust my little can of dot-3 fluid that was threatening to slip down my shirtfront between a couple of quarts of 30-weight oil.

I was, then, a trifle preoccupied, hardly my usual vigilant self, and when I had again a sure grip on my liquids and peered by chance down the utensil aisle, I saw just some girl with a slotted spoon, some girl whose allurements I measured and gauged and who appeared ready cause for a detour. I made out to have a little business of my own, stood before the whisks and the spatulas pretending to be deep in culinary thought while I managed sufficient sidelong perusal to persuade myself that I'd come somewhere across that girl with the spoon before. I was thinking maybe I'd previously observed her in an infraction, attempted to place and classify her, cast back and wondered had she been maybe the creature in the little red Spitfire I'd clocked on the bypass or that girl in the Honda who'd decided on a whim to turn from the right lane left into the Kroger. I seemed to recall it was a brunette who'd parked in front of the firehouse door, but I could not decide if it had in fact been this brunette precisely. Bringing to bear my powers of concentration, I began in fact to squint at her and study her very nearly outright as I prepared the way for my inquiry, set myself to speak.

My regard in fact was such that she became at length sufficiently aware of it to leave off with her slotted spoon and shift about to look full upon me which straightoff served to confirm my suspicion that I was after all acquainted with her since I guessed I knew well enough that nose, those eyes and lips, that dainty chin and was endeavoring to affiliate them with some species of transgression, was about to inquire if hadn't we met on the shoulder of the bypass, when it hit me all at once just where precisely I'd seen those features before, which served, I suppose, to perform upon my squint a considerable alteration that I can't say if she took herself much notice of or not since she looked still fairly blandly upon me and appeared content to allow me, once I'd come to be fit and able, to speak.

It was the blouse of course and the slacks that threw me along with the bright fluorescent Wal-Mart light which was hardly itself so flattering and soft as a shaded incandescent bulb. I guess as well I hadn't been expecting to meet in the kitchenwares there in the flesh the woman whose naked likeness I'd come to be prone nights lately to study. So I had cause, I figure, to be lost at the moment for a suitable thing to say, and I seem to recall that I gave over pretty directly my inquiring squint, settled instead for a slackening of my assorted features and muscles and watched for a time that girl with the spoon just stand there and watch me back until I discovered presently the pluck to tell to her, "Didn't we, weren't you?" which proved to be as far this day as my own particular strain of pluck would take me.

I can't know exactly what she thought but assume she just figured me for a goofy guy in a world where guys as often as not turn out in the end to be goofy. I mean there I stood cradling my fluids and making to have some use for a whisk like maybe I couldn't decide altogether if I'd service my car or concoct a meringue, and then I turn and manage to half let on that I've seen her before and know her very likely from somewhere else which sounded, I'll confess, tired even to me and must have struck her as deplorably common. I wasn't even sure she'd so much as see fit to speak to me back, but at length and in time she lifted her spoon and touched me with the very tip of it, jabbed the thing past my Prestone between the handle and the jug where she found out my platinum badge and tapped with her spoonend upon it.

"I used to be acquainted with a man of the law," she told to me, and I recall I managed to make some manner of oafish reply while I watched her grow not pensive exactly but briefly preoccupied, observed how she cast her eyes away and then brought them again to bear upon me, favored me with her thorough regard as she remarked and declared, "You're not him," which proved occasion for that grin I'd come to know, that ever so slight and scanty smile that suggested how fellows like me could prove a tolerable amusement.

I found myself inspired to a cretinish rejoinder notwithstanding that I'd schemed in fact to be wry and to be catty, managed to make roguish mention of my nightstick I believe and earned for it one indulgent grin further which was better truly than I guess I rated as a parting salute, and I just stood there holding my fluids and watched her turn and stroll away without troubling myself directly to decide what maybe I'd best ought to do now that I'd enjoyed the enormous luck of running by chance across her.

There's not much doubt I was addled a bit. I'd come into the store after fluids alone and had figured on seeing this girl just naked and later in the comfort of my Naugahyde chair and so didn't quite know how best to proceed now that I'd blundered onto her. Consequently, I determined to follow my inclination and just trail along behind her at a distance, and I pursued her after a fashion into the cosmetics where she selected a body lotion and a packet of ear swabs prior to stopping in at the pharmaceuticals for some manner of analgesic on her way to the checkout line where I observed her to make cordial chat with the lady at the register while I lurked a couple of lines over myself and pretended to be captivated by the junk in the checkout rack—the tiny keyring flashlights, the miracle epoxy, the rotary nosehair clippers.

I never was legitimately trained to tail, can't recall having ever even once been advised as to a proper procedure, though I had previously with Wendle staked out a fellow who'd led us on a species of chase. He was a Crutchfield from a decent branch of people, had a wife and a couple of boys and a girl but was saddled apparently as well with a particular stripe of yearning that didn't appear on the face of things to suit him much at all. We'd had word from a man out towards Fries that he was enduring on a tract of his land a couple of regular interlopers. He couldn't say for certain what they might be about but he'd caught once or twice sight of the pair of them slipping together into the woods. He suspected himself they were tending a still and wanted to speak to us of it before we'd found the thing maybe on our own and hauled him in as well. They always parked their green sedan in across the ditch by a phonepole, and that fellow from Fries had crept up one day and taken the license number which led us to the Crutchfield with the wife and the kids and the regular occupation and no cause, as best as I could see, to make as a sideline corn liquor.

Wendle, however, didn't have himself much use for decent people and could not even begin to resist the occasion to undo one. He persuaded the chief we might be afflicted with the princes together of unbonded mash, suggested how he'd had all along suspicions about that Crutchfield himself, and he made to the chief vague reference to some shady and semi-lawless behavior he'd previously found occasion to see that Crutchfield plainly about. Wendle simply figured we should keep for a time our eye upon him and adequately defamed that Crutchfield to bring the chief to his view, the chief who allowed me and Wendle to pass a piece of two afternoons in Wendle's blue coupe down in the lot by the furniture mill where that Crutchfield worked in shipping.

It's a tedious thing to sit in a lot and wait for a fellow who may or may not see fit to step out and oblige you with a bit of intrigue, occasion at least to follow him up to the Arby's for lunch. It's more painful still if you're put upon to pass the time enduring the opinions and the ruminations of Wendle's ilk since Wendle's supreme gift was for holding forth on any of diverse topics about which he could work up impassioned views and abiding beliefs, manage regular homilies that would evermore serve in their particulars to remind him of items further he'd guess he might, while he was up to it, hold forth as well about.

Midway through our second day of sharing the coupe in the furniture mill lot, I'll confess I'd come myself to be in a state, was sick to death of enduring from Wendle his ceaseless estimation of how in fact the world might work were he allowed to operate it. He was advising me, I do recall, as to the feeble and wretched condition of our nation's anti-ballistic canopy, which Wendle of course had a cure to propose and a remedy directly to speak about, when that Crutchfield strode finally forth from the mill, glanced what looked in fact furtively about, and then climbed into his Oldsmobile and motored up out of the bottom. I was myself near ecstasy at the prospect that Wendle might shut up and drive, and he did fairly shortly start his coupe and set out after that Crutchfield who stopped up by the hair salon and fetched away a fellow who'd been standing by the lightpole expecting him to come.

Though we could barely make him out, Wendle didn't care for the looks of him and held forth at some length about the way that people, through little more than personal carriage and bearing, tend to give their blackest secrets away, allowed how a slouch or an odd, ungainly posture often spoke in the end worlds to him.

That Crutchfield made directly for the truck route where he struck out west towards Fries. Wendle lurked back a ways down the road and subjected me to assorted of his hypotheses as to what that Crutchfield and his buddy together were likely to be about. He guessed he'd read already in his day personal carriages and bearings enough to recognize nefariousness and detect deceit when he happened to come across them, and he announced he was persuaded that the Crutchfield and his buddy were very probably cruising into lawlessness. He was still figuring largely on unbonded mash but confided there to me how embezzlement would not startle him much or some other manner of thievery outright. He could see, he told me, they were devious sorts and Wendle wished I'd look how they schemed and connived, indicated the pair of them off ahead of us where that Crutchfield turned and favored his buddy with some strain of remark, his buddy who reached along the seatback and laid lightly to that Crutchfield's shoulder assorted of his fingerends.

We followed that Crutchfield off the truck route on into the countryside, pastureland and hardwood forest intermingled with the odd farmhouse and a bit of scarce truck and tractor traffic. Presently that Crutchfield left the blacktop for a gravel road that he negotiated with a considerable head of steam, churning up grit and dust sufficient to forestall Wendle who found himself obliged to loiter and to lay back until the air had cleared. So we fell appreciably off the pace and did not come again across that vehicle until the Crutchfield had parked it already beyond the ditch over by a phonepole where him and his buddy had left it, we figured, for the woods.

Needless to say, I found myself presented with an exceptional opportunity to creep and slip along after the fashion that was still at the time very much a part of my law enforcement repertoire. Wendle was more of a stalker himself, and he unfastened directly his holster hood and struck out into the trees down along where the scrub looked sufficiently beaten back to have accommodated lately a couple of devious fellows. As was his custom when stalking, Wendle attempted to edify and direct me by means of assorted hand signals which I evermore found to be thoroughly mystifying, so I just rogered as best I was able and followed at some sizable remove so that Wendle might feel a little less inclined to endeavor with his fingers to instruct me and just leave me maybe instead to dodge and creep along as best I might.

Although Wendle fashioned himself a wily tracker, he couldn't turn up much of a trail straightoff and we strayed apparently from the route that Crutchfield and his buddy had taken since we failed for a great while to come across them notwithstanding how Wendle examined twigs and surveyed vines and sniffed every now and again the cool dank forest air, the sorts of techniques that, Wendle insisted, usually served to pinpoint his quarry. He just figured these boys were from a cleverer lot and apprised me of how he meant to corral them, explained by means of a masterwork of vigorous gesticulation that I could not so much as begin myself to penetrate the sense of. So I just followed Wendle once more at a distance and we wandered roundabout the woods revisiting spots we'd circulated through and taking for clues branches we'd broken and scrub we'd crushed ourselves. I believe even Wendle the master tracker was contemplating retiring to the car when we enjoyed together the fine fortune of hearing a telltale discharge, a short sharp throaty cry from off towards a thicket of hemlocks.

Straightaway we crouched and drew our revolvers and Wendle directly mounted an extraordinary dumbshow intended, I suspect, to illustrate to me how we figured we'd best advance to apprehend that Crutchfield and apprehend his buddy, but I couldn't quite distill my role in the proceedings and so acknowledged Wendle's instructions but continued to crouch and to linger until I discovered occasion to follow once more Wendle at my usual distance and approach with him one particularly lush and sizable hemlock with a generous lower canopy that we were able to slip beneath and hide. That Crutchfield and his buddy were plainly hard by. We could hear them struggling together at some enterprise, laboring loudly over a mutual undertaking and straining and grunting with the general exertion. Wendle was persuaded they were moving vats and pouring off skim, made like he could smell the fermentation, and he formulated with his fingers some manner of instruction that I troubled myself to acknowledge and confirm.

Wendle had apparently decided we'd spring on them and we did after a fashion spring on them in fact. Wendle anyhow sprang first himself and I sprang shortly thereafter which served to settle the both of us in a cozy little clearing with a few decorous rocks about and a mossy ground cover. It was a pleasant enough sort of a setting, conducive I guess to romance, had worked anyhow its magic upon that Crutchfield and his buddy who were laid out on a quilt together wearing their socks alone and locked in, what looked to me, a curious sort of embrace. Naturally we were the four of us pretty uniformly flabbergasted. I'll confess I could not directly make much sense of the sight before me, had been expecting troughs and pots and copper tubing and had come across instead purely unforeseen amours.

It was simply all a puzzle to me there at the first, a find-the-unholy-union-in-this-picture manner of conundrum, and I only presently resolved the scene and persuaded myself those fellows before me could be up together in fact to pretty much one thing alone. Wendle, for his part, had a grip on the business from the getgo and managed to grow precipitously disgusted, though he did not forget himself so completely as to fail to provide that Crutchfield and his buddy occasion to explain to him if they might why he should trouble himself to keep from murdering the pair of them which proved just precisely the sort of talk to chase away desire judging from how those fellows uncoupled and grew clearly uninflamed.

Wendle, you see, was one of those flagrant, full-bore heterosexuals who could not for the life of him figure why a man might lay with desire his lips upon or expose with intent his bunghole to any other man on God's green earth. He had to suppose that Crutchfield and had to conclude his buddy were very probably blighted and diseased, were suffering between them some degree of insidious cranium rot that induced them each to take the other for a stunning and savory babe. He couldn't truly find a way to lay their predicament to much cause other than delusion outright and shared with them his hypothesis as that Crutchfield and his buddy scrabbled about for their underpants and their trousers and their shirts, Wendle simply wasn't the type to allow that he'd ever even once found a man so much as vaguely stirring.

So there was, I suppose, a remote danger that Wendle might in fact do some harm, and I guess I would have spoken up and moved myself to dissuade him if I hadn't just then been confused and confounded by the etiquette of the situation, lost for a time as to what might be the mannerly thing to do that I debated and I resolved and determined at length to holster my gun and tell to Desmond my neighbor hello.

She wasn't a heedless manner of driver which I was pleased to remark, signaled to turn and to shift lanes, followed the traffic before her at a safe and suitable distance and did not often appear inclined to drift far above the posted speed which, taken together, served to soften my initial impression of her as a scarlet woman of poor romantic judgment and perhaps unseemly appetites and desires. I was simply, due to my occupation, given to a higher opinion of fine vehicular form and moderate roadway habits than they very likely rated in fact. So I was pleased to observe with what care she exited off the truck route and proceeded west along 58 towards Whitetop where she turned onto an oiled sidestreet back into a little clutch of homes and pulled into the gravel drive of the farthest house where the road gave out into a weedy hummock. I loitered and laid back, stood off in my Chevette a ways until I'd watched her unlock the front door and step full inside when I eased up hard by a forsythia bush from where I could see through the spindly shoots well enough to suit me.

It was a brick house of no size much or distinction, had a slab stoop out front with a little piece of roof above it and pair of doublehung windows either side. There was shrubbery along the foundation, holly and boxwood and hydrangea, all of it left to grow ragged and wild. The storm door was off the jamb altogether and laid across a couple of chairbacks in the yard where somebody sometime had meant I suppose to mend it. The lawn was weedy with onions and purslane, what of it anyhow the leaves hadn't killed, and there looked to be high on the roof near the vent pipe a long-handled shovel pan up on the shingles. It just wasn't an awfully tidy situation with any charm to it to speak of, not anyhow the variety at all of cozy love nest I'd anticipated.

I could see some trifling bit of the interior as the draperies were sheer and gauzy, could make out a portion of the dinette and the shank, it appeared, of the settee, could identify well enough the jittery gray glow from the television and spied every now and again that creature herself as she passed back and forth through the house. Presently, however, I could not discover much worth paying any mind to at all. She appeared to be alone and uninclined, after a time, to circulate out where I could see her. I enjoyed, however, the occasional company of a sizable spotted short-haired dog which was attempting this night to make an occupation of urinating onto my Chevette and was pleased to hose off not just the tires but the fenders and the doorpanels too.

I didn't even know what I was hoping to see, wasn't so much as playing any hunch that I could figure but had just trailed along back of that girl out of failing to be acquainted with what else I might do. Now that I'd seen where she went and was well enough certain how to come back and find her, I can't say exactly why I felt inclined to hang about, just sit there on the roadside in my wretched little vehicle enjoying for diversion hot sour canine breath and the occasional attendant corrosive fluids. But I lingered nonetheless and fetched out in time from back of my sateen flap what I considered anymore to be my Polaroid which I canted to catch sufficient light to reveal to me the features and illuminate the allurements, confirm for me that the creature off in the brick house before me was in fact the one I'd sat home nights and ruminated after a fashion upon.

One of those little import trucks turned presently onto the oiled road. The thing was all trumped up with chrome and no end of gaudy trimwork. It sat high up off the roadway. I could see the undercarriage though not much of the driver himself until he'd coasted down to where the vapor light fell on him and I made him for that Crouse with his bruises and contusions and the stitches in his lip. He turned around at the dead end and stopped before that house, peered up towards the windows and the gauzy sheer white curtains, although I don't believe he could anymore see her than I could see her myself. But he fashioned nonetheless a constant gaze that he favored for a time prior to leaving at length off with it entirely so as to drop his head to the steering wheel, lay it there in such a way that proved to be articulate and managed to be revealing. I mean the turmoil was plain enough and the agitated distress was clear and that Crouse as much as gave himself away to me altogether like people often will if you just shut up and hold still long enough to let them.

He looked to me there on the oiled road inclined to savor his anguish and wallow as best he might in his misery, alternated anyhow between longing gazes out the side window and spells of knocking his bony forehead against the steering wheel which it did not appear that Crouse was fully prepared to give over and leave off at when a vehicle turned from the blacktop onto the oiled road and the sight of it seemed to provoke him unduly. That Crouse, I mean, started and stiffened, directly gave over his turmoil and his agitation together so that he might straightaway find the means to come across low gear which he discovered soon enough and fairly roared away, swerved and skidded and churned up the road and pretty much shot past that oncoming car which pulled presently into a drive up the street.

Of course I didn't need to follow him, wasn't, that is, obliged to attempt to keep in my Chevette pace with him at all since I had directions to that Crouse's house and could find it well enough myself. But I determined I'd pay him a visit and started at my leisure my vehicle, eased out of the ditch and full into the roadway so as to turn around at the hummock and come back to sit and to idle where that Crouse had idled and sat, see maybe in my lowslung compact some of what he'd seen in his truck which didn't in fact prove to be much I hadn't seen before, the ragged shrubbery, the piece of settee, the twitchy gray glow from the television, along with and in addition to the tiniest little bit of herself over in a chair by the wall, a piece of her shoulder, some trace of her hair.

I formulated along the way a suitable procedure, guessed I'd attempt to badger that Crouse and mount a relentless inquiry while his emotions were raw and his blood was up, figuring he might be persuaded to tell once more of his cuts and abrasions and prove this occasion forthcoming perhaps and outright illuminating since I was intending to speak of that girl, stir and unclot him with a little hard talk and assorted loathsome insinuations, was meaning to be prickly and planning to be tough, hoping to manage to do this thing like I had to guess maybe Dewey would do it. Of course circumstances failed me. I mean I was purely set and primed by the time I got to Piper's Gap and had toured around and come across that Crouse's domicile, but that Crouse apparently hadn't deigned to go straight home himself, wasn't yet there when I arrived which left me with one occasion further to ease off the roadway and sit in a ditch from where I considered the Crouse house and holdings which looked to be neat and appeared to be cozy.

I could see that Crouse's wife through the storm door and through the windows as she moved and circulated about with what looked to be a dog trailing after her, one of those little flatnosed creatures that women most especially are prone to adore. It appeared supremely anxious to be picked up and held, seemed by itself to constitute its own manner of swarm, twirled and moiled and leapt and clawed and yapped of course as well at a pitch and with a persistence that rendered me even there across the lawn down in the ditch near about prayerful with gratitude that my own dog only farted.

I was beginning to get my fill this night of surveillance as I watched the travels of that Crouse's wife and the antics of her canine, and I was wondering if maybe I mightn't ought to seek her husband at the motor lodge instead when that Crouse did me at last the service of swinging off the blacktop and into the drive. This time he saw me, appeared anyhow to notice my automobile, and once he'd parked and shut off his truck he struck out for me directly, lumbered on down the grade with his back stiff and his jaw set as if he meant to share with me how little he cared for fellows inclined to sit of an evening in his ditch. But I forestalled and prevented him from favoring me with his opinion, merely opened my door and drew myself upright out of my seat.

"Hey there," I told to that Crouse who'd drawn up and stopped by the postbox at the culvert, and I observed how it seemed he'd put this night some miles on that sharp little truck of his.

He was possessed still himself of pluck enough to muster a snide reply, informed me he wasn't conversant with the law or acquainted personally with the stipulation that might be intended to keep a fellow from riding the roads after dark, which I allowed nobody yet had legislated against and offered myself to congratulate that Crouse on the scope and the range of his travels, let on to find it an inspiring feature of life in this great land of ours that a boy like that Crouse could pass his early evening sitting in the roadway out towards Whitetop and proceed thereafter unimpeded clear here to Piper's Gap so as to pay his respects this selfsame night to one creature further.

"Isn't it this one here you took in holy matrimony?" I inquired of that Crouse and manufactured for him a highly exaggerated quizzical expression, but he'd by then left off with me already, had come to be noticeably unstiffened and bespunked and had suffered plainly the largest share of his surly defiance to drain clean away.

I provided him occasion to speak if he cared to, stepped up before him by the postbox at the culvert and let on to be ready to hear him out, but he didn't talk to me straightoff, considered instead for a spell his shoetops and lifted only at length his head to look once more upon me with his lone bloody eye, exhibit his scabs and his yellowing bruises prior to turning to glance up across the yard and off towards the house where the dog and the wife together had passed for the moment from view.

"All right," he said to me. "All right. She came one night into the lounge. I'd gone over to take a leak and get a Pepsi, no proper crapper in the office, and she was just sitting there, had a table all to herself and was eating cashews and drinking wine and looking at a magazine. I thought I'd might best chat her up. Hell," that Crouse told to me, "you've seen her yourself," which I moved my head enough merely to allow to that Crouse I had.

That Crouse seemed very nearly pleased to share with me how the charm that night had flowed, let on to have been even for him severely debonair. He entertained clearly undue esteem for his personal species of allure and informed me at length with no little pride how once he'd returned to the office in the lot that girl had presently joined him there.

"What's her name?" I asked of him as I drew out my ballpoint and extracted and flung open my pad, but that Crouse just looked past me along the road, gazed in his own dreamy fashion off into the night and gave every indication of enduring the onset of that brand of nostalgia men are prone to, men who maybe caught once a remarkable pass or shot a miraculous basket or landed a huge and extravagant fish or held, even ever so briefly, sway with the stripe of woman they suspect they had no business holding sway with.

"Red," he informed me in time and at last. "Said I could call her Red, told me everybody did."

He said she'd made out to have an itch to see the presidential suite, assured that Crouse she knew for a fact every motel had one and fairly insisted he show to her the provision he was set this night to make himself for the commander-in-chief.

"We've got these rooms that join together," that Crouse told to me and shrugged.

"You took her into the motel proper?"

And that Crouse allowed he had, allowed she wouldn't have it any way else.

"You want to tell me what happened?"

"Well it was me and it was her along with the chief executive's bed. What in God's name you think happened?"

"You had relations," I told him.

"Yeah," that Crouse informed me back. "Relations," he said.

He volunteered how impressed she'd been with his talents and his techniques, and he hinted that he was blessed with the gear to hold most women in thrall which rendered it no surprise to that Crouse that she'd returned the subsequent evening to put once more to some use if she might the presidential accommodations. Then she invited that Crouse to drop by and see her out at Whitetop. "Told me how to get there," that Crouse informed me. "Told me when to come, sent me out the window once that boy kicked in the door."

"What boy?"

"I don't know. Some fellow, had a Pontiac, I think. He came

right on in and went right on back out again, plucked me out of the bushes. I wasn't but half in my pants, hadn't put my shoes on, couldn't do much good at all against him, couldn't but barely make him out."

"And he beat you?" I said to that Crouse who lifted his head so that the light from the pole might fall full upon his stitches, his scabs, his contusions.

I was naturally disposed to figure that fellow had maybe been Wendle himself, guessed he'd burst through the door, suspected he'd scoured the shrubbery, was persuaded I knew what Wendle would do to a boy afflicted with the gall and the gear to horn in on his romance. Consequently, I endeavored to describe to that Crouse Wendle as best I was able, but he cut me short and informed me, "Wasn't that buddy of yours, the shot one, the dead one. This boy wasn't him."

"Well who then?" I inquired of that Crouse who looked set to make his reply when he got interrupted by his wife up back of the door-screen, his wife who called down across the yard, "Baby, that you?"

"Yeah," that Crouse told to her. "I'll be there in a minute."

She wanted of course to hear from him what the trouble might be and called again down across the yard in an effort to find it out which served to give rise to an altogether significant species of lull. I anyhow was impressed myself with the weight and the tenor of the moment, distilled even from it straightaway a manner of illumination, comprehended in an instant how fragile in fact this life can be, not because an organ might flutter and fail or blood might be loosed to flow, but largely because we rarely know when the ground is hollow beneath us until after it's already crumbled and once it's given way.

I mean there was that Crouse's wife at the door with her dog and her home and her man down before her which likely together fueled her belief that she'd almost surely wake up tomorrow with everything she'd woken up with today, and here I was empowered to bring calamity upon her with a word. That Crouse himself watched me to see what maybe I'd do, hear what maybe I'd say, allowed me clearly occasion to reduce the whole business to cinder and ash if I was persuaded to try it. But I didn't move and I didn't speak and heard at length that Crouse call out and tell to his wife a bulb had gone bad as he pointed to the rear of his truck.

"I'll be along," he said to her. "It's nothing," and him and me watched her together linger a time at the screen prior to slipping at last with that agitated canine out of view once more when that Crouse saw fit to favor me briefly with a sour little grin of gratitude I guess in advance of pressing on to tell me how he didn't have any clue himself who'd fetched him from the bushes and beat him. "He was some boy, some kid."

"He say anything to you?"

"Wasn't much to say. I figured out well enough what he meant, came pretty straight on home, told the wife I got set on at the lounge."

"Some boy," I said to him.

"Some kid," that Crouse told me back. "Had a regular mop of hair, smelled like soap and steak sauce, was driving a big sedan, yellow or maybe creamy white. He wasn't your buddy. I seem to recall your buddy was dead already."

"And you haven't seen her since?" I inquired of that Crouse who told me how he'd spied her once or twice just in through the window but hadn't managed yet to conduct any further relations, he called them.

"You ought to stay away from her place," I saw fit myself to advise that Crouse who told to me, "Yeah," told to me, "I ought to," and then entertained further with some little grace my suggestion that he best strike on out for his house and his wife and his worrisome dog.

"Go home," I said to him and flopped shut my pad and jerked my head up towards the housefront, but that Crouse, who'd stiffened and recovered some pluck, just glanced from his house to his yard to his drive to his ditch with my car settled in it and presently troubled himself to inform me, "Looks to me, buddy, I'm here."

5.

My brother claims to enjoy an ever so profitable affiliation with a fabricator in the Roanoke valley, which is his way anymore of saying he works for an outfit up near Salem that manufactures angle irons, stamps them from sheet, bores them with a press, and wraps them on a card in plastic. My brother gives out that he serves a key function in the marketing division of his fabricator, is uninclined to tell plain that he sells for a living angle irons, carries a box of them in his trunk and a board with samples screwed to it. He wasn't raised to be ashamed of working as an angle iron salesman but has lately been persuaded to put on airs and cultivate pretensions, married a woman from Staunton who believes herself descended from an actual baronet and requires for a mate a fellow not merely employed but affiliated.

Clarice didn't prove at the outset the jackass she was ordained to become, managed to make upon our mother a favorable impression and seemed as well an agreeable enough sort of a girl to me. But that was prior to her transformation, before she'd traced her bloodlines back. Her father was a barber, or Clarice at first was willing to allow as much though once her fascination with her royal blood took hold he

154

was given out presently as a stylist instead prior to graduating to coiffeur outright. Clarice's mother suffered from unspecified complaints and, as a manner of avocation, languished in the bed where I was taken in advance of the wedding service to make her acquaintance since she did not believe she possessed the strength to travel to the sanctuary. She was reclining atop the covers in an elegant chiffon robe, was settled in a nest of throw pillows and had dolled herself up with trinkets and rouge. Constitutional decline appeared in fact to agree with her fairly well, and I recall she lifted with grace her fingers for me to take up and clutch, told me how awfully divine it was to have occasion to meet me and then acknowledged her failing condition with a seemly little cough.

Clarice and my brother lived for a time in a duplex out towards Cave Spring, got on pretty much after the fashion of regular people all over while my brother learned the ins and outs of the angle iron game, traveled about with his box and his board and began to cement his affiliation. Clarice was obliged there at the first to seek employment as well and managed even to hold for a bit a job at the shopping plaza, worked I recall at the Rexall where she was put upon to make herself polite and accommodating which Clarice was not afflicted with much disposition for. I seem to recall she got in a fight with a woman about an ointment and made, as was her custom, a couple of rash, unsavory remarks that the pharmacist got wind of and confronted her about and so earned for himself more hard talk than he was inclined to endure.

Clarice probably would have hunted more work if the cementing of my brother's affiliation had not been proceeding apace. He was apparently blessed with a talent and a feel for the angle iron trade and earned by his industry advancements sufficient to allow Clarice to pursue, if she liked, a life of passable leisure, though they did come directly to be engaged in a species of joint venture, guessed they'd attempt to conceive a child which they spoke of like a job or work, as if they were laying a patio or installing a split-rail fence. They took to fornicating by design and charted their copulations, sought to assure that they'd fall in their clenches at Clarice's most fertile interludes.

155

They were together pretty free with talk of the state of Clarice's ovulations, announced in advance which nights of the week they were hoping to stay home and toil, spoke of their techniques and told of their aids and relived through discussion their assorted encounters in hopes, I suppose, of finding some way to economize their exertions.

They made a success of the whole affair, managed to induce conception, and straightoff Clarice applied herself to the business of being pregnant. She read books about babies and enrolled at the Y in a class for expectant mothers where the ladies set out to learn how to breathe and prepare for their dilations but found in time they preferred to drink coffee and eat Rice Krispies squares. Clarice herself got presently to be very little short of unsightly, developed an indiscriminate yen for most anything she could fit in her mouth or tear with her incisors, though she managed at length to settle upon one garnishment alone, grew ravenous for spreadable cream cheese flavored with scallions and chives, slathered it on her cookies and crackers and ate it, when she was feeling full, straight off her finger as a dietary measure.

She got bloated and she got swollen and she got thick and inflated all over which was probably more the cream cheese than impregnation but served nonetheless to as good as confine Clarice to the duplex by day and by night since shortly she couldn't see much fit to carry her bulk outdoors except for the solitary morning a week when the Rice Krispies squares beckoned to her. As a consequence Clarice found herself with occasion to watch some considerable television and discovered shortly she had a taste for the public station on UHF, could tolerate on the regular channels the chat shows and the melodramas but far and away preferred to pass her days with the public station where they ran shows about indigenous snakes and bats the size of buzzards, featured an instructional series that might teach a woman how to paint with just a knife the most enchanting scenes. There was a fellow who on Thursdays customarily poached a fish and proved to be partial in the main to rich and buttery sauces while his counterpart at the bottom of the hour, a woman from the local extension service, created all sorts of ghastly dishes from leavings and leftovers and

demonstrated a pretty remarkable passion for hash with creamed potatoes.

While it was all of it plainly fine enough fare to take with a sleeve
of saltines or a jar of roasted nuts and brought to Clarice some pleasure
in those days when pleasure was scarce, when even her housecoat constricted her and her slippers pinched her feet and her general girth
caused her to lurch and list with the grace of a frigate, she wasn't in fact
touched to her core and plumbed to her inkiest depths until one night
when she came across an installment of imported drama, a show about
people with fine tailored clothes and cavernous homes and impeccable
diction, distinguished men and handsome women with taste and money
and manners as well as aggravations visited by their serving people upon
them which made do in this drama for conflict and distress.

Clarice set out with the episode about the missing fishfork which
most everybody figures that the scullion had very likely purloined
since she was the one whose job it was to buff and polish the silver and
so could spirit away a fishfork whenever the itch might strike her. The
charm of the thing for Clarice lay in just how precisely the presiding
lord and his wife the presiding lady endeavored to get their fishfork
back. The method they chose to employ, the tact they managed to
display when they might instead have rounded up their assorted serving people and near as much as shaken that missing fishfork loose. Of
course it really wasn't so much the fishfork itself that disturbed and
provoked them, and they managed to let on that, if they so chose, they
could likely afford to buy fishforks enough to outfit the entire nation.
They didn't, they said, care even a jot for the extravagant cost of the
thing and weren't themselves sentimentally attached to any of their
utensils, but they allowed they were deeply distressed at the prospect
of having their kindness returned with thievery and deceit.

So they took occasion to speak to their domestics, made out to be
wounded before them, mounted of their disappointment a regular
exhibition and established quite plainly their low regard for dishonesty
in this life in advance of retiring to free their servants to debate where
that fishfork had gone, mount anyhow an inquisition designed to

extract from that scullion an unclouded admission of guilt while the lord and the lady enjoyed in the parlor their customary splash of sherry.

The whole business, as best as Clarice could tell, was ever so proper and refined, and she could not help but admire the bearing of the lord and the grace of the lady who between them demonstrated a gift for nuance and insinuation which held for Clarice no little appeal since she'd evermore hoped to get by in this life without having to screech and to wail. Especially since the Rexall, Clarice had been longing to bring if she might a trifle more tone to her days on this earth, liked to think she was surely herself a woman of charm and of grace, a delicate manner of creature intended perhaps for indulgences and designed for considerations seeing as how she was blessed by nature with seemly noble impulses. She figured in short she'd come very likely from stock like the lord and the lady, grew persuaded there was probably a prince or a marquess lurking in her past, and Clarice resolved to dredge him up, determined in fact to give over her nuts and her cream cheese and crackers and Rice Krispies squares so that she might pursue with singular devotion her claim upon the peerage.

I imagine my brother was simply relieved she'd come across a manner of hobby, had cultivated at last in her bloated state some interest beyond her chafing which she'd been lately wont to speak to him of most evenings at the supper table. So I guess he probably encouraged her and applauded her maybe unduly just to keep from hearing himself further talk of the flakes and of the pustules, and the passion directly took hold with Clarice who sought in the bulk of her waking hours the origins of her people. She consulted her languishing mother and her father the coiffeur as well who unfortunately harbored together little use for their relations, gave them out to be lowly and sorry, a mean and a spiteful lot, hardly a clan fit for a girl to squander her passion upon. But Clarice would not be dissuaded and visited the archives in Richmond where she claimed to discover, on a scrap of foolscap, proof that a couple of the coiffeur's own people had sailed once the sea on a boat.

Clarice, however, failed to discover any evidence much of her ties to the queen, her claims to some species of title outright which led her to enter into consultation with a professional genealogist, a fellow whose advertisement she found in the back pages of a magazine. She wrote him a note and sent him a check, insinuated her hopes and desires, gave even directions as to which way precisely she'd prefer her bloodlines to run which produced I guess the intended effect since Clarice shortly received a document which purported to illustrate the sundry routes and byways of Clarice's own descent with emphasis largely upon the relations of the coiffeur himself whose people, it appeared, had spread pretty much like vermin across the face of the earth.

That professional genealogist had managed to probe clean back into the darkest ages when Clarice's people were living in huts and wallowing still in the mud which Clarice in truth was not herself so keen to dwell upon but found instead what she was after there in the reign of George I where she discovered that the daughter of a woman who'd married one of the coiffeur's people was aunt herself to a child that had managed to land a baronet. I do imagine Clarice very like rejoiced and hosannaed straightoff, and she undertook directly to set about improving her attachment, excised from her chart the intercession of in-laws and cousins and such who served, as best as Clarice could tell, to clutter her route to peerage.

Her genealogist offered for a fee to draw up a heraldic shield designed to suggest the noble ties of Clarice's strain of people, and Clarice quite naturally sprang for the thing and framed it and hung it in the foyer even though it was a cheap and cheesy manner of item and the knight at the bottom was squat and misshapen while the horse at the top had the head of a goat. It made, however, mention in Latin of Clarice's relation's sister's niece who'd baited and taken the baronet and had come thereby to render herself titular by marriage which Clarice guessed a family could hand along just as well as weak chins and hooked noses.

She came, consequently, to feel elected, not fullblown queenly outright but more proper surely than she figured the rest of us had any cause much to feel. Given her native disinclination for rabble and common sorts, Clarice demonstrated pretty directly a talent for condescension and a remarkable gift for haughty airs which she managed in time to hone and perfect as she sat on the sofa before the television and watched the unfolding imported drama which she took anymore with what she called biscuits slathered over with marmalade. She distilled from the lord and culled from the lady tips in how best to project her grace and imply her breeding. She grew, in short, insufferable as her pregnancy came to term, and when she gave in the small hours of a Sunday morning birth at last to a boy, the dimensions of her influence were made plain in the fact that she named him Leslie Algernon Tatum without so much from my brother as a hiccup of dissent.

I have to suppose it was along about then that my brother left off being employed and began instead to consider himself affiliated. I mean it was plain she had his ear and had acquainted him as to the implications of having himself gone and married a woman who descended from people attached to a niece who'd taken the hand of a baronet. She'd schooled him, I guess, in his obligations, had laid out before him his rank and his duties, had even already commenced, I could tell, to groom him and transform his habits by the time I drove my mother up to have a look at the baby since Clarice and my brother proved then to be near about equally snotty and tossed their heads and snorted together at the quaint things me and my mother would say. It was a bitter business to endure, hard most especially on my mother who had not raised her sons either one to be consort to a baronet's heir and had never herself known a boy child to be called "Leslie" or "Algernon." She'd hoped maybe they would have found room for "Wade" which she made so bold as to pass along to Clarice and to my brother who engaged between them in a jolly bout of ever so showy head tossing and wondered directly if wasn't my mother the dearest yokel around.

Clarice bought a Wedgwood service for eight, assorted Water-ford stems, and an electric stainless teakettle so that she and my brother might take their Darjeeling there in the shank of the afternoon once my brother had returned home for the day from his affiliation. They ate often enough organs for dinner and tomatoes in the morning with their eggs, and Clarice usually took a little sherry in the evening while my brother had some claret or a stiff and proper gin. They ordered raincoats from London, sweaters from the Arran isles, and Clarice persuaded my brother to wear a black felt hat with a rolled brim as a regular means of adornment. She encouraged him as well to drape on occasion his topcoat over his shoulders and not go all the time to the trouble to put his arms in the sleeves.

They dressed Leslie Algernon in blazers and shorts and slicked back his hair with pomade. Straightaway he picked up from his mother a gift for wry and patronizing looks and a talent for condescension that was unbecoming in a child. He was a peevish and spiteful little creature and was capable upon the least provocation of the sorts of rancorous displays that I had to figure his mother herself was prone on occasion to pitch.

I didn't as a rule have much at all to do with the three of them, which proved a source of some pain and anguish to my poor mother who wanted me and wanted my brother to still if we might be chums, but there was hardly anymore anything between us we could find to be buddies about, and I hadn't run up on him and Clarice and their little devilish spawn for a considerable while when my mother passed on and so caused us to come together. They drove down for the viewing and my brother saw fit to arrive with his arms in his coatsleeves and his fine black fedora in his hand while Clarice herself took charge of the affair, held court before the casket with my mother's sundry friends and my mother's assorted relations and managed to bring the low mournful talk around to the news of her baronet who she did not suppose the friends and relations could know her ancestor's sister's girl had taken in holy wedlock.

My brother and I stood together at the door and fielded between us condolences along with occasional fond remembrances of things our mother had said and done, saintly acts she'd undertaken, wise advice she'd meted out which my brother largely received and acknowledged with stately nods alone. He entertained on occasion as well with grace and muted pride compliments from departing mourners on the charms of his son, Leslie Algernon, who'd been loosed to circulate about the mortuary and was performing his customary service of identifying for the people he met their assorted unsavory qualities which the mourners at the door insisted they'd found just too cute and disarming for words.

There towards the shank of the affair my brother grew, I have to guess, afflicted with undue feeling, moved and provoked by the circumstances to a sentimental manner of notion, and he invited me up to spend the coming Christmas with him and his wife, suggested what a fitting tribute it would be to the memory of our dear mother who'd hoped we might be close and wished we might stay friendly. Straight-off, of course, I demurred as I am by nature a demurrer, but my brother persisted and swore that Clarice found me to be just the best sort of chap while Leslie Algernon had surely by now wearied of my unsavory qualities and so probably would not make himself extravagantly impertinent.

I figured I probably wouldn't have to go since it wasn't even close yet to the yule season when we buried our mother in the churchyard and cleaned out her house and sold off her goods, but my brother appeared to believe for some reason that his sentimental invitation was in fact his bond even once his undue feeling had long since evaporated. Consequently, he kept after me to drive on up and pass if I might my holiday with them, show up sometime Christmas eve and stay through Christmas night, and he seemed every now and again on the phone a little like my brother of old and so stirred, I'll confess, and affected me and at last won me over altogether since Wade was gone and our mother was gone and I couldn't truly fashion spending my Christmas with a flatulent dog, a bucket of chicken, a quart of High Life and a Nutty Buddy. So I allowed that I'd come, carried with me a toy for my nephew, a bottle of brandy for Clarice and my brother, set out even a plateful of semi-fermented scraps and leavings for Monroe to gorge on and transform, and I'll confess I was near about jolly as I drove in my Chevette up through Willis and Floyd and on over the ridge at Bent Mountain and down into the valley.

We even all got on there for the first hour pretty well. My brother seemed genuinely pleased to see me and Clarice herself mustered a smile that looked maybe two parts happiness and only one part bad oysters. There at the outset Leslie Algernon let on to be devoted to me until I gave him his gift, a truck I'd bought him with a bed that dumped. He rolled it across the floor once or twice prior to clubbing the thing on the doorframe and breaking it in half.

We took tea in the parlor just as the light was failing and puny drams of sherry as well from dainty crystal glasses. Clarice served shortbread and ladyfingers and spoke of the yuletide traditions among her line of people. She played flute music on the stereo and enlisted me and my brother together to throw in with her on a carol or two. Clarice had trained my brother to take his dinner in a jacket and tie and changed herself into an elegant gown, even trussed up Leslie Algernon in a handsome little outfit that he let on to find bothersome and so seethed and pouted by turns. I could only contribute to my ensemble with the cardigan I'd brought in my sack which Clarice appeared willing to make for me allowances about since I did not after all descend myself from the baronet's line of people and so had not probably been bred but for sweaters and such at the table.

I endeavored over dinner as best I might to make some suitable chat, complimented Clarice's side dishes and asked after the delicate seasoning Clarice had used on her turkey which turned out to be pepper and turned out to be salt. I inquired as to the present state of my brother's affiliation which my brother proved gratified to have occasion to hold forth about and apprised me in detail of his own view that the angle iron trade was in truth a barometer of the health of the nation. Clarice, as was her practice and custom, asked after Karen my wife who Clarice like usual claimed to have harbored an exceptional fondness for. She informed me what a sweet and what a lovely girl

Karen my wife had been and suggested to me with her pinched expression the sort of heel and jackass she was obliged to make of me. Leslie Algernon volunteered the occasional unsavory sentiment and brought upon himself assorted consultations which he weathered and endured and responded to usually with a sentiment even less savory than the one he'd been in the first place consulted about.

We came from the wine to be in time more than a little unconstrained, which should probably have made us giddy and gay, given, after all, the occasion, but Clarice and my brother seemed disposed to waste their intoxication sniping across the table, making by turns charges and acrimonious insinuations and inviting me every now and again to take if I might a side.

It's hard to believe that a fellow might, while passing a holiday evening with his brother and his brother's wife and son, long instead for the company of a greasy flatulent mongrel, but we hadn't even left off with coffee before I was lonesome for home. I just didn't much like my brother anymore now that he was married and affiliated, and I couldn't truly find a thing to care for in his wife and child. I could see of course well enough that they didn't among them have any use to speak of for me, as I was, after all, uncultivated and quite utterly undescended, had no attachments left by blood but my brother himself and our Aunt Connie who called sometimes from Orlando once she was full of rum. So we sat for a great while at the table and then retired at length to the front room where Clarice left me and my brother to drink our cordials and chat while she cleared the dishes and got Leslie Algernon out of his suit and ready for bed. But my brother and I just couldn't discover much worth chatting about and spoke of the weather and the state of the nation, touched once or twice on the Redskins, and then sat and sipped and exhaled and grinned and shifted about in our chairs.

The bed in the guest room was too short for me. My feet hung over the end. The aroma from the dried flower petals and herbs in a shallow bowl on the night table proved stifling and unendurably thick, so I stuck that dish deep in a drawer in the dresser and tried to open a window but they were both of them painted shut. There was a knickknack somewhere that clattered and rattled every time a car went past on the street, and the light from the pole entered in through the part in the draperies and lay in a streak on the rug. I could hear for a time Clarice and my brother exchanging talk in the front of the house, transacting between themselves sharp bits of business that were each of them brittle and brief. Leslie Algernon wailed and cried for a spell and so brought upon himself a consultation, and I managed even to fall for a while into an outright slumber but awoke in the night and lay on my back listening to the hall clock and the furnace and the framing and feeling, I'll confess, a little desolate and undone, wholly unaffiliated, orphaned on this earth.

I showed up come morning at the breakfast table with my sack already in my hand and my causes and excuses formulated and refined, but my brother and Clarice couldn't even manage to muster an objection between them and vented their paltry regrets and misgivings while they as good as shoved me out the door, dispatched me to drive up from the valley and over the mountain and along the ridge where I was alone on the roadway since it was, after all, Christmas day.

This was hardly the strain of interlude I was prone to bring up and carry on about. I don't believe I even so much as discussed it with the dog but just directly endeavored to put that business from my mind and didn't find occasion to dredge up the thing and air it until that afternoon when Dale's sister persuaded and provoked me into a lie. It was a couple of weeks after the funeral, a Friday when I was off and free and was out in my Chevette seeping coolant and burning oil and attempting by means of incontinent speed to incinerate deposits in the carburetor. I hadn't been intending to drop in on Wendle's widow. Her house was just adjacent to a straight, flat stretch of road where I was fond of giving the gas to my vehicle and so raced on by one time and spied her in the sideyard, turned around up at the crossroads and raced directly back.

Dale's sister was working her flower bed, was scratching up weeds and spreading mulch and pinching off dead blossoms. Her little girl Catherine was sitting in the grass playing with a piece of a paver. I parked in the drive and crossed the yard, had concocted a jolly and innocuous thing to say about the beauty of the day and loosed it upon Dale's sister who favored me with a wan smile back and, in reaching to sweep her hair from her face, spread grit across her forehead. I tried to make chat with her child in the grass, squatted and spoke sweetly to her, sought to draw from her some talk of her brick, but she treated me to a bout of gurgling instead and sang me a little piece of a song about a flea and a rat and a beetle.

I figured it might be for Wendle's widow that funny time after a calamity when the mourners have pretty much filtered away but this life has yet to return and take hold. I supposed she'd not probably discovered the mix of grieving and living to suit her, was reeling maybe and shifting still between peace and desperation, though she looked well enough in her sweatshirt and slacks with her hair hanging loose and the grit on her forehead. I watched her pull clover and trowel up dirt and listened as she told me of the kindness of her neighbors who'd carried her food and tended her child, freed her to cast about and grieve, lapse into funks and recover, digest at length the bitter news that Wendle was done for and gone. She told me she guessed they'd get along, allowed she was starting to sleep once again.

I'll confess I'm prone in uneasy situations to blather after a fashion. I mean I feel obliged to make polite and suitable conversation although that's hardly the sort of conversation I'm in the habit of making considering how awful much time I pass with my vaporish gutter feeder. As a consequence, I find I'm given in proper company to commonplaces, parrot observations I've heard on the TV or read in the columns of my glamor monthlies. I like to think I can make them sound as if I believe them a little, and as I loosed upon Dale's sister my regular freshet of bromides I could see she was pleased to take me for an earnest and sensitive creature.

I favored her with a sentiment I'd heard one evening from the anchorman in Bluefield along with a pithy piece of inspirational talk

I'd picked up from a football commentator. I saw fit to air a couple of nuggets from the back pages of my spring makeover issue, and I made some sort of declamation on the topic of national moral fiber that I have to believe I'd pilfered from Mrs. Tyree at the *Ledger*. I let on, in short, to be myself blessed with empathy untold, veritable wellsprings of it, and I set in to speaking of all the dead people I previously myself had known, arrived directly at my mother and was somehow moved and persuaded to tell of the anguish I'd suffered, the long bitter nights of torment and pain which led, I suppose, by association to my Christmas eve with Clarice and my brother that straightoff I saw fit to prevaricate about.

The trouble of course is that while I'm intoning a bromide or laboring to adorn a lie I know in my mind the truth all along. I could see that Christmas in Cave Spring as I shared with Wendle's widow what joy and what comfort I'd found there in my time of abject sorrow. I recounted the songs we'd sung and described the gifts we'd given, spoke at length of the many festive dishes we'd dined upon, the lively talk we'd exchanged, the solace I'd carried away. I'd read somewhere or heard somewhere or been by somebody told how good it was to be in fact alive here on this earth and I favored Wendle's widow with the news of it, assured her that her brother Dale and Dale's own wife and child would do very likely for her and her girl what I'd had done for me. I'd learned from a surgeon on a medical drama of the miraculous healing powers of the human heart, and I passed word of it to Wendle's widow who made out to be eased and let on to be instructed.

She tore with alacrity a weed from the bed and pitched it onto the lawn as she conjured for me her own little scrap of sagacity she'd mined somewhere. I countered with a bromide I'd managed to husband and store and then glanced at my watch and made to be pressed and a little constricted for time. I took fond leave of Wendle's widow, pecked her little girl on the cheek and retired to my Chevette in the drive where I laid my head to the steering wheel and lavished myself with loathing.

You could spy them all about, tell just who they were, those fellows that Dewey had seen fit to visit and make inquiries of. They were given to hobbling a little and engaging every now and again in therapeutic squats intended, I suppose, to stretch and expand those parts of themselves they'd suffered to have compacted. I remarked well enough how they seethed, saw the way they watched me as I rolled by in the cruiser, imagined the sort of remarks they aired, the threats they formulated. Clearly Dewey had been busy on his own. I had to suppose he'd lately passed a considerable portion of his working hours down at the river bottom, out at the speedway, up towards the airfield at the dancehall, had toured about acquainting himself with inseams and alibis.

I ran up on one of Dewey's new buddies outside the Dairy Barn, was coming away with a foot-long when I met him in the lot. He was one of those blonde Whitts from off past the parkway, the least one I think. They were the pack of them evermore drinking and brawling and stirring up mischief, but there wasn't much bloodlust among them and they only usually ever thrashed each other. Plainly Dewey had entered into a confab with this least Whitt. He showed still signs of the strain of it, seemed stooped a little and feeble and sported a contusion or two. I knew him slightly, had kept him once from laying open a brother of his which he'd expressed in a sober moment some gratitude about, but he surely hadn't a kind thing to tell to me there in the Dairy Barn lot, loosed instead a regular flood of ever so colorful invective and gimped on over to put himself between me and my cruiser.

I could see well enough he was irritated, and as I came flush upon him he raised at me his finger and said, "Fuck the whole sorry pack of you. Not nearly enough of you dead."

I inquired what his trouble might be and that least Whitt explained that he'd lately enjoyed the occasion to get levitated.

"Well what is it you did?" I asked him.

"What is it I did? I walked down the street. That's what I did," that Whitt told to me and spat and fumed and half stifled an imprecation or two in advance of venting himself outright. "That fucking Dewey," he told me. "You goddam people," and he spat again and favored me with a look I hope not to forget. He was altogether incensed and utterly indignant, and indignation struck me as an odd thing in a Whitt. I hadn't truly figured that a Whitt could get stirred to it given all the turpitude I'd seen those Whitts about. But this one was hot. This one was riled. This one was insulted, and that least Whitt found cause to wish upon me additional damnation prior to turning about and stepping with care up towards the Dairy Barn.

I watched him until he was in through the doors and then climbed in the cruiser and sat there, identified as best I might my options and my choices and endeavored to weigh and compare them. But I can't say I knew just what I'd best do. I don't ever seem to just know, am not near so decisive as I'd like myself to be. I anguish and drift and falter. I'm evermore casting about. I could see well enough what Dewey with his stick and his grip had accomplished and knew I had that girl now and could pump and cultivate her, but I couldn't truly figure how maybe I'd best proceed and so sat and pondered and fretted and unwrapped at length my foot-long which dripped chili grease onto my shirt.

Ellis had a plan, had worked up at the bottling plant a devious scheme outright which Ellis induced his sister to summon me to hear, let on to be full well intoxicated, sang on the landing a bawdy song and retired to unfreight his hanger which gave rise to the call and the nosetoot, the dispatch from Angelene. He hadn't in fact enjoyed but a swallow or two of rye, enough to perfume him a little, and he played the lush out the door and down off the steps to the sidewalk but threw off the act on the lawn and was advising me already by the time we reached the curb.

He'd figured a way to milk that Crouse, a line we might take with him. He'd as much as scripted the things we should say and was laying over the seatback sharing with me my part when I informed Ellis I'd visited that Crouse, had found in fact the girl herself. I told him about the Wal-Mart, spoke to him of my evening passed largely in ditches, apprised him of the things I'd seen, the things I'd had told to me which Ellis absorbed and Ellis digested, which Ellis appeared to mull and consider in advance of scheming afresh.

I was hardly past the hospital and down off the hill to the Magic Wand when Ellis began to air his newly concocted proposal. It seemed now to Ellis we'd be wise to interview that girl straightaway, and he suggested a line of questioning that he had to figure would suit. I tried to remind him that he was himself merely a civilian, but Ellis just insisted we mount together a fullblown rehearsal en route, and we were still shaping inquiries as I turned onto the deadend road and eased down to a stop squarely before the modest brick house with the slab stoop and the ragged bushes and the doorscreen in the yard, the shovel on the roof. Ellis was wanting to make himself out to be hardbitten and he layed upon the seatback and suggested I call him Dan, had considered the matter deeply and had concluded himself that "Dan" was a name with no nonsense much about it and would suit far better than "Ellis" might.

So as an indulgence I sat there with Ellis and practiced calling him Dan, and Ellis rehearsed his sharp responses until he was soothed and satisfied. There proved to be an impediment, though, as her car was not about. I could see a light burning back in the house and the outside lamp was lit at the stoop, but I'd despaired already of raising her as I stepped to the door and knocked on it. There were glasses in the top panels and I cupped my hands and looked in through one but could see just the sofa and the television, a half-dozen magazines strewn on the floor.

I was a little disappointed, but I was more than a little relieved, while Ellis for his part got straightaway that look he gets when he's scheming and was cultivating plainly a plan as we crossed back towards the cruiser. He guessed that fortune was smiling upon us and in the guise of detective Dan, gruff and steely hard, he directed me to drive the cruiser back up towards the highway and pull there at the head of the road off into a clump of trees where we'd be cloaked and hidden. He guessed he knew what we'd best do, had reasoned how we ought to proceed and set to campaigning for his latest concoction, a species itself of misdemeanor. Ellis proposed that I crawl in through a window and nose around. He figured it likely to yield more fruit than even a blunt interrogation, and he assured me he'd stand out behind the house and hoot like an owl if she came so I could climb back out the window and slip safely into the woods.

Quite naturally I was tempted and torn. I tend by nature to go by the book, abide by the rules and the strictures, but the temptation to snoop is always strong, the chance to pry compelling. So I was not any longer my reasonable self and mounted a halfhearted, feeble resistance to Ellis's sundry provisions. He assured me he'd hoot, would keep a strict watch, and I described for him her car as we slipped in the twilight along the road and parked back in the trees. The windows around back weren't most of them locked or shut and the only screen not torn or punched through was laying on top of a bush. I just stepped up on the barbecue and squirmed on over a sill and found myself directly on the bedroom floor. I stood up and waved to Ellis who answered me back with a chirp.

I took time straightoff to commend myself for the idiocy I'd embarked upon and sketched up briefly my circumstances, allowed how I was standing in defiance of the law in the bedroom of a woman whose crime so far was just to take an awfully handsome picture. I remarked as well that I was acting upon the advice of a fellow whose policing experience consisted solely of having once upchucked on a shoplifting migrant, so I stood a time where I'd ended up wondering if I should bail back out, but once I'd begun to look around and soak in the sights and smell the smells, I was altogether ruined for retreat.

This was surely the place itself. I recognized the headboard, the nightstand, the bureau, the photographs pinched snug between the mirror and the frame. She had a gauzy blue scarf draped over the shade of the bedside lamp and scented candles here and there, fat ones the girth of a waste drain. Her clothes were strewn about. Her pants and blouses and skirts and delicates were cast upon the floor and atop the bureau and heaped in a chair in the corner by the closet. The bed wasn't made. The spread and the blanket had been flung partway off and I could see she'd changed the linens but had yet to find a matching set.

I took directly a general tour up the short hallway and past the bath and into the front room and through to the dining alcove and the kitchen beyond it where I paused to inspect the contents of the refrigerator. She had an old brick of cheese, a scrap of butter, brown eggs in the bin in the door, assorted encrusted condiments, a little flat soda, a few light beers, some fuzz and some grunge on the shelving. I was finding myself persuaded to believe that for all of her allure and sultry charm, she was in fact a bit of a pig.

She subscribed to both of the beauty monthlies I received myself on behalf of the Crowders. There were issues of them laying about along with old copies of the *TV Guide* and catalogs for clothing and housewares. She'd left dishes in the front room on the floor beside the sofa, hairclips in an ashtray on a table by the door, and her shoes were scattered and cast about like seed across the carpet. She'd not troubled herself to hang pictures on the walls and didn't appear to have much taste for standard bric-a-brac but just made do, I guess, with clutter for adornment. I wandered about soaking in the ambiance, such as it was, ducked briefly into the bathroom but retired in fright directly and returned to the bedroom where I ventured to peep into the closet and found it to be little more than a hamper with a door.

I plundered through her nightstand drawer which was full of pocket change and straight pins and loose packets of condoms, and then I shifted shortly over to her bureau and made my way from the lowermost drawer to the top one. Her clothes were all balled up and crammed in tight together and I wasn't truly much inclined to poke and probe amongst them and so quickly worked my way to the narrow upper drawer where she kept her socks and her nylons, her bracelets and her rings, her brooches and her lipsticks and, beyond them towards the back, a regular portfolio of candid color snapshots.

Like everything else they were loose and scattered across the drawer bottom, and I collected them up together in a pile and began to sift through them, turned on the veiled lamp by the bed and sat down to pay them some heed. They were Polaroids like mine but whole and complete, and they were all of her in some state of undress, sprawled sometimes purely naked on her bed but upright every now and again and wearing her clothes cast open and unbound. She was sitting in a few in the chair in the corner posed in unladylike postures, and had been captured standing up out of the tub with bathwater sluicing off her. She always had that smile for the camera, that scornful little grin that somehow seemed to enhance her allure, render her more fetching than the parts and the pieces together could manage or the hot white flash could undo.

I worked one time through the entire pile and then laid them all out on the mattress before me. I'll confess at the first I could see in those pictures little aside from herself, was drawn and enchanted, as much as transfixed by the ungirded flesh alone, couldn't seem to get full past the lobes and the contours. But I managed in time to constrict my juices and throttle for the moment my desires, mounted a modest investigation, considered those parts of the pictures before me that were not glands and allurements. Even then I didn't succeed at first in seeing what shortly I saw, passed over the one of her in the chair with her leg cast up on the arm and had come already back to it twice before I noticed there on the rug in front of the closet door a part of a shoe, a piece of a lace-up, a portion of shiny black oxford. I almost let the other pass, the one with the Crouse in the mirror on account, I guess, of the exceptional pose, the graceful languid sprawl which proved an enduring distraction. But I caught sight of him at last high in a corner of the glass. He had the camera against his face and his head turned full in profile, but I saw him well enough for who he was and set that snapshot aside.

I came across the camera itself under the bed on the floor, stepped by chance on the strap of it and was kneeling to draw it out when Ellis climbed onto the barbecue, stuck his head in the window and hooted to a fare-thee-well. I liked to have shrieked a little as well but contented myself with hopping and leaping, hissed at Ellis to learn from him just what he was hooting about. I feared it was her upon us already and set to collecting the pictures and pitching them into the drawer, switched off the lamp at the bedside and was preparing to slip as best I might directly into the yard when Ellis told to me it wasn't her, told to me he didn't know who it was, allowed it was clearly somebody else and then ducked from the window as the cardoor slammed. I was partway out behind him myself when that boy set to pounding the doorrails, worked and jerked the knob a little and then went back to beating the door. For a time I listened from the windowsill but shortly grew a little emboldened and slipped out the bedroom and into the hall from where I could peek around a corner and see to the entranceway.

This boy seemed peeved and frothy, hammered away with a passion, and I could hear him giving vent to his high feeling out on the stoop. He fumed and he swore and then flailed away further. He took up the knob and shook it so as to near about loose the bolt from the keeper. I was fearing he might just spill on in when he seemed of a sudden to yield up his vigor, grew still and fell silent and contented himself with peering in through the doorlight. I could see just his eyes and a scrap of his hair that fell down across his brow, and you wouldn't have guessed he was wild and impassioned given those eyes alone. They didn't let on he was worked up at all as he surveyed the room with a slow, dull gaze and then withdrew at length from the glass and favored the bottom doorrail with a vicious kick in advance of retiring to his vehicle and slamming his cardoor shut.

I crossed directly to the front door myself and peeked through a pane to the drive in time to see that boy guide his big yellow boat of a car out into the street and up towards the highway which proved itself enterprise enough to inspire Ellis to stand again on the barbecue, stick once more his head through the window and hoot at the top of his lungs that I stepped straightaway into the bedroom and sought to advise him about.

I subscribed myself to the sensible notion that a man hoping to be with a bird noise sly and surreptitious ought probably to make it out in the yard with the birds and not stand on the barbecue and stick his head clean into the house to hoot, and I undertook to impress upon Ellis the virtues of my view, wondered of Ellis if couldn't he see the clear advantages of it, and Ellis appeared to weigh the merits of my opinion, stood there on the barbecue gripping the windowsill in what looked to me a thoughtful and pensive attitude. However, when at last he spoke he just told to me, "Dan."

The chief, I believe, was in danger of suffering some manner of neuromuscular collapse due to the self-inflicted strain of so awful many grim expressions. With Wendle a couple of weeks in the ground and no killer yet brought to justice, no official leads turned up, the chief had little to offer but the faces he could pull, and it just appeared to me that the chore of looking dire and anguished was beginning to wear upon him. He'd developed a sort of a twitch, and I came across him several times in private unguarded moments when the chief had dropped his jaw and opened wide his mouth in an apparent attempt to stretch his face and bring himself relief. About the last thing he needed was a local lawless spree but, as is often the way with this life, nothing happens for years on end and then everything happens at once.

It wasn't in truth a spree exactly but got by Mr. Chapman and his sister Mrs. Tyree promoted as a spree and so came to be taken for one by their readers and subscribers. The whole business at the outset looked to be a three-crime affair, but the first two crimes turned out in the end only one thing together that wasn't in fact unlawful itself only curious and semi-salacious while the third one was wholly unrelated and amounted to little more than the theft of a garden tiller. Mr. Chapman and Mrs. Tyree, however, were obliged to take their sprees wherever they might find them and so set up a regular hue and cry and stirred the population who looked to the chief to pull for them just precisely the sorts of faces he was in poor shape to pull.

In the course of one week at the end of the month we had two people to disappear, a woman from up at Elk Creek and a man from down at Baywood. She got gone on a Wednesday sometime after lunch while he didn't turn up missing until Saturday in the forenoon. She was the wife of a Sizemore who owned a little gas and grocery mart out on 21, and I got sent to see him once he called to report her gone. He'd come home like usual in the middle of the day and they'd had dinner together, butter beans and boiled potatoes and chicken from the night before which that Sizemore spoke of with noticeable relish as he sat alongside me at his dinette and made do this evening with a hamburger bun and a bowl full of some sort of coagulated leavings he'd pulled straight out of the icebox. Her car was still in the shed. Her clothes, as best as he knew, were still in the closet and the bureau. She'd not let on to be planning any manner of escapade. He seemed to recall she'd been intending to fertilize her mums.

She'd taken at the very least her handbag and her jacket, didn't appear to have been just abducted from the yard. That Sizemore called her sister and called their girl Eugenia who couldn't either one say where his wife had gone but determined both together to grow wild with apprehension and came each over shortly all frantic and undone. They were not, I have to figure, entirely themselves and issued by turns directives, advised me of what—if they were me—they'd be about by now, labored to provoke me to mount a search and organize a rescue, voiced together their fears that Mrs. Sizemore had been carried off and likely violated. They guessed at the rate that I was moving she'd turn up probably deer season out in the forest under some leaves.

I endured their talk with what grace I could manage and enjoyed shortly the welcome assistance of Mr. Sizemore himself who deflected the ire and rerouted the baleful disdain by wondering if wouldn't his girl or wouldn't maybe his wife's sister step on over to the range and whip him up a little uncoagulated fare. They were together thunderstruck that he could bring himself just now to think of his own stomach, and they visited upon him some appreciable abuse but seemed in time to grow persuaded that I was doubtless myself a little hungry too.

I had the three of them hunt me a suitable likeness of Mrs. Sizemore and they settled on a picture of her standing in the yard. She did not appear a handsome woman, looked more than a little frumpy and plain, had one of those frosted vertical hairdos and a broad back-side and no ankles to speak of. I carried the thing out to the cruiser with me, made like I was meaning to issue an alert, but I didn't take up the handset straightoff, just instead enjoyed the peace and savored the quiet and went for a while unindicted by the sister and the girl. There wasn't of course much we could do there in the opening hours. I'd discovered no sign of mischief, detected no foul play and couldn't myself know for certain those Sizemores hadn't argued. A friend could have carried her off to the triplex, over to the interchange to eat, and I remember flirting with the idea that maybe her beau had whisked her away for an evening of passion at the motor lodge. But I couldn't long entertain such a thought what with that picture before me, at the time simply couldn't imagine that under that print dress and back of that flab there was very much smoldering going on.

When she hadn't turned up come Thursday evening we put out word on the wire while Mr. Sizemore and his girl and his in-law printed up fliers and posted them about. We had a Cobb from Barren Springs carry his hound to the house, but she couldn't seem to pick up a scent and amused herself treeing squirrels and tormenting the Size-mores' cat. Of course Mrs. Tyree and Mr. Chapman saw fit to publish in the *Ledger* the facts of the case as far as they knew them adorned with all gauges of lurid speculation that served to heighten public anxiety and prompt the chief to a harrowing spate of grim and seemly expressions. So the atmosphere was highly charged and the chief already weary and drained come Saturday afternoon when Mr. Womack's wife called in to report her husband missing.

He'd left Wednesday morning on a fishing holiday, owned a

shack up on the river and was in the habit of whiling away his slack times there. As was often her custom, his wife had driven up Saturday morning to join him; she liked to ride in the johnboat and take a little sun. She'd not, however, been able to discover him about, couldn't find truly any sign of him inside the shack or on the river or anywhere around the property. His truck was gone and his boat and trailer were gone with it. The coveralls he kept in the cupboard alongside the toilet were missing, and his rifle and his fifth of Dickel were nowhere to be found.

Dewey spearheaded the investigation, rode anyway up to the shack and satisfied himself that there was nothing in fact to see, no sign of struggle or strife, a couple of soup tins in the trash, some dirty cutlery in the sink, but not much trace of that Womack beyond them, that Womack who we allowed until Sunday to come home and make himself known before putting him on the wire with the Sizemore and bringing thereby to Mrs. Tyree and her brother Mr. Chapman untold delight. Mrs. Womack provided us with a photograph of her husband, a portrait of him taken a couple of years back for the Methodist directory. He had on a navy blue blazer and a striped tie as wide as a plank. His neck pooched over his shirtcollar, and he looked a little bleary-eyed and dazed like maybe somebody had just shaken him awake. He had a broad nose veiny and vivid from too awful much Dickel I guess and a rakish set of sideburns that extended well beyond his lobes and flared out at the bottom. Following the example of Mr. Sizemore, Mrs. Womack had some fliers printed up and she carried them about taping them to store windows and stapling them to light-poles, attaching them often alongside pictures of Mrs. Sizemore who, on account of her pose and posture, appeared usually to be gazing fondly into Mr. Womack's ear.

Aside of course from Clifford, we none of us had much clue as to what had become of the pair of them. Clifford himself was persuaded they'd been as much as spirited away by dark and nefarious forces. It seems Clifford had attended at the triplex lately a supernatural thriller that had impressed him as plausible and persuasive. Evil in the movie had been loosed upon the world in the form of a translucent topical jelly that entered through pores and brought out routinely the worst in people, summoned up the beast deep inside them and caused them to perform acts of violence and commit assorted senseless atrocities which they came in time to rue and regret once they'd soaped up and showered and undone thereby the effects of the jelly.

Clifford just guessed we ought not discount creams and ointments and mysterious potions that might lie at the root of our troubles, and he claimed to have discovered at the Sizemore house and the Womack fishing shack curious bits of crud which Clifford routinely seemed disposed to speculate and hold forth about but suffered himself usually to be curbed and forestalled by Dewey, who would withdraw his nightstick, assume his grip and announce that he was presently under the spell of a moisturizer.

We went on for days not knowing any more than we'd found out straightaway until Lonnie of all people, in idle conversation with that Sizemore's husband who'd dropped by to see what we'd turned up, learned that Mrs. Sizemore had been after a fashion acquainted with Mr. Womack. It seems Mr. Sizemore had hired Mr. Womack to pump out his septic tank and rid his drainfield of roots and obstructions which, along with ditching and hauling, was Mr. Womack's usual line of endeavor. Mr. Sizemore had only spoken to him on the telephone and seen him once or twice at the dinner hour sitting in his truck in the sideyard eating a sandwich. He'd left Mrs. Sizemore to transact the business and informed Lonnie how he'd been in the end obliged to have an entire leach line replaced what cost him no little piece of money.

Lonnie just came to me wanting to know if wasn't this life odd and strange throwing like it had Mrs. Sizemore and Mr. Womack by chance together and them destined shortly, on account maybe of mischief or account maybe of crud, to up and disappear. He just wanted to hear from me if didn't I find this world of ours too curious for words.

I will confess I was myself struck a little dumb, but shortly I discovered tongue enough to encourage Lonnie to tell to me please everything he'd heard from Mr. Sizemore after which I phoned him up to confirm assorted particulars, established that Mr. Womack had spent the best part of a week working with his tank truck and his backhoe in the Sizemores' yard with nobody much for company but Mrs. Sizemore alone. Still, however, the notion I'd hatched seemed to me awfully farfetched, and I visited the stationhouse foyer, out between the glass doors and the steps to the street, where Mr. Sizemore's daughter and Mr. Womack's wife had taped up fliers side by side. I guess I was prejudiced after a fashion against thick homely people of mature years, was loathe to believe that the likes of Mr. Womack with his nose and sideburns and the likes of Mrs. Sizemore with her vertical coif and her spread could burn together with desire.

I couldn't quite fashion how maybe he'd wooed her, cast back to think of what wooing I'd done and was tempted myself to believe I'd have probably been hopelessly hindered and thwarted outright if I'd been obliged to romance a woman and pump sewage simultaneously. I'd had trouble enough in my day with music and candlelight and couldn't suspect I'd have done much good over the hose of a tank truck or from up on the seat of a backhoe. But then I had to doubt that Mrs. Sizemore had lately found occasion to get wooed since Mr. Sizemore didn't seem to me much afflicted to his marrow with romance.

So maybe Mrs. Sizemore had simply been primed for any little scrap of coy and playful talk, maybe she'd had enough of cooking for Mr. Sizemore and cleaning up behind him, maybe she guessed she'd heard everything he could drop his jaw and say, maybe she'd been anxious for a wholesale alteration and here Mr. Womack had up and come along. I'll admit it was just a hunch and, standing there in the entranceway watching Mrs. Sizemore gaze blandly in the direction of Mr. Womack's hairy ear, it seemed at least a little farfetched that Mrs. Sizemore and Mr. Womack had each perceived charm sufficient in the other to throw in together and abscond. I mean she had a home and a husband and a girl and he had a wife and a truck and a backhoe and a shack on the river where he fished. They had between them every reason to be both settled and fixed but just got itchy, I had to suppose, maybe got weary and desperate.

We had a pool going at two dollars a chance. Dewey and Janice and Harnett had thrown in their lot with evisceration and dismemberment and could look to double their money if any little portion of either carcass were, for whatever reason, shipped through the parcel post. The chief himself had seen fit to wager that Mrs. Sizemore and Mr. Womack had become disoriented and had separately wandered off. He liked to believe they were touring the countryside wondering each of them who they might be. The odds for the chief were most extraordinarily long, longer even in fact than the odds for Clifford who was promoting still an ointment or a potion, some sort of semi-satanic pharmaceutical that had worked its evil magic on the Sizemore or the Womack causing the one to butcher the other which had all struck Lonnie as likely enough, considering most especially Clifford's mysterious crud. Angelene herself had the men in collusion, proposed that Mr. Sizemore, with the aid and compliance of Mr. Womack, had murdered his wife and weighted probably the body with block to sink it in the river. She suspected there was money at the heart of the thing, a policy of some sort to cash in which had seemed likely enough to Gooch as well who'd placed with Angelene his wager.

I'd not settled myself upon a theory until the notion began to take hold that maybe that Sizemore and maybe that Womack had embarked upon a romance and had together absconded which I put forth as a proposition and suffered straightaway no little ridicule about. Clifford and Dewey and Lonnie and Harnett wanted to know from me if I'd troubled myself to study that Sizemore's frumpy portrait, while Janice and Angelene were anxious to discover if I'd maybe yet looked upon the Womack who did not remotely appear to them designed for romance. But I had to guess if Clifford could advocate nefarious topical jelly I could probably make a case for a heedless and lusty attachment between the likes of the Sizemore, with her ankleless legs and her vertical do, and the Womack with the veiny nose and the dandruff on his blazer. By then, of course, they were beginning to me to look to

181

be made for each other, but I couldn't bring anybody else around to throw in with my view.

It proved, then, to be a fairly black day roundabout the station-house when an officer in the service of the city of Belle Glade, Florida, spied that Womack's truck and trailer out front of a bungalow on the shore of Okeechobee. As he couldn't know precisely what manner of mischief he might meet, he called in a couple of colleagues and together they flushed that Womack and flushed along with him his partner in sin and carried them into town proper to establish just who they might be. They posed them beside the water cooler and snapped a picture that they sent along the wire. It was murky, of course, and fuzzy but was plain enough the Womack and plain enough the Sizemore with him. He had on a pair of checked shorts and his shirt was entirely unbuttoned. She was wearing knee-length britches and some manner of strapless elastic top. Her hair had deflated and come un-waved and lay down about her shoulders. The Womack appeared to be growing a sort of a moustache and a trifling scrap of beard, and anybody could see plain there in the gap between them that he was holding in his hand a couple of her fingers.

Clifford had to guess still there was some sort of ointment behind it, but the rest of them went ahead and capitulated outright and determined that since I was myself so shrewd and wily a lawman I could be the one to ride up to Elk Creek and share with Mr. Sizemore the happy news. Angelene allowed how she'd see to Mrs. Womack. She'd wagered after all that the woman's husband was likely a mur-derous scoundrel and so guessed she could let on well enough to find him just wretched and conniving. I carried a copy of the snapshot with me and got Mr. Sizemore up from his dinner with my knock. He invited me into the kitchen and had me to sit at the dinette, offered even to spoon me up a bowl of what he was having. He said it was soup and it was sort of yellow and greasy like soup often is, but it was awfully thin, had some navy beans in it and pieces of carrot and little shredded bits of chicken.

I allowed him to pour me some coffee instead and set about

preparing Mr. Sizemore for the news, informed him that we'd found his wife, that she was whole and well but had fallen in, I told him, with a gentleman he knew, and then I showed to Mr. Sizemore the picture from Belle Glade, handed the thing across the table to him.

He made a sort of a quizzical face there at the first, couldn't seem to reason what his wife might be about standing there in kneebritches and a strapless elastic top in the company of the sewer man whose shirt was hanging open and whose belly was exposed. I saw, however, the dawning come upon him soon enough and Mr. Sizemore unburdened himself of a breath and lifted his face in my direction to favor me with a look.

Of course I'd been laboring for a while myself to devise a suitable thing to say to a fellow put upon to digest the news that he lacks even the personal charm and allure of the likes of Mr. Womack, but I'd not yet concocted a piece of talk that seemed to me apt and proper and so mustered instead a face of my own and a breath that I discharged back. He guessed he didn't know what he'd do, couldn't even begin to say how he might carry on, and Mr. Sizemore gazed about the kitchen, eyed the encrusted pots on the stove and the dishes heaped up in the sink, the sack of cookies and the box of Triscuits over by the bread bin on the counter in advance of turning again his attention upon his soupbowl before him, and he stirred with his spoon the greasy broth and watched a bean circulate briefly and sink.

Were Mr. Chapman and Mrs. Tyree down at the *Ledger* not so pliant and adaptable a pair, they might have been distressed to learn that nobody'd been laid open or hacked into parcel-sized pieces. They'd been rooting themselves for evisceration, some species of ghoulish bloodletting which they'd taken no pains much to disguise in their enthusiasm for the case and their pursuit in the *Ledger* of the story. But they were flexible people and enjoyed both the talent for mining the wealth in most any situation. Sure they were hoping for mayhem but they proved to be fairly delighted to settle instead for adulterous union as they had each a special place in their hearts for encroaching moral decay.

The chief even carried the news to them, thinking they'd find themselves obliged to alter the tone of their coverage since nobody after all had been slaughtered and there wasn't a killer afoot. The trouble proved, however, to be that Mr. Chapman and Mrs. Tyree were ever so willing to take their depravity wherever they happened across it, and they weren't themselves so very sure but that what that Sizemore and Womack had done wasn't worse somehow than evisceration. They invited the chief to consider if he might the deceit and the wanton betrayal, encouraged him to take please into account the fiber of the nation at large. Trusts had been breached. Vows had been broken. Commandments had been cast asunder. They simply themselves weren't entirely persuaded that they wouldn't rather live in a world where people were shipped on occasion piecemeal through the mail.

So just when the chief had calculated that he was himself free from blame, had not after all been elected and paid to police the passions and wayward impulses of full-grown consenting adults, Mr. Chapman and Mrs. Tyree began in the *Ledger* to promote the view that the county was in fact a regular sinkhole of beguilers and iniquitous scoundrels evermore tearing at our underpinnings and eroding our national freedoms. They suspected we were not being suitably led and guided, were not being held to firm enough account for the things we did or failed to do, and they implied the chief was as a custom soft on moral decay which the chief directly felt obliged to cultivate a face about, some sort of stern and sullen contrivance meant to suggest that he had in fact no use much for rot himself. Of course it proved a chore for the chief to devise a new expression, bring nuance to his customary grim display, given most especially his weakened condition, and the strain made him ill and peevish and difficult to endure. Consequently, we determined not to tell the chief straightoff when our local lawless spree persevered.

Mrs. Heflin was set upon by an intruder. That is, Mrs. Heflin claimed to have been set upon and there was for once evidence of legitimate mischief about. She'd phoned to the station in more of a state than usually she was prone to, and Janice dispatched both me and Lonnie to drive out and see to her. While I'd not had occasion to visit Mrs. Heflin since before the night that Wendle was killed, I'd gleaned from the log that she'd called in prowlers a couple of shifts I was off, had spied a drug lord out on the landing with a pistol and a spring-loaded knife and had caught sight at the head of the drive of some stripe of ninja marauder, a fellow in black billowy trousers with his head and face wrapped in a rag. Otherwise she'd had a quiet half month until the night she got set upon there in the small hours.

It seems Mrs. Heflin was reading at the time a gangland exposé that she'd bought off the rack at the pharmacy. It was apparently a gruesome and sensational piece of work rife with all manner of blood-letting, lurid descriptions of gunfights and assorted contract killings. There were pictures as well, grainy stills on slick paper in the middle of the book, and they'd produced an effect upon Mrs. Heflin, had struck a bit of terror in her heart on account of how vicious mobsters, in their suits and hats and topcoats, looked pretty much like every-body else, appeared maybe even a little more savory and upstanding than your regular run of people. She guessed they could be just all over and nobody much would know it which Mrs. Heflin confessed was a troubling state of affairs to think upon there in her still house back in the trees where she read of the exploits and looked at the pictures of the dapper, upright mobsters along with those photos of the lately expired ones who were sprawled usually on the pavement with their fluids running into the gutter.

So Mrs. Heflin had promoted herself into a heightened and fretful state, more heightened even and fretful than was customary for her, and she was restive and agitated this night and dozed in fits and starts until just past one in the morning when she awoke and sat up in the bed with a sense, she told it, of foreboding. She heard a noise out on the lawn, what sounded to be footsteps. They seemed the sort that might be made by those handsome leather Italian shoes that Dons and Capos favor. She reached down and plucked up from alongside the nightstand her length of maul handle and clutched it fast to her as she held her breath and listened closely to the shuffling and shifting about. Mrs. Heflin had once previously heard in the night a deer out pawing her fescue and chewing the bark from her crabapple tree, and she'd taken it to be a Latin counterinsurgent which had proven no end of embarrassment to her once Lonnie showed up to shine his light and reveal it to be just a deer instead. She was not, consequently, looking to make the same mistake again and so lay still and listened for a considerable spell until she was fairly well persuaded that there were scoundrels about.

I have to suppose a wallstud shifted or a floorboard creaked and popped. Mrs. Heflin anyway grew persuaded that one of her thugs was raising the window and climbing in over the sill. She seemed to believe she saw the draperies move and slipped from the bed and crept in her nightdress across the floor to the windowbox where she determined to thrash first and inquire later. So she fairly pummeled those curtains and managed to bring down the rod and bust out a pane but discovered that recessed windowbox to be in fact after all thugless. She spied, however, out across the yard up towards the head of the drive a couple of legitimate perpetrators hauling an item between them, carrying some piece of contraband up into the roadway where Mrs. Heflin observed them wrestle it into the back of a van, one of those cut-down customized jobs with running lights and fender skirts and a little nautical bubble window high in the rear sidewall.

They drove away in a hurry and Mrs. Heflin stood in her nightdress amongst the ruins of her windowbox and watched them go in advance of dialing the stationhouse and thereby refueling our spree. Of course Janice was loathe to believe her straightoff as we were not locally prone to mobsters though they did seem to her more likely than drug lords and ninjas and counterinsurgents. So Janice dispatched both Lonnie and me to ride out and see if there mightn't in fact be a mobster or two about. We arrived from opposite ends of the road at almost the same time precisely and loosed each a shriek on our sirens as we eased down towards the house.

Mrs. Heflin came out on the side stoop to meet us with a quilt wrapped about her and her handle in her hand, and though she was more than a little undone she managed somehow the wherewithal to favor me and Dewey together with a brief but illuminating address on the habits and methods of the Cosa Nostra. She guessed some Capo or figured some Don had seen fit to dispatch a couple of lieutenants down here to do her some mischief. The late Mr. Heflin, she took pains to remind us, had been blessed in this life with considerable starch and she couldn't herself guess but that maybe he'd crossed and offended a thug. She claimed from her reading to know for a fact that thugs never forgot a slight.

We were skeptical, Lonnie and me. We couldn't quite figure just how Mr. Heflin, dead now fourteen years, had discovered in life the occasion to insult a Capo or bring grave offense to a Don. He'd been after all a florist, had a little shop by the post office and did largely business in wreaths and sprays and occasional bridal arrangements, kept what native starch he had pretty well hidden and disguised. Lonnie and I were disposed to allow that Mrs. Heflin had seen some more wildlife, a couple of deer or a dog or two or maybe had heard a raccoon, but Mrs. Heflin objected in frantic tones that she rarely employed for assassins or turks or dusky bucks with their dart tips envenomed on toadbellies. She'd seen the pair of them, she'd seen their vehicle, she'd kept them by dint of her hickory handle from slipping into her house. She had to guess they'd probably hoped to have, as an amusement, their way with her, but she'd driven them off and had watched them retreat hauling some sort of an item between them.

I checked at the road and could see for myself just where that vehicle had sat, and Lonnie found evidence there in the yard that some fellows had tromped about lately which was all very novel and un-foreseen as we'd not before answered a call at Mrs. Heflin's and come across trace of a culprit. We toured as a trio the property, inspected the garage and scanned the lawn and nosed about the brick barbecue but discovered no trace of wrongdoing until we'd passed through the sideyard beyond the cultured laurels to a peaty patch of ground with a wire fence about it where Mr. Heflin in life had planted his beans and his squash and his big boy tomatoes. I didn't myself notice much amiss and Lonnie detected no mischief but Mrs. Heflin seemed to sense that something was wrong and wandered about that garden patch with her handle at the ready until she noticed hanging from a post an ancient galvanized tub with the grips gone from it and the bottom partway punched through and corroded. The sight of the thing inspired her to a fairly extravagant display, and Mrs. Heflin leapt after a fashion about and darted as best she was able beyond that post and around that corner to the place where her late husband's garden tiller had sat with that tub upended upon it to keep off what of the rain it might.

Of course the thing had been stolen. We could see where those boys had dragged it off, the tracks anyway where the tines had caught that ran down around the far post and clean up to the edge of the drive where I guessed they'd elected to lift that tiller and carry it to the roadway. Mrs. Heflin was fairly beside herself with anger and distress and wondered of me and wondered of Lonnie if we could likely either one know the affection she'd had for that tiller, the sentiment she'd attached to the thing since it had, after all, aside from his Toro, been Mr. Heflin's favorite contraption. She confessed, though, that she lacked herself the strength and leverage to pull the cord.

"You mean then you haven't used it lately?" Lonnie asked of her, and Mrs. Heflin informed us that she'd not in fact ever used that tiller at all which inspired Lonnie to calculate that Mrs. Heflin's tiller had been sitting almost a decade and a half out in the weather with just a corroded washtub for protection.

"Bound to be seized up by now. Those boys just junked it for you," Lonnie told to Mrs. Heflin who took pains again to explain to me and explain as well to Lonnie how she harbored herself a warm and special fondness for that machine which she doubted we'd come to understand until our spouses had kicked off and left us with just their contraptions.

The thing that Mrs. Heflin couldn't quite figure was why maybe a Don or a Capo might have call for her late George's tiller, which she

fretted and puzzled about as we circled the house and inspected the
bushes for signs and traces of thuggery but found nothing out of the
ordinary even there at the bedroom window where the mulch was
undisturbed and the screen still whole and secure. Mrs. Heflin took us
into the house and had us look under her guest bed and into all of her
closets. I inspected her window myself and could see that the lock was
fastened and an eightpenny nail was driven through the sash. I collected what broken glass I could find and disposed of it in the trash
bin, and I set to straightening the curtain rod and rehanging Mrs.
Heflin's draperies while Lonnie had Mrs. Heflin sit on the bed and
narrate in coherent fashion the sundry events of the night, tell to him
what she'd heard exactly and tell to him what she'd seen, describe for
him the customized van in the road with the fender skirts, the lights,
and the bubble window.

I was hardly paying them any mind until she up and said it, was
fiddling with the curtains and only half heard Lonnie ask after the
height of the culprits and probe for distinguishing features, something
in addition to the fine Italian leather shoes, and he ventured to submit
to Mrs. Heflin the theory that maybe those boys had come by before
just to see what was about. Lonnie suggested to Mrs. Heflin that
perhaps that ninja she'd spied in the drive or that boy with the sword
in the bushes had been only one of these fellows here scouting around
for loot.

But Mrs. Heflin could hardly see clear to subscribe herself to
Lonnie's theory and corrected him directly about the implement, told
to Lonnie, "Scimitar," and allowed how the man who'd carried the
thing had been a little dark and mysterious and at least a trifle exotic.
"And he drove a big sedan," Mrs. Heflin told Lonnie. "A yellow one,"
she said and allowed how she'd seen it go by on the road, figured he'd
parked maybe up at the dumpster and cut through the woods to get
at her. She still didn't guess she could say for certain why she'd not
been ravaged and filleted.

In the Friday edition of the *Ledger* Mrs. Tyree and Mr. Chapman ran a story devoted to what they elected to call "Mrs. Iris Hef-

lin's Night of Terror." It was a fairly shrill piece of work and exceedingly atmospheric, touched upon even the particulars of the night of terror itself in advance of veering onto the topic of our general moral decay and settling at last upon the sorry and dilapidated state of local civic authority. Of course there was an accompanying picture of Mrs. Heflin taken in harsh, incandescent light, a portrait of her in slacks and a blouse from along about her saddlebags up. The chief let on to be untroubled by the tone of the commentary and made out to harbor yet wellsprings of suitable grave expressions. I happened, however, onto the chief in the washroom late in the day, found him before the towel dispenser working forlornly his mandible muscles.

Desmond goes through phases when he's persuaded that he's portly, most usually a solid month before his annual trip to the keys where I guess he means to be, if he might, slender and alluring. He starts in usually asking me to comment on his profile, pops down from upstairs and knocks on the door, poses for me on the landing. I evermore make as if to find him sleek and willowy, but by the time Desmond has seen fit to pop down he's decided already he's fat. That means of course for Desmond a broiled chicken diet, a moratorium on daiquiris, celery stalks for snacks. But there's only one thing that comes to my mind when Desmond shows up to pose for me. I know then that I'm in for about a month of Dancercise.

While ordinary, aimless, circulating Desmond is surely plague enough, stationary, concentrated, semi-syncopated Desmond is something else altogether. He performs as a custom his calisthenics before his television just above my Naugahyde chair, manages his three-quarter-hour routine with all the dainty grace of a jackhammer and sounds usually to me to be inflicting some manner of structural damage. I keep expecting the Sheetrock to give way or the fire wall to collapse and bury me. He wears a little outfit to Dancercise in, answered the door in it there that first night when I thought he was being attacked and beaten and had rushed up the stairs to his aid to find Desmond in black tights and bright red leggings and with the trunk of his T-shirt cut short leaving his hairy belly exposed. I explained that he'd sounded to me to be in some sort of imminent peril, but Desmond informed me he'd been simultaneously toning his deltoids and firming his glutei by waving about his extended arms and leaping into the air which he indicated an instance of over on the television where the leggy instructor and her charges were waving and leaping still.

So at least anymore I know what it is, have the visit on the landing for warning and preamble, but I can never quite get used to Desmond's Dancercising. The thunderous clamor of it is simply overwhelming, attracts even the wholesale regard of Monroe who sits venting vapors by the laminated table with her snout elevated and her eyes upraised as she waits for the ceiling to give way. I suppose it's all just the price we pay for the subsequent ten days of Desmondless peace while he's off sunning in the keys, but Desmond in training surely takes a toll and inflicts no little distress.

A bout of it happened to come upon us at an unfortunate juncture, full in the midst of my surreptitious investigation when I was in need of my faculties and had call for my concentration. I was in fact passing my first full evening with my new Polaroids when Desmond showed up on the landing to turn sideways and invite appraisal. Consequently, I wasn't permitted by Desmond to reflect and deduce undistracted but was obliged to endure the clamor of Desmond's initial workout while I sat in my chair beneath him and watched the Bluefield newsman's hair in the whitehot studio lights. I laid out my pictures on the chairarm and studied them each in turn, took up the one with the Crouse in the mirror, the one with Wendle's shoe, the original trimmed and excised shot I'd found in Wendle's wallet.

I managed even not in fact to look always at her, scanned the background and the margins, recalled that boy in the doorlight, the one with the bangs and the yellow sedan, endeavored to conjure his face through the glass, made to cement my suspicions, though I have to confess I suffered unbidden visions of Desmond my neighbor bounding about in his half-shirt and tights with his stomach hair catching the breeze.

6.

I think too much. I eat too many fried foods and wear the same socks too often, watch more television than a sensible man should and breathe more dog wind than anybody ought to, but mostly I just think too much when I should by now know better. I simply find I'm prone to believe that people are complex and clever, scheme and connive and calculate and plan to do what they've done. I've always liked myself to suppose that if I were provoked to some desperate act, driven to some criminal enterprise, I'd take occasion to map the thing out and weigh and consider my prospects which demonstrates what little I know of being provoked and driven.

Consequently I've no gift much for proper investigation. I'm evermore wanting culprits to prove at least a little shrewd and devious and so entertain theories and allow for angles that tend to lead me astray. I mean there were nights I sat in my Naugahyde chair with incentive enough for homicide laid out in full color before me, but I couldn't believe that girl alone was sufficient to get Wendle killed, wanted to think there were riches involved or some manner of contraband, kept trying to complicate the whole business with wayward suppositions, I'd simply forgotten what it was like to be a boy in this life, not so much a boy like that Crouse or a boy like Wendle had been but an actual chronological legitimate adolescent, the sort of verifiable boy who drove that yellow boat of a car, smelled like soap and steak sauce, was given to agitation. You see I'd made the mistake of supposing that he was thinking too.

So I wasn't in much of a place myself to foresee what might happen even once we'd found that boy and knew just who he was. Maybe somebody else would have moved in sooner and saved him, saved us all, but I had my angles to nurture and my theories to entertain and could hardly myself hope to predict what probably would come about when I couldn't even make useful sense of what had transpired already. She as much as gave him up, told me who he was, had gotten I think to be herself a little frightened of him and couldn't quite work and reign that boy the way that she preferred. She didn't let on to know what he'd done, and maybe she didn't know it. More likely she simply didn't care as she was finished with him by then and set to move along.

Of course I was meaning to tell the chief, intending to let them all know, and I did in fact discover occasion to put Dewey onto the car, apprised him of how I was after a boy who drove a yellow sedan and suggested it was a grave business without truly allowing just how. Dewey was anxious to do what he could to be a help in the matter and proposed himself to interview what yellow car owners he found and discover thereby the manner of mischief they'd lately been about. So I guess I provided a service in constricting Dewey's scope and supplying him a focus group to levitate and query. But I'd been planning to speak to the chief and lay the thing full out before him, told myself I'd tell it all clean up until the end when I couldn't at last see cause anymore to open my mouth and speak.

Me and Ellis rode round nights working our surveillance, but it was hardly like we either of us only lurked and spied. Ellis regularly took time off to sluice out and scour his gullet while I rode in the cruiser my regular route and policed when called to the population. I attended at a knife fight down along the river, arrived, that is, for the leavings of one, and recovered a stolen Eldorado in a pullout off the interstate just beyond the ridge. Me and Lonnie together quelled a dispute at the roadhouse up towards Fries where a couple of fellows had differed as to the murky intentions of a female patron who'd proven herself too drunk to declare which one of those boys she was meaning to bed.

I had myself no end in fact of duties and distractions, and I pulled my shifts and went about my regular line of work, just spent some free nights off in the ditch back of the bush with Ellis where we together performed our surveillance on that house with the door in the yard, the shovel up on the shingles. We were hoping the boy with the yellow car would pop by again for a visit, but he didn't happen to come around while we were keeping our watch and would likely have been himself left just to kick at the door once further and glare again through the glass since that girl didn't turn out to be much disposed to pass her evenings at home.

She'd come by, we had to figure, from work and would freshen herself and change her clothes and be often gone again already by the time we eased into the ditch. So we'd sit and hull peanuts and trade fabrications and chase by turns that spotted dog back up towards the highway where he'd see fit to loiter until he got to feeling sleepy again. I heard at length about Ellis's duchess with assorted revisions and per-mutations, and Ellis shared with me erotic techniques he'd gleaned from his wealth of relations, but I didn't collect much information per-tinent to the case and wasn't truly certain from listening to Ellis just where exactly he meant a man might lay the tipend of his tongue and induce thereby some unambiguous rapture in a woman. Ellis simply wasn't much up on proper anatomical names and phrases and so failed to promote his erotic techniques with any precision to speak of.

She must not have usually come home until sometime in the small hours since she rarely returned before we'd decided to pack it in for the night, though she did happen back an evening or two while we were still about, arrived on both occasions with a gentleman in tow.

That first night, Ellis saw her coming, had gotten out to stretch himself and iron with his palms the creases in his handsome clawhammer jacket when she turned in off the highway in her little blue Toyota and with her headlamps chased and drove him on back into the car. We both together laid low until she'd passed us by and were obliged to stay both scrunched and hunkered while she lingered at the culvert down along the drive and waited for the boy who did directly join her, some fellow in a 4x4 who pulled up in the yard. I didn't recognize him and Ellis didn't know him. We couldn't say between us if we'd seen his truck before though she made straightaway herself to be acquainted with him, greeted him on the driveway with a singular sort of embrace, laid one hand upon his neck and saw fit with the other to trail her fingers down his shirt and grip him at his buckle.

She appeared to give him a little push, worked and turned him like a mule and sent him towards the landing where he was made to stand and wait while she unlatched the bolt and then ushered him into the house and shut the door behind them. We couldn't see anything of them to speak of, had a view of a piece of the mantel through the front and a portion of the dining room wall through the side and now and again we'd manage to spy a little scrap of somebody, but we were chiefly obliged to content ourselves with lascivious suppositions, proposed by turns what we expected they were probably about and charted each of us the course we imagined their amours were taking.

My personal version of events was highly economical in keeping with my nature and my own experiences, and I had them naked on the bed coupled in consummation almost before Ellis could figure they'd left off with their cocktails. He gave that boy credit for being an accomplished romantic force with an altruistic interest in giving rapturous pleasure which, as a consideration, served to slow and hinder Ellis, and he was mired up still in foreplay when the camera first went off and the flash lit up the bushes at the far end of the lot.

We attempted to wait that boy out but he failed to accommodate us, and we left for the night with the 4x4 parked still in the yard. I stayed away for an evening or two but was called upon late in the week to drive out west of town and enforce a restraining order, remind a Hege that a lawful and duly authorized judicial decree had been drawn up and processed to keep him from stopping whenever he pleased at his ex-wife's house to piss on her peonies and hose down her columbine, which that Hege every now and then just managed to forget. So as I was a little out towards Whitetop anyway, I determined to swing on by that girl's house and see if maybe I could get lucky and find that yellow sedan, and I guess I enjoyed after a fashion some manner of fortune as she was sure enough entertaining a guest.

I saw straightoff his truck in the yard, the little imported variety all trumped up with chrome and oversized tires and extravagant suspension, and I sat there in the middle of the street where just anybody might come upon me and tried to reason how much of a throttling that Crouse would have to endure to get to be sufficiently curbed and instructed to go maybe deaf to his urges. I mean I know there are the sorts of men about who are essentially quiff-propelled, and I figured that Crouse was very probably prone to follow his nose, but how many times can a fellow need to trip on a root in the woods before he gets illuminated or broken at least and tamed?

I suppose that I was prodded at last and provoked to take some action by the news of Dewey's liberal view of just what made for yellow. Dewey professed himself no grasp much of primary colors and at length allowed that beiges and creams and assorted shades of greens and blues all looked yellow enough to him given a suitable light, or rather newly hobbled members of the general population began to stop in at the stationhouse and allow it on his behalf which bestirred the chief to inquire what Dewey was about, and I did not know how long in fact that we could put him off. So I prepared myself to confront her the first evening I was free, and Ellis joined me for it, came reeling off the porch and uncorked a vile remark for the benefit of his sister who'd been led by Ellis to believe I carried him in my leisure hours to the pancake house at the interchange and filled him full of coffee and flapjacks with whipped butter which had served of course to advance me in Ellis's sister's regard. She tended most nights to advise me what a saintly creature I was.

We were on our way to Whitetop when we met that girl on the road, and I brought my Chevette around sharply and followed her towards town. She drove up past the fish house and beyond the Magic Wand, proceeded on by the Hop-In and the bank and the remnant shop and turned just past the triplex into the lot at the bowling lanes where I eased around to the side of the building and parked hard by the dumpster. As we watched her get out from her car and cross over towards the landing, Ellis collected the wind to confess that he'd not, in his assorted evenings of sitting in the ditch and observing her abode, ever once suspected her the type for league play which I allowed was pretty much the case with me as well.

We were a fairly conspicuous pair there in the doorway of the bowling lanes. Ellis most especially garnered some regard since, here in the modern day and age, hardly anybody bothered anymore to bowl in evening wear. So Ellis earned for the both of us appreciably more perusal than we wanted or required, and I expected to cast around and find probably that girl herself soaking us in as well, but she didn't appear to be about. I didn't see her down around the ball returns or at any of the scoring tables or up by the register and the rental desk, didn't see her anywhere at all and sort of eased about the vicinity in an effort to turn her up and discovered in fact just where she was before I actually laid eyes upon her.

I saw a fellow watching her. He was standing by the bar in this little saloon they had off at the far end of the alley. It was up a couple of steps from the main floor, and they served chiefly beer and hamburgers and kept the place tidy and welcome. This boy was leaning against the barrail drinking a High Life and looking off towards the booths along the far saloon wall, was paying the sort of heed that only a creature like her could inspire, was moving his gaze along her length and settling temporarily on those features that happened to catch his fancy. He shifted about and made once or twice to be watching the television, but he evermore came back to favor her again with his regard.

I stepped around to where I could see into that saloon a little better and found it to be fairly full of men pursuing a common course of study. Even the ones in the company of women appeared a trifle distracted and leered at their peril towards the far wall where she'd settled into a booth. I caught at last full sight of her in fact and just for a time watched her along with the pack of them otherwise who largely persevered at their semi-surreptitious perusal, drew on their bottlenecks and tended to their butts but kept shifted and situated about so that they might only roll up their eyes to see her. It wasn't like she was mounting some sort of gaudy display. I mean she was hardly preening and puckering and favoring indiscriminately the clientele with pouty, come-hither gazes. No, she was just sitting there nursing a watery light beer and amusing herself with the bottlecap which she flicked with her foremost finger to send skidding across the Formica.

She just seemed to have a fairly mystical effect since there was no clear cause for men to be so routinely smitten with her. Looking at her there in the bowling lane saloon, I couldn't see much reason why she should prove magnetic even as I felt well enough the pull of her myself. I've had, of course, occasion to reflect upon her charms and consider as deeply as I might care to the nature of her allure, and all I can figure is she filled a niche that otherwise would have been vacant. You see we have no end of proper women about, the sort raised right by decent people, polite and mortifiable creatures who can surely be tempted to transgress but are too well acquainted with guilt and shame to take much pleasure in it and have a way of regretting the things they sometimes relent and do even before they manage in fact to full well finish doing them.

We have of course our share of sluts on the opposite end of the spectrum, the Spivey sisters being themselves a pure and prominent instance. They are together essentially glands with appetites for wine cooler and embark upon services and engage in transactions to make each their way in this world. We just aren't blessed with too many girls who occupy the middle ground there between belle and slattern, which I have to guess is largely why she seemed so rare an item as she was handsome and presentable yet careless as well of what the general run of people might happen to think about her. She didn't attempt to disguise her itch and was hardly ashamed of indulging her urges.

She struck, consequently, the men about as exotic and unforeseen while the women appeared inclined themselves to seethe at her instead and were likely as not to favor her with that sour, constricted expression that seems often enough to serve for women in the place of an outright blow. It proved just about impossible to be indifferent to her. Nobody local anyway could appear to pay her no mind, and as I stood there in the bowling lane looking into the saloon I could see for myself the sort of attention she was able to command just by sitting alone in a booth and playing with a bottlecap. The men about watched her when they thought they could be sly at it and the women winced and puckered when they figured she might see. They all, that is, paid to her their personal regard and suggested acquaintance with that girl's reputation, her talent for seduction, her taste for Polaroids.

Ellis was the one to spy that Crouse off at a table short of the bar. He appeared to be primping, tugged at his locks and tested the hang of his hair, looked to have had more cuts to close and a couple of bruises to fade though he was still a little unsightly even across the way. I had to figure he'd soon rise and attempt at least to join her, lacquer her with his manner of charm and settle on into her booth if I didn't move to prevent him and leave the way clear for myself. So me and Ellis figured and schemed and determined at last to fetch him out the best way that we might, concocted between us a ruse and set it into motion. Ellis, that is, entered the saloon and closed upon the Crouse to inform him that he had a call on the phone back by the toilet, that his wife was on the line in a wild and frantic state which served well enough to spur that Crouse who charged out of the saloon and down the little hallway towards the public phone where he only at first saw the receiver that hung still in the cradle but managed at length to broaden his scope and take me in as well.

"Hey there, bud," I told him, and that Crouse who'd been glib with me and short with me before, that Crouse who I'd allowed to say most anything he pleased snorted and glared and looked to me to be building to a remark which I saw fit somehow to interrupt and move to frustrate him at.

The chief had attended a seminar in Meridian, Mississippi, where he'd made himself acquainted with a manner of restraint, a wicked bit of business that a fellow with his fingers might inflict upon the windpipe of a restive restrainee. We'd all been obliged to learn the thing though I'd never myself employed it except for that time when me and Dewey set upon Clifford in fun and levered and restrained him as a sort of an amusement. I mean I'd not had yet a practical occasion to make any use of the technique, and I can't say I'd been lurking there hard by the phonebox devising a plan to spring out and catch that Crouse at the throat. It was just an unpremeditated sort of an undertaking, and I was probably as surprised myself as that Crouse could likely have been to find of a sudden his windpipe snug between my fingers.

The effect was almost magical. As I stood there holding that Crouse at the throat and watched him struggle for breath, he began in a manner of speaking to wither and to shrink. He turned as well a little purple on account of the constriction, but largely my impression was of a man deflating, a fellow enduring his pluck and bluster to abandon him all at once. That Crouse grew ever so agreeable and attentive to my wishes and desires, let on to be inclined himself to entertain my views, and failed to make to be so much as even the least contrary as I shared with him my notion that he might best hurry home.

That Crouse allowed Ellis to escort him out of the bowling alley, and I watched them cross to the double doors, prior to looking on while a left-handed woman rolled a strike outright and managed a difficult spare, and then I stepped on over to the entranceway of the saloon proper and endeavored to propel myself directly up the stairs.

I hung back, however, and loitered, inquired after my intentions and reconsidered my plans, simply saw fit, as is my custom and habit, to hesitate and draw up short. I just happen to count ambivalence as probably my favorite emotion, and I'm often given to finding a way to run hot and cold together.

By the time I'd managed to climb the steps she was spurning an advance, visiting anyhow some torment on a fellow in loafers and poplin slacks, a boy with a sort of a weaselly moustache and a labor-intensive coif, the type who looked to sell for a living some item that nobody had cause to buy. I couldn't hear precisely what she told him but could see well enough the effect of it and gauge the alteration since he came pretty much to look as if he'd had his windpipe constricted and he ever so sheepishly withdrew, retired straightoff from the field.

I'd worked up a sort of an introduction, was meaning to refresh her as to where we'd met before, remind her of how I'd been the one eyeing the whisks at the Wal-Mart, when she forestalled me from speaking by wondering herself, "Lawman's league night, is it?" And she gave her cap a potent flick and bounced it off the ashtray.

I tend to smile at handsome women, am likely as not to lay wide my lips and present a jolly grin when I mean instead to slay them with a measure of cunning talk or divert them with a delicate dose of clever repartee. The trouble seems to me to reside chiefly with my tongue which is often enough a useful and obedient sort of an item but becomes headstrong and mulish at the most unfortunate junctures. Consequently, I've found it best simply to lay wide my lips and grin until the spasms pass and the saliva gets replenished. So I sat there across the booth from that girl wanting to cut loose and turn a phrase but fearful, if I dropped my jaw, of just what might come out.

She was placid enough herself, sipped at her beer and fingered her cap and considered me at her leisure, waited for me to tell her whatever I'd come to tell and looked set to sample if she might my own species of banter, but I couldn't myself oblige her and so only looked at her back until I determined I'd likely best draw from my pocket the items I'd carried and lay them before her on the Formica to see how she might respond. I set them out one at a time, the two whole ones first and that pared down, well-thumbed piece of a picture beside them, and I observed her to see if maybe she'd give anything away.

But she didn't so much as suggest surprise or indicate dismay. She just seemed a little unhappy with the general arrangement and moved and shifted those pictures about until they suited her better, put the clipped one in the middle and the whole ones on the ends. Subsequently, she took up each in turn to study it more closely and was looking at the one of her in the chair with her leg thrown over the arm, the one with the piece of Wendle's shoe off at the edge of the frame, when I managed to bring myself to speak, saw fit to ask her, "Who are you?"

"Me?" she said and laid that picture back where she'd plucked it up from. "Why I'm just a girl who can't say no."

"I mean what do they call you?"

"Red," she told me and then picked up the clipped and pared-down picture, ran her finger along the scissored edge.

"Well Red," I said to her, "you take a fine photograph," which I guess I meant to serve for cunning and make do in a pinch for clever, but she held up the shot with the Crouse in the mirror, high up where just anyone might see, and announced how she did not much care in fact for that exposure herself.

"My eyes are about closed," she told me. "I look a little flabby."

Ellis arrived just in time to see that picture as well. She indicated with her fingerend just where she guessed she could stand to do a little slimming and toning up. Being a gentleman, Ellis of course protested straightaway and held forth as to just how svelte she looked to be to him, indicated in the Polaroid an ever so admirable contour which Ellis paused to allow me occasion to throw in with him about. Him and that girl together shifted to look upon me and as much as invited me if I might to name my favorite flabless part which I mustered pretty directly my jolly grin about, managed in fact my jolly grin alone until I succeeded at wondering of Ellis if wouldn't he maybe retire for the moment as me and that girl had been ourselves just in the middle of something.

Of course that girl could hardly see why anything she might tell to me she couldn't just as well turn round and share with my wine steward, she called him, and she reached out and tugged with her fingers at one of Ellis's shiny plate buttons which pretty much had the effect of setting Ellis off, Ellis who announced it was queer and peculiar how much that charming young thing before him put him in mind of a woman he'd met previously on a train. I suspected he was meaning to speak of her lineage, feared he was hoping to tell if he might of the cramped, contorted rapture they'd conspired together to enjoy, and so I moved to intercede, wondered of Ellis if didn't he feel like stepping to the bar and having a beer.

"Thank you," Ellis told to me, "no," and he went on to wax rhapsodical as to the heady, intoxicating effect of the sleek, well-formed creature before him.

"Ellis," I said and endeavored as best I was able to be emphatic, "why don't you go bowl a frame or two, rent yourself some shoes." But Ellis confessed how he had in truth no love himself for bowling.

"Ellis," I said, "step on if you will out in the lot for some air," and Ellis appeared to me likely to speak of his disinclination to breathe when I said to him once more, "Ellis," and secured at last his regard, pulled even enough of a face to persuade him to admit that a cold beer after all might just hit the spot.

So he left us at last and she set straightaway to speaking to me of him, applauded his features and the cut of his coat. She lamented that nobody much was graced with manners like his anymore, and she sought to learn from me who he was and where I'd turned him up, but I suggested that maybe we ought to speak of somebody else instead.

"Well officer," she said to me, "who might that be?"

"How about Wendle," I informed her. "You remember him."

"Do I?" she asked me and sent her beer cap skidding across the Formica.

"Used to come round," I told her and tapped with my finger on the portion of oxford in the picture of her in the chair. "Doesn't come round anymore."

"Wendle?" she said to me. "Wendle," she told to herself.

"Had a stick, had a badge, had a gun. Wendle," I reminded her and shortly she made to recall in fact an acquaintance with such a fellow.

"About yea high?" she asked me as she made an indication with her nose. "Kind of thick around the middle? Thinning on the top?" and I nodded myself in confirmation. "Oh that one," she told me. "I can't say he's been by in a while. What ever went with him?"

"I found a piece of his head in a bush down along the branch near the highway. Came across the rest of him off in the vines up at the edge of the woods."

"Dead?" she asked of me and feigned an expression of abject shock, pulled a face of ever so gaudy highblown consternation.

"Oh yeah," I told her and suggested that she'd probably read about the thing in the *Ledger* or heard about it maybe on the radio, though she allowed directly that she often failed to keep up with the local goings on.

"But you'd made his acquaintance," I said, "and Wendle, he'd made yours," and I invited her to eye with me if she might herself in the chair in the corner with her clothes in a pile on the floor and her leg flung over the arm.

"I'm a friendly girl," she told me. "I meet no end of people."

"I see you are," I told to her back. "I imagine you likely do. As a matter of fact I'm hoping you can point me to one of your buddies. He drives a big yellow sedan. He's hardly more than a boy."

"Is there any other sort of man about?" she inquired and took up her bottle, sloshed her backwash in a way that served to annoy me.

"You think this is all just foolishness, don't you? Me here nosing around on account of some fellow who happened to get dead and some fellow who happened to kill him. What do you care. You're a friendly girl. You meet no end of people."

"That's right," she told me and shook that bottle just one damn time too many as I was provoked to reach out and catch her at the wrists, hold her hard and tight.

"Who the hell are you?" I said to her. "Where in God's name did you come from?" And I jerked her so as to make if I might a stout impression, caused her to lurch and exclaim, vent anyway noise enough to set off all the boys about who rose to their feet as a body. Even the ones with wives and dates got up out of their chairs, and they all of them glared in my direction and made with their chins and shoulders, with their knuckly hands that they knotted and clenched, to be each prepared if called upon to thrash the life out of me. Ellis at the bar seemed full well set to do me no small damage, and I guess they would have raced to see who could dismember me first if she'd favored them with a look or a cry, just any little indication that they could be of service.

Of course I turned her loose, purchased I imagine my salvation by opening my hands and allowing her to draw her arms free, and she favored me with that little grin of hers I'd come to know, that paltry, disdainful curl of the lips with just a trace of amusement about it.

"Aren't they ever so quaint," she said and managed by gazing around the saloon to return those boys to their ease.

"Well, I'm not blind," I assured her and studied for a moment the pictures on the table, looked for a bit upon her as well. "There's no mystery much to what they see in you, but what in the world do you see in them?"

"Oh they've got charms enough, officer, and here and there you'll find one that's slick and even clever."

"Wendle?" I said. "That Crouse?" I asked her.

"Here and there," she told me. "Just here," she said, "and there."

I advised her how it seemed to me an awfully large net she cast to take in so few keepers, and straightoff she saw fit to wonder how I myself had come to be expert in her affairs. Then she looked for a time with renewed attention upon the snapshots before us prior to raising her head to favor me with a wholly unsettling gaze.

"You," she said at last when she spoke. "You," she told me at length. "Back of the bushes, off in the ditch. You," she said again. "I'm hardly blind myself."

"Been getting an eyeful, have you?" she asked and of course I offered my protestations and aired my strident denials but she just smiled at me after her fashion and made me to feel considerably other than slick and less than clever. She offered to arrange if I liked an occasion where I could hide myself under her bed or lurk if I cared to out of view in her closet and observe relations between herself and some fellow of my choosing if that was the sort of an enterprise that tended to work up my lather. She was soft, she confessed, on men afflicted with wanton inclinations.

"I'm with the police," I told the girl. "I look into bits of business."

"So you've been sitting off in my ditch back of my bushes policing?"

"That's right," I said. "We've had a man killed. We've got us a homicide. You admit you were acquainted with Wendle well enough, and I figure maybe this boy with the car had a thing to do with the killing. I'd just like to speak to him if I might. Tell me who he is."

She confessed that she'd not ever herself had much of a memory for names, but she allowed that she could usually call up physical details, faces, she told me, and the like. So I offered up what little I knew of that boy with the yellow sedan, his height and his hair that hung in the front almost to his eyes. I added how I'd heard he was a fellow with fiery passions, a boy with a bit of a violent streak who'd impressed well enough his disposition upon at the least that Crouse. "This one here," I informed her and laid my finger to the Polaroid, the one with the Crouse plain in the glass, the camera against his face.

"Oh yes," she told me. "Boys, boys, boys," she said and wagged her head as if to suggest that some things were a puzzlement even to her.

She couldn't recall his name outright, doubted she ever knew it, but seemed to remember he went by Buck or Buzzy or Buddy or something. She was persuaded his people ran a bank, had gotten that somehow in her mind, recalled they lived up on the bluff in one of those fine old houses with the stone chimneys and the tiled roofs, the grand porticoes and the terraced grounds.

"He's a little high-strung," she volunteered and suggested how it appeared to her that he was accustomed to having things play out usually to suit him.

"And you flung a wrench in the works," I offered and earned for myself one time further that bilious little grin.

"I hate to be the one to tell you this," she said and drained off from her bottle a dainty dram of beer, "but I suspect you're a little more like me than you'd probably care to let on." I guess I squirmed and shifted and made plain my dissent since she saw fit to tell me, "Oh don't let your bunghole pucker and knot. I just mean there are only really two sorts about. There's people like us who can't be happy unless we're running the rodeo, and there's people like them," she told me and with a nod took in the patrons about, "just looking to mount up and ride."

"So that's how it works, is it?"

"That's how," she said. "Either you go round policing or you stand to get policed."

"And you go round policing."

"As best as I can tell, this life's just one big manhunt," she told me and bounced her bottlecap off the sugar jar.

She offered up how Buck or Buzzy or Buddy, whichever he was, had turned out a manner of hybrid, came from a line of people accustomed to cracking the whip but was, on a personal level, inclined to allow himself to be driven. She wondered if couldn't even I comprehend the conflict bound to ensue, the internal struggle of Buck or Buzzy or Buddy, whichever he was, his torment and confusion, his assorted throes and pangs. I decided, however, to volunteer an alternative opinion and suggested that maybe the boy with the hair and the big yellow boat of a car had just been obliged to go around with his sap up for too long and as a result had suffered his brain to get strangled a little for air.

"So," she told me, "that's how it works."

And I informed her that sometimes that was exactly how, let on to have known men's juices and hormones to full well intoxicate them and drive them to all manner of unlikely undertakings.

"If you're trying to tell me a man can on occasion think with his dick, I'll have to confess I'm stunned and a little flabbergasted." And she drew down her beer and burped for godsakes and announced to me that she was in fact ever so mortally shocked.

I just let it go, just let it pass and asked her if maybe she had about a picture of that boy even if only reflected in the mirror over the chest, but she was quick to apprise me that the photographs were hardly intended for her and served instead as keepsakes for those fellows she came to know.

"Memories," she told me, "of love."

"Love?" I asked and she offered in reply a gesture with her hand, a slight, wavering movement meant, I believe, to communicate her low regard for pure precision in matters of the heart.

I told her I figured she simply might have squirreled away a picture or two. "You know," I said, "trophies," and she informed me straightaway, "Ouch."

"Just keepsakes, huh? Just memories," I told her, "of love. And you think that'll feed and hold them, a little evidence of the act?" which sparked her to that smile of hers I didn't have much use for. "Hell of a thing to be doing just now."

"I told you already, I'm a friendly girl."

"Yeah, you meet no end of people."

"I'm fond of these boys in my way."

"I can see you were nuts for Wendle."

"After my fashion," she said.

"After your fashion," I told her and so as to keep from reaching out and jerking her again, I slid from the booth and stood to my feet, looked about at the patrons who were paying me still some regard. "You must think they can't bite back, or do you just figure they won't?"

"I can't say I think much about it at all."

"No," I told her, "No. I don't suppose you would."

And she suggested as I turned to leave that next time I was back of the bushes, parked off the road in the ditch, I ought to pop in for a visit, stop by for a little talk, she told to me, or something.

On my way down the steps I called over to the bar and invited Ellis to come on if he was coming, and he trailed me the breadth of the alley and out into the lot, allowed me even to sit for a time in silence in the car before he undertook to probe and began after a fashion to inquire, set to fishing for what she'd said, what she's said about him. He wanted to hear if she'd told me much that he could construe as adoring, was anxious to learn if she'd seen fit to speak of her regard, and I informed him I didn't intend to find him out at Whitetop, come across him in the bedroom playing the shutterbug.

"You stay away from her," I warned him, and I made it plain I'd thrash him myself, do him some genuine harm, made it plain I'd very likely even tell his sister which so thoroughly rattled and stung him that he dropped off in a funk, sprawled and moaned and pulled assorted long and woeful faces, let on to be full well inclined to languish in despair which induced me to confess she'd been admiring of his jacket, and I made out to recall that she'd found him slick and clever.

"Did she?" Ellis wanted to know.

"Oh yeah," I told him. "She did."

There was nobody else much up on the bluff but Rumsfelds and Tillmans together along with a household of imported Farradays thrown in for variety largely. You see the Rumsfelds and the Tillmans had between them accumulated most of the wealth to be had about. They counted among their holdings the furniture mill and the lumber yard, the Ford dealership on the truck route, and the savings and loan in town, and one or the other of them owned the shopping plaza outright and collected rent from the Revco and the Pic 'n' Pay, the Diamond Mine and the Wal-Mart. They had a pair of feuding mausoleums out in Gooch's memorial park where most everybody else just laid under slabs, and they'd seen fit in tandem to give to the city a tract of land that they'd timbered and graded which the town lacked the funds to further improve and so had left it to come to be pretty much a monument to erosion.

I can't say I personally knew any Tillmans or was acquainted myself with a Rumsfeld beyond of course the one they called Dink who's developed a talent for sloth and an appetite for fortified wine. They tried for a time to straighten him out, packed him off to private hospitals and prestigious institutions where notable doctors and therapists attempted to implant some gumption, but Dink just usually came back with his color a trifle improved and his belly a little larger from the wholesome regular meals. He evermore started in again with whatever he'd been about, went back to whoring and drinking and stealing from his father, and we'd find him blind one place or another and carry him up to the house where I guess his people just grew weary of having to take him in and so devised some means of disposal that I've yet to come to know.

They just got rid of him somehow, shipped him I guess away or hired perhaps a professional to prepare him for the mausoleum where I figured sometimes they'd shut him up and gotten him out of their hair. He didn't, at any rate, show himself around town anymore and beyond what Clifford gleaned from a cousin, we never knew where he went. Clifford happened to stop one time a Rumsfeld on the bypass, a girl with an expired county sticker who Clifford quizzed and Clifford queried and heard consequently from that cousin that Dink was off on holiday, that Dink would not be back.

They kept to themselves that way rich people do, spread on occasion some money about in a charitable sort of a way and showed up every now and again on the social page of the *Ledger,* but they largely ran with a different pack than the most of the rest of us ran with, and they rarely found cause to call in the law, settled most usually their own disputes, resolved the bulk of their quarrels and had early on set a useful example for the thieving scoundrels about, had hired some boys from out of state to track down a fellow who'd hot-wired a Ford and driven it off of their lot. They found him, I believe, in South Carolina and presently shipped him back to us more than a little chastened, I'll call it, and persuaded of his error. So everybody pretty much left them alone and they rarely bothered to come down to mix but just kept to themselves high on the bluff where you couldn't even so much as see their houses except from the far rise beyond the river, high on the knob where the road leveled out. If the wind was right you could even sometimes hear scraps of talk or music, and one evening I recall I saw from the knob a Tillman or a Rumsfeld or a Farraday chasing a dog across his yard with a rake raised over his head.

I made a few special amendments once I decided to visit the bluff, had Lonnie to wait for me back down the hill while I drove ahead to scout around for that yellow sedan. I just figured with the two of us it would seem a proper and serious business, a unit-wide sort of an undertaking and not just me alone come to the bluff on a lark. It was nearly dark when I eased the cruiser up through the masonry gateway and in among the houses and grounds. I didn't have much notion myself as to who lived where precisely except of course for Dink's own people with the elm in the yard and the rose arbor. The still and the quiet up on the bluff were fairly arresting together. No noise came up from town below and I could hear just the birds and the grit on the street as I slipped along the roadway and I looked up the drives and across the yards and in when I could through the windows.

The truth is I almost didn't see it as I was watching a woman upstairs next door fiddling with her earring, standing in her slip with her hand to her lobe, and I couldn't somehow bring myself to not look at her anymore until I'd nearly passed it. But there the thing was sitting next door partway around a wing of the house and hidden a little by the shrubs but not so much that I couldn't be sure it was a sizable yellow vehicle. I parked down front at the edge of the road and walked up the drive to inspect it, found it to be a Cadillac, one of those models well after the fins but long in advance of the shrinkage. The windows were tinted. The tires were new. The thing had been buffed to a luster.

I called Lonnie up to join me and laid out just where he was to stand and what he was to do, told how he should lurk back and choke off his remarks or just whisper to me in confidence whatever he might have to say. We wanted, I told him, to be polite, to be ever so proper and seemly, and I instructed Lonnie to pay careful mind to that boy if he was at home, watch what he did and observe how he looked and heed the way he responded. I let on to be suspicious myself that he'd been up to some grave mischief. So we advanced together up the walk and I found the chime and rang it. A Rumsfeld answered the door, a semi-ancient, doddering model in an old white cardigan that he appeared to have fairly incinerated with cigarette ash or coals from his pipe. There were sizable stains here and there as well as if he'd maybe extinguished himself on occasion with helpings of casserole.

I believe he was very nearly stone deaf though he never came out and told us as much, but his responses were always a little askew and evermore wide of the mark as if he hadn't quite managed precisely to hear just what we'd asked him. So I put to that Rumsfeld questions about the Cadillac in the drive and he made to me answers I'd hardly sought on topics I could not quite fathom, but he seemed otherwise a sensible creature and gazed with patience upon me as I tried to make him understand just what I wanted to know which all produced an effect upon Lonnie who'd been, as instructed, lurking back but stepped up to confide how he was himself befuddled beyond recall.

A woman came out from somewhere off in the depths of the house and joined Mr. Rumsfeld. She was of such an age that she might have been his daughter outright or by marriage. A man anyhow could be forgiven for not detecting straightoff that she and the Rumsfeld were wed themselves since she hardly acted towards him like a wife, didn't let on, that is, to be familiar with the Rumsfeld but just came up to stand alongside him as if he wasn't there.

She was, I guess, a handsome woman that way some women are handsome, most especially women of leisure who seem on occasion to manage to make of their upkeep an occupation. She was awfully thin, not fit so much and sleek but just wiry and underfed, and she had one of those rigid defiant hairdos that might crack or shatter but would surely never muss. Her dress was becoming and simple and looked a fine item even to me, and she wore pearls around her neck and a diamond on her finger and whenever she moved her bracelets tended to slap together and ring. There was something forbidding about her. She was too old to be ever girlish again and too young to be yet a grand dame but appeared to be pretty well hard set herself to call back the one and forestall the other.

Lonnie stepped up and attempted to confide to me some manner of news, but as nothing much had transpired and few queries had been put, I didn't suppose I was wanting myself to hear just yet from Lonnie and so rebuffed him after a fashion, made signs enough and gestures sufficient to send him back where he'd stepped up from while I embarked myself upon a delicate line of talk, endeavored to learn if there was perhaps a boy about somewhere who answered to Buck or answered to Buzzy or answered maybe to Buddy, and I provided what physical description I could, guessed at his height and spoke of his hair, and endured from Lonnie a spell of throat clearing that earned him a meaningful glance.

Mr. Rumsfeld, in an effort, I suppose, to cooperate with the authorities, delivered himself of some manner of wholly inconsequential remark, provided me with a piece of news about one of his neighbors across the way who'd suffered a rabbit to eat his lilies until he'd caught the thing in a trap and drowned it in his fountain. He set then to prattling a little about his personal affection for wildlife which earned him a corrosive glance of his own from his wife alongside him who informed me at length how her husband was deaf, how I seemed to be speaking of Walter, their boy.

Lonnie seemed full well afflicted with phlegm and coughed and wheezed and honked a little until I turned and squelched him so as to entertain from Mr. Rumsfeld's wife a comment about their Walter who was lively, she said, and full of spunk and evermore into mischief that way, she told me, boys will be. She suspected I knew what she meant, wagered I'd kicked up a fuss myself back in my own salad days.

"Is your son here at the house?" I asked her and Lonnie behind me near about choked but recovered from his distress in time for me to hear Mrs. Rumsfeld inquire why I might want to know, ask after the sort of hijinks precisely I figured their boy had been about.

This, of course, was the troublesome and thorny part of the enterprise since I couldn't just come full out and say how I was myself persuaded to think their Walter had shot a man twice in the face. It seemed, however, safe enough to suggest that maybe her boy Walter had witnessed by chance the crime without implying that probably he'd seen it from back of the hammer and back of the pin. So I told her, in case she didn't know, what lately had happened down by the branch, told her, in case she hadn't heard, just who it had happened to, and I allowed how we'd been led to believe that her boy Walter had been about in the Cadillac in the drive. We thought he might have seen somebody, hoped he might have heard something, had come by to learn if he could tell us what maybe he'd happened upon.

She stood for a moment and appeared to be considering what I'd said, undertook shortly to speak on her own, as much as declared to me, "Walter," and directly from up on the landing he told to her, "What?" in reply and I lifted my head and saw at last what Lonnie had been dredging and wheezing about, spied him there at the head of the stairs where I had to suppose he'd been standing a time and watching us talk in the foyer. I can't truly say how she saw him herself since her back had been to him the while, don't even know that she saw him at all though she knew well enough he was there, and they managed together an odd sort of chat. I mean she never in fact turned around but just looked instead at me as she spoke, as she told him what I'd told to her, narrated for him the bulk of our business in a loud, flat, unmotherly voice.

In the end I proved to have no need for Lonnie much at all since from down where I stood with my back to the door I could study him on my own, consider the play of his features as his mother told him the tale, described the grisly encounter down on the road by the branch which did not appear to disturb or affect his original slack expression. He just stood where he'd been standing, looking like he'd looked, and failed to appear much disposed to exercise his features. He simply gazed a little dully at the back of his mother's head and told to her, "Yeah," on occasion when she paused to allow for a Yeah, when she sought to discover if he was in fact digesting what she said.

I'd like to say I gained some sense of the sort he was at heart. I'd like to claim I managed to plumb and penetrate his depths. I certainly watched him close and hard, as did Lonnie behind me, and maybe we should have come away with more than we carried off. Anymore Lonnie tends to make out he was onto him from the start, that a look alone informed him of all he needed to know, but I'm hardly even persuaded myself that Lonnie is onto him yet. I have to believe I was looking for him to do what I might do, act anyway at least that way that culprits around here act and favor me from the landing with a twitchy, strident denial. But he wasn't like me and wasn't in fact much like many culprits about, notwithstanding how he tended to seem just a regular sort of a boy planted there up on the landing in his sneakers and his jeans and gazing down at the sternend of his mother's lacquered coif.

He looked pretty much like I'd once looked, was fit and sleek and bony and had bangs that he flung to situate, jerked his head to arrange. So it was natural, I guess, to figure that maybe he'd think the way I'd thought back when I was lanky and hard and too awful fond of my hair. He proved, however, to be in fact deficient after a fashion, and I imagine I could have watched him for days and failed in the end to detect it. You see I was on guard for even just the merest sign of regret, not so much a show of guilt or an indication of shame but only a feeble trace at best of practical remorse. I didn't truly require him to care that he'd done what I figured he did. He just had to bring himself to wish that maybe he'd best not done it if simply to forego the inconvenience of officers in his foyer and the ever so troublesome prospect of a trial and a conviction. He had to fear just what we might see fit to inflict upon him, had to have a thing he wanted to keep that we could take, a way of going through this world he hoped he might preserve.

He just had to be like people are and the truth is that he wasn't. While he looked himself a regular boy, an ordinary sort of fellow, he proved inside to be hollows and reaches and no firm ground to speak of. He wasn't, I don't think, evil. I don't even believe he was mean. He just happened instead to be empty, had managed to get somehow cored. Where we are the most of us guilt and shame, avarice and longing, he was chiefly disregard leavened with adequate vanity to keep him tossing his hair. How could I have guessed at that? How could I have seen it?

He never said anything much at all. His mother said everything for him. She allowed that we were permitted on occasion to make mistakes, show up at places we shouldn't go and pry where we'd best not be prying. She talked to us like we were schoolboys, scolded us after her fashion, and let on to be willing in this instance to let the whole thing drop.

There came to Mr. Rumsfeld's mind a neighbor up the road who he wasn't persuaded to believe he had awful much use for either, liked in fact a good deal less than the one who'd drowned the rabbit, and he was casting about to attempt if he could to recover the reason why when his wife stepped past me and swung wide the door so that me and Lonnie might plainly see where we were intended to go. Lonnie retreated straightaway, backed directly out onto the porch, but I stood firm for a moment or two and soaked in those Rumsfelds before me, the Mr. in his shabby sweater, the Mrs. in her encrusted do, and up on the landing Walter their boy with his hands shoved deep in his pockets and his hair, for all of his enterprise, hanging straight down in his face.

❦

The chief counted himself a connoisseur of apt and seemly deportment, laid claim to a personal instinct for what one best ought do. He preferred to believe he'd instilled in his men a certain sense of refinement, liked to think that in delicate matters he could rely on our judgment and taste, had trained us to know who we'd best never trouble with our presence. So probably I would have been in deep with the chief the following morning when Mrs. Rumsfeld called to the station hoping to have with him a word. But the chief was away at a conclave, had gone to a conference in Charlotte where he'd been enlisted to test with his peers a teargas delivery system and was scheduled himself to speak at the banquet, had prepared, according to Clifford, a rousing salute to Mace.

At any rate he wasn't around to hear from Mrs. Rumsfeld, and Angelene took down her message and brought it directly to me which was hardly her custom and practice but Mrs. Rumsfeld had set her off, had talked to her like an imbecile, had talked to her like a fool, had said her own name four times together lest Angelene be at all deceived as to who was on the line. She'd set forth item by item the barbs of her displeasure which could largely be reduced and distilled to the fact of lawmen at her door, the fact of lawmen in her foyer, the fact of lawmen harboring suspicions against her son.

Apparently she'd paused here to make quite clear to Angelene that her son just happened to be himself a full-blown Rumsfeld too, Rumsfeld which it seems that she'd seen fit at last to spell. So Angelene hunted me up to say a Rumsfeld wanted my pelt. "R-u-m," she told me, "s-f-e-l-d," and I allowed how I'd attempt as best I might to watch myself which seemed on the face of it pretty completely hopeless to Angelene and she favored me with an altogether skeptical expression which I guess was meant to remind me of the way that Rumsfelds worked, Rumsfelds, that is, and Tillmans together whose assorted designs and wishes existed often enough like smoke and seeped and filtered wherever they pleased, touched and tainted whoever they might.

"R-u-m," Angelene informed me, "s-f-e-l-d."

So likely I would have served for the chief as a source of no little displeasure, probably he would have invited me to join him for a chat, called me into his office proper and shut behind me the door so as to lay before me not simply my latest affront but all of my transgressions, as he was wont to do. He'd remind me of that boy I'd caused to pass out at the triplex, the woman I'd pulled at the interchange who'd claimed I'd made a remark, those fellows from the sawmill I'd let off with a warning—the ones who'd wrecked the buffet out at the Western Steer—and he'd lament my inability to master the inseam lever, the playful tone I seemed to him to favor on reports. He'd wonder why I couldn't be a grimmer sort of lawman, advise me to take some care to watch the way that Dewey worked.

However, he wasn't around to hear what lately I'd been up to, was off with his brethren in Charlotte celebrating riot control. So I figured I had a day at least to mull my sorry prospects, to discover a way to explain to the chief just what I'd been about, and it seemed I'd be presented with occasion for rehearsal since Clifford had gotten wind enough of something odd afoot that he'd begun to nose around and make of me inquiries. He'd learned that Dewey had been out lately trolling for sedans and had managed in fact with the aid and assistance of the last remaining sweet roll to extract from Lonnie a murky account of his foray to the bluff, heard how he'd been instructed to stand with me in a foyer and watch a boy at the head of the stairs toss and fling his hair. So Clifford got piqued and Clifford got prodded and Clifford got hungry to know what was up and put to me queries and suppositions, hypothetical formulations, conclusions he'd found cause to draw already, theories he'd cultivated, staged in fact a regular pageant of squandered penetration and labored, I felt, to dazzle me with wayward strains of thought.

I auditioned on Clifford a modest assortment of semi-legitimate facts in hopes that I could get some feel for what the chief might say, but that was like beating a pig with a stick to see if a dog would bite.

The worse news was that Dewey had discovered a boy with a car, some fellow from out past the airfield in a renovated Impala that, under the lights at the car hop, had looked to Dewey pure yellow, hadn't anyway seemed to him green until only after a while. Dewey allowed how it would have likely turned out a harmless encounter but for the fact that that boy proved to be an awfully cheeky sort. Dewey inquired if I was acquainted with his own opinion of lip, and I confessed I seemed to recall that he had little use for rejoinder, no personal threshold, truth be told, for quips and wry asides.

"We tussled," Dewey admitted.

"Tussled?" I inquired, and straightoff Dewey favored me with a devilish manner of grin.

"He had a girlfriend with him, some buddy in a Ford. He was wanting to amuse them, was just looking to be cute. I couldn't persuade him to tell me even the first simple thing outright."

"But you fixed him," I said to Dewey, and Dewey allowed that he had.

"He drove me to it," Dewey insisted. "He wouldn't let anything lay."

"Aw Dewey," I said, but Dewey assured me this boy from out past the airfield didn't himself come very likely from anybody much to speak of. "Probably that trash that lives out by the quarry. You know how they can be."

"I got trouble already up on the bluff. I just don't need that boy of yours to set up a fuss as well."

"I could speak to him," Dewey proposed.

And I told to him, "No, Dewey," told to him, "no. I really don't think you could."

It just looked to me that I was destined to hear at length from the chief, and throughout the morning I set to reliving my history of chastisement, all those times I'd been by the chief taken aside and advised, summoned to find him hunched over his blotter signing letters or reading reports. He'd permit me just to stand for a time and watch him at his work but would presently pay me some heed, raise up to see fit to wince as a means of suggesting, I have to suppose, the bitter suffering I'd inflicted. The chief had a way of crossing the room to shut the door behind me, a way of crossing back to his desk and settling into his chair which evermore touched off in me a sublime sense of dread that no dressing down he might concoct could possibly live up to. He'd get shrill of course and unsavory once he'd started in, but there at the first, in advance of the talk, a fellow could be persuaded to think that doom was surely high.

I suppose I was faced with at least a full day of delicious anticipation, a reliable twenty-four hours before word got back to the chief that I'd been behind an unbidden visit to the money atop the bluff which was the species of transgression to truly set him off. I couldn't be sure he'd manage to keep sufficiently calm just to breathe and make his stately way to the door, his stately way back from it. But I proved to have no leisure much to dwell upon my prospects, attended a collision in the turning lane out front of the remnant shop and fetched a besotted Reavis home from the superette where he'd eaten the most of a package of wieners and then stretched out full in the meatcase to take himself a nap. I investigated the thievery of a cement lawn adornment, a toad in a chair with an umbrella that turned up in a ditch, and I arbitrated a dispute between a couple of Dog Ridge Pfaffs who'd become embroiled in a quarrel out at the DMV.

Dewey, pulling a double shift, relieved me just past six, and I stopped for some chicken and carried it home, was planning a quiet evening. I parked by the dumpster alongside Monroe who'd nosed up a rotten tomato and a rancid chunk of fat and had discovered a puddle of nectar in a sinkhole by the curb. Desmond had lately come to favor some stripe of Teutonic opera, had gone on a sort of Germanic jag and was inclined to play excerpts and extractions that tended to feature strident sopranos in the throes of some semi-melodic distress. I could hear, however, my television if I turned the knob dead loud, so I sat this night in my Naugahyde chair and ate supper straight from the box as I caught the shankend of the Bluefield news and the bulk of the worldwide report.

The pseudo-magazine show was featuring an actor, a brawny type famous largely for his muscle tone though clearly he enjoyed as well a wealth of teeth and hair. He'd purchased lately an estate that he was proud to own and took the correspondent roundabout the house and grounds, showed off his furnishings, his pool, his stable and his gym, and he trotted out his present wife who joined them on the lawn to contribute, when the need arose, sympathetic noises as that fellow revealed the strains and demands attendant to being him.

With no little effort and appreciable guile, the correspondent prevailed at length on that actor with the torso to speak if he might of his upcoming film which was set, he told it, on an ore-rich planet in the galaxy of Andromeda where him and his buddies find themselves obliged to take part in a mining dispute with unsavory beings from Ektar. That fellow with the teeth and hair and the present wife on his arm, couldn't say when last he'd had a script touch him to his core the way this ore rights treatment had managed itself to touch him. He felt the thing to be saturated with passion and with truth, and he was praising the man who'd designed and manufactured the Ektarians, who were latex largely with people inside and looked like silverfish, when my telephone rang and so drew me away from him and his wife and his grounds and brought me into earshot of Ellis's sister instead, Ellis's sister who offered to me the wan and pitiful toot she most usually reserved for Angelene, most usually reserved for Janice.

It seems she'd figured since I was myself Ellis's own special friend and had taken particular interest in her brother's sorry affliction that she'd call me directly to tell me he was drunk.

"He's loaded?" I asked her, and she assured me that he was gone with rye, had broken a piece of crockery in falling against the hutch and had vented a scandalous proposition at the weather girl in Roanoke as she was standing beside her map explaining an occluded front.

"Let me just talk to him," I suggested and she supposed I might as well though it seemed more likely to her that flapjacks would serve better and a tour of the county with the windows down and a pint or two of mini-mart coffee. But she went ahead and put Ellis on the line and I told him how I was meaning to pass my evening in peace at home couldn't figure what purpose we'd serve sitting in the ditch or interviewing that girl again, troubling ourselves with that Crouse. I informed him I'd come across the boy with the car, the boy with the hair and the temper who'd stopped by that night and kicked at the door, but I hadn't found him much of a help and was allowing again that maybe we'd do just as well at home when Ellis, who'd not but breathed so far, saw fit to offer reply, delivered himself of one of his more lengthsome and resonant belches, loosed over the phoneline the manner of noise an Ektarian miner might make.

"Ellis," I said, "are you drunk for real?" and Ellis directly favored me with some manner of declaration that was long on spit and volume but elsewise sorely wanting, and I was asking him to repeat himself as he threw, I think, the receiver, bounced it off the floor or the wall and left his sister to fetch it up and plead for me to come.

So I wouldn't even have gone out, would have stayed at home and not had occasion to see what I saw, do what I ended up doing if not for the way that forces conspired like forces sometimes will. I ate the rest of my slaw from the cup, finished my whipped potatoes and plucked my windbreaker off of the knob as I proceeded out into the lot. I deposited the better part of a thigh against the curb by the dumpster where I meant for it to spoil and decay and become thereby a savory snack for Monroe that greasy mongrel who was licking at present the residue off a hamburger wrapper and favored me as I passed with a glance and a dose of extemporaneous vapor.

I did a little carburetor work along the way, was guilty on the truck route of undue acceleration and incinerated, I have to think, at least a deposit or two before I turned up past the Magic Wand and

climbed beyond the hospital to Ellis's sister's street where Ellis's sister
came down to meet me halfway across the yard and spoke, as was her
custom, of the perils of hard liquor, fretted as to what just might
become of Ellis her only brother. I comforted her as best I could,
assured her that out of all the drunks I'd personal cause to squire, Ellis
was doubtless the pleasantest one, was clean and polite and outfitted,
clearly, like no other local inebriate which Ellis's sister appeared in fact
to take no ease about but favored me still with her knotted, her pained
and constricted expression as she led me up across the porch and
steered me into the house where I climbed the stairs to find Ellis
standing alongside his chair.

A fellow can sometimes arrive at a place where even a tale of
inflamed abandon and coitus in a railway toilet holds no charm much
for him. Full well saturated with rye, Ellis was of an inclination to cast
back fondly and reminisce, ply me again with the very yarns he'd plied
me with before, the ones about his member and where he'd found to
put it, the ones about the boys he'd known with members of their
own. I wasn't, however, of a mood to listen this evening to Ellis even
though I could usually sit with grace through whatever he had to say.
Maybe it was gas from the chicken and spuds, dread on account of the
Rumsfelds, some corrosive and unsettling combination of the two. I
just know I was uneasy and ill disposed to hear of Ellis's amorous
duchess who'd straddled the water taps.

As a consequence I made an alteration in our route, decided to
break with custom and head directly for the mini-mart. You see
usually straightoff I carried Ellis the length of the bypass and back,
drove him at carburetor-scouring speed with the windows rolled down
to ventilate him as prelude to the mini-mart brew since I was persuaded it might be cruel to spring that concoction on anybody who'd
not been roused and made ready first. This evening, though, I couldn't
dredge up much in the way of compassion and drove headlong down
the hill and onto the truck route proper where I turned north past the
branch bank and the Pizza Hut and the tire center and cut up behind
the Pontiac lot on the short route to the interchange, came out there

at the middle school and pulled onto the highway where Ellis was reminded by the scent of the bushes in the schoolyard of a woman he'd met on another conveyance, a woman he'd met on a bus who he threatened to conjure and began to describe with exhaustive anatomical precision.

So I was a little benumbed and I was a little distracted while racing with Ellis under the overpass and up the rise towards the mini-mart. I mean I wasn't terribly sharp and attentive and can't say I was paying much mind to my assorted fellow travelers as I pulled into the turning lane and stopped there at the light. It's possible, then, I wouldn't myself have taken notice of them if Ellis, in casting around for an adjective to suit him, hadn't happened on his own to spy that yellow sedan. It was up a little ahead of us in the adjacent lane, and once Ellis caught sight of that vehicle he said to me, "Hey!" a couple of times in a tone that hardly suited the salaciousness he'd been about.

So I swung around and looked for myself at that Cadillac up ahead of us in the thru-traffic lane though all I could see of the driver was his near hand on the wheel. I eased forward a trifle, allowed my Chevette to roll until Ellis and I could make out together just who was driving that car. I'll confess I'd expected probably those bangs or maybe that lacquered do and was more than a little surprised to find that Crouse behind the wheel. Ellis for his part vented himself of a supplemental "Hey!" and appeared disposed to comment further or exclaim at least again when pressing gastric considerations caused him to belch instead.

I couldn't tell who was with that Crouse but could see he wasn't alone, made out a piece of somebody beside him—a part of a shoulder, a bit of an arm. I was torn as to what I might best do, was half inclined to toot my horn and make myself known to him, was of a mood to demand outright what he might be about and show him the fingers I'd only lately crushed his trachea with. But then I was tempted to lay back and watch him in secret as well and hadn't quite reconciled myself to the one or to the other when that Crouse put an end to my quandary for me, turned his head what, I guess now, was only as far as he dared and showed to me and Ellis the near side of his face. His eye was fairly closed again. He had a knot on his brow and a gash along his cheekbone that had bled in some profusion clean down onto his neck, was seeping clearly still. He was just a gaudy, pulpy mess as best as I could tell.

Directly as the light changed that Cadillac shot forward and I endured from Ellis instructions and proposals as to how he figured me and him had ought best to proceed. He seemed to be anxious we stay put and charge ahead as well, was a little too besotted yet to know just what he thought and so objected and applauded both as I slipped out of the turning lane and followed that yellow sedan up past the mini-mart, beyond the shoe outlet and the pancake house, out of the bright mercury lights roundabout the junction and into the dusky failing day. I could see from behind there were three of them—that Crouse back of the wheel, that Rumsfeld against the far door, and her between them sitting straight up with her hair hanging loose to her shoulders.

Ellis was anxious to hear what I guessed they were about, was growing fairly frantic with all manner of misgivings, confessed how he was likely not competent himself to tangle with the sort of boy who'd tangled with that Crouse. He wondered if shouldn't we maybe best stop and phone downtown, fetch Dewey out to join us and help us with the case. Ellis owned up to an admiration for Dewey's gifts and talents, that way he had of raising people clean off the ground.

I reminded Ellis of the effect I could have upon a windpipe and fashioned with my fingers my windpipe-crushing grip which Ellis did not find he liked so well as a baton, suspected the boy who'd beat that Crouse could get by without breathing. He was apprehensive that me and him would end up thrashed ourselves and began to grow, from fear and rye, tumultuous and frantic, wondered if I was aware myself of the sort of toll a beating might take on a fellow with looks like his, a fellow who tended to make his way on charm and on appeal. He didn't care what they were up to, hadn't from the outset liked that Crouse, encouraged me to fall back and observe them from a distance, not press so close, not tail so tight. I figured I'd best ought to soothe him and so reached into the glovebox and drew out from under the roadmap and back of my windshield scraper my .25-caliber pistol with no bullets and no clip, my scant and dinky firearm that I showed off to Ellis, neglecting of course to tell him how I'd nothing to load it with.

"What is that?" Ellis wanted to know, and I was pleased to identify it as in fact a gun, but Ellis objected and Ellis disputed, insisted he'd had cause to see guns before and knew just how they looked.

"It's a pistol," I told him and showed him the hammer, showed him the trigger and the bore, advocated it was indeed an outright lethal item, but straightoff Ellis scoffed and ridiculed my gun and we entered together into an acrimonious debate, argued the relative merits of such a minuscule firearm, which served in fact to put Ellis off from that Rumsfeld entirely, Ellis who grew inclined to speak of guns that he had known which led to talk of a woman of his acquaintance who'd packed in her purse a Browning, a woman he described at considerable length from the blousefront down and back.

Ellis, then, was engaged in a fashion and hardly took much notice as I turned off the blacktop back of that Caddy, followed it down an oiled road that went over in time to gravel. It was bordered by pastures on both sides that gave way to woodland at last as we dropped down off the spine of the ridge towards the branch bottom below. I laid back as best I might, figured I knew where they had to be going, allowed them to stay a bend ahead and watched the brakelights through the leaves. Ellis recalled he'd been fond of that woman, the one who'd owned the Browning and, lubricated like he was, he got to be remorseful that he'd ever let her go, aired with feeling his regrets, appeared inclined to blubber, set in to cataloging assorted of his woes and ills which wouldn't, he figured, be his lot had he not thrown her over. He was working himself into a state by the time I pulled off the road and parked just back of that Cadillac in a little clearing at the head of a trail.

They were gone already from the vehicle. I climbed inside and poked around, found a cup from the dairy barn under the seat, a black shoestring and a slotted screwdriver in the glovebox with the manual. Ellis had sufficiently collected himself to be fretful and uneasy once more, and he charged me to explain if I might just where those people had got to.

"Through here," I told him and led Ellis down to the mouth of the trail where I warned him he'd best check himself and rein in his misgivings as we couldn't go unnoticed were he to fret and whine. I earned in response a smart salute, and Ellis followed me past the locusts, through a crease in the fledgling oaks and down to the ruins of the rolling mill with the branch and the trestle beyond it.

They were out on the span already, stepping from tie to tie. She was in the front and turned her head to speak once or twice to that Rumsfeld who was walking behind her escorting that Crouse, clutching a handful of hair. I couldn't hear what she said to him or what he said to her back. The night was coming on and the bugs about were setting up a fuss. The branch even made, with its trickle of water, a little racket itself. They drew up and stopped in the middle and stood for a time along the rails. That Rumsfeld appeared to be holding forth. That Rumsfeld who I'd watched on the landing saying next to nothing at all looked positively chatty out over the branch on the trestle, spoke at some length and waved his arms in considerable animation which was when we got sight of it, and Ellis leaned in and told to me low, "Now I'd say there's a gun."

It turned out to be a .45, an ornamental model plated with nickel and etched all over, had handles of genuine pearl. That Rumsfeld's daddy had bought it at a show, had never even shot it, forgotten that he owned it. When later Dewey carried that pistol to the bluff, he said that Rumsfeld held the thing for a quarter of an hour, turned it about and examined it and said only presently, "Oh."

Squatting in the scrub, lurking behind the leaves, me and Ellis watched that boy wave his gun about. He didn't look hot exactly, hardly seemed crazed and undone as he lectured that girl and that

Crouse together who stood by both and allowed him to speak at whatever length he pleased. They suffered themselves to be instructed, were advised, it would seem, where to go stand. That Crouse anyway stepped out between the tracks while the Rumsfeld escorted that girl to the rail, helped her to climb up onto a girder and perch herself on a steel tie high above the branch. He was very nearly gallant and courtly, took great care to see that that girl was suitably situated prior to setting back in with his monologue, pacing about on the trestle, working his arms and airing his views which me and Ellis, from back in the scrub, could hear the noise of a little.

Notwithstanding the plated pistol, he looked inclined just to talk, appeared inexhaustively supplied with personal views and opinions. And it wasn't that I was faltering in my faith that he'd done Wendle in. I guessed still he could kill, assumed he'd killed before. Plainly he had the gun and potential victims handy, but he didn't seem worked up enough to use the one on the other. You see I thought he had to be all fiery and indignant, eaten up with jealousy and palpably enraged. I supposed maybe even I could see fit to kill a fellow myself if he'd managed to stir and anger me beyond my normal bounds, but I guessed I would do it at the height of passion, be altogether wild and out of my head. This Rumsfeld was almost sedate, paced about on the trestle, struck professional poses, and approached in time that Crouse and favored him with a word. That Rumsfeld anyway said a thing and that Crouse picked up his pulpy face and appeared to make reply. You might have thought they were only trading news about the weather, might anyway have thought it until that Rumsfeld raised his daddy's gun and laid it to that Crouse's jaw, touched him with the bore of it and squeezed off two quick rounds. Then he just turned and stepped away.

I believe I even knew already everything was changed, that nothing would be for me again the way it had once been. There in the scrub, back of the leaves, I felt the chill straightoff. "So this," I recall informing myself, "this is what people can do." You see it wasn't so much the act; I mean we've been killing each other forever. It was more the manner, the tone of it. I'd seen a polite, a civilized slaughter—calm, deliberate, efficient—and directly I was scarred, directly I was branded. Doubtless for stretches I'm able now to put from my mind that it happened, but I don't believe I'll ever for even a moment forget that it can.

Ellis stood up, couldn't apparently reason what else to do. He gurgled a little, wheezed a bit and shortly gave us away.

"What!" he yelled toward the trestle. "What!" he turned and screeched at me and raised his arm to point down where that Crouse now lay. Plainly stark murder and Old Overholt didn't much blend and mesh, and Ellis grew directly a little unhinged on account of what he'd just witnessed, that crimson cloud of atomized fluids and exiting sludge and nuggets, the collapse of that Crouse who'd as much as caved in and lay partway atop the timbers, partway dangling between. Ellis made a low and mournful noise and stepped full onto the trail where that Rumsfeld watched him from down on the trestle and that girl on the girder watched him as well.

I stepped out shortly alongside of him, drew my pistol from my trouser pocket and attempted to mount a display and stage an exhibition, was hoping my gun would look from the trestle like maybe some manner of firearm. After eyeing us, however, for just a few seconds that Rumsfeld went back about his business, set in, that is, to speaking once further to that girl on the girder before him and began, it appeared, to grow emphatic and work up a measure of feeling. He almost yelled a time or two, made agitated motions and stepped back over to that Crouse to fire into his carcass.

Ellis was torn between his desires to whip some butt and save his hide, was outraged and terrified together and figured I should be the one to take charge of this business since this was precisely the sort of thing I was paid to mix in with. Consequently, he gave me a little push, attempted to goad me with a shove and suggested to me, "Go on," suggested to me, "Fix him."

I eased down to the old railbed but was obliged to step back and

curb Ellis who'd set to yelling threats and provocations at the Rumsfeld out on the trestle, the Rumsfeld who turned and fired a shot up
over us into the treetops which brought home my point that Ellis
should probably fall for the moment dead silent.

I made it so far as the footing where the trestle joined the bank
before that Rumsfeld turned again and fired another time just, I could
tell, to keep me off. I identified myself as an officer of the law, tried
once further to show to that Rumsfeld the pistol in my hand, wondered if couldn't me and him just have a little chat, but he didn't
appear to pay me any heed at all, went back to talking to that girl,
expressing, I could make out now, his lowly opinion of her. He spoke
with rising feeling of the faithless way she'd done him, called her a slut
and a cunt and a tramp, allowed he wasn't the sort at all to tolerate her
pastime. He aired a few sentiments they'd exchanged naked in bed
together, invited her please to analyze if she might the things she'd
said, wondered what maybe she'd have thought if she were in his
place.

For her part, she looked remarkably calm given what he'd just
done, given how he'd simply touched that Crouse with the bore of his
daddy's gun and then had turned and stepped away. Plainly she didn't
herself much hold with that Rumsfeld's opinions and views and offered
there from atop the girder to bristle and contradict. I couldn't quite
hear what she told that boy but there didn't appear much tenderness
to it judging from the way she wagged her foremost finger as she
spoke.

I believe he meant to kill her. My suspicion is he'd very likely
planned to do her in, soften her up a little with the slaughter of that
Crouse, bring her around to see him for the nervy sort he was. Clearly,
anyway, he'd not remotely figured on a scolding when he was the one
himself with the ornamental pistol in hand. I guess he'd thought she'd
yield and give, fall at length into his arms and plead for him to spare
her, own up to her faithlessness, vow to be transformed. That was
what he had to have, all that he required, an abdication from her so

that he might take the throne. I mean how could he hope to shoot her when she had her hooks still in him. He needed for the reins to pass, had call, if even with a gun, to put himself in charge.

But she just wouldn't play. She had us down, had us cold. He stuck that pistol in her ribs and made his accusations, and she just wagged her finger back, gave him all she got. It didn't have a thing to do with where the bullets were. He was simply overmatched, and the longer he stood on the trestle ties and threatened and abused her without drawing back the hammer and offering to fire, the less he seemed the fellow who'd just laid waste to that Crouse. He began to look, from where I was, pathetic and undone, and I endeavored to engage him in some stripe of conversation, called to him, "Walter," from the trestle end, announced how awfully pleased I'd be were he to drop his gun.

He heard me. He turned and looked upon me, and I figured for a moment there I'd probably gone and done it. A boy like him just couldn't hope to kill a girl like her. Boys like him killed each other. Boys like him killed themselves. I figured he was wondering was I maybe a boy like him, looked to me to be taking my measure, stood there and just gazed for a time, and I was shifting about to propose to Ellis that probably he'd best retire when that Rumsfeld gave me over and made up at last his mind. He ran right at her, raised that shiny nickel-plated pistol and vented a sort of a cry as he charged straight towards the rail. I don't know what he thought she'd do that she hadn't done already, don't know if he was even truly thinking anymore. She held to a stanchion on one side, a guyline on the other. She just stood there and watched him come, let him touch her with that bore, lay that pistol to her. But he couldn't shoot a girl like her. He simply wasn't able. He turned that gun around and pulled the trigger with his thumb.

The sound of gunfire does some funny things up in these mountains. It pops and cracks from peak to peak, pulses along the gullies and sounds to be tearing the air. It hangs sometimes on a creekbed, echoes and lingers and fades at last, and I recall I was hearing still that report long after the Rumsfeld had dropped to the ties and loosed his daddy's fine etched pistol to fall to the rocks below. Ellis, of course, set in straightaway with an assortment of throaty discharges tinged largely with rank moral outrage and personal consternation though he found occasion to put on exhibit a dose of peevishness too, managed to wonder of me why I'd brought him to this place when all he'd needed truly was some coffee and some air.

I stepped full onto the trestle proper, left Ellis behind me up on the bank and moved out onto the span. She was standing yet on her girder holding to her stanchion and her line with that Crouse and that Rumsfeld sprawled before her, sagging a trifle each of them down between the sleepers and oozing still their fluids and their gore. There's more than a little enchantment to actual, true-life carnage, a manner of magnetism that movie carnage lacks. At the triplex when the blood flows and the corpses begin to mount, people tend to squint and are prone to turn away at the ghastly sights they have to know are only manufactured, while out on the street a carcass can prove an exceptional attraction. You can't even hope to drive people off. They come to study and stare, consider the gashes and examine the wounds and manage to engage, often enough, in pitched anatomical exchanges. I know I came to be at least a little enchanted myself and expended no shrinking regard on that Rumsfeld and Crouse together.

I mean to say I didn't just then exactly know I was angry. You see at the time I was pretty completely under the spell of the carnage and so wasn't keeping much of a watch on my personal indignation. It was only when she called me that at last I came around.

"Officer," she said in a calm and steely voice like probably she'd say it anywhere, like I'd known her to say it before, and I drew myself off from the corpses, the shattered skulls and the seepage, and looked to see her standing with her arm upraised and her fingers extended. It was that pose women strike sometimes when they're set to be helped and aided, assisted out of a car or drawn up off a settee.

"Officer," she said to me again and wiggled at me her fingers.

I've cobbled together over time a plausible explanation, and I manage every now and again to believe it even a little. First I like to think I was unbalanced from the slaughter. Watching two fellows get their brains blown out through their cowlicks is doubtless enough to cast a person into a singular humor. So I was already out of sorts when she saw fit to beckon to me. I was mindful of the waste and the senselessness, had given in passing thought even then to that Crouse's wife out at Piper's Gap, those Rumsfelds up on the bluff. I was anguished, I guess, and aggrieved, not worked up beyond all reason and sense, but appropriately tormented at the sight of such boys cut down and squandered, at the thought of the suffering they'd cause. And then she says to me, "Officer," and flutters at me her fingers and manages thereby to set me off. I think it was chiefly the tone she took, sort of blithe and sprightly as if she'd suffered an inconvenience that, thankfully, had passed. She couldn't even manage to seem affected, concoct a little alarm. "Officer," she says to me and shows to me her hand to take.

I suppose I was hoping to impress upon her that even in fact if this life is trivial and hollow at heart there are still some things that count and matter like two fellows dead on a railroad trestle, one fellow dead in the woods. Anyway now I make out that that's pretty much what I hoped as I left off with the carnage and crossed to where she stood. Were I a glib and able sort I might have explained it to her, but I could only manage instead to raise my feeble weapon and press the muzzle close, lay it flush against her ribs where she took notice of it. I guess she thought I was meaning to help her, had come to squire her away. Straightoff she didn't recognize just what I was about but laid in time her hand to mine and felt that trifling item, ran her finger along the barrel and down around the hilt to the hollow in the grip where the bullets should have been. Then she stuck her finger up inside and smiled at me that smile.

I didn't push her. It might even be easier, better if I had, but I didn't push her off. You see I just wanted loose and free, wrenched myself away and served by jerking and twisting about to throw her out of kilter. She'd been holding to me, pulling against me, you know, so when I turned she lurched and shifted, pitched straight off the girder. It happened awfully fast, not in an instant truly but surely quick enough. I dissect it anymore, slow it down to suit me, but out there on the trestle it happened in a hurry. I can't even say I could in fact have caught and maybe saved her, though I'm certain of an instance when I might at least have tried. But I just stood there. I just watched. It suits me too damn well. I didn't shove her or pull her in. I just let her fall.

Ellis was hooting and hollering again before she even hit the rocks, couldn't so much as begin to believe his own miserable fortune. All he'd wanted after all was fresh air and some coffee, and here he'd been made party to an out-and-out bloodbath. The rye and the incredulity were working together upon him, began to render him speechless though they failed to strike him dumb, and he stood on a sleeper just shy of the span and moaned and whined and howled.

At length I managed to secure the nerve to look down into the bottom where I found she'd hit full in the branch, landed, that is, on the damp, dark rocks instead of the dusty dry ones. I called to her. That's right. I leaned out over the rail and yelled to her, "Hello!" even made to listen to hear what she might muster the breath to say back. It was, however, a considerable drop down into the bottom and she looked to me to have been herself rendered speechless too.

Ellis elected to follow me down the embankment to the branch even after he'd already indicated he'd stay perched on his tie. She had a dent in the back of her head and was twisted oddly about. Ellis and I together endeavored to hunt a vein, but we were both queasy and squeamish and directly gave her over.

"She slipped," I said and raised my head to look up to the girder. "She fell," I told to Ellis who informed me shortly, "Yeah," told to me, "she did."

Ellis refused to walk under the bridge for fear that some gore would drip on him, so I stepped up the branchbed alone and hunted that plated pistol, found it wedged between two rocks with the grips both busted free. I took it up at the barrel and carried it out of the bottom, climbed to the trestle with Ellis and advised him of the plan, allowed how I'd decided that he would take my car back out to the interchange and phone in to the station.

"Have them send Dewey," I told him. "Tell him we're out on the trestle, the one hard by the mill. Dewey knows just where it is," and I laid upon Ellis's upturned palm the keys to my Chevette which he regarded and remarked with extravagant attention.

"I can't drive your car," he said when presently he spoke. "I'm still about half-drunk and I don't have a license."

"You want to stay here instead?" I asked him. "One of us surely has to."

"So it's right out on the road here and then back up to the left?"

"Right," I told to Ellis, "and then left up at the crest."

I could hear him for a long while following the roadway, over-accelerating, fishing for the gears, and then he cleared the ridge and traveled out of earshot leaving just me on the bank with them out on the trestle, her down in the creek. At first I was unsettled, nervous and uneasy, occupied myself in turning to each noise. I grew, however, calm in time, walked onto the span, laid against the girder, looked up and down the branch. The air was cool and misty. The sun was long since down. The light was wan and meager, what you'd look out from a lit house and take to be the night. I remember the jarflies, the toads on the creek, her bright blouse down on the rock bed, the drip and trickle of the branch. The smell of blood, like metal, was thick upon the air. The lightning bugs were putting on a show along the bank. I found directly overhead the first star of the evening. It all seemed worth remarking, even at the time, and has proved to be enduring, crisp and stark and clear. It was like I'd been asleep forever, woken up at last.

I can't say just how long it took for Ellis to come back, but I don't believe he was even out of the Chevette when Dewey pulled in behind him. I could see the beacon. I could hear the siren. I could detect the clamor of the semi-controlled skid. They came together through the scrub following Dewey's light beam, proceeded onto the trestle proper and called together to me. Dewey didn't himself have much to say, whistled once between his teeth as he looked upon those boys and made a sort of a noise in his neck while he peered down to the creekbed. I showed him the gun, raised by the barrel that handsomely engraved pistol with only the grip rivets left.

"Her too?" he asked which earned him straightoff from Ellis the news that she'd just somehow slipped, that she'd just somehow fallen.

"Yes sir," Ellis told him. "Her feet went out. I saw it."

"All right," Dewey said. "All right. She slipped then. She just fell."

He joined me at the girder, laid against the steel, and I was half prepared to mount a full description, was trying to determine just where I might best start when Dewey declared he could hardly remember his last trip to the branch.

I seemed to recall he'd come with that boy who'd made off with the Vega. "Little wiry fellow," I said, "from over past the gap."

"Why yes sir," Dewey told me, "I do believe it was," and he gazed off towards the treetops, said nothing at all for a time in advance of announcing, "Light as a feather, not but a husk of a thing." And Dewey looked fondly from the rails and the ties to the girders and the ledgy branchbed. "Weren't those the days?" he inquired of me.

"Weren't they now," I said.

❦

Being son to the chief's wife's sister served, as best as Clifford could tell, to saddle him with duties and obligations that the unrelated employees just could not hope to know. That anyhow was his explanation for getting patched through to Charlotte and attempting to page the chief in the middle of the banquet at the Sheraton where the conferees had enjoyed a meal of pork loin and potatoes and were taking with their apple crisp, were taking with their coffee, the chief's own tribute to the compounds and to the purified gases that, when combined and mixed together, make for chemical Mace. But the girl at the desk simply could not see clear to interrupt the presentation even if the caller did claim to be the son of the chief's wife's sister. She proved in fact for a desk clerk firm but sympathetic and answered Clifford's mounting abuse with news of the Eastern techniques she tended to employ when gathering tensions and pressures became a plague and affliction, caused her to snap and be peevish and short that way that tensions and pressures can.

By the time that me and Dewey had come back off the trestle to haul the generator out of the trunk of Clifford's car, he was fairly sprawled across the seat with the handset in his hand. He was telling that girl his hair was brown, his eyes were greenish blue, added those inches to his height he'd deducted from his waistline. He was speaking in fact of the many times he'd call to be in Charlotte when Dewey interrupted him, stuck his head through the window and said, "Get off that goddam radio. Drag your sorry ass out of this car."

It was pretty much all on this occasion the same as it was before, minus of course the mystery and the reckless speculation. We set up the halogen lights on the trestle and illuminated the bottom. Lonnie came out with the camera and took pictures of the scene, and I mounted a manner of briefing off alongside the girder. I told them that me and Ellis had been on our way for flapjacks, told them we'd seen this crowd at the light over by the interchange.

"That one there was bloody already." I jerked my nose at the Crouse.

"He was," Ellis said. "I saw him. Looked beat up to me."

I aired the suspicions that Rumsfeld had managed himself to inspire, and Lonnie piped in to figure that we'd likely smoked him out, made him to know we were onto him, made him to know we were wise.

I let on it all seemed plain enough, let on it all seemed clear. "You get two boys like these together with only one girl between them and one of them's bound to be rubbed raw and find himself set off."

"Three boys," Clifford told me. "Wendle," Clifford said.

And before I could snort and cast my doubts that way that I'd intended, Dewey peered down in the branch and declared she didn't look to him Wendle's type at all. He managed a truly masterful pause before he turned back to us and told to Clifford, told to Lonnie, told to Ellis and me, "No pulse."

I guess maybe Clifford would have pressed and Clifford would have persisted, ferreted after his aimless fashion until he'd struck some ore, but Gooch showed up in his wagon and provided a reprieve. He passed through the scrub in his fine blue suit and stepped out onto the span where the halogen light fell upon him, served to transform his toupee, and the ensuing spectral shimmer and shine proved for Clifford bewitching.

Of course they got around at length to attempting to flatter and woo me. Dewey and Clifford and Lonnie as well mounted together a rapturous tribute to my special charm in times of sadness, my native grace in times of loss. They wished they could manage even together to be maybe half so consoling, and they took each occasion to testify to the comfort they'd known me to bring, supposed I was blessed and gifted and as stupid, I guess, as a stump. I told them I'd had my turn already delivering dire news. I supposed all you needed was a tongue in your head and spit enough to work it.

I helped them to pack off the bodies, haul that girl up from the branch, and Clifford was just undertaking to recommend a grid when I declared I'd probably best carry Ellis on home, allowed that we were both a little shaken and undone given the baleful slaughter that we'd stumbled on together. Ellis contributed a burp, a low dyspeptic rumble that sounded as much the product of strain as rye and gastric juices, so nobody offered objection as I escorted Ellis away, called to remind them I'd be on come morning, called to remind them I'd be fit by then. In my Chevette as we crested the ridge and made towards the interchange, Ellis and I spoke in fits and snatches. We sat for great spells silent and still, and when Ellis climbed out at last at the curb and laid in the window to say his goodnight, we ended up just eyeing each other and failed to speak at all.

I meant, I think, to go straight home. I don't, that is, remember having planned to call upon her but just failed up past the remnant shop to make my lefthand turn and proceeded on the truck route into the county proper where the clutter of town gave way in time to hayfields and to pastures, to acres of sewn white pines, stretches of timbered forest, and cabbages presently where the road flattened and leveled out.

You know I don't believe I'd ever before called her by her name. She was always just Dale's sister. "Her" would do, or "you." So it sounded peculiar to me and seemed almost mistaken as I knocked upon the doorrail and spoke in through the screen.

"Here," she said and I turned round to find her on the glider off in the dark at the end of the porch with her child asleep on her lap.

Without my uniform, my belt, I couldn't rest my hands upon my pistol and my stick and had hardly struck a proper place to have them light and lay as I closed upon the glider, adjusted to the dark, tried again to reason just what I'd come to say.

I set in with a bromide, some tripe about the night, but caught myself and forestalled a rising commonplace, fell in fact dead silent and stood there like a fool as she asked me, "Yes?" asked me, "What?" and made inquiring faces.

I stuck my hands into my pockets. I pulled them out again. I said we'd had a glider once that squeaked just like hers did.

"Sit," she told me. "Please," she said.

I loosed a breath. I sat.

7.

They lived clean out in Newport News. Angelene hunted them down from the envelope of a birthday card that Clifford found in the house. They had a boy too who'd settled hard by in Chesapeake. He took a week off from the shipyard and drove them out in his Dodge. It wouldn't do but we should call her Marge and call him Clayton. They kept giving their boy out as Ricky but he'd shake and tell you, "Dick." He was missing the tops of two fingers and had a tattoo on his arm. It was some sort of serpent though, due to his shirtsleeve, I never saw more than the assend. Dick didn't have much to say. He wasn't sour or surly but simply preferred to sit and smoke and let Marge and Clayton hold forth, Marge and Clayton who seemed to give voice to whatever popped into their heads.

She'd been, they told us, a sweet child, never a quarrelsome thing. I carried them out to Whitetop that afternoon they arrived, let Marge and Clayton into the house and sat on the stoop with Dick who failed to speak for the longest while but just fairly ingested his Winstons, smoked like a service veteran, covered the coal with his hand. In time, though, he loosened up. After about a quarter hour he pointed across the yard and asked, "What kind of tree is that?"

"Tulip," I told him.

"Tulip," he said and informed himself shortly, "yeah."

I can't say just what Marge and Clayton were up to in the house. I could hear sometimes the sound of them speaking lowly back and forth but could only every now and again make out what they'd say. Clayton called to wish that Marge would look please in the icebox. Marge asked Clayton if wasn't in fact the paper in the hall the very same pattern they'd had in their bedroom in Manassas. I expected them just any time to undertake to quiz me, figured that, standing among her things, they might become resentful, enlist me to explain again just how it all transpired, tell them why we'd let their girl arrive at such an end. There didn't, however, seem to be much they wanted to know. I'd provided my sketchy version in the cruiser on the way and the chief had told them on the phone the gist of what had happened which I'd thought would seem inadequate and strike them both as slight, but Marge and Clayton appeared to guess they'd heard all they should hear.

They were religious people, which I like to think explains them. Marge, that is, and Clayton. I can't speak for Dick who really didn't say enough to let on what he was. But his parents were afflicted with a manner of devotion, a firm and binding faith in His judgment and His will which resembled, truth be known, some sort of brain impairment. Whatever the Lord and Maker decreed they swallowed with a smile and never made like it was rank or let on it was bitter. They seemed almost delighted that their child had flown to heaven, informed me that they meant themselves to see her there some day. They appeared to think that they were being tried, were being tested, hoped to put the best face on a prickly circumstance. Maybe at the motel when they woke up in the night they felt a little different, weren't so gracious and content. I can't say. I only know that in the house at Whitetop they reminisced about the place they'd lived in at Manassas, decided that the paper had been in fact the same.

That evening on the glider I'd enjoyed a revelation. I'd gone not knowing what exactly I might up and say, just meant to tell Dale's sister some version of the truth, excised, of course, and tidied, a delicate rendition, but studded and encrusted with essentially the facts. I just guessed it was important that the thing be real at heart no matter the exclusions, the vile items left unsaid. I simply hadn't figured I could get by with a lie until there upon the glider as I set myself to speak when suddenly it struck me that, once all you've got is corpses, there's no overwhelming reason to be honest and precise. I mean when everybody's done for, when everybody's dead, the culprits and the victims, the whole lot in together, where is the inducement for giving out just why? Sometimes the truth is fine enough, and so much as consoling, but every now and then it's likely worlds worse than a lie.

The chief's idea of decent and of honorable treatment was for me to drive those people to the fish house for a meal, Marge, that is, and Clayton along with Dick their boy who picked at their fried platters and undertook to chat, made out to have an interest in our handsome little town. Marge said her and Clayton had been meaning once to come, had been planning on a visit that they never somehow made. Marge drew from her pocketbook her big blue vinyl purse, sorted through it for a picture that she plucked out and displayed, a photograph of their sweet child wearing in fact clothes and standing by a treetrunk outside in the sun. The sight of their girl seemed to shake Marge up, appeared more trial than she wanted. She didn't quake or cry outright but yielded up that look of toothy rapture and devotion as she laid her finger to their girl and vented from her throat a low, unprayerful noise.

I said I'd heard she'd been in fact a lovely sort of creature. I said I'd met a friend of hers, a girl she'd known from church which produced upon Marge and Clayton together a wondrous effect, galvanized them both at once and prompted them to join me in lamenting how young guileless things can often serve as prey for men guided by their appetites and led by their desires.

"The devil's own," Clayton said.

"The devil's own," Marge added.

"Yes ma'am," I told to her. "His minions I don't doubt." While for his part Dick just sat and smoked and covered up his coal.

I never showed them the Polaroids that Clifford and Dewey and Lonnie together had turned up at the house. I did carry them back to the station and into the conference room where the chief had intended I break the news their girl had been a tramp, but I just served them thick scorched coffee from the urn by the water cooler and showed them instead the pictures our Clifford had found on the dresser mirror. There was one of Clayton and one of Marge, one of the boys with the teeth and the hair who proved to be Dick's sons and who Marge and Clayton and even Dick carried on some about. I assured them if I was in Newport News I'd stop by and pay them a call, and I accompanied them out of the station and down to their car at the curb where Clayton and Marge together blessed my eternal soul. Dick their boy just raised a hand and pulled into the street.

The chief and Dewey and Janice all met me at the door and announced their own consensus that the news had gone down well. I laid it all to Jesus, to the balm of steadfast faith which was as much as drove the chief to a jowly, grave expression, that face of his that hints at Billy Graham in repose. I just couldn't see the harm since all we had was corpses and innocent relations who'd been knocked about enough. If we had to lay it somewhere, why not lay it on the Rumsfeld. His folks had managed taints before, could make it go away. They'd already orchestrated a grand obituary, a front-page piece below the fold in Thursday morning's *Ledger* with a picture of their Walter in a jacket and a tie and pomade enough upon his hair to hold his bangs at bay. Mrs. Tyree had been toothless. Mrs. Tyree had been sweet. How could she puncture and undo the son of plutocrats?

You see they knew just what I told them, and I told them dick and squat. I can't say I decided to keep people in the dark. I can't say Ellis and I conspired to lead them all astray. I mean I didn't ride out to the bottling plant and draw Ellis aside for instruction. I don't believe we ever so much as spoke on the topic at all. They just went ahead and made their assertions and cobbled together their theories without troubling themselves to consult on the matter, without troubling themselves to inquire. And they got it almost right. Most anybody could have. It was bloodlust and high humor, romance and betrayal. They saw this sort of thing at the triplex all the time and so had the surface of it figured pretty much. I mean there were at least two boys, that Rumsfeld and that Crouse, tilting for the favors of a girl of easy virtue, a handsome, comely creature who was weak and largely faithless. There were camps of course that figured Wendle'd had a taste himself, but they were small and muted and got overcome in time. Most people thought it ghoulish to throw Wendle in the mix.

The chief allowed a Polaroid or two to circulate. Seemly portions of them were printed in the *Ledger*. I kept of course my own three back home in a drawer, was not remotely meaning to explain how I'd come by them. The women about appeared as a group to detest her instantly while the men, for their well-being, claimed pure blindness to her charms, let on they couldn't figure how some boys had come to bullets over such a thing as her. Those fellows she'd had dealings with, the live ones still about, failed to venture forward and confess to their acquaintance, had wives, I guess, and girlfriends and didn't need the trouble. But a Greer from up past Willis, a Greer from in the hills, a foul and filthy sort you'd not touch but with a pole, attempted to persuade us that he'd married her in secret and owned by rights her bureau, owned by rights her bed. It turned out that he had himself a fine settee already.

So they got it mostly right. It was bloodlust and high humor. It was romance, was betrayal. It was faithlessness. But they missed the sport entirely, the sense of gamesmanship, the way she snagged and played those boys, the way she had them figured. They decided she was wanton and driven by desire. The woman who'd employed her in an office in Mt. Airy confessed to Mr. Chapman that she'd seemed a lusty sort. They guessed she'd had more appetite than just one boy could feed while that Rumsfeld was accustomed to more honorable creatures. They seemed to think she'd led him to believe that she'd be true, that he'd simply lost his wits when he'd found her with that Crouse. They liked to think it passion that prompted and inspired him, but they didn't see him at the branch, how calm he was, efficient, the way he touched the muzzle to the cheekbone of that Crouse, the way he turned that pistol, pulled the trigger with his thumb. How could we explain it, me or Ellis, to them? I had a sort of feeling it was privilege gone wrong, breeding come unraveled, though I couldn't say just why. I let them figure what they would. They liked to think she jumped.

The Crouse and the Rumsfeld got dispatched in consecutive ceremonies. The Crouse was remembered at the mortuary chapel and then carried in procession on back out to the gap where he was laid with his people in the family cemetery on a knoll in a pasture high among the cattle with cedars for an accent and fencing roundabout. I stayed down at the roadway, had led them in the cruiser, could hear the preacher talking, could hear the hymn they sang. I could see the widow with her tissue to her face. I could see those boys who'd come to stopper up the vault. They laid against the backhoe. They waited and they smoked.

The Rumsfeld got a grander do at the new church on the bypass. The crowd there had some tone to it. They'd come in from all over to send away that Walter, pay his people their respects. Harnett from the state patrol hired out himself for traffic, did duty at the light where the truck route intersects. Dewey led the mourners while I brought up the rear, and we paraded clean through town, drew a crowd along the street. The choir even went to the memorial park, arrayed themselves by the mausoleum and opened the proceedings with "All the Way My Savior Leads Me." That Rumsfeld's mother looked elegant in black. The collar of his father's coat had caught and turned up somehow. The place was saturated with handsome wreaths and sprays, and the way that preacher carried on you'd have thought that boy had been done in honoring the flag, had given up his life so that others might be free. The Rumsfelds put a feed on in their backyard at the bluff, had a bar and had a buffet, some sort of string ensemble, hired a boy from down the hill to park and fetch the cars. Gooch got shed that selfsame day of Marge and Clayton's girl, shipped her on a flatbed truck east to Newport News.

Dewey himself never even saw fit to ask me for the skinny, didn't bother to draw me aside to see if I'd come clean. I feared the chief would press me when he got back from Charlotte, but the general intoxication of his triumph at the banquet could not be altogether defeated and dispelled. It seems his tribute to chemical Mace had been capped by a rousing ovation, and the chief was at the outset too flushed with pride and rapture to be his old grim self and mount a stern inquiry. I was fearful of the chief's gift for long and studied silence, nervous he would call me in and sit me down before him and wait until the quiet just served to suck me dry. You'd talk so as to fill the air and make some sort of racket. A fellow couldn't always know what he might up and say. But the chief was well distracted by the memory of his triumph and satisfied himself with my lean account of things.

It worked out that he never had occasion for reflection. You see this thing was news all over. Rumsfelds got around. Naturally the woman with the square teeth came from Roanoke and interviewed the chief at the Grange hall by a shrub, but in the end she proved in fact the least of the attention. A crew came up from Charlotte, a crew from Winston-Salem, a crew from out in Richmond drove down to see the chief. He had his version to work up, his faces to rehearse. He didn't have the leisure to worry much with me.

The chief's gift for dramaturgy is in the dinner theater range. I mean he's awfully broad and gaudy when you see him in the flesh, but the camera serves to work upon the chief a transformation, filters and improves him to remarkable effect. Those times he'd made the Roanoke news you never had occasion to see the chief hold forth and perform at any length. That woman with the square teeth preferred to be on camera as if regional calamities were largely just a backdrop designed to set her off. But these other correspondents weren't so hungry for exposure and allowed the chief to hold forth and mount a full performance.

He had his version down, his expressions, his demeanor, his
earnest silences, his heartsick exhalations, and I guess they lit him well
and posed him to effect, because the segments they broadcasted plain
scared me half to death. He looked somehow sincere, seemed genuine
and forthright. You couldn't on the TV tell he was a fraud. His faces
all looked natural. His voice was deep and pleasant. Even those rare
moments when his recitation left him and he squinted and attempted
to remember what to say, he appeared to be just thinking that way
other people think, the sorts who tend to speak unscripted, hold forth
unrehearsed.

People about who were themselves acquainted with the chief
communicated to him and to his wife as well how awfully fine a figure
he'd seemed to them to cut, and nearly everybody threw in to agree
that they'd never known a camera to adore a fellow so. Now the chief's
wife golfed with a woman who had a sister who'd married a man who
worked in California and knew people in TV, and she was the one who
encouraged the wife of the chief to give her a tape that she proposed
to ship off to her sister on the coast who'd have her husband show it
to his buddies in TV, which wasn't quite so farfetched as maybe it
might sound on account of the state along about then of ordinary
television fare.

You see that was just when TV shows, dramas and sit-coms both,
had become at last so dull and stupid that even the public noticed.
Nobody much seemed interested in watching anything anymore until
TV types discovered the appeal of real-life docu-drama, shows on the
cheap about firemen and cops, rescue squad workers and federal of-
fenders. People just seemed to take to them, grew keen on reenactments and revelations of the sorry actual things some sorts can do.

So that Rumsfeld's bit of gunplay proved timely for the chief,
and the husband of the sister of the chief's wife's golfing partner must
have pressed in fact that tape on somebody or another because it wasn't
awful long before we heard from California. Janice took a call one day
from Mort of Malibu. You'd have thought he'd phoned from Mars to
see the fit that Janice threw, and the whole thing just got better when

Mort at length confessed that he'd dialed up on his car phone, was sitting in thick traffic on Ventura Boulevard.

The chief and Mort had themselves a lengthy conversation. The chief shut fast his office door and Janice watched the panel light, confirmed for us at intervals that Mort was on the line. Clifford speculated as to the mounting charges, explained the way the signal bounced into space and back, while Janice, who'd met once the weatherman from Greensboro, came across him in a restaurant having supper with his wife, determined the call from Mort to be in truth a grander thrill. She was herself persuaded that the chief would be a star, and once the light went out the chief joined us straightaway, flung his door wide open, fairly posed against the jamb and appeared to be persuaded he would be a star himself.

It turned out Mort produced a brand-new show about policemen that featured reenactments of assorted villainy along of course with stilted, uninflected narration straight from the lips of lawmen acquainted with the crimes. Mort had been quite taken with the chief's on-air persona, his pleasing resonances, his pauses and his gaps, and Mort had never seen a lens caress a fellow so. He liked the crime, the concept, the glamor and the gore, the murders and the suicides, the shooting and the leaping. He planned to be on our coast, had business in New York, and he hoped to fly on down and have a look around, meet the chief, see the scene, hear about the carnage.

"Mort's coming here?" Janice asked, and the chief allowed he had from Mort assurances he was.

Mort brought with him an associate when at last he came to see us. The chief had Lonnie fetch them from the airfield up in Roanoke and carry them to the station where we all made their acquaintance. Mort seemed decent and hale enough, was short and thick and loud, had a moustache and a cough and when he came in through the doorway he went straight to the phone. His associate introduced himself as Richardson Pike, the director. He had studs in his ears and a ponytail and was wearing a purple sportscoat. Richardson Pike named for us a show he'd worked on lately. It was the one set in the cleaners where people came by to drop off their clothes and hijinks somehow ensued. Richardson Pike had directed the installment about the buxom blonde who'd spilled wine on her blousefront. He was sure we would recall it if we'd seen it when it ran on account of how it had a look, Richardson Pike informed us. He'd moved the camera on a boom. He'd employed yellow gels. He was, of course, the Richardson Pike known for his cutaways.

Clifford was fond of a show on Tuesdays set in a used car lot. They had a buxom brunette and all sorts of jolly fun, but even before Clifford could ask if Richardson Pike had worked on it, he told us he knew of that show himself. He told us that show was just trash.

The chief drove Mort and Richardson Pike about the county, showed them where Wendle had died on the roadway, showed them where Wendle had been dragged through the woods, carried them out to the house at Whitetop, down to the trestle over the branch and then brought them back to the station where Mort made use of the phone while Richardson Pike told me and Janice about the feature he meant to make whenever his money came through. It was to be a space adventure about some boys on Neptune, fellows sent off for a couple of years to run a refinery. They get attacked by potent beings from the fourth dimension, and I wondered of Richardson Pike if they looked like silverfish.

I'm not even sure our carnage would have taken hold and endured had Mort not decided to bring in a crew and film a reenactment. I mean people about were worked up already, but had largely a sense of the shame of the thing. The killing, the bloodshed, it all seemed a waste, a shabby bit of business. However, when Mort decided to shoot the reenactment for TV, people about couldn't help but feel that maybe in fact it was something. Even Mrs. Tyree and Mr. Chapman left off for a time with our moral fiber and the woeful inclinations of America's youth and ran instead a profile of Mort and an interview with Richardson Pike.

By the time they rolled in with their trucks, their RVs, their equipment, people about had undergone a sort of a transformation.

The pride was apparent whenever citizens gathered to speak of the slaughter. It was our own mayhem anymore, prompted by passion, touched off by deceit, and it said a thing about our pluck, a thing about our spirit. People just seemed disposed to believe that local blood ran hotter than maybe they'd ever imagined local blood could run. Now everybody wanted to see the thing staged out on the trestle, and it was all me and Lonnie and Dewey could do to keep them off the span that night Richardson Pike set up at last to film down by the branch.

The crew laid track for the camera between the railroad steel as Richardson Pike had ambitious plans for one long rolling take that he could dice and chop up, leave off with and come back. Mort had imported some actors, flown them in for the shoot. There was a kid with bangs to play the Rumsfeld, a sort of a wiry and weaselly type to take on the part of the Crouse. The boy who played me looked almost like Dewey, and they had a girl of course for her. She'd flown in from Columbus where she'd been lately playing a calico in the traveling show of *Cats*. She was pretty and slight and strawberry blonde, hardly looked a temptress, but Mort's people slutted her up pretty good, fitted out in Spandex and treacherous heels and a wig.

I had a chat with her by an RV, was coming out of the john. She thought I'd been hired on like her and greeted me with a bilious appraisal of Mort and Richardson Pike. She said she'd done a cleanser spot for a nonabrasive scrub, said she was in the running for a television movie. She wondered had I seen her on the show about the nurses. She was the one they'd rolled in with the superficial burns. There was talk they'd have her back next year to get maimed in a wreck. And then she asked me where I'd been, what I'd been working at. I said I'd not been up to much, was coming from the john.

As the sun dropped off behind the ridge, the sunset turned out murky, and Richardson Pike determined they'd best make themselves a twilight. So they shifted the standards and tested some gels and came up with a kind of a dusky look that Richardson Pike figured would do. Once they got around to shooting I could see it was all wrong. I mean she was on the girder and they were on the ties which suited well enough, but they'd made the Rumsfeld wild-eyed and that Crouse got played too spunky while the girl up on the girder seemed too awful near to tears.

They pushed the camera down the track. They drew it back again. That boy with the pistol capered pretty madly about the span and endured at intervals bold talk from that wiry little Crouse, put up with spells of whining from that girl up on the girder and was appearing himself prepared to burst when Richardson Pike interrupted the scene. Richardson Pike had his technicians situate the sacks of gore, tape to the heads of those boys on the span a bag each of thick and giblety pulp while Richardson Pike had the camera rolled in for a tight and intimate shot. There wasn't any report to hear, no pistol crack to warn us. A boy on the bridge from the catering truck told me they'd put that in later. All we could hear was a muffled pop as that Crouse's sack exploded and the manufactured blood and brains sprayed into the air, and then once the Rumsfeld stepped to the girder and delivered a line to that girl, he turned the prop pistol on himself and his sack went off too. That girl in the Spandex and spindly heels fairly quaked with emotion.

Ellis had gotten deleted early on from the script, so the boy who played me stepped alone out onto the trestle. He had a line. He had a word. He told to that girl, "Hey," but with professional inflection so that it said truly worlds.

He stepped to the rail and reached for that girl who'd begun to turn and twist away when Richardson Pike stopped the scene and called for the stunt double who I can't say I'd taken previously any notice of. I think he'd been off out of sight back behind a lightbox, and who could really blame him since he'd not been made for Spandex. He wore a wig and heels like her, but that dress just chewed him up. He couldn't help but mince across the sleepers to the rail where three boys together hoisted him up and helped him to his mark once they'd lifted down that girl and set her on the span. I couldn't guess there was a gel to maybe make him girlish. Richardson Pike just had them draw the camera back away until the guywires and the stanchions served to hide him some. He had that fellow playing me to raise his arm again, and once they'd switched the camera on, Richardson Pike just pointed and that fellow in the dress pitched back into a net.

I think if they'd only done it once, I could have let it go. The atmosphere was jolly as that man climbed to the decking. People cheered and whistled and assorted wags about aired unseemly propositions, but Richardson Pike wasn't pleased at all, was unhappy with his angle and couldn't be certain of his gels now that the ambient light had changed. So they did it again and then did it again and then did it another time, and after a while it didn't seem just TV anymore. Most everybody else hooted and yelped, made amorous declarations, cheered as that boy climbed from the net and took his bows on the decking, but for me I think I'd found that place where life and TV meet. He was just a guy in a dress and heels until he started to fall.

I've yet to see the thing on television proper. Mort's supposed to call us a week before it runs, but I heard from Clifford who heard from the chief that there's a complication. Mort found a case in Utah of some gunplay on a bridge, a similar sort of slaughter though with more appeal than ours on account of how the gunman had been worshiping the devil. Mort called from his car and explained to the chief that he was personally torn. It seems the sheriff out in Utah had no polish much about him, but of course the devil has some draw, more even than a Rumsfeld. So I haven't seen the thing myself, am doubtful it will run, though the chief still campaigns for it. He stalks out of his office once every week or so and tells Janice or tells Angelene, "Get Mort on the line."

❧

I'm persuaded the truth got lost for a time, vanished into the fiction —the gels, the fades, the cutaways, the artful framing shots. Of course I thought about it all. Thinking is what I do, sat at home in my Naugahyde chair and relived the entire business. I sorted and weighed the elements and took heed of the factors, tried to decide just why at the trestle I'd done the things I did. I was chiefly looking to lay it to her, believed she could explain it, preferred to suppose she'd had it all designed and orchestrated. I half believed she'd been wanting to go, thought of herself as done for. I mean there she was rutting with whatever boy it struck her to carry home and this world anymore ripe with danger and riddled with disease. It was plain suicide from the getgo. I forgave myself a little. I figured she'd needed someone like me to help her to get delivered.

Along about this same time, in the aftermath of the carnage, Desmond my neighbor upstairs took himself a lover. He met a boy he fancied at a swap shop up in Wytheville and beguiled him I guess with the splendid news of his personal orientation. That fellow's name was Warren and he would come and stay with Desmond, spend weekends upstairs overhead and weeknights on occasion. He was small of frame and bony and considerably lighter of foot though Warren had a cackle that could travel through cement and Desmond proved at first a source of grand amusement for him. I got invited upstairs early on in the affair, Desmond called and summoned me to meet his new love object. Warren turned out nice enough if not so very dashing, but then Desmond was no prize himself even those few weeks a year when he was sleek and Dancercised.

It seems that one of Warren's loves was Shirley Bassey records, though he was fond of Eartha Kitt and Nancy Wilson too. But Shirley Bassey was the one who really set him off and he'd carried his collection down from Wytheville with him, played some numbers for me as I sat and had a drink. Desmond made like he was awfully fond of Shirley Bassey, pretended he could hardly hope to ever get his fill. They were sweet and giggly together right there at the first, quarreled a bit and bickered some but only in treacly tones. For even I think four weekends straight I never heard a showtune or shrill Teutonic opera and only, on the part of Desmond, infrequent stomping about. As Warren wasn't of a mind to muck up Shirley's timbre, he played her at low volume. I could barely make her out, which left for me to endure just those penetrating cackles and even they waned shortly as the weekends went along.

I guess the bloom just faded that way it often does. First Desmond set in to touring again, goosestepping about his apartment, and then the treacle vanished from their sundry disagreements. I could hear them some nights shrieking about a minor matter. The peas were oversalted. The beef was underdone. Nobody'd sung up-tempo songs the way Gwen Verdon had. It got to be that they were on each other all the time. They howled almost like yardcats, Desmond and Warren did. I believe they even got into a fight on one occasion and wrestled with each other, rolled across the floor. I can't say what the matter was, but I guess the tussling proved erotic since shortly I heard Warren setting up his fuss. Warren was a moaner, often sounded like a cow.

Some evenings I'd get in my car and call on Dale's sister, make often like my neighbor and his lover were the cause, that they'd provoked me with their racket and driven me away. She'd let me join her on the porch and sit and watch TV. She didn't need to hear from me. She wasn't one to make me talk, appeared to have no use for chat or idle conversation. It wasn't hard to sit with her. I never felt uneasy, even on the glider when all we'd do was breathe. She had me in one Sunday for dinner with her parents, and it was just like in the old times, the way they carried on. Dale's mother kissed me on the cheek. His daddy grabbed my neck. I stayed until the evening, helped put the child to bed, sat with Dale's sister on the porch and watched the night come on.

I like to think that I'm just fine, have Marge and Clayton's girl to blame. It's little chore to reason that she brought on her perdition, had a Rumsfeld figured wrong, earned precisely what she rated. Then I'll have a long, bad night. That's all it takes sometimes. I remember once I'd gone to bed, was suffering through my dream, the dream about the car I stop out along the bypass, nothing but a rolling heap kept whole with wire and putty. I climbed out from my cruiser. I hung my stick. I donned my hat. I laid, as was my custom, my hand upon my gun.

That car was fairly crammed full up and I knew everybody. Karen my wife was in the front sitting on Wendle's lap. That Crouse and that girl were next to him. The Rumsfeld was back of the wheel. The boys had their bullet holes already, their punctured skulls, their matted hair. My mother was in the backseat with her pocketbook in her lap. She was deep in conversation with the Bluefield anchorman who was sitting himself beside the girl who suffers from diarrhea, the one on the commercial who's too pretty for the runs. She seemed to be having a word with Ellis on the topic of gastric distress.

"Well hey," I said and bent so I could look into the window.

"Evening, officer," they told me back and lifted up their guns, nickel-plated pistols, handsome, engraved items. I saw their knuckles whiten. They shot me all at once.

I as much as levitated, nearly jumped out of the bed. I could hear the motor in the lot, see the headlights through the window. That boy in the refuse truck had come and flung the dumpster down. I was rattled pretty good, got up and walked around. Monroe loosed from behind the bowl a weary exhalation as I passed along the hallway and stepped into the kitchen to open up the door and stand before the Frigidaire. I wandered to the front room and drank milk from the jug, sized up my sorry holdings, my table and my chair, my second-hand TV with the aerial wrenched from it, my former wife across town, my job down at the station where me and Lonnie did whatever Dewey wouldn't do.

The ruckus from the dumpster must have roused the boys upstairs. The toilet flushed and briefly Desmond drilled along the hallway in advance of retiring and having, I would guess, his amorous way with Warren who began after a fashion to bellow. His rhythmic, bovine cries of pleasure were nearly themselves as penetrating as Warren's giddy cackles though, muffled as they were by the Sheetrock and the carpet, it didn't sound precisely like I lived beneath a stockyard. I mean there was something doleful in the way that Warren wailed, something almost ghostly by the time it got to me.

The noise was loud enough still to irritate the dog who stood up off the bathroom floor and ambled down the hall, came to offer me a snort and gaze upon the ceiling in a show of unadulterated canine disapproval. So there we stood together in the front room in the dark listening to Warren fairly lowing overhead, and maybe it was only me and my own circumstances, but shortly I just couldn't any longer hear the pleasure. Desmond would prod Warren who'd volunteer a moan and it would filter down to me sounding like despair.

❦

I don't mind midnights anymore. I'll swap a shift to get one. You see everybody wants to draw me off and have a word on account of how they've cultivated theories and opinions, saw for themselves the sacks of gore that blew up on the trestle, that man who bailed into the net, and so they think they know, consider that they have now a fair notion of events and are fit to try on me their concocted formulations. They ask me for my version. They make me sit through theirs. So I'm pleased to have occasion to work a midnight now when they're all at home and sleeping and just leave me to myself.

As a consequence I can't say that I see too much of Ellis, though I picked him up the other week and took him on an airing. We chatted right there at the first the way we used to do. He laid up on the seatback where he boasted and he lied, recalled a pair of sisters that he'd dazzled with his charms, but once he'd had his coffee and had gotten ventilated, Ellis couldn't seem to think of anything to say. When we'd pass beneath the lightpoles I could see him in the mirror just peering out the window and chewing on his cup.

Last week Mrs. Heflin called in with a demon in her shrubbery, some variety of hellhound that I got sent to rout. I waded through the bushes and beat them with my stick while Mrs. Heflin stood out on the lawn clutching her maul handle. When I fail to get dispatched to her or sent out to the speedway, I can't say that there's awful much I'm put upon to do. I stop drunks on occasion or follow them clean home, cruise down along the river, rattle knobs in town, tour the shopping plaza where I dodge carts in the lot. I rode back out to Whitetop once to see her house again. It had been relet already—a truck was in the drive. Somebody had climbed up on the roof and brought the shovel down.

I tend to close my midnight shifts over on the parkway at the turnout in the poplar grove up above the branch. You can see the ridge back to the west, Mt. Airy in the valley. It's a place the lovers like to go and watch the lights blink on. I switch the cruiser off and sit. I turn the two-way down. Sometimes the air is crisp and clear, but usually it's misty. A fog boils off the branch below and thickens towards the dawn, closes off the valley and shuts away the stars. It settles in along the ridge. It spills into the creases. The poplars drip, the nightjars sing and I am swallowed up.

ABOUT THE AUTHOR

T. R. Pearson was born in Winston-Salem, North Carolina, in 1956, and now lives in Virginia. He is the author of *A Short History of a Small Place, Off for the Sweet Hereafter, The Last of How It Was, Call and Response,* and *Gospel Hour,* and is currently working on a new novel.